THE THIRST FOR IMMORTALITY

Athas, world of the dark sun. Ruled for thousands of years by power-mad sorcerer-kings, the cities of Athas have become vile centers of slavery and corruption. Only heroes of the greatest strength and bravest heart can stand against the might of these overlords. The Prism Pentad is a tale of such heroes....

Sadira—the ebon-skinned enchantress, imbued with the dark powers of the Pristine Tower and determined to free Athas of its greatest evil.

Neeva—the beautiful and deadly veteran of Tyr's slave arena, mother of the mul-child destined to kill the Dragon.

Tithian—the usurper of Tyr's throne, whose thirst for the immortal powers of a sorcerer-king may destroy the world—or save it!

PRISM PENTAD

Troy Denning

Book One
The Verdant Passage

Watch for the next DARK SUN™ Series

Tribe of One
Simon Hawke
beginning in December 1993

The Cerulean Storm

TROY DENNING

THE CERULEAN STORM

Random House and its affiliate companies have worldwide distribution rights in the book
trade for English language products of TSR, Inc.

Distributed to the book and hobby trade in the United Kingdom by TSR Ltd.

Distributed to the toy and hobby trade by regional distributors.

Cover art by Brom.

First Printing: September 1993
Printed in the United States of America.
Library of Congress Catalog Card Number: 92-61097

9 8 7 6 5 4 3 2 1

ISBN: 1-56076-642-5

TSR, Inc.   TSR Ltd.
P.O. Box 756   120 Church End, Cherry Hinton
Lake Geneva, WI 53147   Cambridge CB1 3LB
U.S.A.   United Kingdom

Dedication:

For Jim Lowder, with thanks for his many
contributions to the series.

Acknowledgements:

Many people contributed to the writing of this book
and the creation of the series. I would like to thank you
all. Without the efforts of the following people, especially, Athas might never have seen the light of the
crimson sun: Mary Kirchoff and Tim Brown, who
shaped the world as much as anyone; Brom, who gave
us the look and the feel; Jim Lowder, for his inspiration
and patience; Lloyd Holden of the AKF Martial Arts
Academy in Janesville, WI, for contributing his exper-
tise to the fight scenes; Andria Hayday, for support
and encouragement; and Jim Ward, for enthusiasm,
support, and much more.

BEYOND THE LAND

THE GREAT RIFT

LAKE OF FIRE

THE VALLEY OF DUST AND FIRE

THE BROKEN LAND

DRAGON'S SANCTUM

ISLE

THE MOUNTAINS OF FIRE

THE BAXAL SHOALS

SEA OF SILT

N

PROLOGUE

Most men called it shadow, that dark stain visible only as an absence: the cold gloom cast upon the ground when their bodies blocked the light of the crimson sun. Wiser minds referred to it as the Black, and they knew that it separated everything that existed from everything that did not. It lurked just beneath the surface in all things, like the leathery shell of some great egg, buried shallow and about to hatch. Outside lay the barren mountains, the endless sand wastes, and the bleak, windswept plains that were the world of Athas. Inside lay the Hollow, filled with the languid albumin of nothingness.

Within this colorless ether floated the bones of an ancient skeleton. It lay curled into a tight ball, its shoulder blades fused into a large hump and its gangling arms wrapped around its knees. The skull seemed remotely human, though the slender jawbones, drooping chin, and flat cheekbones insinuated that this was not entirely true.

The skeleton filled the Hollow completely, but it

1

would have been wrong to call the thing huge. In this place, size had no meaning. Only existence mattered, and by the mere fact that it *was*, the skeleton occupied all of the vast emptiness inside the egg.

The skeleton scratched at the murky shell with long barbed talons, dreaming of the day it would be reborn. For the first time in an eternity, it felt confident of escaping its timeless prison. Forks of lightning circled its misshapen skull like a crown. Sparks danced in the empty sockets where once it had possessed eyes.

Beneath the scratching talons appeared a pair of blue embers and a long slitlike mouth. The features were all the skeleton ever saw of its servants. The shadow people were part of the Black, as trapped within the dark shell as their master was inside the emptiness of the egg.

We felt your summons, Omnipotent One.

The servant used thought-speech to report, for sound did not exist within the skeleton's eternal prison.

I have been thinking, Khidar, the skeleton replied. It slowly twisted its oblong skull around to stare more directly into the shadow's eyes. *The sorcerer-kings must be near when the Usurper frees me.*

That's too dangerous! The servant's eyes grew larger and brighter. *The six of them have grown stronger than you know, Rajaat. They'll destroy us!*

A ball of lightning formed above Rajaat's head. *They won't destroy me!* he snarled. *If you hesitate to sacrifice a few lives so I may return Athas to its greater glory, perhaps you should remain in the Black.*

Khidar winced, his eyes and mouth sliding down the inside of the black shell. *Our fates are bound together,* he said, with more regret than enthusiasm. *We have no concern except the future of Athas.*

Never forget that, Rajaat hissed, the blue rays in his empty eye sockets flickering in ire. *Think of all that I have sacrificed to return the world to your people, and follow my example.*

We are most grateful, Khidar assured him. *We'll see to whatever you wish.*

Good. It would be best to avenge the sorcerer-kings' betrayal before proceeding with the Restoration, Rajaat said. The lightning began to crackle more steadily and calmly over his head. *After that, we'll cleanse Athas of the most profane strains of the degenerate races. The half-breeds shall die first.*

Which ones? asked the servant.

All of them: half-elves, muls, half-giants, every filthy abomination produced through an unnatural union. We must kill them as soon as possible.

As you wish.

The New Races come next, Rajaat continued, knotting the barbed talons of both hands into tight fists. *There are so many! It may take us a century.*

We must expect opposition, Khidar warned. *Sadira and Rikus—*

Are half-breeds. They'll die with the others! the skeleton pronounced. *I'll destroy them as soon as I finish with the sorcerer-kings.*

What of the Usurper? asked Khidar. *Will you make him a sorcerer-king?*

Yes, I'll keep my promise, provided he honors the cause of the Pristine Tower, Rajaat answered.

And if he betrays us like Borys and the others?

My new champion will never do such a thing, the skeleton replied. *After he witnesses the fate of the other traitors, he will not dare.*

ONE

Samarah

King Tithian of Tyr gnashed his teeth in vexation, accidently crushing the sweet chadnut upon which he had been sucking. The pulp filled his mouth with sour, peppery seeds that burned his tongue and made his eyes water. He swallowed the kernels in a single gulp, hardly noticing the fiery aftertaste that chased them down his throat.

"It's a whole damned fleet!" His old man's voice was hoarsened by the spicy chad seeds.

The hunch-shouldered king stood behind a low stone wall, peering through a curtain of swirling dust. A thicket of masts had just appeared in Samarah's tiny harbor. While the thick haze prevented a reliable ship count, Tithian could see so much billowing canvas that the flotilla looked like a cloud bank rolling in from the Sea of Silt.

"Why should the fleet anger you, Mighty One?" asked Korla, clinging, as always, to Tithian's arm. She was the fairest woman in the village, with ginger-colored hair and a sultry smile. That did not mean she was beautiful. A life of heat and dust had framed her brown eyes with deep-etched crow's-feet, while the sun had baked her skin until it was as creased and rough as a man's. Korla clasped the king's elbow more tightly. "Your retainers wouldn't dare come for you with anything less than a dozen ships."

Tithian pulled free and straightened his shoulder satchel.

She frowned. "Soon you'll show me the wonders of Tyr—won't you?"

"No." Tithian fixed a disdainful glare on her weather-lined face.

"You can't leave me behind!" Korla objected. She glanced at the small crowd of villagers gathered behind the wall. "After what I've been to you, the others will—"

"Quiet!" Tithian ordered. He waved a liver-spotted hand toward the harbor. "That isn't my fleet. Rikus and Sadira will come by land, not ship."

Korla lowered her eyelids and sighed in relief.

"Don't be too relieved," said Riv, Korla's brawny husband and Samarah's headman.

An elf-tarek crossbreed, Riv had a square, big-boned face with a sloped forehead and a slender nose. Standing so tall that the village wall rose only to his waist, he cut an imposing figure. Normally, Tithian would have killed such a rival outright, but the headman had taken pains to make himself indispensable as an intermediary to the villagers. Besides, the king enjoyed flaunting Korla's adultery in front of him.

"Your reign as whore-queen will end soon enough." Riv glared at his wife.

"Why's that?" Tithian demanded, shuffling around Korla to confront the huge crossbreed. "Is there a reason I should fear those ships?"

Riv shrugged. "Everyone should fear Balican armadas. But I see no reason they should concern you especially," he replied. He raised the thin lips of his domed muzzle, showing a mouthful of enormous canine teeth. "I only meant that Korla shouldn't expect to go with you when the time comes. I've seen enough of Athas to know she'd only be an embarrassment in the city."

"You may have seen the brothels of Balic, but you know nothing of life in Tyr's royal court," Korla spat back. She regarded her husband suspiciously, then continued, "Now answer the king's question. We haven't seen a Balican fleet for more than a year. Why now?"

Riv sneered. "Ask your lover," he said. "He's the mindbender."

"I'll know the answer soon enough," Tithian said, thrusting his hand into his shoulder satchel. "And if you ever again refer to me as anything but *King* or *Mighty One*, you'll beg for your death."

Riv blanched. The king had pulled spell components from the sack often enough that the headman recognized the gesture as a threatening one. What Riv did not realize was that Tithian could also withdraw a venomous viper, a vial of acid, or any one of a dozen other tools of murder from inside. The sack was magical, and it could hold an unlimited supply of items without appearing full.

Riv glared at Tithian for a moment, then hissed, "As you wish, *Mighty One*."

Tithian spun toward the center of the village, signaling for Korla and Riv to follow him. As they moved through the dust haze, they passed a dozen stone huts shaped like beehives. Inside most buildings, haggard women furiously packed their meager possessions—sacks of chadnuts, stone knives, clay cooking pots, and bone-tipped hunting spears. Outside, the men gathered the family goraks, knee-high lizards with colorful dorsal fans. It was a slow, difficult process, for the stubborn reptiles were engrossed in overturning rocks and catching insects with their long sticky tongues.

The king and his companions reached the village

plaza. In the center was the communal well, a deep hole encircled by a simple railing of gorak bones. A small crowd of children surrounded the pit, arguing in panicked voices and elbowing each other out of the way as they struggled to fill their waterskins.

On the far side of the plaza, outside the hut the king had confiscated from Riv, lay an obsidian orb larger than a man, with languorous streaks of scarlet swimming over its glassy surface. It was the Dark Lens, both the source of Tithian's power and the means through which he would achieve his greatest ambition: to become an immortal sorcerer-king.

The Dark Lens had once blonged to Athas's first sorcerer, Rajaat. Thousands of years ago, the ancient sage had started a genocidal war to cleanse Athas of races he considered impure. To assist him, Rajaat had used the lens to make a group of immortal champions, each dedicated to destroying one race.

After dozens of centuries of fighting, the champions had learned that their master intended to strip them of their powers. They had rebelled, using the Dark Lens to lock Rajaat into a mystical prison. Then they had transformed their leader, Borys of Ebe, into the Dragon, appointing him to guard the prison forever. The other champions had each claimed one of the cities of Athas to rule as immortal sorcerer-kings.

Tithian intended to kill the Dragon and free Rajaat. In return, he had been promised that the ancient sorcerer would bless him with the immortal powers of a champion. Unfortunately, the Tyrian king could not hope to kill his prey alone. Borys was a master of the Way, sorcery, and physical combat, and the Dark Lens would make Tithian powerful enough to challenge the Dragon only in the Way.

The king knew who could help him: his former slaves Rikus and Sadira. A champion gladiator, Rikus carried a magical sword that had been forged by Rajaat himself, while Sadira's body had been imbued with the magical energies of Rajaat's mystic castle. Together, the three of them would have the power to destroy Borys.

Of course, Tithian realized that it would not be easy to induce his ex-slaves to help. For their own reasons, they were as anxious to kill the Dragon as the king was, but they were also smart enough not to trust him. So, to lure them into helping him, Tithian had sent them a fraudulent message in the name of their friend Agis of Asticles. In it, he had claimed that Agis had recovered the Dark Lens and asked them to meet the noble in Samarah. To convince them the summons was real, he had included the Asticles signet ring. Once they arrived, he would make up a lie about how the noble had died after sending the message. Then the king would convince them to let him take Agis's place and help them kill Borys.

Tithian had reached the far side of the village square. The sentry the king had left to watch the Dark Lens showed himself. He was a disembodied head with grossly bloated cheeks and narrow, dark eyes. He had a mouthful of broken teeth and wore his coarse hair in a topknot. The bottom of his leathery neck had been stitched shut with black thread.

"What'd you find in the harbor?" the sentry asked, floating toward Tithian.

"It's a fleet, Sacha," the king reported.

Sacha's dark eyes opened wide. "That's impossible." He glanced at the obsidian orb. "As long as we have the Dark Lens, Andropinis can't find us."

"Then what are his ships doing in the harbor?" Tithian growled.

"How should I know?" sneered the head. "You're the one who controls the lens. I suggest you use it."

Tithian lashed out to snatch Sacha's topknot, missed, and silently cursed. His slow reflexes still surprised him occasionally, for his body had grown frail and old just a few weeks earlier. In the course of stealing the Dark

Lens from the giant tribes in the Sea of Silt, the king had been forced to outwit its guardians: a pair of dwarven banshees named Jo'orsh and Sa'ram. Before he could send them away, the spirits had stolen what remained of his youth, burdening him with aching joints, shortness of breath, and all the other afflictions of old age.

Leaving Korla and Riv behind, Tithian spread his arms and stepped toward the Dark Lens. As he approached, waves of blistering heat rose off the glassy orb and seared his old man's body clear to the brittle bones. Clenching his teeth, he laid his hands on the scorching surface. From beneath his palms came a soft hiss, and the smell of charred flesh filled his nostrils. The king did not cry out. He looked past the surface and gazed into the utter blackness of the Dark Lens.

Tithian opened himself to the power of the black orb. His hands seemed to meld with its surface, and its blistering heat ceased to burn his flesh. A torrent of energy rushed from the lens into his arms, flowing down into his spiritual nexus, the place deep within his abdomen where the three energies of the Way—mental, physical, and spiritual—joined to form the core of his being.

Tithian focused his thoughts on Samarah's harbor, concentrating on what he would see there if the dust haze were not obscuring his vision. In the black depths of the Dark Lens rose an image of twenty schooners, each depicted clearly in ghostly red light. The first ship was just sailing into the narrow strait that served as the harbor's mouth. Inside his mind the king heard the creaking of masts and the pop of flapping canvas. The visual image was so clear that he could see the gaunt slaves shuffling along yardarm ropes as they furled the sails. On the main deck, hairless dwarves labored around a capstan as they struggled to raise the keel boards, and in the stern the shipfloater stared into a black dome of obsidian. From his own experience aboard Balican schooners, Tithian knew that the shipfloater was using the Way to infuse the dome with the spiritual energy that kept the ship from sinking into the dust.

"Find out if Andropinis is with them," suggested Sacha, hovering at Tithian's side. "If he isn't, even an incompetent like you can destroy the fleet."

"And if he is?" Tithian demanded.

Sacha did not answer.

Tithian shifted his attention to a particularly large schooner near the center of the fleet. Unlike the other ships, this one had narrow banners snapping from the top of its masts, identifying it as the flagship. The king focused all his attention on the craft, closing the others out of his mind. He felt a surge of mystical energy rush from deep within his body, and the ship's image gradually enlarged until it was the only one visible.

On the foredeck, four ballistae sat ready to fire, massive harpoons nocked in their skein cords, with a pair of lumbering half-giants standing nearby. Two sorcerers stood in the prow, inspecting the dust-swells ahead of the ship for signs of buried obstacles. To aid in the search, each man held the base of a large glass cone to his eyes. The glass cones, Tithian knew, were king's eyes, unique lenses especially enchanted so the viewer could peer through the dust hazes so common to the Sea of Silt.

To the king's surprise, there did not appear to be any slaves on the main deck. Half-giants stood next to every catapult, while the crew struggling to turn the capstan wore the plain togas of low-ranking Balican templars. Even the men and women crawling over the yardarms showed no whip scars on their bare backs.

When Tithian's gaze fell on the quarterdeck, his stomach coiled into a tight knot. "In the name of Rajaat!" he cursed. "It can't be!"

Behind the helmsman stood Andropinis, sorcerer-king of Balic. He was muscular and huge, with a fringe of chalk-colored hair hanging from beneath his jagged crown. He had a slender face, a nose so long it could almost be called a snout, and dark nostrils shaped like eggs. His cracked lips were pulled back to reveal a mouthful of teeth filed as sharp as those of a gladiator. Beneath his sleeveless tunic, a line of sharp bulges ran down his spine. Small pointed scales covered his shoulders and the backs of his arms.

What disturbed Tithian more than the sight of Andropinis were the five people standing silently at the sorcerer-king's side. Two were male, two female, and one of uncertain gender. All stood close to Andropinis's height and appeared just as menacing. One man had a thick mane around his neck, with slit pupils and the heavy nose of a lion. The other seemed remotely avian, with a scaly, beak-shaped muzzle and recessed earslits on the sides of his head.

The taller woman appeared as cold as she was beautiful, with long silky hair, dark skin, and narrow eyeslits extending from the bridge of her nose around to her temples. She had a small, oval-shaped mouth, with dainty fangs pressed against the flesh of her lips. The other woman was of lighter complexion. Her huge eyes constantly roamed about and never seemed to focus on anything. Save for the curled claws at the ends of her fingertips, she looked more completely human than anyone else with Andropinis.

The last figure stood half-again as tall as the others. It seemed a miniature version of the Dragon, with a gaunt build neither male nor female. A glistening hide of leather and chitin covered its willowy limbs and androgenous body, while huge claws with knobby-jointed fingers hung from the ends of its skeletal arms. At the end of its serpentine neck was its head, little more than a slender snout with a glassy, bulbous eye on each side and a bony horn at the end.

"Who are they?" asked Korla, coming to stand at Tithian's side. She held her hands out to shield her face from the blistering heat of the lens.

"The six sorcerer-kings and queens of Athas," supplied Sacha.

The head had hardly spoken before Korla glanced toward her husband. "Riv!"

Sacha faced Tithian and growled, "You should have killed the half-breed when you decided to bed his wife."

"It wasn't me," Riv objected, joining them. Over at the well, the children had formed a neat line and were working efficiently to fill their waterskins. "The last thing I want in Samarah are sorcerer-kings. Most of my villagers are slaves who came here after escaping the cities."

"I've seen jealous fools risk more," pressed Sacha.

"Riv didn't summon this fleet," Tithian said. Inside the Dark Lens, he could see Andropinis's ship passing between the two spits of land that formed the mouth of the harbor. "Even if Riv has a way to contact the sorcerer-kings, he has no reason to think they'd be interested in me—unless you told him, Sacha?"

"Don't be absurd," snapped the head.

"They must have found a way to track the lens," the king surmised.

"Impossible," Sacha said. "As long as Jo'orsh and Sa'ram still walk Athas, their magic prevents any sorcerer-king from finding the lens—by any method."

"Then what are all six doing here?"

When the head didn't answer, the king shifted his attention from Andropinis's flagship back to the whole fleet. He felt a surge of energy course through his body, then his field of view expanded to take in the entire armada. The ship in the lead was furling its sails and slowing to a stop under the shouted guidance of the first mate. The end of Samarah's single quay lay just a short distance ahead of the bowsprit.

Fearing that a Balican watchman would soon be able to see him, Tithian searched the sky over the harbor for the silhouette of a mast or crow's nest. To his relief, he found nothing but a pearly sky full of blowing dust.

Samaran mothers began to pour into the plaza with heavy satchels of household belongings slung over their shoulders. The fathers waited at the edge of the square, clubbing their goraks with bone spears in a futile effort to keep the flocks from drifting.

"Where are your villagers going, Riv?" Tithian asked.

"If we stay here, the Balicans will seize everything we have—even our children," the headman reported. "We'll scatter into the desert until the fleet leaves."

"We'd better do the same," urged Sacha.

"And forgo a chance to spy on my enemies?" The king shook his head. "We're staying."

"We can't eavesdrop on sorcerer-kings!"

"Of course we can," Tithian replied. "You said yourself they can't find us as long as we have the Dark Lens."

The king returned his gaze to the black orb, then gasped. Several schooners had come to a dead halt in the middle of the harbor, but that was not what had alarmed him. Borys had appeared next to the flagship, his willowy frame so gaunt it would have made an elf seem stout. Though the Dragon stood waist-deep in silt, his slender head loomed as far above the ship's deck as the highest mast, with a spiked crest of leathery skin running up the back of his serpentine spine. A menacing light glowed in his tiny eyes, and wisps of red fume rose from the nostrils at the end of his slender snout.

Andropinis stood at the gunnel, conversing with Borys. "How can you be certain Tithian is here, Great One?" the sorcerer-king asked.

"I'm not," the Dragon replied. "But my spies in Tyr inform me that Rikus and Sadira are preparing to leave for Samarah. Why would they come so far, if not to meet the Usurper and retrieve the Dark Lens?"

"And you summoned us to help you ambush them?"

"Perhaps, if my agents in Tyr fail to stop them," Borys said. "But first, I want you and the other sorcerer-kings to find Jo'orsh and Sa'ram."

"The dwarven knights?" asked Andropinis.

"The dwarven banshees," Borys corrected. "Now that the Usurper has stolen the lens from them, they should not be so difficult to find. Bring them to me, and my spirit lords will force them to undo the magic hiding the Dark Lens."

"Perhaps it would be easier to destroy the banshees where we find them," suggested Andropinis.

"These banshees cannot be destroyed by you—or even me," said Borys. "Only my spirit lords can do that—which is why you must bring them to me."

"You'll be here?"

The Dragon nodded. "Waiting for Tithian."

With that, Borys stepped away from the ship. The crew began to lower the skiffs, and the sorcerer-kings prepared to disembark.

"Now will you leave?" asked Sacha. He was hovering near Tithian's shoulder, watching the scene inside the lens.

"No. It wouldn't do any good," Tithian's heart was pounding, pumping fear and panic through his body, and it was all he could do to keep control of his thoughts. "Running into the desert won't save me, not from Borys and his sorcerer-kings."

"So you'll fight them?" Korla asked in an anxious voice.

Tithian looked up from the lens and glared at her. "Don't be absurd," he spat. "One or two sorcerer-kings, I could kill easily. But not all of them, and not with Borys here. Even I can't kill the Dragon alone."

"I don't suppose you'd do us the courtesy of surrendering outside Samarah?" requested Riv. "It might spare my people some trouble."

"Why should I care about your people?" growled

Tithian. "I have no intention of surrendering."

"I'm happy to hear that," said Korla.

Smirking at her relief, Riv scoffed, "Why? If he's not going to run or fight, what else can he do?"

"The last thing Borys expects: hide in the very place he's trying to ambush me," Tithian was untroubled by Riv's obvious delight at his plight. The headman would pay for his insolence soon enough.

Tithian thought his plan stood a good chance of seeing him through until help arrived. If Borys thought his agents could stop Rikus and Sadira, the Dragon was underestimating them badly. As long as the pair believed they were coming to meet Agis, they would find a way to reach Samarah. Once they did, they would have no choice but to help him slay Borys.

The king studied Riv's brawny form for a moment, then used the Way to visualize himself growing as large and strong as the headman. A torrent of searing energy rushed from the lens into his body. The king's arms burst into agony as his muscles began to swell, taking on a knotted, bulging shape. After his arms came his shoulders and neck, then his chest, back, and stomach. Each transformation brought with it a fresh surge of pain. Tithian clenched his teeth and waited for the Dark Lens to change his thoughts into reality, until at last his legs felt as thick and bandy as Riv's.

The king slipped his arms, now as sinewy as those of a half-giant, around the heavy lens. He lifted it easily, then moved toward the center of the plaza, shuffling to keep from banging his knees on the huge orb. The crowd of Samaran children backed away, their half-filled waterskins dribbling precious liquid onto the dusty ground.

"Where are you going?" Sacha demanded, floating at Tithian's side.

"I told you: to hide," the king replied.

"What good will that do?" the head whispered into

Tithian's ear. "There isn't a villager here who'd hesitate
to tell the Balicans where you are."

"I've thought of that already," Tithian replied.

As he spoke, the king concentrated on the people
ahead, fixing their faces firmly in his mind. He used the
Way to visualize them clasping at their throats, choking
and gasping for air. He felt the energy of the Dark Lens
flow through his body and into the ground. A column of
brown mist whooshed from the well, spreading over the
plaza with the fetid, caustic odor of charred flesh. The
sound of coughing and gagging filled the air, then
Samarans started to drop, their strangled voices calling
for help. The instant a body hit the ground, its flesh
grew ashen and began to wither.

Heavy steps sounded behind Tithian. The king turned
and saw Riv charging, his muzzle twisted into a snarl of
rage. "Murderer!" The headman flung himself into the
air.

Tithian shifted the Dark Lens to one hand and raised
his other arm. He opened himself to the lens's power.
He felt a streak of mystic energy rush through his body,
then Riv's chest hit his hand. A dark flash erupted from
beneath the king's palm, engulfing his attacker in a pall
of absolute blackness. The headman howled in pain, but
the cry was strangely muted, as if the ebon fire of the
lens had swallowed it. Riv's scorched bones clattered to
the ground, trailing wisps of greasy, foul-smelling
smoke.

Hardly seeming to notice her dead husband or any of
the other dying villagers, Korla stumbled to Tithian's
side. "I'm choking," she croaked. "Save me!"

Tithian shook his head. "You must die as well."

Korla's eyes widened in disbelief. "No!"

"If Borys finds you, he'll tear your mind apart with
the Way," Tithian explained. "You'll tell him where to
find me."

"I would never," Korla said, stepping back in fear.

Tithian caught her hand and pulled it to the lens. A flame flashed beneath her fingers, then her body erupted into a column of crimson fire. The blaze died away quickly, and all that remained where Korla had stood were her bones, a pearly heap of ash, and a handful of cracked teeth. Recalling that they had once nibbled his ear and made him feel young, the king stooped over and picked up the incisors, slipping them into his shoulder satchel for safekeeping.

As Tithian glanced around the square, he saw that most of the people near the well had already died. Their bodies were shriveling into piles of dust and white bone that even Borys would find impossible to interrogate. Farther away, the mist had just reached the edge of the plaza. The stunned fathers were thrashing about on the ground, their purple tongues hanging out. The goraks accepted their fate with more dignity, dropping to their bellies and turning their yellow eyes away from the sun.

The king did not worry that the Balicans would find it strange that an entire village had perished, for such catastrophes were far from rare on Athas. When the sailors walked among the bones, it would be coins and chadnuts they sought, not answers.

Tithian grabbed Sacha and slipped the head into the satchel, then walked over to the well and peered back toward the harbor. Above the huts of Samarah, he could see the faint outline of dozens of masts showing through the heavy silt curtain. From outside the village came muffled Balican voices demanding that the gate be opened.

The king stepped into the well, using the Way to lower himself and the Dark Lens gently into the pit. The gloomy depths swallowed them both, and Tithian settled into the tepid waters to await Rikus and Sadira.

TWO

Pauper's Hope

A deep boom rumbled over the butte, and golden cascades of sand spilled down the bluff's waferlike ledges. The sound passed over the road, rolling across a salt-crusted lake bed until it echoed off the craggy flank of a distant mountain.

Rikus looked up and frowned. The sky remained clear, the crimson sun blazing through the olive-tinged haze of dawn. To the west, Athas's twin moons hung low over the Ringing Mountains, silhouetting the distant peaks against golden crescents. A harsh wind hissed over the top of the butte, but there was not a thunderhead in sight.

The mul passed his hand over his kank's antennae, bringing the mount to a halt. The insect was twice the size of a man, with a chitinous body and multifaceted eyes bulging from the sides of its head. The wicked mandibles protruding from its maw made it look as though it could have destroyed a pack of lirrs, though in truth it was a timid and rather gentle creature.

Rikus sat astride the kank's thorax, his feet dangling

among its six legs and almost touching the ground. With a rugged, heavy-boned face and a hairless body that seemed nothing but knotted sinew, the warrior looked even more dangerous than his mount. In his case, however, appearances were not deceiving. He was a mul, a dwarf-human half-breed created to live and die as a gladiator. From his father, he had inherited the incredible strength and endurance of the dwarves, while his mother had bestowed on him the size and agility of the humans. The result was an ideal fighter, combining both power and nimbleness in a single frame.

When another boom did not sound from behind the butte, Rikus lowered his hand to the Scourge of Rkard. As his fingers touched the hilt, the sword's magic filled his ears with discordant sounds: the roaring wind, the rasp of falling sand, and the pounding of his own heart. From the shadowed cracks of the butte cliffs came the clamor of chirping crickets. Somewhere out on the lake bed, a snake's belly scales whispered across the rough surface of a hot stone.

Rikus also heard something that disturbed him more: the drone of human voices, no doubt coming from a faro plantation that lay on the other side of the butte. The words were muffled by distance and the high bluff. Still, the mul could tell that many of the farmers were yelling, some even screaming. As he listened, a loud, sonorous laugh drowned out the human voices, and he knew that something was terribly wrong at Pauper's Hope.

Rikus took his hand away from his sword and faced the inhuman figure at his side. "Do you hear that, Magnus?"

Though Magnus called himself an elf, he did not resemble one. Born in the magical shadows of the Pristine Tower, he had been transformed into something that looked more akin to a giant gorak than an elf. He had a hulking, thick-limbed body covered by a knobby hide, ivory-clawed toes, and hands the size of bucklers.

His face was all muzzle, with an enormous, sharp-toothed mouth and huge round eyes set on opposite sides of his head.

"The boom? It wasn't thunder," Magnus answered.

"It doesn't take a windsinger to know that," Rikus replied. "What about the voices? Use your magic to find out what's going on."

Magnus turned his eloquently pointed ears toward the butte and listened. After a moment, he shook his head. "The butte's too high for me to understand their words," he said. "Even a windsinger cannot listen through rock."

Rikus cursed. He and Magnus were due at a meeting of the Tyrian Council of Advisors by midmorning. Normally, it would not bother him to make the council wait, but today he and Sadira were asking for a legion of warriors to take to Samarah. Being late would not put the advisors in a mood to grant his request.

A damson-colored shadow fell across the road. The mul looked up to see a cloud of ivory dust drifting over the summit of the bluff. Although the wind carried most of the scintillating mass out over the dry lake, some of the powder fell toward the road like a soft rain.

Rikus held out a hand and caught a light dusting in his palm. The stuff was the color of straw, with the silky texture of finely ground flour. Rikus touched his tongue to the powder. It tasted dry and bland.

"This is faro!"

The mul held his hand out toward the windsinger.

"It looks freshly ground," Magnus observed. "The boom we heard could have been a collapsing silo. That would explain all the excitement."

"I don't think so," Rikus said, remembering the deep laugh that he had heard over the concerned voices. "We'd better have a look."

The mul dismounted.

"Is that really necessary?" Magnus protested. "When

she contacted me last night, Sadira made it clear that she wants you present when the meeting starts."

Rikus scowled at this. "She should have thought about that before she sent us to inspect the outpost at the mine," he growled. "She'll just have to handle the council on her own until we arrive."

He led his kank off the road and tethered it to a boulder.

Magnus sighed in resignation. "At least let me send word that you'll be late."

"After we see what's happening," Rikus said. "It'll be better if we can tell her how long we'll be."

The mul led the way up the butte, clambering over sharp-edged rocks that had already grown hot in the morning sun. The boulder field soon gave way to a talus slope dotted with quiverlike clusters of arrow weed. Magnus grabbed whole handfuls of the yellow stalks and used them to pull himself up the steep pitch. As the canes snapped between his thick fingers, a tangy, foul-smelling odor filled the air. Rikus could only look on in envy and scramble up the loose gravel on all fours. His skin was not as tough as the windsinger's, and the stems of the plants were lined with razor-sharp ridges.

When they reached the cliffs near the top of the butte, it was Rikus's turn to gloat. He crawled up the vertical crags easily, while Magnus cursed and groaned with the effort of pulling his heavier body up the precipice. At times, the windsinger had to use his fist to beat a suitable handhold into the rock face.

Upon climbing onto the summit, Rikus found himself looking out over a wide, shallow canyon flanked on one side by this butte and on the other by the ashen crags of the Ringing Mountains. The orange soil was speckled by thickets of gray-green tamarisk and spindly catclaw trees, while crests of dark basalt wound across the valley floor like the shattered vestiges of some ancient and long-forgotten rampart.

The highest crest in the valley stood as tall as a small mountain, and was known locally as Rasda's Wall. Tyr's newest relief farm, Pauper's Hope, lay behind its bulk, completely hidden save for the green stain of a faro orchard spilling from behind the immense barrier. The field was made verdant, Rikus knew, by the waters of a deep well that the new farmers had laboriously chiseled through a hundred feet of granite bedrock.

More than a dozen figures were splashing down the shallow ditches of the faro field. Though the distance was too great for Rikus to tell the race or sex of any of the people, he could see that they were running hard, occasionally glancing over their shoulders at something hidden from view by Rasda's Wall.

"I was right. There's some kind of trouble." Rikus looked down at Magnus. The windsinger was only halfway up the cliff, hanging by a single hand thrust into a narrow fissure. "I'm going ahead," the mul said. "Follow me as soon as you can."

Without waiting for a response, the mul drew his sword and rushed down the gentle side of the butte. As before, a tumult of sounds filled his ears: gravel crunching beneath his feet, the hot wind sizzling through the brush, the alarmed hiss of a lizard scrambling for cover. Now that the high butte did not stand between him and Pauper's Hope, the drone of the farmers' voices came to Rikus more clearly. Some yelled for help, while others called the names of missing loved ones. Most simply screamed, their cries hoarse with terror.

Rikus heard other voices that worried him more. These were much louder than those of the farmers, with deep timbres and booming laughs like the one he had heard earlier. After dodging past half a dozen clumps of arrow weed, the mul reached the valley floor. He was close enough now to see that the fleeing farmers still wore the paupers' rags in which they had dressed as Tyrian beggars, and were sunburned and haggard from the struggle of adjusting to life outside the city.

From behind the fleeing paupers reverberated a sharp command, as loud as thunder: "Come back, you little vermin!"

At the shoulder of the ridge, where the crag was not as high as the rest of Rasda's Wall, a pair of huge heads appeared above the crest. The size of small kanks, the heads had shaggy brows and greasy braids of matted hair hanging off them. They had eyes so huge that, even from an arrow's flight away, Rikus could see that they had brown irises. Their teeth resembled long yellow stalactites. One of the figures had a hooked nose as large as a kank mandible, while a pair of plump, bulbous lips distinguished the other's face.

"Giants!" Rikus hissed, hardly able to believe what he saw.

Though the mul had never before seen a giant of the Silt Islands, he did not doubt that he was looking at two now. They were as tall as gatehouses and twice as broad, with huge barrel chests and limbs as thick as an ironwood. As they walked, they crushed faro trees and smashed irrigation ditches, leaving a series of small ponds behind where their feet had sunk into the ground.

Rikus didn't understand what the giants were doing here. Their race lived near Balic, in the long estuary of dust that twined its way inland from the Sea of Silt. From what he had heard, they were an aloof people, using the dust sea to insulate their island homes from visitors. Occasionally they journeyed to the Balican peninsula to sell their hair, which made excellent ropes, or to raid caravans and farms. But he had never heard of them traveling inland as far as Tyr.

The mul's puzzlement did not change the fact that the giants were here, and he knew it would not be easy to chase them away. As he sprinted across the valley floor, Rikus studied the terrain ahead, pondering the best way to save the farmers. He still could not see the plantation itself, for the buildings and most of the faro orchards remained hidden behind Rasda's Wall.

A careworn woman holding a baby in her arms reached the end of the faro field, then sprinted into the rocky desert. The hook-nosed giant chuckled in mad delight and stooped over to reach for her. His knuckles scraped along the ground, raising an orange cloud of dust. She dove to the side, barely escaping the long fingers.

The woman cradled her infant against her body and rolled several times. Rikus thought she might come up running, but upon righting herself, she stopped to look up at her attacker. The giant was already reaching for her again. She laid her infant beside a nearby bush, then fled in the direction opposite Rikus. As she ran, the woman screamed loudly to keep the titan's attention fixed on her.

"This way!" Rikus yelled, still running.

The woman continued away, apparently unable to hear him. The giant's hand descended and grasped her. As the brute plucked the woman off the ground, Rikus could see nothing of her except a pair of kicking legs. The titan chortled madly, then slipped her into his bulging shoulder satchel and reached for the infant. As the giant pinched the baby between a massive thumb and forefinger, it seemed to Rikus that he could hear nothing but the child's wailing voice.

The rest of the farmers came spilling out of the faro field. With the Scourge's magic, Rikus could hear their individual shrieks of panic as the second giant stooped over to scoop them up.

Suddenly, Magnus's voice howled over the valley, amplified by the power of his wind-magic. "You giants, leave those people alone!"

The command filled Rikus's ears with a painful ringing. His first instinct was to drop his sword, but he forced himself to retain his grip and concentrated on the cries of the farmers. As the windsinger's voice faded away, the mul heard their voices crying out in astonishment. The paupers turned toward the butte and two pointed toward the summit.

Rikus waved his arm to attract their attention. "Come this way!"

This time, the mul was close enough to make himself heard. Several farmers looked in his direction, then the whole group began to run toward him.

The hook-nosed giant stooped over and smashed half a dozen farmers beneath his fist.

"Don't run no more!" The words were loud enough that even without the Scourge, Rikus would have had no trouble understanding them.

The giant raised his hand to strike again. To Rikus's relief, the other one grabbed his partner's enormous arm before any more paupers were smashed. "Patch said to catch them, not smash them," said the second titan. He pointed at Rikus. "Besides, here comes a dangerous-looking one."

"That's right!" Rikus yelled. Though he was still two dozen steps away, the mul raised his sword. "Hurt any more of my people, and I'll make your death a slow one!"

The first giant crinkled his hooked nose and glanced at his partner. "I'll smash him, Tay?"

"No, Yab," Tay countered, pulling Yab back. "Your brother would crack my head if I let a little man cut you."

Tay stepped past the farmers and lumbered forward. The giant stood taller than the four-story townhouses that lined the streets of the nobles' quarter in Tyr. As he came within striking range, the mul had to crane his neck back to keep a watch on the titan's enormous hands.

The giant reached down to grasp Rikus. The mul waited until the palm filled the sky above him, then voiced his mightiest war cry. The Scourge flashed up, its enchanted blade slicing cleanly through the sinew and bone of three sword-length fingers.

Tay bellowed in pain. Rikus dove forward and rolled. Hot stones scraped at his shoulders and back, then the mul was on his feet again, running toward the open space between the titan's ankles.

"Stomp him!" yelled Yab.

Tay lifted a foot high into the air. Rikus dodged toward the opposite leg, and the giant's heel crashed down behind him. The impact was so hard that it bounced the mul off the ground.

Rikus swung his sword at Tay's leg. Again, the ancient steel passed through the giant's flesh easily, slicing through the vulnerable knee joint. The mul whirled around instantly, striking at the back of the giant's other ankle. There was a sick sort of pop as the tendon separated, balling up into two gnarled masses beneath the titan's skin. Rikus pulled the Scourge free and ran as fast as he could.

Tay screamed and spun around to catch him. The giant's slashed knee buckled as soon as he set his foot back on the ground. When the titan tried to steady himself with his other leg, his severed ankle flopped about uselessly. He pitched over sideways, hitting the ground with a thunderous crash. He thrashed about madly, clutching at his wounds and raising a billowing cloud of orange dust.

The farmers fled toward the butte, giving Tay a wide berth and cheering Rikus. The mul waved them on, then turned his attention to Yab. The giant's crag-toothed mouth hung open, while his gaze flickered back and forth between his injured partner and Rikus.

"You've had your fun," Rikus called. He stopped and pointed his sword at the giant's satchel. "Put those people down."

Yab's face turned crimson with anger. "No," he boomed. "First return our Oracle."

"What Oracle?" Rikus demanded.

"The giants' Oracle," the giant replied, glowering. "The one you Tyrians stole."

"We never stole anything," Rikus snarled, starting toward the giant again.

"Liar!" Yab bent over to scoop a boulder off the ground.

Magnus's lyrical voice rang out from the base of the butte. He sang a deep, somber ballad that filled the entire valley with a strain of melancholy notes. The morning grew still for a moment, then the windsinger raised his voice in a pulsing vibrato that sent whirls of dust scurrying across the desert. Rikus heard a gentle whistle behind him, then felt a strong wind blowing toward the giant.

Yab hurled his boulder.

Magnus's voice rose to a crashing crescendo, and a tremendous gust blasted past Rikus, so powerful that it swept the mul off his feet and hurled him to the ground. In the same instant, the gale caught Yab's boulder and flung it back into the giant's face. The stone bounced off the titan's cheek, raising a shiny lump and opening a long gash below the eye.

Yab ran his hand along the cut, then licked the blood from his fingers as if he were checking to make sure it was real.

Rikus returned to his feet. After glancing back to see Magnus's thick-limbed form plodding toward him, he resumed his walk toward Yab. "Put those people down," he yelled. "I won't tell you again."

The giant reached into the satchel and withdrew a gray-haired half-elf. He hurtled the man to the ground, smashing the man's frail body on the rocks.

Snarling in anger, Rikus sprinted forward. Yab thrust his hand into the sack again, this time withdrawing the careworn mother Rikus had seen earlier. "Stop there!"

The mul came to a reluctant stop, realizing that he

could not save the woman by continuing his charge. He would have to find some other way to make the giant obey.

Yab grinned maliciously. "Now drop your little knife and come over here."

Rikus glanced back at Tay's groaning form. "I don't think so."

The mul retreated toward the wounded giant, keeping his sword ready in case Tay lashed out at him.

"What're you doing?" Yab demanded.

"The same thing you are," Rikus replied, stopping a few paces from Tay's head. The wounded giant growled and reached toward Rikus with his uninjured hand, but stopped short when the mul placed his blade between the titan's fingers and himself. "What you do to those people, I do to your friend."

Yab frowned and scratched his ear. He stared at Rikus and muttered to himself in muffled tones, then shrugged and stepped into the faro fields.

"Where are you going?" Rikus asked, puzzled by the giant's peculiar retreat.

"Don't hurt Tay, or all these people die. And I can find plenty more, too." The giant stepped behind Rasda's Wall and disappeared from sight.

Rikus started to pursue, then thought of the plantation behind the ridge and decided to wait. By pursuing immediately, he would only provoke Yab into a fit of destructive rage. Instead, the mul thought it wiser to interrogate Tay about the condition of the farm and its inhabitants, then decide what to do.

Before Rikus could begin his inquiries, Magnus stepped to his side. "I sent a wind-whisper to Sadira."

"Is she coming?" Rikus asked.

"Not yet," the windsinger replied. "She and the others were just leaving for the council meeting, and at the time it looked like you had things well in hand. Should I tell her I was wrong?"

Rikus shook his head. "Let's see what Tay has to say." He waved a hand toward Rasda's Wall. "Keep a watch and let me know if you see Yab coming back from the farm."

"He's probably too busy gathering more hostages, but I'll keep an eye turned in that direction." The windsinger positioned himself so that one of his round eyes was directed toward the ridge and the other toward Rikus.

Gripping his sword with both hands, the mul laid the blade across the giant's immense gullet. "What are you and Yab doing here?"

"We c-came for our Oracle." Tay could not keep his plump lips from quivering as he spoke. "Two Tyrians stole it, your king and a nobleman."

Rikus frowned. "Tithian and Agis of Asticles?"

"That sounds like what our chief called them." Tay kept platter-sized eyes fixed on the mul's face.

"Don't lie to me," the mul said. He pressed down until a trickle of blood ran from beneath his blade. "Agis is no thief. Besides, he wouldn't help Tithian."

"Not even to kill the Dragon?" asked Magnus, still watching Rasda's Wall.

"What do you mean?" Rikus asked.

Instead of answering, the windsinger asked Tay, "What does this Oracle of yours look like?"

"A ball of black obsidian, no bigger than you," replied the giant.

"It sounds like the Dark Lens," Magnus noted.

"The Oracle!" the giant insisted. "If you don't return it, we'll raze every farm in the valley."

Paying the giant's threat no attention, Rikus asked the windsinger, "How did you know he was talking about the lens?"

Magnus shrugged modestly. "Tithian had to be looking for something when he snuck out of Tyr," he said. "My guess is that Agis caught him, and they both found the lens in the giants' possession."

"They stole it!" Tay growled. "And you've got to give it back—or something bad's going to happen to us all."

"What?" Rikus demanded.

"Only the chiefs know," Tay answered. "But giants won't be the only ones to suffer. We were guarding the Oracle for everyone on Athas."

"You're going to have to do better than that," Rikus threatened.

"Not at the moment," said Magnus.

The windsinger pointed toward Rasda's Wall, where Yab's head had just appeared above the low shoulder. He was looking back toward the plantation, yelling, "Come quick, Sachem Patch! Tay's hurt."

"What hurt him?" From the faintness of the reply, Rikus guessed that this giant was a considerable distance away—probably in the fields on the far side of the farm.

"A little bald man," yelled Yab. "He looks kind of like a dwarf."

"Tay let a *dwarf* hurt him?" chuckled a fourth giant. "What did Tay do—slip on the blood when he stomped it?"

A storm of laughter erupted behind the outcrop, and Rikus knew he had seriously underestimated the number of giants attacking the plantation. Apparently, while Yab and Tay chased down the escaping paupers, most of the war party had remained behind to destroy the farm itself.

Rikus looked back to Tay. "How many warriors in your group?"

"Eight," Tay said. He smirked at the mul.

"We'd better run for it," Rikus said. He stepped away from Tay, pulling the windsinger along with him.

"No!" boomed Tay. "Stop!"

Rikus looked up and saw the giant's hand descending toward their heads, balled up in a tight fist as large as a shield. The mul shoved Magnus in one direction and dove in the other. Tay's fist landed between them, cracking stones and raising a plume of orange dust. In the next instant, they were both on their feet and scrambling over the rocky ground at their best sprint.

It took a dozen steps and two more close calls before they were safely out of the crippled titan's reach, and even then they continued toward the far end of the valley at their best pace.

Magnus came over to Rikus's side. "Should I send for Sadira now?"

Before answering, the mul glanced over his shoulder. Yab was stepping out from behind Rasda's Wall, no longer carrying his shoulder satchel. Behind him came another giant, much larger than either him or Tay. This one wore a black shawl draped over one eye.

"Call her," Rikus said. "But tell her not to do anything until she sees eight giants. If we let any of them escape, it could take days to track them down."

The windsinger nodded, then a soft, lilting strain rose from deep within his throat. So perfect was his breath control that his voice betrayed no hint of strain, even though he was still running. As Magnus repeated the message, air whirled around the windsinger's head with a hushed, melodic hissing that sounded to the mul like whispering ghosts.

Magnus completed the message, finishing with, "To my brother the parching wind I commit these words. Carry them to the ears of Sadira and no one else."

An eerie silence replaced the hissing of the wind. Then Rikus saw a series of dust-whirls skipping across the desert as Magnus's spell streaked toward Tyr.

The mul and the windsinger ran another dozen steps before boulders began to crash down to all sides of them, filling the air with flying chips of stone and the mordant smell of powdered rock. A billowing cloud of sand and dust engulfed them, and Rikus heard Magnus cry out. The windsinger slammed to the ground amid a mad clatter of rocks.

"Magnus!" Rikus called, whirling around.

"Here," came the reply. Through the clearing dust, Rikus saw Magnus pushing himself to his knees. "It just glanced off me."

Rikus went to the windsinger's side and took his arm. "Can you still run?" He helped his big friend to his feet.

"Perhaps a little slower than before," Magnus replied, looking back toward the farm. "But we'd be wiser to duck."

Following his friend's gaze, Rikus saw Patch, Yab, and five more giants charging past Tay. The titans were all struggling to retain their balance, having launched another flight of boulders while on the run. The jagged shapes were already descending toward the mul and his companion.

Rikus dropped to the ground and covered his head. A tremendous crack sounded ahead as a boulder smashed into a huge, half-buried stone and shattered it. A jagged shard of basalt scuffed Rikus's back, then he heard the boulder clattering across the rocky ground and felt warm blood flowing down his ribs.

"Can you stand?" asked Magnus, clasping his huge hands around the mul's waist.

"It's just a scrape," Rikus said, struggling to get his feet underneath him. He looked toward the giants and saw that they were charging. "Let's keep—"

The mul was interrupted by a loud whoosh, and a large sphere of black haze appeared in the air. It hovered there for a moment, then gently settled onto the ground and began forming the shadow of a slender woman.

As it drained from the air, the dark fog left a winsome sorceress standing in its place. She had waves of amber hair spilling over her shoulders, and her skin was as dark as ebony. Her eyes had no pupils and glowed like blue embers, while wisps of black shadow slipped from between her lips whenever she exhaled.

"Good timing, Sadira," Rikus said, accustomed to seeing his wife arrive in this manner. Like Magnus, she had also visited the Pristine Tower. As a result, she had been transformed into something the mul did not understand—and that he was not entirely sure he liked.

Sadira slipped past Rikus and Magnus. "I see only seven giants," she said, kneeling on the ground. "I thought there were eight."

Turning back toward their attackers, Rikus saw that his wife's conspicuous arrival had caused the giants to stop and reach for more boulders to throw. The mul was not surprised, for even the dullest warrior would recognize Sadira as a sorceress and approach her with caution.

Rikus pointed at Tay's prone form. "The eighth is lying over there."

"Good."

Sadira turned one ebony palm into the sky. Rikus was surprised to see the signet ring of her other husband, Agis of Asticles, glimmering on her finger. Before the mul could ask where it had come from, a string of mystic syllables flowed from the sorceress's blue lips, and a wave of pulsing red energy sizzled into the valley floor. The glow fanned outward from her fingers in a brilliant flash. Stone and sand began to melt into a hot, viscous mud, sending yellow wisps of acrid smoke curling into the sky.

The spell swept out to Yab and his company. Screaming in terror and confusion, the giants sank to their waists in the mush. The boulders they had been grasping turned to liquid and drained from between their fingers. Then the whole field gradually hardened into a steaming orange plain as smooth as glass. The titan wearing the patch roared in anger and began to pound at the lustrous ground, but the stuff was as hard as granite and showed no sign of cracking.

Sadira withdrew a ball of yellow wax from her pocket

and began working it between her fingers. Rikus knew from experience that she was preparing some sort of fire spell.

Rikus laid a hand across her wrists. "How long will your first spell hold them?"

"Until the sun goes down."

Rikus nodded, for it was the answer he had expected. Sadira's powers lasted as long as the sun was in the sky, and generally so did any spell that she cast during the day. There were exceptions, however, so he had thought it wisest to check before making his next suggestion.

"You might not want to kill the giants," he said. "They seem to know something about Agis and Tithian. They also claimed that the Dark Lens was stolen from them, and that if we don't give it back, something terrible will happen."

Sadira's eyes flashed a deeper shade of blue. "Do you believe them?"

Rikus shrugged. "I didn't have time to ask many questions," he said. "But I don't think we'll solve anything by killing this bunch. The giants will just send more warriors to recover the lens. We'd be better off to convince them that we don't have it."

Sadira considered this for a moment, then nodded. "We'll talk with them later," she said. "But I must return to Tyr now. The warder had just opened the chamber doors when I received Magnus's message, and I should be there."

Rikus nodded. "We'll stay here."

Sadira shook her head. "You're needed in Tyr, to lead the legion out of the city," she said. "Return as quickly as you can. I'd take you with me, but the spell I must use can carry only one."

"Don't worry about it," Rikus said, just as glad he would not have to endure the touch of her strange magic. "But what about the giants?"

"They can't escape—and if they could, you couldn't

stop them."

The sorceress raised both hands toward the sun. Her shadow formed a circle around her feet, then rose up to swallow her body in a dark fog.

THREE

The Council of Advisors

When Sadira stepped into the vaulted murkiness of the advisors' chamber, she saw that the entire host of Tyrian councilors stood shoulder-to-shoulder on the orator's floor, while the feather-stuffed chairs in the gallery sat empty. She knew instantly that this morning's session would be a trying one, and that her opponents on the council would use her tardiness to make it even more difficult. Although her trip to help Rikus and Magnus had delayed the meeting less than a quarter hour, many advisors made a point of shuffling around to cast impatient glares in her direction.

Sadira started across the floor. The advisors were divided into four different groups, each gathered around a podium in a separate quarter of the floor. In the far corner, with the rays of the morning sun spilling through the windows behind them, were the guildsmen. Mostly humans and dwarves, they were dressed in sooty aprons and clay-specked tabards appropriate to their various professions. Next to them stood the free citizens, consisting of hemp-robed muls, half-elves, tareks, humans, and anyone else who had been either a slave or pauper before Tyr's liberation. Closer to the entrance were the nobles, dressed in exotic silks of every color and description, and the templars, who embellished their black cassocks with bronze neckchains and breastpins of precious copper.

As Sadira passed between the noble and templar podiums, she found her way blocked by a double-chinned templar. He had a shaved head, eyes as shadowy as her own skin, and a long silver chain hanging around his corpulent neck.

"Sadira, here you are—at last!" he said, smiling just enough to bare his gray incisors. "How kind of you to come so promptly to the meeting you called."

"If a short delay matters so much, then I suggest you let me pass so we can get started, Cybrian." Sadira tried to step around the heavy templar.

"I think we can excuse your tardiness," said a blue-frocked noblewoman, moving forward to block the sorceress's way. She was a handsome woman with gray eyes, silver hair, and a patrician nose. The lady eyed Sadira's dusty robe, then clucked her tongue and added, "But your raiment is another matter. By now, you should realize that your apparel reflects your respect for the council itself."

Sadira suppressed the urge to make a sharp reply, suspecting that the noblewoman's purpose was to disrupt the meeting by starting a senseless argument.

"To the contrary, Lady Laaj," the sorceress said. "I came as I am because I have no wish to keep the council waiting."

Sadira stepped between the noblewoman and Cybrian. When her adversaries tried to stand their ground, the sorceress chuckled at their foolishness. While her ebony body was steeped in the power of the sun, even a half-giant could not have blocked her way. She brushed the pair aside easily, sending them stumbling into the midst of their respective groups, and walked over to the free citizens. Here, the sorceress found her three guests waiting.

"Who were those two?" asked Neeva. A former gladiator with blond hair, deep emerald eyes, and a figure as powerful as it was voluptuous, she wore only a breechcloth and halter, with a cape of green silk thrown over her shoulders to show respect for the council.

Sadira cast a contemptuous eye upon the two advisors she had just shoved aside. "The lady fancies herself the leader of the noble faction in Agis's absence, and the templar is one of several who claims to speak in Tithian's name," the sorceress explained. "Because I asked the legion to stand ready this morning, they must think we're going to find Agis and Tithian. Neither one would like that; they enjoy playing leader too much."

"Never mind them," interrupted Rkard, Neeva's mul son. "What about Rikus?"

Though only six years old, the boy already stood as tall as most dwarves, with long graceful limbs, a sturdy frame, and cords of muscle running across his chest and arms. Like Rikus, he had sharply pointed ears and a hairless body, but he also had the distinguishing marks of a young sun-cleric: red eyes and a crimson sun emblazoned on his forehead.

"Both Rikus and Magnus are fine," Sadira said. "They'll be coming along later."

"What happened?" Rkard pressed. "If Rikus needed help, it must have been bad trouble."

"We can talk about that later, son," said Caelum. He had the blocky features, pointed ears, and hairless body typical of a dwarf, with the same red eyes and crimson mark his son Rkard bore. In his hands, the dwarf grasped a closed ironwood box that Sadira had asked him to hold during the council meeting. "Right now, we have business to conduct."

Caelum offered the box in his hands to Sadira. "Do

you need this?"

"Not yet."

Sadira climbed onto the podium and peered over the heads of her fellow advisors. The nobles and templars quickly grew silent, for Lady Laaj and Cybrian already stood on the respective pulpits for their two factions. But the guildsmen did not stifle their contentious discussions for several moments, until a bony, slender-faced man climbed onto the last platform. With the sooty apron of a blacksmith strapped over his chest, he looked as though he had come to the meeting straight from his shop.

"Charl Birkett to speak for the guilds," he declared. "Gar won't be coming today."

"Then we can begin," said Cybrian.

The templar raised his arm toward the murkiness of the vaulted ceiling, as did Lady Laaj. Their hands were closed, save that they held their index fingers open enough to form a small circle with their thumbs.

"What are you doing?" Sadira demanded.

"You may have convened the meeting, but any orator has the right to call for the wrab," replied Lady Laaj.

"Surely you haven't forgotten," added Cybrian. "The tradition's as ancient as Tyr itself."

"I remember council practice better than you remember common courtesy," Sadira replied, thrusting her own hand into the air. "Since Kalak's death, it's always been the one who called the meeting who controls the floor first."

A shrill screech echoed off the stone arches. A tiny winged serpent dropped out of the ceiling's shadowy coves. The creature glided around the room, barely distinguishable from the gloom above it. Everything about the flying snake was black: the leathery wings, the huge eyes, even the scaly body and barbed tail.

The wrab passed low over Sadira's hand and circled back once. She thought it would perch on her finger, but its tongue suddenly flickered in Cybrian's direction. It flapped its wings and sailed over to the templar. After coiling up on his hand, it thrust its tiny head down inside his curled fingers and remained motionless.

Sadira lowered her hand, not entirely discouraged. Cybrian would control the meeting's agenda for now, but the wrab was notoriously restless. A natural user of the Way, it was trained to sense whether or not the assembly approved of the speaker's topic. When the crowd's interest began to ebb, it would seek a new roost from the upraised fingers, and control of the session would pass to the person it chose.

"Sadira, will you explain why you were late to your own meeting?" Cybrian asked, smirking.

"Perhaps later," said the sorceress.

Her refusal to answer the question was in disregard for council rules, but it was also a common tactic used to gain control of the wrab. If she could interest the other advisors in her topic quickly enough, the creature would leave Cybrian's hand and roost on her finger before he could call for a vote of censure and ask her to leave the chamber.

The sorceress motioned for Rkard to come up and stand with her, then continued, "I think my fellow councilors will be more interested in hearing how this boy is going to kill the Dragon."

The advisors greeted her statement with snorts of derision and even a few guffaws, but her tactic worked. As skeptical as they were, the councilors were also curious. The wrab quickly left Cybrian's hand and came to Sadira's. The creature weighed almost nothing, and, if not for its damp scales tickling her flesh, the sorceress would hardly have noticed its presence.

Cybrian glared at Sadira, but did not object. He had used the same technique too many times to cry foul. "By all means, tell us," he sneered. "I'm certain my fellow advisors will appreciate a good jest."

The templar's tactic was an effective one, playing on the crowd's skepticism to such an extent that the wrab raised its black wings as if to leave Sadira's hand.

"Perhaps you would waste the council's time on a jest, Cybrian. You've certainly wasted it on many things just as trivial," Sadira said sharply. "But I assure you, I would never do such a thing."

The wrab folded its wings and pushed its tiny head down into her fist. Seeing that she had won the assembly's support, at least for a time, Sadira laid her free hand on Rkard's shoulder. The boy stood straight and tall, looking out over the volatile throng with an unflinching gaze.

"This mul boy is the son of Neeva, whom many of you will remember from her days as a gladiator, and of Caelum, son to the late *uhrnomus* of Kled," Sadira said.

"Ten days ago, Rkard was visited by a pair of dwarven banshees, Jo'orsh and Sa'ram," the sorceress continued. "Those of you who are familiar with the *Book of the Kemalok Kings* will recognize the names as those of the last two dwarven knights, who died before they could avenge the Dragon's destruction of their city."

"And they told the child to do what they could not—kill Borys?" asked Charl, incredulous.

"Not exactly," replied Sadira. "They said that he *would* kill the Dragon."

"And who heard them say this?" asked Lady Laaj.

"I did," Rkard replied.

This prompted the noblewoman to give Sadira a patronizing smile. "My dear, since you have no children, you may not realize that young boys create make-believe friends," she said. "Why, when my own sons were his age—"

"He did not make up Jo'orsh and Sa'ram," Neeva reported. "I also saw the banshees."

"And we have another harbinger as well," Sadira said. She raised her hand, displaying the ring on her finger. "Last night, a messenger arrived bearing my husband's signet."

"Which husband? Agis, Rikus, or someone we haven't heard about yet?" mocked Cybrian. "Maybe that dwarf?"

The comment drew a few crude laughs from the same pedants who always thought ill of Sadira for loving two men, but it failed to shake the crowd's interest enough to dislodge the wrab.

"The signet is Agis's," Sadira said patiently. "With it came the message that he had found the Dark Lens."

For the first time that day, the room fell completely quiet. Despite the efforts of Sadira and her husbands to keep the nature of the Dark Lens secret, they had spent five years searching for it and word of what they were seeking had eventually leaked out. By now, most of the advisors knew not only what the lens was, but why Sadira was seeking it. She intended to kill Borys, thus ending his practice of collecting a thousand slaves a year from each city of Athas. If the sorceress and her friends succeeded, not only would they save untold numbers of lives, they would also eliminate the greatest danger to Tyr itself: that the Dragon would attack the city for refusing to pay his gruesome levy.

It was Rkard who broke the astonished silence. "Jo'orsh and Sa'ram said I will kill the Dragon." The boy addressed the advisors directly, utterly composed and confident. "But they also said I would need an army—an army of humans and dwarves."

"Kled's militia is prepared to fulfill this prophecy," Neeva said. "After I learned of Rkard's destiny, I summoned them to guard against attempts on his life. Even as we speak, they are at the Asticles estate, preparing to march."

"And that's why you have commanded Tyr's legion to stand ready for action?" demanded Cybrian. "To give it to a child?"

"The legion will remain under Rikus's command, as

always," Sadira replied.

"Speaking of Rikus, where is he?" asked Lady Laaj. "I'm sure that all of the advisors want to hear his opinion of this plan before voting."

Sadira took a deep breath, knowing that her answer would send the council into an uproar. Still, she did not even consider concealing the fact that there were giants in the valley. The advisors had a right to know about any threat to Tyr, even if it meant it would be harder for her to get what she wanted.

"Well?" Cybrian asked.

"As they were returning to attend this meeting, Rikus and Magnus happened across some rampaging giants at our newest relief farm," Sadira explained. "I've trapped the invaders for now—"

The chamber broke into a tumult as astonished advisors began yelling questions across the packed floor:

"You mean half-giants?"

"How many?"

"What do they want?"

The wrab slithered completely into Sadira's hand. The sorceress felt confident that it would rather have retreated to its lair in the ceiling alcoves, but it was too well trained to flee while a speaker had commanded such rapt attention.

"Quiet, please!" Sadira shouted. "We can't accomplish anything like this!"

The furor slowly faded to a drone.

As soon as it was possible to speak without screaming, Lady Laaj asked, "How many giants are there, and what are they doing so far from the Sea of Silt?"

"There are eight of them, and they want the Dark Lens," answered Sadira.

"Then I suggest we tell the giants where to find it—before they destroy us," said Cybrian.

"I can't do that," Sadira said. "Not only would that endanger Agis—"

"Agis would be the first to sacrifice himself for the good of Tyr," Lady Laaj interrupted. "Every noble knows that."

"True—if his sacrifice would save Tyr," Sadira agreed. "But it wouldn't. Unless we kill the Dragon—"

"We won't discuss such nonsense!" declared Cybrian.

"Would you rather let him destroy the city?" Sadira countered. "Or are you willing to sacrifice a thousand lives a year to him?"

"Your scare tactics won't succeed here," Cybrian said. "We have nothing to gain by attacking the Dragon. He hasn't been to Tyr since Kalak died."

"That's because Tithian has been paying the levy in secret," Sadira replied.

"With what?" scoffed the templar. "His personal staff?"

"With men, women, and children kidnapped by his slavers," said Neeva, stepping forward to stand at Sadira's side. "They attacked our village less than four months ago."

"How dare you speak such a lie!" Cybrian stormed. "King Tithian freed the slaves. He'd never—"

"He did, and I can prove it," Sadira interrupted. She looked down at Caelum. "Open the box."

The dwarf obeyed. A shriveled, ash-colored head with sunken features and cracked lips rose out of the box. It hovered in the air for a moment, its sallow eyes roaming over the assembly, then floated up to Sadira's level.

Gasping in disbelief, the advisors pressed close around the sorceress's podium, craning their necks to peer up at the disembodied head. Though many of the councilors had heard rumors that King Tithian kept a pair of disembodied heads as companions, few of them had ever seen one in person.

"Some of you may recognize the king's confidant, Wyan," Sadira said. "He's the one who brought Agis's signet ring to me."

Wyan regarded the assemblage with a sneer, then rotated around to face Sadira. "What do you want?"

The sorceress nodded toward the crowd. "Tell them about Tithian's slavers."

Sadira did not worry that the head would disobey or lie. Wyan was one of the Dragon's most ancient enemies, for Borys had separated him from his body more than a thousand years ago. Since then, the head had been condemned to a miserable existence where his sole physical pleasure was the drinking of warm blood. The sorceress had no doubts that Wyan would do whatever it took to destroy the Dragon, even if it meant betraying one of Tithian's most carefully guarded secrets.

When Wyan did not speak up quickly, Sadira reminded him, "The sooner you talk, the sooner we can attack Borys."

With a weary sigh, Wyan looked out over the advisors. "The king was only thinking of Tyr," he said. "Anyone who thinks the Dragon would be denied his levy is a fool. Tithian did what was necessary to protect the city."

The chorus of outrage that followed came mostly from the free citizens, but many of the guildsmen also added their voices. The nobles looked more frightened by Wyan's admission than angered, while the templars quietly exchanged whispered comments of concern.

Wyan cautiously floated higher in the air, apparently fearing that one of the free citizens might try to hold him responsible for Tithian's acts.

"Let me see if I understand this correctly," said Lady Laaj. "You want the council to give you the legion so you can go off to battle the Dragon—leaving Tyr to defend itself from eight full giants?"

At this, the wrab crawled out of Sadira's hand and launched itself into the air. For a moment, the sorceress didn't understand why it had abandoned her, since everyone in the room seemed to be interested in the same thing. Then she realized that it was a matter of emphasis. Lady Laaj was talking about the defense of Tyr, while Sadira was still trying to convince the advisors to kill the Dragon.

Hoping the wrab would return to her, Sadira kept her hand in the air. "As I was saying earlier, I have the giants under control for now," she said. "Before we take the legion out of the valley, they will be under control permanently—one way or another."

The wrab settled on Lady Laaj's finger. "And what if there are other giants?" the noblewoman asked. "The Dark Lens must be very valuable to them. Surely, they'll send more warriors when these don't return."

"We should be back by then," Sadira said, reluctantly lowering her hand.

"That's not something you can guarantee, my friend," said Charl, the guildsmen's speaker. He shook his head sadly. "I'm sorry, but what Lady Laaj says is right. It's foolish to worry about the Dragon when angry giants are about to storm the city."

The noblewoman smiled. "We'll put the matter to a vote," she said. "All those in favor of telling the giants where to find the Dark Lens—"

"There's no need to vote," Sadira said. With the other three orators supporting it, the sorceress knew without a doubt that Lady Laaj's motion would pass. "I won't reveal the location of the lens—none of us will. You'd be condemning Agis to death."

"You'd defy the council for the sake of your husband—the same husband who has lectured this body so many times on the importance of lawful rule?" asked Cybrian.

"How dare you speak to me about the law!" Sadira spat. "You're only doing this because you hope to see Agis and Tithian dead. You want control of the council."

"Maybe that's true of them, but not of me," said Charl. "If you defy Lady Laaj and Cybrian on this matter, you're defying the entire council. You, more than anyone, should know that when someone of your power does that, the city is on the path to despotism."

"Tyranny of the many is tyranny nonetheless." Sadira hissed the words, spewing wisps of black shadow over the heads of those standing between her and the guildsman. "If this council betrays Agis, voting to do it together makes the act no less wicked."

"We have already discussed the matter," said Lady Laaj. "Your magic is powerful enough that the council cannot compel you to obey, but we *can* strip you of citizenship. Will you comply with the council's wishes or not?"

When Sadira replied, her throat was tight with anger. "No."

The sorceress stepped off the podium, motioning for Rkard to follow.

"What are you doing?" demanded Caelum.

"Leaving Tyr," Sadira replied, starting for the door.

"But what about Rkard's destiny?" asked the dwarf. "Jo'orsh and Sa'ram said that he would have humans as well as dwarves in his army."

The sorceress cast a cold glance over the council chamber. "Apparently, those humans will not be from Tyr," she said. "We'll gather them somewhere else."

"There isn't time to find another army!" snapped Wyan. "The giants won't be the only ones searching for the Dark Lens. Every day we delay increases the chance that the sorcerer-kings—or Borys—will find it before we arrive!"

Sadira turned around and faced the head, who was still hovering high over the free citizens' podium. "We can't have Tyr's legion," she said. "You can see for yourself we don't have the votes."

Wyan ignored her and glared down at the advisors.

"The city was better off under Kalak!" he yelled. "We will have our legion!"

The head floated closer to the ceiling, placing himself directly in the sun's rays streaming through the window. His shadow fell in the center of the chamber floor, covering the heads of more than a dozen councilors, and began to expand. Crying out in alarm, the advisors pushed their way into the gallery seats. As the floor emptied, the black shadow spread across the granite blocks like an ink stain.

"Wyan, no!" Sadira commanded, hardly able to believe what she was seeing. She had known for some time that the head could communicate with the shadow giants, the nebulous beings of the Black, but she had never before seen any evidence that he could summon them to Athas. "Stop!"

When Wyan did not listen, Sadira pulled a glass rod from her pocket and pointed it at him. The head's eyes went wide. Before she could begin the incantation to her spell, he left the light and flew up into the murky alcoves of the ceiling.

It did not matter. The shadow on the floor had taken on the shape of a tall thin man with ropy limbs. A pair of sapphire eyes began to shine from the head, and a blue gash opened where the thing's mouth should have been.

Sadira pushed Rkard toward his mother. The sorceress did not need to utter any warning, for both women had seen such creatures before. Neeva had fought a shadow giant named Umbra during the war with Urik, while Sadira had visited the shadow people's home in the Pristine Tower.

As Neeva took the child, she asked, "Are you going to allow this, Sadira?"

"It's not for me to allow or disallow," the sorceress replied. "The shadow people are the ones who bestowed my powers on me, and my magic won't work against them."

"But you've got to do something!" Caelum said. "We need Tyr's legion."

"I have no way to interfere," Sadira snapped. "When I can do something, I will!"

The shadow rose to its feet, taking on a full three-dimensional body as tall as that of a half-giant. It stepped toward Cybrian and Lady Laaj, who defiantly remained standing on their podiums.

"Your tricks won't fool us." Cybrian looked past the shadow to Sadira. "You won't win your way with a simple illusion."

"The Black is no illusion!" hissed the shadow giant, stretching a hand out to each of the pair.

Recognizing the voice as that of the chief of the shadow people, Sadira stepped after the dark being. "Khidar, leave them alone."

"You are not the one who asked me to take them," the shadow replied.

Khidar wrapped his sinuous fingers over the pair's skulls. As their faces disappeared into darkness, the wrab took wing and disappeared into its shadowy lair. Cybrian screamed, then Lady Laaj, their voices harmonizing into a single pained, fearful howl.

Sadira grabbed the arm holding the noblewoman. The shadow giant's flesh felt misty and cold, and holding it was like trying to grasp water. Still, the sorceress came closer to touching it than most beings, and when she pulled, tendrils of the arm came away in her hand. The black filaments evaporated into the air, vanishing like a dawn mist in the morning sun.

Khidar's murky substance continued to swallow the templar and noblewoman, slipping over their shoulders, then down their wildly thrashing arms. Finally, the shadow consumed even their hips and legs, and they were gone.

For all of her magical powers, Sadira was helpless to stop the shadow giant. Casting a spell against him would have been useless, like trying to pierce the sun with a ray of light, and she knew better than to try. If she accomplished anything, it would only be to enrage Khidar to the point where he attacked more councilors.

Instead, the sorceress looked toward the ceiling. Though she could not see Wyan, she had no doubt that he was still up there in the murk. "This accomplishes nothing, Wyan. An army coerced into fighting is an army of slaves," she said. "You know that neither Rikus, Neeva, nor I will have anything to do with that."

"Then let the council vote," Wyan countered. "They can do it here, or in the Black."

"Why bother?" demanded Charl Birkett. He stepped onto the floor and crossed to Sadira. "You and your friends have the power to take the legion, whether we like it or not—but I won't lend my name to a sham." The guildsman spat on the sorceress's sandaled feet and turned toward the exit.

Khidar blocked his path. "The council has not voted," said the shadow giant.

Charl glanced over his shoulder and glared at Sadira. "Tell this thing to stand aside."

"I had no respect for Lady Laaj or Cybrian, true, but this is not my doing," Sadira said. "You saw me try to stop him."

"I saw you pretend to try," the guildsman retorted. "Do not take me for a fool."

Charl tried to step past Khidar. The shadow giant raised a hand to stop him. Sadira lashed out, closing her powerful fingers around the guildsman's shoulder, and pulled him back. She shoved him roughly toward the gallery seats, drawing a murmur of angry comments from the other advisors.

"I suggest you vote." The sorceress looked at Khidar, knowing that by now Lady Laaj and Cybrian would be half-frozen with the cold of the Black. "And do it now."

Without taking his narrowed eyes off her face, Charl

growled, "All those who think we should give our legion to Sadira?"

"Aye," came the response.

Though the chorus was far from deafening, Charl said, "The motion carries. Now can we leave?"

Sadira glanced up at the ceiling. "Are you happy?"

Wyan came down out of the shadowy alcoves just far enough to be seen. "Your duties are finished, Khidar."

"What of the noblewoman and the templar?" the shadow giant asked.

"Keep them," Wyan sneered. "They'll serve as an example to those who cross me."

"As you wish."

The shadow giant began to shrink. He quickly lost his human shape and melted onto the floor like a puddle of black water. Sadira waited until his blue eyes and mouth disappeared, then dropped to her knees and pressed her palms into the center of the dark stain that had been Khidar. The cold she felt was not that of the stone. It was more bitter and biting, numbing her flesh to the bone and stiffening her joints so that she could hardly bend her fingers.

"Caelum, keep Wyan out of the light!" she yelled, not looking up.

"I'll burn him to cinders if I see him poke so much as his nose out!" the dwarf promised.

Sadira uttered a string of mystic syllables and her hands sank into the Black up to her elbows.

"Lady Laaj, Cybrian, take my hands!" Sadira directed her words at the floor, and began to shiver as the circle of shadow slowly contracted around her arms. "I'm here to help you!"

Whispers of astonishment echoed down from the galleries as the advisors started to return to the floor, but Sadira hardly noticed. Her whole body ached with cold, and her teeth chattered uncontrollably. She began to fear that the noblewoman and templar had been gone too long, that the Black had turned their bodies into frozen lumps of flesh.

Then, as the stain on the floor contracted to no more than a pair of small circles around her arms, Sadira felt a weight at the end of each hand. Her frozen flesh no longer had any sensation of touch, so the sorceress had no way of knowing whether or not the missing advisors had finally found her. Nevertheless, she willed her fingers to close, not sure whether the digits were obeying her wishes, and rose.

As Sadira pulled her arms from the floor, each of the dark circles around them expanded to the size of a human body. Out of the shadowy stains came the shivering forms of the two advisors. Their flesh was as pale and shiny as alabaster, and their muscles were so stiff that their own legs would not support them. With each breath, plumes of white steam rose from between their quivering lips, and hundreds of gleaming ice crystals clung to their clothes.

Murmuring reticent words of gratitude, several allies of the two advisors stepped forward to take their shivering friends from Sadira's arms. Charl studied the sorceress thoughtfully, then asked, "Why'd you do that? You already got the vote you wanted."

Sadira shook her head. "No," she said. "Not the one I wanted—only the one I needed. If Khidar had taken any more of you, I wouldn't have been able to pull you all back."

"Then you really meant what you said about not taking the legion if it was coerced from us?"

Sadira nodded. "And what I said about leaving Tyr before I would be part of betraying Agis."

The sorceress started to turn toward the exit, but Charl caught her by the arm. "Wait a minute. Tyr can't afford to lose a citizen like you," he said. "If we let you take the legion to fulfill the boy's destiny, can you really keep the giants away from the city?"

"Yes," Sadira replied. "And if we can't, not only will we send the legion back, Rikus and I will return to fight with it."

Charl raised his finger to summon the wrab. "Then before you leave, there's one more vote we should take."

FOUR

The Cloud Road

Neeva crawled forward on the Cloud Road, a long ribbon of black slate hanging across the face of an enormous cliff. She reached the jagged brink where a section of the bridge had fallen away, and peered down into an arid valley. Far below lay the missing section of road, a jumble of broken rockwork strewn across a drift of red sand. The warrior saw no indication of what had caused the collapse, only a handful of limestone buttresses half-buried beneath shattered slabs of paving stone.

"This road's as old as Tyr," she growled, more to herself than the companions waiting behind her. "Why'd it have to collapse today?"

Coming as it did at the start of their journey, the breakdown did not bode well for their mission against Borys—nor for the legion's chances of reaching the giants before nightfall. Already the sun hung low over the western mountains, its rays striking the granite cliff at a direct angle, while the Tyrian warriors waited impatiently at the beginning of the Cloud Road. There were a thousand of them, all human, armed with huge obsidian axes, bone tridents with serrated tines, saw-toothed scimitars, spiked balls hanging at the ends of long coils of rope, and a variety of other weapons as deadly as man's infinite desire to murder.

Neeva looked across the missing stretch of road. A brightly cloaked merchant stood on the other side, his image dancing in the heat waves pouring off the cliff face. The man was staring into the breach and scratching his ear, his face hidden beneath the broad brim of his great round hat. Shaking his head in despair, he looked over his shoulder at a pair of inixes, wagon-sized lizards with horny beaks, pincerlike jaws, and serpentine tails. The reptiles were harnessed to a cargo dray, so large that one side was pressed tight against the cliff, while the other hung over the outside edge of the Cloud Road.

Neeva backed away from the gap.

Magnus took her arm and helped her to her feet. "What did you find?" he asked. The windsinger and Rikus had joined Neeva and the others in Tyr, shortly after the council had voted to send the city legion to help Rkard slay the Dragon.

"I didn't see much," Neeva reported. "There was nothing in the rubble to suggest something heavy made it collapse."

"I thought as much," Caelum said. He pointed at the square cavities where the buttresses had been mounted into the cliff face. "Those joining holes are in perfect condition. There aren't any broken posts sticking in them, or any chips around the edges."

"Which means?" asked Magnus.

"That the supports didn't snap because of a load or sudden impact," Caelum answered. "They came straight out. The buttresses were pulled—intentionally."

"Could be more giants," Rikus suggested. The mul was just returning from the beginning of the road, where he had gone to fetch a rope from the legion's supply kanks.

Neeva shook her head. "We're twice as high as a giant stands," she said. "Besides, why would they bother? If giants didn't want us to get across, they'd just smash the road, not pull it apart."

"Well, whoever did it, they aren't going to stop us." Rikus glanced at Rkard, who stood near his father's side, and asked, "You're not afraid to cross that gap on a rope, are you?"

"No." The boy answered sharply, frowning as though insulted.

Rikus chuckled, then said, "Good. If we don't reach the giants before dusk, our plan won't work."

They had decided the best way to make the giants leave the valley was to lure them away. While the legion surrounded the titans, Rikus and Sadira would interrogate the invaders about Agis, Tithian, and what they knew of the Dark Lens. During the questioning, the mul would let it slip that the lens was not in Tyr and that they were on their way to recover it. Then they would allow one of the titans to escape. Sadira would use her magic to spy on him and be sure that he returned to his fellows with the news that their Oracle was not in the city. Once Sadira was certain their ruse had worked, the legion would leave an obvious trail for the giants, so that any further war parties would go after the legion instead of attacking the city.

Rikus sat down on the road's jagged brink and wrapped the rope around his waist. Magnus watched him for a moment, then scowled.

"Have you thought this out?" the windsinger asked.

"Of course," Rikus answered. "Clavis said it would take a day to fix the road, and we don't have a day. So, we'll have to rope across."

"And then what?" asked Magnus. "You can't expect the whole legion to crawl across that rope. It would take too long—and with so many warriors, dozens are sure to lose their grip and fall."

"The legion can take its time, if it needs to," said Neeva. "We can fetch my militia from Agis's estate. Our numbers aren't as great, but there should be enough to support Sadira while she attacks with her magic."

"Speaking of Sadira, I'm sure she could solve our problem easily enough," Caelum suggested. "Maybe Magnus should send a message to her?"

Sadira had stayed behind in Tyr, making provisions with the Veiled Alliance to help defend the city in the legion's absence. She had promised to catch the legion long before it reached the giants, and Neeva was surprised that the sorceress had not joined them already.

"That's the wisest thing anyone has suggested yet," Magnus said. He went a few steps up the road and began to work his magic.

"I'll take a line across anyway," Rikus said, finishing his knot. "We don't have any time to waste if Sadira can't come yet."

After handing the other end of the rope to Caelum, Rikus reached out and thrust his hand into the square hole where the first missing buttress had been lodged. The mul swung out onto the cliff and reached for the next hole, grimacing as his face rubbed over the hot stone. His fingertips barely caught the bottom edge of the dark square. He worked them deeper into the cavity, then released his first hand and slipped it into the next hole.

Rikus shrieked in fear and surprise. He jerked his hand out of the far hole and began to fling it around madly. A silvery creature about as long as a stiletto had attached itself to his middle finger.

Neeva pulled her dagger and kneeled at the edge of the road. "Hold still, Rikus!" she ordered. "I can't see what you've got."

"I've got nothing!" the mul roared. "It's got me."

In spite of his shock, Rikus managed to steady his hand. A huge scorpion had clamped its pincers onto his middle finger, cutting him clear to the bone. The barb of the tail was buried deep into the back of his hand, with a great cone of red flesh already swelling up around the puncture.

"That scorpion's huge!" Caelum observed. "It couldn't have been in the hole when the buttress was there."

"Who cares?" Rikus growled. "Just get it off!" The mul pushed his hand toward the road, but could not quite reach because he had to cross his arm in front of his body.

Neeva laid down on her belly and stretched out to cut the pincers. The scorpion pulled its tail from Rikus's hand and struck at her. It moved with such blinding speed that she barely managed to twist her blade flat and deflect the venom-dripping barb. She changed targets and sliced at the thing's body, but the creature was every bit as quick as she was. Its tail lashed again, this time arcing at her wrist.

Neeva pulled back to avoid being stung. "I've seen lightning strike slower!"

"I could've told you that!" Rikus growled.

Pulling his hand back toward his body, the mul lowered his head and opened his mouth. There was a crunch of splintering carapace, then Rikus turned toward her and spit the scorpion's severed tail from between his sharp teeth. The mul extended his arm toward her. Already, his hand was so swollen that it looked more like a bear's paw.

"Get the damn thing off—now!"

As Neeva reached for the scorpion, its carapace suddenly changed from pearly gray to yellow. The color did not fade so much as it slipped off the arachnid's body like a passing shadow. For an instant, the formless apparition hovered in the air, then it floated down to the hole into which Rikus had been sticking his hand when he was stung.

The scorpion itself turned gold and began to shrink, until it was so small that its pincers would no longer fit around the mul's thick fingers. It fell free and tumbled away, its tiny body vanishing from sight long before it hit the ground.

"By the sun!" cursed Caelum.

Neeva tossed her dagger on to the road, then grabbed Rikus's arm with both hands. She felt her husband's powerful arms slip around her waist, then the dwarf pulled both her and the mul back onto the road. Caelum kneeled in the dust and grabbed Rikus's wrist with both hands, his stubby fingers pressing down on the veins to shut off the blood flow. Neeva did not need to ask why the sun-cleric was so concerned. Of all the poisonous beasts in the Athasian desert, gold scorpions were among the worst, with venom powerful enough to drop an adult mekillot in five steps. Of course, such creatures did not normally change sizes or disguise their color beneath silver shadows, but Neeva was too concerned with Rikus's welfare to dwell on the matter right now.

"Hold his wrist, tight!" Caelum ordered.

Neeva did as commanded, and her husband raised his own hand to the sky. "The sun's heat will boil the poison away."

Rikus grimaced. "This is going to hurt, isn't it?" The mul's eyes were glassy and his words slurred.

Caelum lowered his hand, fiery red and smoking from the fingertips. It glowed so brightly that it was translucent, save for the dark bones beneath the skin. The dwarf laid his palm over the scorpion puncture and squeezed Rikus's hand as hard as he could. There was a soft sizzle, and streamers of greasy black smoke rose between his fingers.

Rkard slipped over to watch, placing his back to the cliffs. His face paled at the sight of Rikus's scorched skin, but he did not look away. Neeva considered sending him elsewhere, but decided against it. Her son was as much a sun-cleric as he was a warrior. If she attempted to shield him from the unpleasant sight of a wound, he would never learn his father's art.

When an involuntary hiss slipped through Rikus's clenched teeth, Rkard stepped closer and laid his hand on the warrior's shoulder. "Don't worry," he said. "The sun demands pain in exchange for its magic."

"I know." The mul winced, then added, "Your father's done this to me before."

Caelum continued to hold his hands over the wound for many moments, until Neeva could no longer see the bones outlined beneath his flesh and the fiery glow had completely faded. By then, Rikus was only half-conscious and hardly seemed to realize where he was.

"What happened?" asked Sadira's voice.

Neeva looked up to see the sorceress coming toward the small group, trailing black wisps of the shadow spell that she had used to answer Magnus's summons.

"A gold scorpion stung him," Neeva explained.

The sorceress kneeled at her husband's side and took his injured hand between hers. Although the swelling had gone down, the flesh remained black and scaly.

"Is he going to die?" Sadira asked.

"No. Father won't allow it!" said Rkard, his hairless brow furrowed in determination.

"That's right," said Caelum. "He'll be a little sick for a few hours, but he'll live."

The sorceress's blue eyes seemed to glow a little brighter. "Thank you."

Sadira rose, cradling her husband's limp form in her arms. Although the mul probably weighed half-again as much as a normal man, the sorceress showed no sign of strain at lifting his heavy body.

She passed Rikus to Magnus. "If you'll bear Rikus for a while, I'll get us across this gap."

The sorceress took the rope from around Rikus's waist and lay down at the end of the road. She leaned over the brink and tied one end to the last buttress, then returned to her feet and tossed the coil toward the merchant standing on the other side of the gap.

At first, Neeva thought the rope would fall short of its target, but Sadira uttered a quiet incantation that sent the line drifting straight into the merchant's hands. "If you'll tie that off, I'll bring you and your wagon across," she called.

For a moment, the man seemed too astonished to reply. Then he dropped down and fastened the line to a buttress beneath the road. Sadira smiled and yelled for him to stand back, then took the rope in her hand and spoke the words to another spell. A sheet of crimson light spread outward from both sides of the cord. Within moments, a red, flickering ribbon of luminescence spanned the gap, connecting the two severed ends of the Cloud Road.

"Come on ahead," Sadira called. She continued to kneel, holding one hand on the rope. "My spell is more than strong enough to hold both you and your beasts."

The merchant stared at the scintillating patch and did not move.

"I'll go across and show him it's safe," Caelum volunteered.

"No, I'll go," said Neeva. She checked her harness to make sure both of her steel short swords were readily accessible. "With buttresses slipping from their joining holes and gold scorpions disguising themselves as something else, there's something strange here. The merchant might be part of it."

The warrior stepped onto the bridge and started across. With each footfall, the road swayed slightly under her weight. Through the soles of her sandals, she felt a strange, pulsing heat rising off its shimmering surface, and she understood the merchant's reluctance to lead his inixes onto the unstable road. Even if it would support the weight of his huge wagon, coaxing the skittish draft lizards over a hot, vibrating surface would not be easy.

After Neeva had taken a dozen paces, the merchant stepped onto his end of the shimmering bridge. The inixes kept their gazes focused straight ahead and pulled the heavy wagon with no sign of spooking. As each set of wheels settled onto the road, the pathway swayed and undulated beneath Neeva's feet, making her feel as though she were standing on water. She continued forward, thinking it wiser to meet the stranger in the middle of the link.

The man kept his eyes on the road, hiding his face beneath the broad brim of his hat. He wore a striped robe of many bright colors, though its vibrance was dulled by a gray coating of road dust. His gloves were worn and black, as were his belt and boots. The inixes behind him had silver-gray hides, which served to reinforce Neeva's fear that this was a trap. Usually, the beasts were covered with a mottled assortment of scales ranging from rusty red to murky brown, hues that camouflaged the beasts in the rocky wastelands of Athas.

Neeva stopped at the halfway point. "Hail, trader," she called. "Have you waited long?"

The man did not look up.

"Before you come farther, I'll know the name of the man who wishes to pass over this bridge." She rested her hands on the pommels of her twin swords.

The merchant continued forward, his hat shielding his eyes. Neeva drew her swords and stood ready to defend herself.

"Speak," she ordered.

The man was now so close that she could see that his clothes were not covered with road dust, as she had thought earlier. They seemed immersed in a pale shadow, as if he were lurking in some back alley in the Elven Market. The same was true of the inixes, for Neeva could now see dim blotches of much-faded color on their hides.

"Stop and show yourself!" she demanded.

The merchant raised his arms to about chest height. Though he carried no weapon, Neeva took the gesture as a hostile one. She waited for the man to close within two steps, then raised both her short swords. The merchant threw his arms up to ward off the expected blows. She slipped one blade over his guard and slapped the hat away, baring his head.

The warrior gasped at what she saw. The man was a corpse, with a swollen tongue protruding from between his cracked lips and the hollow expression of death in his eyes. A gray pall covered his flesh, not in the fashion of his inherent color, but like a silken shroud clinging to his lifeless features.

"It's a wraith!" Neeva yelled.

Having fought similar creatures during the war with Urik, the warrior knew instantly that she was in trouble. Wraiths had no bodies of their own. Instead, they took control of other beings, such as the corpse before her or the gold scorpion that had stung Rikus. She had even seen them animate marble statues.

The wraith launched itself at her, the corpse's arms outstretched and its filthy fingers slashing at her eyes. Neeva swung her second sword, twisting her whole body to increase the force of the blow. Her blade sank deep into the neck. There was a pop as the head came free, but the corpse's momentum carried it forward. She caught the brunt of its charge on her shoulder, then dove away and rolled.

Neeva came up facing her companions. Sadira continued to kneel at the edge of the road, holding onto the rope to keep her spell activated. Caelum was just charging past the sorceress with a raised mace, while Rkard followed a few steps behind with Rikus's sword clutched in both hands.

"Rkard, no!" she yelled.

Caelum's crimson eyes went wide, and he spun around instantly, almost impaling himself on the Scourge as his son crashed into him. He swept Rkard off the ground and started back up the road.

A shiver rolled down Neeva's spine as a pair of cold hands touched her neck. She raised a hand above her head and spun. As she came around, she brought her arm down and trapped her assailant's wrists between her elbow and body.

Neeva found herself staring into a pair of sapphire eyes, set into a face of ghostly gray shadow that sat upon the stump of the corpse's severed neck. The wavering visage was that of a sneering man with a sharp chin, an arrowlike nose, and hollow cheeks.

The boy! it commanded. Although the wraith's lips moved when it spoke, no sound came from them and Neeva heard the words inside her head. *Borys commands it!*

Neeva's mouth went dry as she realized that not only did her attacker resemble the creatures she had encountered during the war with Urik, it was one of them. Before their deaths a thousand years ago, the wraiths had served as knights in Borys's campaign to eradicate the dwarven race. They had even fought at his side when he had used the Scourge to mortally wound the last king of the dwarves, Rkard. Now, having returned to their master's service, they had come to destroy Rkard's namesake and heir, her young son.

"This time, Rkard shall not fall!" Neeva yelled.

Still holding the corpse's forearms trapped beneath her elbow, the warrior plunged the sword in her free hand into its stomach. The weapon sank deep and true, the tip driving up into the heart. Blood, cold and dark with death, oozed from the wound.

The dead thing simply raised its arms and clasped its hands around Neeva's throat. The cold fingers sank deep into her flesh. Her temples began to pound, and she felt dizzy. Her vision narrowed to a tunnel, a hissing roar filled her ears, and her knees grew weak.

Leaving her second sword buried in her attacker, Neeva snaked her hand over one of his arms and under the other. She clasped her hands together around the pommel of her other weapon and pivoted. The motion sent the dead merchant swinging toward the side of the road, and the warrior used all her strength to pry the thing's arms from her throat.

The corpse's grip broke, and it soared away, tumbling over the edge of the road toward the red sands below. After the body hit, a gray shadow drifted away and began a slow rise back toward the road. The warrior watched the wraith long enough to be sure the thing would take many moments to reach her again, then turned her attention to a more immediate danger: the inixes.

The gray-mantled beasts were only a dozen steps away, scrambling forward as fast as they could pull the heavy wagon. Their eyes sparkled with gemlike light, one's red and the other's yellow, leaving little doubt in the warrior's mind that the beasts were also controlled by wraiths.

Neeva turned and ran. Had the things been normal inixes, it would have been a simple matter for her to find a vulnerable spot and kill them both, even with her small sword. But, animated as they were by wraiths, the only way to stop them was by cutting their huge bodies to shreds or pushing them off the bridge, and she would need help to do either.

"Borys sent them for Rkard!" she called, pointing at her son. "Take him and go!"

Caelum passed their son to Magnus. The windsinger started up the road with Rikus tucked under one arm and Rkard under the other, and the dwarf raised a hand toward the sun.

Neeva glanced over her shoulder and saw that the

inixes remained a dozen paces behind. Normally, the lizards would have caught her in a matter of steps, but with a heavy cargo dray harnessed to their shoulders, they were not as swift as usual.

"Sadira will help me, Caelum. You go with Rkard!" Neeva commanded. She pointed at the many fissures lacing the hard granite next to the road. "The scorpion that stung Rikus was possessed by a wraith. There may be more."

Caelum stopped short of casting his spell and ran after Magnus, positioning himself between the wind-singer and the wall.

"Hurry, Neeva!" Sadira called, her hand still on the rope. "I can't cast another spell until I drop this one."

As Sadira spoke, a flurry of gray forms streamed out of nearby crevices and streaked over to her. Before Neeva could cry a warning, the wraiths attacked, their immaterial hands sinking into the sorceress's flesh as though it were air.

A cloud of black shadow billowed from Sadira's mouth. Her glowing eyes flared white, and her ebony body trembled with the pain of the onslaught. She did not release the rope to save herself.

One more gray streak flashed up from the valley below, slipping over the side of the Cloud Road to join the attack on Sadira. Neeva looked down and saw that the wraith that had animated the merchant's corpse was gone. It had been waiting to join its fellows in the assault against the sorceress.

The wraiths had played her for a fool, Neeva realized. They had never intended to take Rkard, but had only demanded him so that the company would concentrate on protecting the child. Then they had struck at their true target: Sadira.

Behind the sorceress, Magnus was rushing back to help, leaving Caelum to guard Rikus and Rkard, whom he had dropped upon the Cloud Road. Neeva did not think he would arrive in time. She kneeled and felt the roadway shuddering with the heavy footsteps of the inixes.

"Drop the spell!" Neeva yelled.

Sadira shook her head and did not release the rope. Her emberlike eyes burned with pain. She flung her free arm about madly, trying to shake off a pair of wraiths clinging to it. Her ebony body had turned gray in many places.

"I'm fine!" Neeva yelled. The warrior pressed her hand to the pulsing road, directly over the rope, and called, "Save yourself!"

Neeva faced the inixes and found the huge beasts upon her. The first beast snapped at her head. She ducked, thrusting her sword into the lizard's maw. The reptile closed its jaws on the steel blade and whipped its head around, ripping the weapon from the warrior's hand. The second inix opened its sharp beak, pushing the first reptile aside.

The surface of the road suddenly grew cold. It stopped shimmering, and Neeva knew that Sadira had dropped the spell. The warrior felt the bite of the rope across her palm, then she was falling. She closed her fingers around the cord, all that remained of Sadira's bridge, and caught herself.

The dray dropped onto the rope, causing a sharp jerk, then tipped to one side. As the wagon fell past Neeva, the second inix snapped at her dangling legs. She kicked its beak away, and the beast was gone.

When the warrior looked back to her companions, a sick feeling filled her chest. Sadira was engulfed in a swirling ball of black shadow and gray haze, just transparent enough to reveal that she had risen no farther than her hands and knees. The sorceress's limbs were all shaking violently, while her weakly glowing eyes stared blankly at the road's slate surface.

Magnus stood behind her, singing an angry, tempestuous song, while a hot wind tore at the gray wraiths in a vain attempt to rip the apparitions away. Caelum was cautiously approaching the pair, taking care to keep himself between the wraiths and his son.

Neeva hauled herself toward her companions, traveling along the rope hand over hand. The two wraiths that had been animating the inixes streaked up to join the attack. As soon as they rose above the surface of the road, Magnus's searing windsong sent them tumbling away.

They circled back to approach from below the surface.

Neeva reached the edge of the gap and transferred her hands to the slate roadway. "The last two are coming from underneath!" she warned.

Magnus's shoulders drooped, and Neeva knew that the windsinger's spell would not penetrate through stone. Nevertheless, he did what he could to help Sadira, directing his voice down at the surface of the road. The hot gusts simply curled up into his own face. As the last two wraiths passed through the stone directly beneath Sadira and joined the attack, Neeva pulled herself onto the road.

A groan of exhaustion escaped Sadira's lips, and the sorceress collapsed to her side. The ball of shadow and haze settled over her like a veil, leaving nothing exposed except her flowing locks of amber hair and her ember-like eyes, now blazing a sickly hue of greenish-blue. The murky shroud turned completely black, then flashed to gray, and began to alternate between the two colors at rapid intervals.

"We've got to do something!" Neeva said.

"We can't," said Caelum. "The wraiths are swarming her spirit. Any attempt to drive them away will harm her more than it does them."

"Then we have to attack them another way." Neeva stepped past her husband and took the Scourge from Rkard, who still held the enchanted sword.

"What will you do with that?" asked Magnus.

"I saw Rikus slice a shadow giant's hand off with this blade," the warrior explained. "Maybe it will work against wraiths, too."

Neeva studied Sadira's flickering shroud for several moments. Finally, the warrior felt confident she could predict the changes. She waited for the pall to turn gray and gently drew the tip of the Scourge along the sorceress's shoulder, hoping it would slice through a wraith's insubstantial body without harming Sadira.

A vicious screech echoed off the cliff wall, and a gray ribbon flew off the whirling mass. It shot up the Scourge's blade in a pearly streak, then expanded to form a gray, cloudlike mass around the weapon.

The warrior thought she had destroyed a wraith. The gray cloud slowly assumed a shape vaguely resembling that of a human female. A pair of orange eyes appeared in the head, and the hazy figure began to shrink. Neeva felt a searing sting as the apparition passed through her flesh, then the sword's hilt twisted in her hand.

"Get back!" she yelled. "The wraith's trying to animate the Scourge!"

The sword wrenched violently against her thumb and came free. It did not fall to the ground, but floated tip-down in front of the warrior. The entire weapon had turned gray, and a pair of angry orange eyes burned out from the pommel. The point slowly began to rise toward Neeva's heart. Caelum started to reach for the hilt, but pulled back when a line of blue frost shot down the length of the blade.

The Scourge stopped rising. The steel began to quiver, filling the air with an eerie, high-pitched wail.

"What's happening?" Neeva asked.

"The Scourge's magic is too powerful for the wraith," Magnus replied, a note of urgency in his voice. "Perhaps we should move—"

Before the windsinger finished, the sword emitted a blue flash of cold. The blade stopped vibrating, and the shrill wail of quivering steel was replaced by a howl of pain. Ribbons of gray shadow flew in all directions, trailing droplets of sleet.

Neeva and the others threw themselves to the ground. The Scourge continued to float, wobbling madly. The blade flexed almost in two. It straightened with a deafening knell, and the sword's shroud exploded into a cloud of gray haze. For an instant, the road seemed very quiet. Then the weapon clanged to the ground, and the cloud dissolved into a squall of ash-colored snowflakes. The tiny crystals did not even last long enough to fall. In the blistering heat of the day, they evaporated long before they reached the Cloud Road.

Neeva retrieved the Scourge, then gasped in alarm. The sword was as cold as ice, but that was not what troubled her. The blade had lost its silvery sheen. It was now covered with a dull gray stain that made it look more like tin than steel.

"What have I done?" she gasped.

Magnus came and stood at her side. After studying the sword for a moment, he gently took it from her hands. "The wraith's touch has tainted the blade."

"Can we fix it?" Neeva asked.

"Perhaps, with time," answered the windsinger. He kneeled next to Sadira, who remained covered beneath the murky shroud that Neeva had been trying to remove. "But for now, we have more pressing problems. The giants are still trapped at Pauper's Hope, and the Cloud Road remains impassable. Once the sun sets, we can't stop them from rampaging—especially with Sadira and Rikus both unconscious."

"Rikus might be well by then," said Caelum. "As for Sadira . . ."

"Even if we can help her prevail against the wraiths, I suspect she will be unconscious until morning," said Magnus. "Still, we can hope. I see nothing else we can do."

"I do," said Neeva. She turned and looked toward Agis's farm, where the Kledan militia was awaiting their return. "Find me a runner who can show my warriors the way from the Asticles Estate to Pauper's Hope."

Magnus folded his ears in doubt. "Your men are brave, but are they a match for giants?"

Neeva shrugged. "I don't know," she said. "But I've learned never to underestimate a dwarf."

FIVE

The Gray

Sadira had gone to the Gray.

She stood on a narrow stairway, looking out over an immense abyss filled with a haze that stretched from far below her feet to the zenith of the sky. It was the color of ash and as still as the midday sands. There was nothing else out there.

The steps had been carved from a spire of porous white rock that rose out of the gray murk far below. The stairway spiraled up the pillar to Sadira's feet, then continued above her head with no apparent end. The column simply grew smaller and smaller, until both the stairs and its tip vanished into the ashen haze far above.

Sadira recognized the pillar as the Pristine Tower, but did not think for an instant that she had truly returned to the distant spire of white rock. If she had, the sky would have been yellow-green, with puffy silver clouds drifting past. Lush thickets of bogo trees would have surrounded the base of the column, and in the distance there would have been fields of silver-green broomgrass. Instead, all she saw was a sea of ashen haze.

The sorceress studied the area carefully, searching for the wraiths who had attacked her on the Cloud Road. The Gray was their natural home, and the whole point of their ambush had been to push her into the ashen haze. Here, the spirits of the dead were dissolved and absorbed into the Gray, much as corpses on Athas were slowly obliterated by rot and decay. Some spirits did not suffer this fate, however. They were sustained by a force even more powerful than the Gray: their everlasting faith in a cause greater than themselves. The wraiths had dedicated themselves to Borys's service many centuries earlier, and they were such spirits. It was clear that they intended to use their special natures to force her to fight at a disadvantage.

The sorceress was far from panicked. While she would not be as comfortable in the Gray as her foes, she knew more about this place than the wraiths realized. If they expected her to assume they had killed her simply because she found herself in the Gray, they were badly mistaken. The Pristine Tower served as ample evidence that Sadira was alive. A reminder of the most significant event in her life, the spire of white rock acted as a lode-stone for her spirit, holding it together and preventing it from dispersing into the haze. Before they could destroy her, the wraiths would have to drive her off its steps.

Magnus's voice began to toll out of the haze. He was singing a ballad with melancholy strains as loud as thunder and as sweet as morning dew. Though she could not understand the words, Sadira quickly realized that her friend was trying to help her find a way out of the Gray. Unfortunately, the music came from all directions at once, from the front and back, both sides, above and below, even from inside her own head. She cupped her hand to an ear, trying to locate the source of Magnus's sonorous voice. It would have been easier to chase down the wind.

The sorceress pulled her slender stiletto from its

scabbard. A magnificent weapon with a blade of etched bronze and an iron handle beset with tourmalines, it had been in Agis's family for centuries. She fished a piece of twine from the deep pocket of her robe and tied it around the crossguard. The other end she looped over her wrist, then held the dagger out at arm's length and let it dangle from the string. She spoke a magical incantation that would make it lead her to the source of Magnus's voice.

Sadira felt a strange tingle in the hand with the twine, and its ebony color began to fade. The sensation slowly spread up her arm. What she could see of her flesh, from the fingertips to the wrist, paled to its normal tawny color, and the dagger began to spin wildly.

Though she had not expected the reaction, the sorceress was not really surprised by it. Normally her skin remained black with mystic energy during the day, then returned to its usual color the instant night fell. But in the Gray, day and night did not exist. Without the sun in the sky, her spell had drawn its power from the only available source: her flesh. Then, unable to replenish what it had lost to the spell, her arm had remained pale.

Of more concern to the sorceress was the dagger. It continued to spin madly, attempting to point in every direction at once. Sadira watched the blade for several moments. When it showed no sign of settling down, she decided that her spell had failed, and she caught the hilt.

As the sorceress started to slip the weapon into its sheath, the tower lurched beneath her feet. Sadira stumbled and nearly pitched over the side, but managed to drop to her hands and knees in time to keep from falling. Her stomach rolled in one direction after the other, and a sick, queasy feeling rose into her throat. Although she saw no hint of motion when she tried to fix her gaze on the haze around her, she felt like the spire was spinning as wildly as her stiletto had a moment earlier. By plunging her dagger into a fissure and twisting the blade against the edge, she barely managed to keep herself from flying off the steps.

For a long time, all Sadira could do was cling to the hilt and pray the blade would not slip from the crack. If she lost contact with the Pristine Tower, she feared that the haze would begin to eat at her spirit, and that her life-force would seep away. Even if that did not happen, the wraiths would certainly find it easier to prey upon her as she drifted aimlessly through the Gray. Perhaps they were even responsible for knocking the tower into its crazy spin.

Magnus's voice began to waver, growing much louder each time the gyrating tower pointed in a particular direction, fading to a mere whisper when it pointed away. At first, the volume increased every few seconds, but gradually the rotations slowed and the spire continued to point in the same direction for a little bit longer, until the sensation of movement ceased and the song came to the sorceress's ears from one direction only: the top of the stairs.

Sadira breathed a sigh of relief. The wraiths had not caused the wild spinning after all. The dagger had been unable to point in a single direction because doing so would have led her not to Magnus's voice, but away from the tower and into the dangers of the Gray. Instead, her spell had reoriented the whole tower, so that the exit lay in an obvious direction: up.

Listening attentively to Magnus's beautiful song, Sadira peered under the collar of her robe. The flesh of her arm had paled clear up to her shoulder. The sorceress guessed that the magic energy in her body would be completely drained after five or six more spells—even less, if they were powerful ones. After that, she would have to find a different source for her enchantments. And in the Gray, she doubted that she would find any plants from which to draw the mystic force of life.

Wondering if she would have enough magic to defeat

the wraiths when they finally showed themselves, the sorceress started to climb. The stairs were small, barely wide enough to accept her foot from the toes to the arch. Often, they were cracked and so worn that they formed more of a ramp than a staircase. A thousand years of dust lay upon the treads, and she passed over the ancient grime without leaving a track. It took more than a footfall to disturb the torpor of the Gray.

The sorceress climbed for a long time: minutes or hours or days, she did not know. Progress, if she was making any, came slowly. The summit remained veiled by distance, and the base of the tower seemed no nearer. Still, she continued to climb, reassured by the increasing volume of the windsinger's voice that she was traveling in the right direction. In the stillness of the haze, distance and time were mere illusions, but not Magnus's song. It came from the outside, and it was real.

After a time, a glowing emerald floated into view. It hovered next to the wall, several steps above, and a large eddy of darkening haze slowly circled it. A pair of green pinpoints appeared in the haze, at about head-height and twinkling with a sinister glow.

Sadira stopped climbing, anxious and ready for battle. Like her, wraiths needed something important from their lives to serve as magnets for their spirits. Although the sorceress had never encountered these particular apparitions before the attack on the Cloud Road, Rikus had. From his description, she knew that for Borys's followers, a brilliant gem served this purpose. Though she could not be certain, she guessed that Borys had given one of the stones to each of his knights when he took them into his service.

The sorceress thrust a hand into her robe pocket, watching dark haze coalesce around the emerald above. The cloud soon formed the cumbersome figure of a woman in a full suit of plate armor. The warrior wore the visor of her helmet up, so that she could focus the green specks of her eyes on Sadira. The woman's face was stern and hard, with a cleft chin, sneering lips, and broad flat cheeks.

The wraith pointed the tip of her sword toward the haze below. "Go down," she ordered.

Sadira pulled a tiny satchel of copper dust from her pocket. The sorceress tore the packet open with her teeth, then waited as the wraith charged. When her attacker was almost upon her, she blew the brown powder toward the warrior's open visor. The stuff coated the woman's face.

The wraith's sword came down.

Sadira twisted away, diverting the blow with a crashing block to her foe's elbow. From the solid feel of the armor, it was hard to believe the warrior had coalesced out of gray haze just a moment earlier. The wraith stumbled, then caught herself and braced to swing again.

The attack came too late. Sadira spoke her spell's command word, and the copper dust covering the wraith's face flashed blue.

A tremulous, ear-piercing shriek burst from the wraith's lips. She dropped her sword and clutched at her face, pitching forward. Before she could clatter to the ground, a blue glow ran through her armor. Her body instantly dissolved into a gray fog and drifted away, leaving a glowing emerald floating where her head had been an instant earlier.

The sorceress plucked the gem out of the air. It was as large as her thumb, cut into an eye-shaped marquise oval and deeper in color than any emerald she had ever seen. The sheen of its many facets looked almost black, while a faint green light glimmered in the center.

Sadira laid the stone on a step, drew her dagger, and smashed the pommel into the gem. The stone did not shatter so much as crumble into a coarse, lime-colored powder. A shimmering radiance hung over the crushed stone, slowly expanding outward in a cloudlike mass.

Save for its green tint, the light resembled the mystic energy that normal sorcerers drew from plants to cast their spells.

The cloud burst apart with a deafening crash. Bolts of green light shot through the Gray, lighting it with a spectacular show of brilliant flashes. The storm continued to rage, filling the vast abyss with a tempest of resounding booms and effulgent flares, stirring the ashen haze into a froth of swirling green light.

Sadira was surprised by the tumult. She had known crushing the gem would release a certain amount of life-force, for even wraiths needed some energy to bind their spirits together. But the stone had contained at least as much power as she would expect to find in a living woman. Perhaps that was the reason Borys's knights had been so dedicated to him. If the gems served as repositories for their life-forces, it would be possible for him to resurrect them.

After a time, the storm gave one last rumble and died away in a wave of flickering color. Once more, Magnus's voice descended from the tower summit clear and unimpeded. Before starting up the stairs, Sadira paused long enough to look under her robe to see how much mystic energy her spell had consumed. The enchantment had been a costly one. Most of her upper torso had paled to the normal hue of her flesh. If she was going to get past all the wraiths, she would have to find a more efficient way to use her magic.

The sorceress began climbing. By this time, Magnus had repeated his sibilant rhymes so many times that she knew the syllables by heart, even if she did not understand the meaning of the words. Sadira began to sing along. The melody lifted her spirits, and, keeping a watchful eye for more wraiths, she bounded up the stairs two at time.

Finally, the sorceress rounded a curve and the staircase broadened into a small apron, which sat before the open gates of a white bastion. The ramparts were built of alabaster and finished with undulating caps of ivory. Beyond the entranceway, a pool of shimmering blue water filled the inner ward of the citadel, with a single pathway of limestone blocks leading toward the center. The walkway stopped at the base of a minaret rising directly out of the water. This slender steeple was faced with white onyx and crowned by a crystal cupola.

Although she had reached the summit of the Pristine Tower, Sadira's singing croaked to a stop. Between her and the gate stood ten wraiths, all armored in gray plate similar to the first woman's. They wore their helmet visors down, so that all the sorceress could see of their faces were the jewel-colored slivers of light emitted by their burning eyes: ruby, sapphire, citrine, amethyst, and more. None of them carried weapons.

The largest wraith stepped forward. He extended a mailed hand and, in a raspy voice, ordered, "Go down."

Sadira reached into her robe and shook her head. She was vaguely aware that Magnus's booming voice had grown urgent. Directly above the citadel's minaret, the pearly haze swirled about in two great eddies, each spinning in the opposite direction.

"Stand aside—" She paused to clear a nervous catch in her throat, then continued, "Let me pass."

The wraith shook his head. "Borys is aware of what you and Rikus are doing," he said. "He has demanded your death."

Sadira tensed, her limbs cold and aching. She wanted to ask how much the Dragon knew, and whether he had found Agis, but realized that it would be futile. If the wraith replied at all, his answer was sure to be misleading.

"Then Borys should come for me himself." The sorceress pulled a tiny, two-tined fork of silver from her pocket. "You won't stop me."

She struck the fork against the wall and pointed the quivering tines at the wraiths. The leader's purple eyes flashed brightly, and he threw himself to the ground. Several of his fellows followed his lead, but not all were quick enough to react before Sadira finished her incantation.

A shrill, painful screech shot from the end of the fork and blasted over her foes. Blinding flashes of colored light flared inside the visors of the wraiths who had not yet hit the ground. First their helmets, then the rest of their armor burst apart, the shards instantly dissolving into wisps of gray fume. The whole tower shook with the violence of the explosion, and the air erupted into a maelstrom of streaking colors: red, blue, yellow, and all the hues of the prism. Only the leader and four other wraiths, all lying on the stony apron, escaped the destruction.

The blast knocked Sadira from her feet, making her ears ring and sending her tumbling down the stairs. The sorceress dropped the silver fork and clawed at the porous stone, breaking off half her fingernails. As soon as she brought herself to a stop, she reached into her pocket for another spell component.

By the prickling sensation of her skin, she knew that her first enchantment, one of the most powerful she could cast, had drained her mystic energy down to her hips. She had expected that, gambling that the attack would destroy most of her enemies in a single blow. But she had not expected so many of them to drop to the ground, where the tower's stone would absorb the magic vibrations she had sent to shatter the gems holding their life-forces.

Sadira came up ready to attack again, the stairs still trembling beneath her feet and the maelstrom tearing at her clothes. In her hand, she held a small iron hammer, the first syllable of her incantation already spilling from her mouth.

When she looked toward the wraiths, she held her spell. To her surprise, they were not charging. Instead, they stood on the apron between her and the gate, their feet planted wide to brace themselves against the raging tempest. Behind them and directly above the minaret, a faint gleam of pink was beginning to show through the swirling haze.

The sorceress raised her hand toward the light, hoping it came from the sun and that its rays would restore the mystic power to her body, but her flesh remained pale. Sadira started up the stairs again, catching a few notes of Magnus's song between the storm's booms and crashes.

The leader of the wraiths held his hand out toward her. Sadira felt her stiletto slip from its sheath. She lashed out, but the dagger was gone before she could catch it. The weapon sailed straight to his hand, coming to rest with the iron handle in his palm.

"I believe this weapon once belonged to Agis's mother," he said, lifting the stiletto. He had to raise his voice only a little, for the tumult was beginning to fade.

Sadira scowled and stopped a dozen steps below the wraiths, still holding her small iron hammer. Although puzzled by the warrior's action, the sorceress was less interested in what he was doing than in selecting her next attack. She estimated that her body contained enough energy for only one more spell. If she wanted to escape, she would need to pick a good one.

"What does it matter who owned it?" Sadira asked.

"You shall see."

A pearly cloud of haze began to swirl around the dagger, coalescing into the face of a handsome human, a man with even features, a patrician nose, and long black hair streaked down the center by a single band of silver. The rest of his body took form below the dagger, and soon he stood with his sinewy arms hanging limply at his sides and his shoulders slumped forward.

Forgetting about her spell, Sadira gasped, "Agis!"

The noble said nothing. The pupils of his eyes remained milky and vacant.

"Don't worry, he's still alive," the wraith said in a reassuring voice. "The Gray often disorients the spirits of the living."

Sadira's heart felt as though a hand of ice had closed around it. The wraith was lying. Agis's spirit had coalesced out of the Gray, not been drawn through it. Had the noble come from Athas, he would have arrived fully formed.

The wraith continued his lie: "Your husband valued his mother's weapon highly. I used that attachment to summon his spirit from Samarah."

For a moment, Sadira did not move, too shocked to react. Then she cried out and almost collapsed, her whole body convulsing with grief. *Samarah.* She repeated the name over and over. That one word confirmed her worst fears. The wraiths had found Agis, or Borys had, and they had killed him. All that remained of her husband was the glassy-eyed apparition at the wraith's side, a spirit that could not remember his own name.

"Go down," the leader said. "Step into the Gray, or I'll take your husband's life."

"Take him!" Sadira yelled. Her chest suddenly felt constricted and hot. "What good is he to me now?"

The words had barely passed her lips before the sorceress felt sick with guilt. She could not have said such a thing. It had to have been some other woman, a weak woman who had not truly loved her husband.

Sadira knew that she should be sorry for Agis's death, concerned about the portents it held for the future. She should be worried that Borys had taken the Dark Lens, and that now she and her companions would have no defense against his mastery of the Way. She should be seeing young Rkard, his red eyes blazing with determination, standing before the beast that had killed Agis and a million others. She should be thinking of what came after Borys killed her and Rkard and the others, of how he would raze Tyr and murder its citizens, of how, too soon, an immense pile of rubble would lie where Athas's only free city had stood.

But Sadira did not feel any of those things. She only felt angry, angry at the husband who gone away and died so far from her.

Magnus suddenly stopped singing, and an eerie silence fell over the tower. The wraiths cast nervous glances back toward the minaret, where a pink band had appeared between the swirling eddies in the sky. The leader motioned to his companions, then started down the stairs, pushing Agis's spirit before him. The other wraiths followed, taking no chances that Sadira would make a run for the gate.

Magnus's voice boomed out of the sky. "Sadira, you're almost out!" he yelled. "Help me. Sing!"

The leader looked up, as if his amethyst eyes could actually see the words booming out of the sky, then halted two steps above Sadira. "Stay silent!" he ordered. "The time has come for your decision."

The sorceress opened her mouth and sang, though her thoughts were more on the small hammer of iron in her hand.

The leader stepped back, pulling the hand with the dagger out of Agis. The noble's spirit looked toward Sadira, his mouth half-open and his eyebrows arched in sadness, then dissolved into haze.

Sadira stopped singing and threw her hammer past the leader's head, crying out an incantation. The weapon smashed into the next wraith with a resounding boom. The impact knocked him into the one behind him, and they both fell to the ground.

The hammer hovered over them for an instant, then enlarged to the size of a kank and crashed down. The impact flattened their helmets and demolished the stairs beneath their heads. As the gemstones containing their life-forces shattered, a tremendous blast rocked the tower. The explosion hurled the leader into Sadira and blew the other two wraiths off the stairway.

The sorceress and the leader crashed down the steps together, locked in a tight embrace. Each time they rolled, the wraith's armored body battered Sadira. She fought desperately to throw her attacker off, while he struggled to drive the stiletto into her heart. Finally, they came to a rest with Sadira lying on her back, her head lower than her feet. The wraith kneeled astride her, the dagger still clutched in his fist.

Sadira looked past his leg and up the stairway. Her magical hammer had disappeared with the two wraiths it had destroyed. The two who had escaped the blast were nowhere in sight, but the sorceress could see her own feet lying five steps above. They were as pale as ivory, clear down to the toes. She had used the last of her mystic energy.

"No more spells," hissed the leader, following her gaze.

His purple eyes flashed malevolently from behind his visor, then he tossed the dagger aside. He grabbed Sadira by the shoulders and started to rise.

"Now you go to the Gray."

"Hardly!"

The sorceress drove the heel of her palm into the bottom edge of the leader's visor, forcing it up and away from his face. Sadira lashed out with her other hand and grasped the wraith's withered visage. She began to pull, as though she were drawing mystic energy from a field of Athasian plants. A warm, stinging sensation rushed up her arm. Had the wraith been alive, it would have been impossible for her to draw the life-force directly from her foe. But the creature was not alive, and the energies that held him together were not bound into the gemstone nearly so tightly as they would have been fastened into a true body.

The wraith screamed, and his leathery skin began to

flake away beneath Sadira's fingers. He tried to push her away, his arms already trembling from the loss of vital energy. The sorceress wrapped her free arm around his neck and held tight. The leader stepped toward the Gray, gathering himself up to leap off the tower edge.

Sadira thrust her hand deep into the papery mass of his dissolving head and grasped the dark amethyst inside. The leader's flesh turned to dust. He jumped, but the sorceress felt her feet drop onto the coarse rock of the tower and knew she would not be carried with him. The wraith drifted past her in a dun-colored cloud, which quickly dissolved into hazy wisps as it drifted out into the Gray.

When the sorceress saw no sign of the other two wraiths, she quickly picked up her dagger and used the pommel to smash the leader's amethyst. This time, there was no storm of escaping energy. She had already drawn all the life-force from the stone, and could feel it tingling in her flesh, which had assumed a faint purplish cast.

Keeping a watchful eye, Sadira started up the stairs. She began to sing again, and pulled a small lump of green clay from her pocket. After she dribbled a few drops of saliva onto the mass, it began to hiss and pop, burning the palm of her hand with tiny droplets of corrosive fluid. The sorceress did not care. She had not yet destroyed the last two wraiths, and when they attacked, she intended to be ready.

By the time Sadira reached the open gates of the bastion, a crevice of crimson light had appeared above the minaret's crystal cupola. Magnus's voice sounded clear and pure. There was no sign of the wraiths on the path anywhere between her and the center of the citadel. Nor did she see them in the blue pool that filled so much of the bastion, but she knew that did not mean much. Her enemies could be hiding anywhere beneath the water and the shimmering waves would make it impossible to see them.

The sorceress started to step through the gates, then thought better of it and stopped. Borys's servants had not become wraiths by easily forsaking the tasks he assigned to them. If the survivors had not yet assaulted her, it was because they were lying in ambush inside the bastion itself.

Using the life-force she had drained from the leader's gem, Sadira cast her spell. The purple sheen faded from her skin, and a caustic-smelling mist began to rise from the lump of clay in her hand. She waited until the green fumes condensed into a hissing stream of vapor, then stepped through the gate.

The first thing she noticed was the quiet. She could not hear Magnus's song, the hiss of the vapor rising from her palm, or even the sound of her feet shuffling over the limestone cobbles. Then she glimpsed a wraith pulling himself out of the shimmering pool beside the path. The water dripped from his armor without making a sound, and the sorceress realized that a magic pall of silence had been cast over the area—no doubt to keep her from voicing the incantation of her own spells.

Congratulating herself for avoiding the trap, she held her hand out toward her ambusher and blew a stream of green vapor into his face. The wraith's visor dissolved instantly, and she saw him open his mouth to curse before his head was swallowed in the green fog. Without waiting for the magic acid to finish its work, Sadira spun, fully certain that the last of Borys's knights was behind her.

The sorceress found a pair of mailed fists reaching for her neck. The wraith at the other end of the arms wore the armor of a broad-shouldered female, with yellow rays of light pouring through the eye-slits of her visor. Sadira twisted to the side, thrusting the hand with the magic acid toward her attacker's face. At the same time the sorceress protected her vulnerable throat behind her shoulder.

The tactic succeeded only partially. Sadira planted her hand squarely in her foe's visor, which instantly began to dissolve beneath a billowing cloud of green vapor. The wraith switched her attacks at the last minute, however, smashing one mailed fist down on Sadira's collarbone and bringing the other around in a vicious uppercut to the ribs. The blows landed with such force that the sorceress felt bones crack in both places.

Sadira's body erupted into such agony that she barely noticed when her magic acid dissolved the gem inside her first ambusher's head. She felt the path buck beneath her feet and saw streaks of ruby-colored light flashing past in the silence, then she dropped to the cobblestones gasping for breath. The wraith reached down to pick her up, attempting to carry out Borys's orders even as the sorceress's green fog ate away the repository of her lifeforce.

One mailed hand clasped onto Sadira's wounded shoulder, and the other reached for her throat. Then a silent yellow flash flared from inside the acid cloud. The wraith dissolved. A tremendous shock wave crashed down on the sorceress, spraying her with droplets of acid vapor and driving her tormented body into the unyielding cobblestones.

The sorceress did not care. Pain would not stop her from escaping the Gray. She forced herself to her hands and knees and turned toward the minaret. Sadira slowly crawled forward, the syllables of Magnus's wind-ballad pouring forth from her silent lips.

SIX

The Dark Canyon

As the crimson sun slipped behind the purple crags of the Ringing Mountains, long streaks of shadow stretched across the valley outside Pauper's Hope. The sheen slowly faded from the glassy plain that Sadira's magic had created earlier. The smooth field of rock slowly reverted to its true nature, filling the air with a soft murmur as orange stone crumbled into orange dirt.

To half the titans who had attacked Pauper's Hope that morning, the change no longer mattered. The one that Rikus had wounded, Tay, lay motionless and blank-eyed at the edge of the field. Three more, including Tay's comrade Yab, had succumbed to the searing heat of the Athasian day. They were slumped over at the waist, the tips of their thirst-swollen tongues protruding from their blue lips.

That left only four living giants to rejoice in the disintegration of their magical prison. Bellowing in gleeful, thirst-parched voices, they began to dig their hips and legs free. They hurled each handful of rock-filled dirt to the ground just out of arm's reach, where a company of dwarven warriors had surrounded each of them only moments before.

Despite the steel breastplates and helmets protecting the warriors, the giants' barrage savaged through their disciplined companies, opening great holes in their neat ranks and sending armored figures rolling away like tumbleweeds. The dwarves countered with a volley of crossbow fire. Their iron-tipped bolts were about as effective against the thick hide of the titans as cactus needles would have been against mul gladiators.

"Call Neeva back," Rikus said. "Their crossbows are useless."

Caelum shook his head. "They've just begun," he said. "She'll never retreat so soon."

"If she waits much longer, she won't have a chance," said Magnus, his ears twitching with tension. "I'm afraid we arrived too late. The wraiths may have failed to kill Sadira, but the delay they caused might prove fatal to us all."

The trio stood about a hundred paces from the battle, facing the butte over which Rikus and the windsinger had climbed when they first heard the giants. Caelum and Magnus were waiting in reserve, ready to cover the retreat as soon as the battle turned against the dwarves. Unlike Sadira's sorcery, their clerical magic was primarily defensive in nature, and not of much use in destroying titans.

Rikus had been forced to stay with the clerics because, up until a few minutes ago, the ill effects of the scorpion sting had left his vision too blurry to fight. Thanks to his hardy mul constitution and Caelum's magic, however, Rikus was recovering rapidly—even if he still had a queasy stomach and sporadic bouts of dizziness. In spite of his condition, the mul would rather have been with Neeva, standing near the dwarven companies and directing the attack from close range. Unfortunately, she had ordered him to stay behind, saying he would only be a liability, and the mul had been in no position to protest. Neeva had organized the assault, and it was under her full command.

As Magnus had explained to Rikus, Neeva had reacted quickly after the wraith attack on the Cloud Road. Perceiving that the original plan for dealing with the giants was in jeopardy, she had sent a half-elven runner to fetch the Kledan militia from Agis's estate. Then, while the windsinger helped Sadira fight off the wraiths, she and Caelum had discussed their options. When it became clear the sorceress would survive but might not regain consciousness before dusk, Neeva had carried Rkard across the rope that spanned the gap. Caelum and Magnus had followed close behind, with Sadira and Rikus tied to their backs in the case the pair awakened in time to help confront the giants. The Tyrian legion would follow as soon as possible, but it seemed unlikely that they could get two thousand warriors safely across the breach in time to stop what was about to happen.

The largest giant, the one-eyed fellow Rikus had heard called Patch by the others, braced his enormous hands at his sides. He pushed down, and a gentle tremor rolled through the field. The orange dirt bulged slightly upward around his hips. The dwarves peppered him with crossbow bolts, but he only twisted from side-to-side, trying to loosen the ground and free himself.

Before the battle, Rikus had made a point of reminding Neeva to leave the one-eyed giant alive so they could interrogate him about Agis and what would happen if the Dark Lens was not returned to them. Now, the mul was beginning to worry that it would be the titans who left no one alive.

"Caelum, I want to stop the giants as much as anyone," Rikus said. "But your dwarves can't do it."

"Kled's warriors are as brave as any in Tyr," the dwarf replied sharply. "Wait until you see their axe-charge."

"Neeva wouldn't waste good warriors like that!" Rikus considered his objection for a moment, then started forward. "Maybe I'd better go talk some sense into her."

Before the mul had taken his second step, Magnus's huge fingers dug into his shoulder and brought him to an abrupt halt.

"If you go out there now, Rkard will have another sleeping Tyrian to look after." The windsinger looked across the valley to the top of the bluff, where the young mul was hiding with Sadira's unconscious form. "Wait until you're stronger."

"I'm ready now." Rikus tried to pull free, but the windsinger's powerful fingers held firm.

"Save your strength," advised Magnus. "If this doesn't work—"

A tremendous rattle sounded from the battlefield as the ground around Patch's hips loosened. Bellowing with delight, the titan leader stretched forward and slapped his palm down with a thunderous clap. Three dwarves died instantly, lacking the time even to scream.

Rikus saw Neeva barking a command, though it was impossible to hear her over the din of the battle. He reached for the Scourge's hilt, but Magnus had already tilted his eloquent ears forward to catch her words.

"She's come to the same conclusion as Rikus," the windsinger reported. "Signal the retreat."

The dwarf raised his hand. A pillar of crimson light shot from his palm and arced westward, casting a luminous glow over the battlefield. The Kledan militia disengaged instantly. They rushed toward the signal, assembling themselves into loose squares as they moved.

"At least their discipline's good," Rikus commented.

Caelum shrugged. "Yes, but what now?" he asked. "We've lost our best chance to stop the giants. They'll raze every farm in the valley."

"Not if we keep them busy with us," Rikus said.

Patch grabbed another handful of rubble and hurled it at the fleeing dwarves. A hail of stones rained down on the trailing company, denting more than a dozen helmets and leaving dazed warriors scattered over the field. Magnus began one of his ballads. A powerful wind howled down out of the mountains. It swept just a few feet above the dwarves' heads, with enough force to drive any more such barrages back the way they came.

Rikus continued speaking to Caelum. "I have an idea, but it'll mean leaving Rkard alone until Sadira wakes."

"Rkard will be fine. He has a sun-spell he can use to summon us if he has trouble," the dwarf said. "What's your plan?"

"There's a dead-end gorge on the other side of Pauper's Hope where I hid once, after escaping from Tithian," the mul said. "It's full of ancient mines. If we can make it into the canyon and harass the giants enough to keep their attention focused on us, we might keep them busy until morning."

"And by then, Sadira should be well enough to help us." Caelum nodded. "Let's give it a try."

They waited a few moments for Neeva and her dwarven militia to arrive. Without the dwarves harassing them, Patch and the other giants concentrated on digging their legs free. Soon, they were each ringed by mountainous heaps of dirt, and Rikus knew that reaching the gorge would be an uncertain proposition.

When the first company of militia arrived, Rikus saw by their clenched jaws and narrowed eyes that retreating grated on the dwarves' pride. He waved his arm at them, yelling, "The battle's not over yet. Follow me! I have a plan."

Neeva winced, no doubt remembering his disastrous plan to invade Hamanu's city during the war with Urik. Nevertheless, she took a long breath and ordered her dwarves to obey. The mul started toward Pauper's Hope at a sprint, padding over the ground in near silence.

Neeva joined him and ran just as quietly at his side, but Caelum's feet slapped the ground loudly with every step, and Magnus's heavy footfalls actually shook the ground. The four companies of militia spaced themselves out across the field and followed at a short distance, armor clanking and booted feet stomping.

By the time they reached the edge of the field, Ral and Guthay had risen. Both moons were in a crescent phase. The flaxen light they cast over the broken ground was so pale Rikus found it difficult to distinguish between shadows and stones. Nevertheless, he continued to run at his best pace, finding his way as much by feel as by sight. The queasiness in his stomach was fading with the exercise, but the bouts of dizziness came more often. Several times, Neeva had to reach out to steady him, not because he had stumbled, but because he had lost his balance and was listing to one side or the other.

As Rikus entered the faro field near Rasda's Wall, Patch dug himself completely free. Instead of chasing after the fleeing warriors, the titan went over to his companions and began pulling them out of the ground like a crop of tubers.

Keeping a wary eye fixed on the giants, Rikus turned to Neeva, "Have your warriors drop their shields and whatever else they can discard on the run—aside from their weapons. Right now, speed's more important than armor."

Neeva shook her head. "They're well disciplined, but they *are* dwarves," she replied. "That equipment came from Kemalok's armory. They'll die on the spot before they cast any of it aside."

"I was afraid of that," Rikus grumbled, starting down one of the paths between the faro rows.

Behind them, Patch's voice cried out in an angry howl that seemed to shake the sky. Rikus looked back to see him kneeling over Yab's body and remembered that Tay had said something about the young titan being the leader's brother. The rest of the giants were racing after Rikus and the militia, their heavy steps reverberating through the valley like thunder.

The ground between the faro rows was packed hard. Rikus and his followers crossed the orchard at an all-out sprint, quickly passing around the shoulder of Rasda's Wall. If Rikus had possessed any regrets about the fate of Yab or any other giant, they quickly faded when he saw what had happened in the farm buildings of Pauper's Hope.

The night air was thick with the stench of corpses that had lain rotting in the sun all day long, and it was apparent that Patch's brutes had taken great delight in killing the inhabitants. The bodies of men and women lay heaped at the bottom of Rasda's Wall, while dark smears of blood, barely visible in the pale moonlight, speckled the cliffs above. As if mere slaughter were not enough, Patch and his warriors had also stomped every building flat, usually with the inhabitants inside. They had even destroyed the irrigation dam, leaving a shallow depression of cracked mudcakes where once the pond had been.

A short distance beyond the farm lay a moonlit wall of foothills. Covered with little except jagged stone and flakes of clay-rich soil, they rose steadily upward to form the lower slopes of the Ringing Mountains. A narrow gorge twisted its way into the hills, the blackness of its depths creating the impression of a snake crawling up the steep scarps.

As the militia neared the far side of the compound and started toward the dark canyon, the giants reached the other end of Rasda's Wall. The titans stopped long enough to lift several boulders off the outcropping and hurl the huge stones at the fleeing dwarves. Two of the rocks landed just ahead of Rikus and shattered harmlessly into a hundred pieces, but the others were better aimed and came down in the midst of the trailing company. Several of Neeva's warriors died amidst the crinkle of steel armor.

"Loose formation!" Neeva called. "Spread out!"

As the dwarves scattered, Rikus saw the giants start forward again. They covered half the distance across the compound with a single stride, then stopped to pluck more boulders off the cliff. The mul was tempted to fight them here, on the site where the brutes had slain so many helpless people, but resolutely resisted the temptation. Nearly a decade earlier, during the war with Urik, he had learned the foolishness of allowing emotions to guide his tactics.

Instead, he waved the dwarves on toward the canyon, but stopped Magnus near the dry irrigation pond. "Can you slow them down?" he asked. "We're two hundred paces from the canyon, but they'll cover the distance in ten."

The windsinger nodded. "I have a powerful song that will give you time," he said. "Go on."

"Don't get yourself—"

"I have no intention of dying tonight," Magnus replied.

Flecks of dried mud stung the mul's face as a rock crashed into the irrigation pond just a few yards away, then he heard a crumple as heavy stones crushed the armored forms of several more dwarves. Magnus raised his voice in a thunderous song, summoning a tempestuous wind from the depths of the desert night. It roared down from the mountains in the blink of an eye, bringing with it a thick fog of cold mist. The blast surged across the compound, hurling broken mudbricks and dead livestock high into the air. It slammed the debris into the outcropping with a deafening boom, loosening a slide of rock to come pouring down on the giants' heads.

Magnus pushed Rikus toward the canyon. "Go! This will hold them for only a few moments. You must show the others what to do when they reach the canyon."

The mul obeyed, sprinting for cover. Once, he was overcome by dizziness and fell. Nevertheless, with his longer legs and lack of heavy armor, he caught up with the dwarves easily and led the way into the gorge.

The place was really more of a gash than a canyon, a sheer-sided crevice of crumbling rock that twisted its way less than a mile into the base of an enormous mountain. There were no smooth bends or gentle curves in the entire course. It changed directions at unpredictable intervals and at sharp angles. In some places, an entire dwarven company could have stood in dress formation across its breadth. Then, less than a dozen paces later, it grew so narrow that a giant would have to turn sideways to pass between its towering walls.

At last, Rikus came to a bottleneck in the gorge, where the cliffs stood so close together that he could have leaped from the brim of one to the other without a running start. Although it was not possible to see much in the pale moonlight, the mul knew that those cliffs were pocked with dozens of caves, the portals of ancient mines that had been worked, abandoned, and forgotten centuries ago—perhaps even before Kalak had conquered Tyr.

On the other side of the bottleneck, the canyon opened into a large circular valley. It was enclosed on every side by sheer walls of red-stained stone, many times the height of a giant. Like the cliffs of the bottleneck, these were pocked by mine openings. Those near the top could be seen as dark circles on the moonlit rock faces. Rikus knew that there were also several mine tunnels near the bottom of the cliffs, though they were hidden behind huge mounds of waste rock that covered most of the valley floor.

An angry bellow echoed up the stony canyon, then the walls began to shake with the steady crash of heavy footsteps. Rikus looked back down the gorge. The dwarves of the first two companies were beginning to peer nervously over their shoulders. The mul could not see the two companies bringing up the rear, for the gorge took a sharp bend.

Rikus joined Neeva, telling her, "There's a huge tunnel on the far side. I think it connects to most of the others, so lets go over there. Once the giants think they have us trapped, we can duck inside, then come out the other mines and harass them from behind. With luck, we may even be able to circle back and block the canyon."

Neeva nodded and passed the order back. The mul entered the valley, picking his way between mounds of red-stained waste rock and the stone foundations of several huge buildings. Neeva and the dwarves came close behind him, their armor filling the still valley with a clatter such as had not been heard there in a thousand years.

Finally, upon reaching the back of the gorge, they slipped from between two piles of rubble and came upon a small area of open ground. It was located beneath a towering cliff that seemed to rise straight to the crescent moons. At the base of the scarp, a tunnel ran toward the heart of the mountain. Though the passage was easily broad enough for three dwarves to walk down, and high enough that an elf could have stood inside it at his full height, it was not so large that a giant would be able to do more than thrust an arm inside.

From the far side of the valley rumbled Patch's deep voice. "There they are, Fosk!"

Rikus looked toward the entrance in time to see the giant's immense form stepping into the valley, his shoulders turned sideways so he could fit through the narrow gap. He was pointing toward the open space in front of the tunnel, where the dwarven companies were gathering.

"Let's draw them closer," Rikus said. "Make it look like we'll fight here."

Neeva traced a line in front of the cavern entrance. "Form ranks by companies!" she ordered.

The dwarves rushed toward the place she had indicated, milling about purposefully. Although the scene seemed one of utter confusion to Rikus, each of Neeva's warriors seemed to know exactly what he was doing.

While they arranged themselves, Patch and one warrior, probably Fosk judging by the name Rikus had heard a moment ago, entered the valley. In three steps, they had already walked more than a quarter of the way across. The mul did not see the other two giants.

At Rikus's side, Neeva suddenly cried, "Sult? Where in the name of Ral are you?"

The mul looked toward the tunnel entrance, where he saw three ranks of dwarves standing with axes drawn and bucklers guarding their chests. "What's wrong?"

"Sult Ltak and his Granite Company are missing," Neeva reported.

Just then, a giant's angry bellow rolled across the valley, followed by the distant sound of crumpling armor. Rikus looked back toward the canyon. Beyond the lumbering forms of Patch and Fosk, he saw a third titan kicking madly at something on the ground.

"They're still in the canyon!" Rikus said. "They must have fallen behind!"

"Either that, or stayed on purpose," said Caelum, coming to the mul's side. "The *yalmus* of the Granite Company is a brave man—sometimes overly so."

"You mean he'd hang back on purpose?" Rikus gasped.

Neeva nodded. "If he thought he could kill a giant, he would."

In the dark shadows of the narrow canyon, the mul could see little, only the silhouette of a huge knee rising and falling as the giant stomped at his attackers. Curt death cries and the creak of folding armor suggested that the brute's foot found its target all too often, but Rikus could also hear a softer sound: the incessant thump-thump-thump of dwarven axe blades biting into tough flesh.

Looking back to Patch, Rikus said, "Call him back, Neeva. They'll be wiped out."

Neeva shook her head. "I can't do that, even if Sult Ltak's men would obey," she said. "They've *declared for honor*."

"Declared for honor?" the mul asked.

"You remember how Yarig fought?" Neeva replied.

Rikus groaned. "They wouldn't do a thing like that."

He and Neeva had trained with a dwarf named Yarig during their days in Tithian's gladiator pits. Before each match, the squat gladiator would make victory over his opponents his life focus.

Neeva nodded. "In Kled, they call that declaring for honor," she said. "Sult and his warriors must kill the giant or die trying. If they retreat now, it's the same as breaking their life focus. They'll become banshees when they die."

"I thought your militia was disciplined!" Rikus snapped. He cursed and kicked at the ground. He barely noticed as his callused foot sent a melon-sized stone rolling away.

"It's not Sult's fault," Neeva said. "Every *yalmus* has the right—even the responsibility—to act on his own initiative."

"Sult is dividing the enemy's forces, just as Neeva taught him," added Caelum.

The mul cursed the dwarf's initiative and tried to think of a way to save the company. During the war with Urik, too many brave warriors had died needlessly for him to want to see the same thing happen to the Granite Company.

Before anything came to mind, Patch and Fosk surprised the mul by stopping their advances. The giants stood thirty of Rikus's paces away—only five or six of their own—and glared down at the three ranks of dwarven warriors.

Rikus drew his sword and stepped forward. The blade remained gray with the stain of the wraith attack, and the weapon's magic did not seem quite as powerful as before. Although the Scourge brought the dying screams of Sult Ltak's dwarves to his ears more clearly, he still could not understand their words—as he would normally have been able to do.

"Where is our Oracle?" demanded Patch.

"If you want to talk, call off your warrior's attack," Rikus countered, pointing toward the gorge.

Patch peered over his shoulder, then looked back down at Rikus with his one uncovered eye. He smiled, revealing a cruel set of filed yellow teeth. "Not until you answer."

Rikus sighed, then said, "We don't have it here."

"We knew that when your ugly little dwarves started shooting needles instead of giving it to us," sneered Fosk, standing a step behind his leader. "Where have you hidden it?"

"If you make us call the rest of the tribe to break into Tyr, we'll raze the city," warned Patch. "We won't leave nothing standing."

"There are many powerful wizards in Tyr—including the one who imprisoned your war party this morning," Rikus bluffed. "Besides, we only need to borrow the lens. We'll give it back as soon as we kill the Dragon."

Patch's single eye went as round as the sun, and Fosk could not stop himself from stepping forward.

"No!" boomed the giant leader. "Especially not for that!"

Rikus frowned. "The Dragon is everyone's enemy," the mul said. "He may not take giants to fill his levy, but it's his magic—and that of his followers, the sorcerer-kings—that turned Athas into a wasteland."

"Better to live in a wasteland than die in a paradise," countered Fosk.

"What's that supposed to mean?" Rikus asked.

Patch and Fosk looked at each other with blank expressions. Then, as if it would explain everything, the leader said, "That's what Jo'orsh and Sa'ram say."

"What do you know of Jo'orsh and Sa'ram?" demanded Caelum, stepping to Rikus's side.

"They gave us the Oracle," Patch informed him. "They said if we lose it, almost everyone on Athas could die."

"Then they must have changed their minds," Neeva said, joining the pair. "Because they're the ones who told us that it was time to kill the Dragon."

Fosk's cavernous mouth dropped open, and Patch raised the brow of his uncovered eye in disbelief. "They're here?" asked Fosk.

"They visited us ten days ago," Rikus said. He carefully avoided any mention of Rkard, deciding that he would leave it to Neeva to reveal or keep secret what the banshees had said about the boy's destiny. "They said nothing about returning the lens to the giants."

Patch scowled doubtfully. "If you really saw them, what'd they look like?"

"They were the size of giants—not quite as big as you, but close," Neeva replied. "They were nothing but bone, all twisted up. One had a skull, and the other didn't. Neither one had any skin, but both had orange eyes and long gray beards."

Patch ran a hand through his snarled hair braids. "And they didn't take our Oracle back?" he gasped. "Where are they?"

Neeva started to answer, but Rikus raised a hand to keep her from speaking. "First, stop your warrior from smashing any more of our friends."

Patch motioned to Fosk, who turned and bellowed, "Galt, leave them guys alone for a minute—but don't let 'em out 'til Patch says."

Galt reluctantly stepped back. He grabbed a huge

boulder and dropped it into place at the mouth of the canyon. Rikus heard the sound of crumpling armor, then dozens of angry dwarves screaming for the giant to come back and fight.

"Right now, we don't know where Jo'orsh and Sa'ram are," Rikus said. "We haven't seen them since they said it was time to kill the Dragon. But I suspect they've gone to protect the lens until we get there."

"Get where?" Patch demanded. "Our Oracle isn't in Tyr?"

Rikus smiled, proud of himself for salvaging their original plan. Even with Sadira unconscious, it seemed he would be able to lure the giants away from Tyr—perhaps even convince them to abandon their demand for the lens altogether.

"No, Agis didn't bring the Dark Lens back to Tyr," Rikus said. "He sent word for us to meet him someplace else."

Fosk scowled, and Patch narrowed his eye. "Agis told you meet him?"

"Yes," Rikus replied. "We'll leave as soon—"

"Liar!" Fosk thundered. He stooped down and scooped up an entire pile of waste rock.

Caelum touched his palm to the crimson sun on his forehead and pointed his other hand at the giant. Rays of scarlet light shot from between the dwarf's fingers, illuminating the valley in eerie, flickering hues as they streaked over and enveloped the titan's hand.

When Fosk whipped his arm forward, no stones flew from his hand. Pink balls of sticky, bubbling gel arced off the ends of his fingers, igniting small circles of flame wherever they spattered. The drops that fell on the ground flared briefly and faded, but the burning sludge stayed in Fosk's hand. The giant screamed in pain and slapped the hand at his thigh, kindling a fire even larger than the one he was attempting to put out. Finally, he simply dropped to the ground and began to roll, sending clouds of dust high into the sky.

"Nicely done, husband," said Neeva.

Rikus grunted his agreement. Keeping a watchful eye on Patch, who was studying the fallen giant with a wary scowl, the mul asked, "How many other spells do you have like that?"

"That was my most effective. That's why I saved it," Caelum replied. "It may not kill him, but it should keep him from bothering us for now."

"Perhaps Magnus will have some wind-magic—"

"I doubt he'll be coming," Rikus interrupted. "I assigned him to slow the giants back at the farm. He must have gotten trapped on the other side, or he'd be here by now."

As the mul spoke, Patch looked back toward the gorge. "Kill the dwarves, Galt!" he yelled. "All of 'em!"

Neeva spun around, commanding, "Into the tunnel. Now!"

As the dwarves obeyed, the mul shook his head in bewilderment. "Stop it, Patch!" he yelled, trying to keep the anger out of his voice. "I thought you understood. Jo'orsh and Sa'ram don't want the lens back."

"Be quiet, little liar!" Patch countered. He picked up a huge boulder and stepped toward the mul. "Agis died in the Bay of Woe."

"You're the one who's lying!" Rikus yelled. "Agis is alive. He just sent us a message!"

"Tithian stole our Oracle," Patch insisted. "And you're trying to hide him."

The titan hurled the stone with both hands. It arced toward Rikus. He had time to see that it was easily large enough to flatten both him and his companions. The mul brought the Scourge up and slashed at the rock with all his strength.

Rikus did not feel the enchanted blade biting into the boulder, as he had expected. His arm just went numb. A loud, clanging knell punched at his eardrums, and a black flash erupted from where his sword had met the rock. The dirt vanished from beneath his feet, and he felt himself being slammed into the ground by a tremendous blast. Everything fell quiet, and he expected to feel the crushing weight of the boulder smashing down on his body.

Instead, he was pelted by a stinging hail of gravel shards. He found himself gasping for breath as he struggled to draw air back into his lungs, and marveled that he had survived.

"Rikus!" Neeva screamed.

"I'm fine," he groaned. The mul ran a hand over a stinging cut above his ear, then picked himself up off the ground, nearly fell, and put out a hand to steady himself.

It was then that he realized he no longer held the Scourge.

"My sword," he growled, shaking his head and glaring in Patch's direction.

"There," Neeva replied. "It exploded."

She pointed to the ground next to where Rikus had landed. The Scourge of Rkard lay in two pieces, still tainted gray and disjoined about midway between the tip and hilt. From the jagged ends of the blade oozed a stream of black fluid, thicker than syrup and smelling as foul as a briny well. Instead of sinking into the dirt, the liquid drew up into glistening beads, which immediately rolled toward each other and began to form a single, much larger glob.

A cold ache rolled over Rikus's entire body. "No!" he cried, snatching the two pieces of his sword off the ground.

The mul spattered his fingers with several drops of the black fluid. The beads quickly rolled over his hand and started up his wrist, leaving a stinging trail of blisters in their wake. He yelled in surprise and whipped his hand downward, flinging the liquid onto the ground.

"What is that stuff?" he gasped, watching the beads

crawl toward the larger blob on the ground.

"What does it matter now?" responded Caelum. He pointed toward Patch, who had grabbed another boulder and was raising it to throw again. "Let's go!"

With that, the dwarf seized the mul's arm and pulled him into the tunnel. Patch's boulder crashed down outside and bounced off the cliff wall, filling the mine with a resonant boom.

Caelum led them into the deep recesses of the cavern, where the three remaining companies of Kled's militia waited safely beyond the giant's reach. The dwarves had not bothered to strike torches. When there was no true light available, their eyes detected the ambient heat emitted by all objects. It was an ability they had inherited from their ancient ancestors, who had lived out their entire lives in the black snugness of subterranean depths. Since he was a half-dwarf himself, Rikus was also blessed with this gift.

From outside came Patch's distant voice, deriding the dwarves as pointy-eared cowards, backstabbing thieves who couldn't grow a hair braid between them, and a dozen other names that he considered insulting. Each time the giant uttered another indignity, the tunnel trembled with the impact of another boulder hitting the cliff face outside. Once, a stone even entered the mine and rattled around the collar for a few moments before coming to a harmless rest.

Caelum stepped over to Rikus's side, his hand already glowing with crimson light.

"My healing magic is not as strong at night," he said, gesturing toward the gash above the mul's ear. "But at least I can stop the bleeding."

Rikus pulled away. "Wait a minute. I have an idea."

The mul looked at the Scourge's broken blade. The black fluid continued to drip from its jagged breaks. Enough of the stuff had gathered on the tunnel floor to create a knee-high blob of the stuff.

Rikus fit the two pieces of his sword together and held it toward Caelum.

"What do you want me to do?" the dwarf asked. He stared blankly at the blade and the dark fluid dripping from it. "I'm no smith."

"If you were, you'd know steel doesn't bleed." Rikus pointed his chin at the oozing seam between the broken pieces of blade. "So heal it."

"Mend steal?"

"Just try it," Rikus interrupted. "What can it hurt?"

The dwarf shook his head, then reached for the seam.

Rikus put out a restraining hand. "Can't you do it without touching it?" he asked. "That stuff stings."

"Pain is nothing new to me," the dwarf replied, closing his fingers around the Scourge.

As his hand contacted the black liquid, Caelum drew sharp breaths between his teeth and squeezed his eyes shut, but did not pull away. A soft sizzle echoed off the tunnel's stony walls and sparks spewed from between the dwarf's fingers, filling the dark passage with fleeting flashes of orange light. Sweat poured off Caelum's brow and his muscles trembled, but still he did not pull away.

"Is that going to work?" Neeva asked, stepping to her husband's side.

"I hope so," replied Caelum. "Without the Scourge, I don't know how Rkard is going to kill Borys."

The dwarf held his hand over the seam for several more moments. Finally, when no more black fluid dripped from between his fingers onto the blob at his feet, Caelum took his hand away from the Scourge.

The blade separated into two pieces, but the ends had ceased to drip. Disappointed, Rikus slipped the broken tip into his scabbard for safekeeping. "At least you stopped the bleeding."

"Whatever that liquid is, it's not blood," hissed

Caelum, staring at his hand.

The dwarf's palm was covered with the black ooze, which now bubbled and spewed as though on fire. More grotesquely, the bones beneath Caelum's flesh seemed to be writhing about like worms.

"Get that off my husband!" Neeva screamed.

Rikus grabbed the dwarf's hand and used the back of the Scourge's broken blade to scrape Caelum's hand clean. The black fluid hit the floor with a splat. It gathered itself into a bead and joined the largest glob.

"By the sun!" gasped Caelum. "What's happening to me?"

The mul looked back to the dwarf's hand and saw the cause of Caelum's alarm. Thick, pointed scales had sprouted along the outside edges of the palm. In the center gaped a fang-lined maw, with bright red lips and a forked tongue that rose up from the abysslike depths of its ebony throat.

"Release me." Black wisps of shadow slipped from between the mouth's lips. "Come and free me."

Caelum closed his hand. He grew very pale and said nothing.

"What is it?" Neeva demanded. She pulled them all away from the blob on the floor.

Rikus studied his broken blade for a moment, then shuddered. "It must have something to do with the Scourge's magic," he said, slipping the broken blade into his scabbard with the tip. "Sadira will know more— I hope."

"Come out!" yelled Patch's voice.

Rikus looked toward the entrance. The giant was lying on his stomach and looking into the tunnel with his one good eye. He peered into the darkness for a moment, then pulled away.

"Then you can stay in there, cowards!" he bellowed.

A moment later, a huge boulder came careening down the passage. It bounced off the walls a few times, and finally came to rest twenty or thirty paces inside the portal. The huge stone filled the tunnel so completely that Rikus could not see even a sliver of pale moonlight shining around its edges.

"I guess we won't be leaving that way," Rikus said.

The mul turned around and waited for his eyes to adjust to the dearth of light. Within a few moments, he was viewing the tunnel in a dozen radiant hues: the dwarves and Neeva in luminous red, thick veils of broken spiderwebs in shining green or yellow, the cold stone of the tunnel walls in shimmering blue.

"So how are we going to leave?" asked Neeva, peering around blindly. As the only full human in the group, she was the only person present who could not see in the dark.

"It won't take us long to find another exit," Caelum said. With his good hand, the dwarf grasped his wife's arm and began to lead her deeper into the inky depths. "That's true, isn't it, Rikus?"

"There are hundreds of ways out," the mul assured Caelum. "I suggest we divide the militia into three groups. Two of the companies should find exits as quickly as possible, then attack Patch or any other giant they see. We don't want them to go for a kill. Just let them know we're still alive, then retreat and try it again from another portal."

"What about the other company?" Neeva asked.

Rikus could see that she was gripping Caelum's arm tightly, and had squeezed her ineffective eyes shut so that her mind would not automatically strain to see what it could not and would be more open to her other senses. The technique was one that he had taught her long ago, while they were training for a special match of blindfolded gladiators.

"We'll take the rest of your warriors and try to reach the mines opening into the mouth of the gorge," Rikus said. "With a little luck, maybe we can find our way through in time to help Sult and his Granite Company."

"That shouldn't be difficult," said Caelum. He touched his fingers to his sun tattoo. "I've just the magic to lead us through this warren."

SEVEN

The Banshees

Rikus gnashed his teeth, trying to be patient and not succeeding very well. He stood at a tangled intersection of mine tunnels, holding his hand out in front of him. A single tongue of scarlet flame flickered in his palm, scorching his flesh and rising straight up into the gloomy air. The tiny fire cast just enough heat to wash out his dwarven vision, and its small sphere of scarlet light was barely large enough to illuminate the black maws of a dozen passages gaping at him from all directions. Beyond that, he was as blind in this murk as Neeva.

At last, Rikus looked to Caelum, who was standing at his side. "The flame's not pointing anywhere," he growled. "Your spell isn't doing anything except burning my hand."

"I'm sorry you find my fire-beacon uncomfortable," said Caelum. He raised his own hand. "I would have held it in my own palm, but . . ." He opened his fingers, revealing the scales and red lips that had formed there when he tried to heal the Scourge.

Rikus looked away. "Good enough," he said. "But which way now? The flame's not pointing toward any tunnel."

"Isn't it?" Caelum asked, looking up.

Rikus tipped his head back and saw a circle of blackness.

"Wonderful," he grumbled, raising his hand over his head. The flame's light revealed a man-sized cavity, roughly circular in shape, rising straight up. "How am I going to climb that without smothering the fire-beacon?"

The mul said nothing about the sporadic dizziness he had been suffering earlier, for it had all but disappeared during the long walk. Occasionally, he would feel light-headed for a moment or two, but the sensation no longer caused him to stumble or fall.

"You're not going to climb anything, Rikus," Neeva said. She turned to the dwarves at their back. "Brul Siderite, present yourself with a rope."

A young man promptly came forward with a coil of rope. Compared to the boulderlike shape of most dwarves, Brul was rather gaunt and lean, with gangling arms and bowed legs. Neeva had him remove his armor and sling the rope over his shoulder, then boosted him into the shaft. The warrior began to climb, his long arms and bowed legs flickering over the rough-hewn walls in search of secure holds.

Rikus waited in the musty darkness with the others, the mine's humid air forming cool beads of water on his bald head. Every time a groan or scrape sounded from above, he cringed, fearing Brul was about to come crashing back down.

Though Rikus recognized Neeva's wisdom in sending the dwarf up first, that did not make waiting any easier. Even with Caelum's fire-beacon guiding them through the maze of mine tunnels, he feared that it was taking their group too long to work their way back to the

mouth of the valley. The Iron Company had not gotten
lost once, but it had encountered many obstacles that
delayed its march. Several times, the dwarves had
crawled through long spans of partially collapsed tunnel on their bellies. Once, after the fire-beacon directed
them into a passage filled with foul-smelling air they
could not breath, they had found it necessary to back-
track and find a different route. Neeva had even been
forced to ferry the entire company of dwarves across a
stretch of flooded cavern, wading back and forth
through fifty paces of muddy water as deep as her chin.

At last, Brul's panting voice echoed down from the
top of the shaft. "Rope!"

As soon as the end of the line dropped into the tunnel,
Neeva tied it around Rikus's chest. "Haul away!" she
said.

The coarse rope bit into the mul's chest, and he felt his
feet leave the ground. Brul hauled him up in a steady
cadence of long pulls. The shaft was small enough that
the fire-beacon lit it completely, revealing rough-hewn
walls cut from red rock. Once, Rikus got stuck in a narrow section and could not free himself until he had
taken off his scabbard belt—no easy feat with one hand.

Near the top of the shaft, Rikus felt an arid breeze
blowing across his skin, sapping the dew that had col-
lected on him in the lower, more humid depths of the
mine. He resisted the urge to cheer, knowing there were
a hundred portals in the valley. Just because he felt an
outside breeze did not mean they had reached one of the
exits overlooking the gorge where the Granite Company
was trapped. The mul glanced at the fire-beacon in his
hand but did not find the answer to his question there.
The flame was flickering, but it still pointed upward.

A moment later, Brul pulled Rikus into a small passage, so cramped that the mul's broad shoulders barely
fit between the walls. Rikus scrambled onto the ledge.
He did not even try to stand, for the ceiling was so low

that it scraped his back even when he rested on his hands and knees.

"Is this the way?" asked the dwarf, shielding his eyes from the fire-beacon. "I think there's an exit here, but the shaft also continues up for at least another hundred feet."

Rikus looked at his hand and saw the flame pointing straight down the side passage.

"This is it," the mul reported. He pressed his palm to the wall and sighed in relief.

Once Rikus had smothered the fire-beacon, he saw a square of moonlit night at the other end of the tunnel, about a hundred paces distant. He untied the rope around his waist and squeezed past Brul, anxious to see what had become of Sult, the Granite Company, and the giants.

There was no need to wait. Patch's muffled voice sounded from the other end of the tunnel. "Nasty dwarves! I'll kill you like you killed Galt!"

Rikus heard a distant crash. A muted rumble rolled through passage, shaking dust and loose stones from the ceiling.

"It sounds like the Granite Company killed one giant," the mul said, turning to Brul. "Have Neeva bring me an axe, and we'll see if we can't get another."

While the dwarf lowered his rope back into the shaft and relayed Rikus's request, the mul strapped on his scabbard belt. By the time he finished, Brul was heaving on the rope again. With the fire-beacon gone, the mul's dwarven vision had returned, and he saw a halo of rosy light appear as Neeva's head rose out of the shaft. She carried a pair of battle-axes in her arms and an extra rope over her shoulder.

Rikus reached past Brul and grasped the weapons. "Over here."

The mul pulled the axes past the dwarf, then took one and started up the passage. Neeva followed close behind. As they crawled, Patch's voice continued to rumble down the passage, punctuated by muffled crashes and distant booms. The noises did not seem to grow much louder as they neared the exit, which made Rikus fear the battle had already moved farther down the canyon.

Rikus finally reached the end of the tunnel. Directly ahead lay the moonlit crags of the gorge's opposite wall. He looked to one side. He and Neeva had come out as intended, where the narrow canyon opened into the valley. In the other direction, the gorge ran for only a short distance before kinking sharply. Had he not known better, the mul would have sworn the chasm ended there. He saw no sign of Patch in either direction.

"Make room," said Neeva, crawling alongside Rikus.

As her flank pressed against his, the mul could not help smiling at the warmth of her soft flesh. It reminded him of times past, when they had lain pressed together all night, too tense to sleep or talk, knowing the next morning they would leave the arena as they were then, victorious or dead, but together still. Rikus had never thought he would miss anything about being a gladiator, but now, with Neeva pressed against his side, he realized he did miss one thing.

The crack of a shattering stone sounded from somewhere below, reminding Rikus that dwelling on his past with Neeva would do him no more good than wishing the Scourge's blade had not been snapped. The mul looked down and saw that they had come out much higher than he had hoped, as he could tell by the sight of a tangled nest of giant braids far below.

Rikus squinted, trying to see what was happening more clearly. The moonlight reflecting off the gorge's walls washed out his dwarven vision, so even after careful study he could distinguish little more than a hulking pair of shoulders filling the canyon from wall to wall. Nevertheless, it appeared that Sult and the Granite

Company were giving the giant a good fight. Patch's head was tilted forward to look at the ground, and he seemed oblivious to anything but stomping and cursing the dwarves at his feet.

"Rikus, didn't you see that?" Neeva asked, a note of urgency in her voice.

"What?" the mul asked. He scoured the gorge's shadows for something he had missed.

"Up there," Neeva corrected.

She pointed into the sky, where a crimson sphere hung just above the opposite rim of the gorge. The ball was flickering and sputtering, like a torch that had burned all its oil, and was so faint it barely stood out from the night.

"What's that?" Rikus asked.

"Rkard's sun-spell." Her voice cracked as she spoke. "He's in trouble."

"It's about to go out," Rikus observed. "How long does it last?"

"A quarter hour," Neeva replied. She looked at Rikus, then asked, "Do you think there's any chance Sadira's awake yet?"

"If she was awake, there would be no need for Rkard to cast his spell," the mul replied.

Neeva started to back down the tunnel. "We've got to help him!"

Rikus grabbed her shoulder. "It'll take too long to return," he said. "But I know a faster way."

Neeva allowed herself to be pulled up the passage. "How?"

Rikus took the rope off her shoulder. He began tying it around himself, looping it first between his legs, then around his hips, over his shoulders, and beneath his arms so it would spread the impact of a long fall over the strongest points of his body.

"Leave about ten arms of rope between us," Rikus said, finishing his harness off with a secure knot. "Fasten yourself into the other end of the line like I have. Then come up here next to me."

By the time they finished, Caelum was crawling up the tunnel toward them. "What's wrong?" he asked, eyeing the rope strung between his wife and Rikus.

"Your son's in trouble," the mul answered.

Rikus checked Neeva's harness, then twisted himself around so that he sat at the mouth of the tunnel, his legs dangling over the edge. Neeva passed him his battle-axe and sat next to him, cradling her own weapon in her arms.

"Wait!" Caelum cried. "That rope isn't tied off. You'll fall—"

"Not now, husband," Neeva snapped. Without looking back at the dwarf, she peered down at Patch's shoulder, which was just a little bit ahead of their perch. "I know what to do."

"Just like old times," Rikus answered, smiling. "Go!"

Gripping his axe with both hands, he slipped out of the tunnel. He pushed off the gorge wall with his legs, driving himself to the side so that he would fall in front of Patch's body. In the same instant, Neeva also slipped from her perch, though she launched herself straight ahead so she would come down behind the giant. The rope stretched out between her and Rikus, keeping them connected as they plummeted into the shadows.

Rikus heard Caelum cry out, then the roar of the wind filled his ears and drowned out the dwarf. The mul felt his own voice vibrating inside his skull and knew he was screaming, but he simply ignored the panicked part of his mind and focused his thoughts on one simple task: clutching his battle-axe.

Rikus plunged past a tangle of hair braids, and Neeva passed out of sight behind Patch's massive collarbone. The mul hit feet-first, then glanced off the giant's breast and bounced away. The rope caught him an instant later, his makeshift harness biting deep beneath his legs and arms as the cord stretched with the force of the fall. It squeezed tight around his ribs, filling his chest with a terrible ache and driving the air from his lungs in an involuntary groan. He heard a similar grunt from Neeva's side of the shoulder, then felt himself arcing back toward the titan's chest. As painful as the stop was, Rikus knew that it would have been much worse—possibly even snapping his back or breaking his ribs—had he not taken the time to tie himself into the line as he had.

Patch roared in surprise and wrenched around to see what had fallen on him. The motion sent Rikus swinging toward the gorge wall and the rope skipped as his weight hit the end. Fearing the line would slip off the huge shoulder, he swung his axe as hard as he could. The steel head drove deep into the titan's breast, instantly stopping the mul's flight and drawing a pained howl from the giant.

Releasing his weapon, Rikus grabbed a fold of the giant's smelly sheepskin tunic and pulled himself forward. Patch's hand slapped down behind him. The back edge of the double-bladed axe sank deep into the titan's palm and the giant bellowed in anger. While the titan plucked the battle-axe from his palm, the mul climbed for the opposite shoulder. He saw Patch raise a hand to claw at him, then the giant abruptly stopped as a flurry of dull thumps sounded at his feet.

"Stomp the Granite Company, will you!" cried a dwarf's angry voice. "We'll chop you off at the ankles, you lout!"

Patch hopped from one foot to the other. Each time he changed legs, a dwarf cried out in pain, and the sound of folding steel echoed up from the dark gorge. Determined to make the most of the diversion, Rikus continued his climb and soon pulled himself over the giant's shoulder. He met Neeva coming from the other side. Like Rikus, she remained harnessed into the rope.

"Everything okay?" Rikus asked.

"It will be, when we choke this giant," Neeva replied.

The warrior scrambled away, crossing in front of the titan's throat. The mul jumped over the back of the shoulder. Patch did not attempt to stop them, his attention fixed on the dwarven axes hacking at his ankles. Rikus waited until he saw Neeva appear behind the giant's other shoulder, then braced his feet and pulled. She did the same. The rope, now looped around the huge throat like a garotte, tightened.

Patch forgot the dwarves and tried to pull the rope away. His efforts were to no avail. Rikus and Neeva had pulled the cord so tight that it bit deep into his flesh, and the titan could not slip his fingers beneath the taut line. A deep gurgle rumbled from the brute's throat.

Patch stumbled around, turning his back toward the cliff. Anticipating the giant's next move, Rikus called, "Cross and over!"

Still pulling on the rope, the mul shuffled across Patch's spine. Neeva did the same, and they crossed. The giant leaned back toward the cliff. They threw themselves over his collarbone and narrowly avoided being crushed as he slammed into the rock wall.

Patch kept his back against the cliff, his rasping chokes echoing down the canyon. He raised one hand toward each of his tormenters.

Rikus could not see what Neeva was doing, but the mul tried to draw his dagger. He found the hilt tied into place beneath his harness. The giant's fingers encircled his body. Rikus grabbed the rope with both hands and pulled, kicking at the enormous hand with both feet. He almost slipped free, then Patch caught his legs. The titan squeezed, filling Rikus's knees and hips with agony.

The choking giant had already grown very weak, and the torment was not as bad as it might have been. None of Rikus's thick mul bones cracked, and he did not even feel anything pop out of socket. Deciding he could bear the pain until Patch fell unconscious, the warrior braced himself against the titan's thumb and index finger, concentrating his efforts on keeping himself from slipping deeper into the huge fist.

The mul peered around the giant's gullet and caught a glimpse of Neeva. Somehow, she had braced her feet against the back of the hand and wrapped both her arms around the titan's little finger. She was pulling it back against the joint, though Rikus suspected she had little chance of snapping it.

A series of deep, racking coughs shook the giant's torso. He tried to jerk Rikus and Neeva away from his throat. They were still connected to the rope, and he succeeded only in drawing it tighter. Patch began to sway, then dropped to his knees.

Cheering madly, more than a dozen dwarves began hacking at the giant's thighs.

A long convulsion ran through Patch's body, then his hands opened and he pitched forward. His face slammed into the gorge wall, leaving his killers dangling from the rope around his neck.

Rikus and Neeva pulled themselves up the rope to Patch's collarbone, where they freed themselves from their harnsesses. They tied the ends of the cord together so the garotte would not loosen before it had done its work completely, then slid down the unconscious giant's back. Their feet had barely touched the ground before Neeva was yelling for Sult to report.

"Here, commander." A grizzled dwarf stepped forward, wading through a river of blood that was pouring from a wound in Patch's thigh. He had a weather-lined face and a thin, crooked nose that looked as though it had been broken a dozen times. "Fifteen survivors for the Granite Company."

"Never mind that," Neeva replied. "How many giants did you kill in this canyon?"

"One, aside from this one," the dwarf replied. "The

fourth one stayed at the farm to fight the windsinger."

With a curse, Neeva turned and started down the dark gorge at a sprint.

* * * * *

From his hiding place on the butte, Rkard saw Magnus run out of the faro orchard below Rasda's Wall. The windsinger looked utterly exhausted, stumbling over rocks and flailing his massive arms as he tried to retain his balance. He veered away from the four giants who had died during the day and raced for the far end of the valley.

A series of thudding footsteps echoed behind him. A single giant appeared from behind Rasda's Wall, carrying a stone he had torn from the ridge. The titan looked as exhausted as Magnus. He had two jagged cuts on his brow, and his body was covered with huge bruises so dark Rkard could see them even in the pale light of the moons.

The marks were evidence of the terrific brawl to which the young mul had been listening until just a few seconds ago. After the four surviving giants had followed Kled's militia toward Pauper's Hope, a terrible storm of whirling winds and rumbling thunder had erupted behind Rasda's Wall. The din had been answered by the clatter of breaking stones and angry bellows. A moment later, most of the titans' voices had begun to grow more distant and muffled, and Rkard had guessed they were chasing the militia into the mountains. One brute had stayed behind, however, and the sounds of battle had continued to rage for a long time.

Now, it was finally clear who had won. As Rkard watched, the giant braced himself and hurled his stone. The rock glanced off the windsinger's shoulder and tumbled away. Magnus dropped in midstride, tumbling head over heels for the length of a dozen strides. He finally came to a rest flat on his back, with his head toward his attacker.

Rkard almost forgot himself and cried out, but at the last moment managed to choke his scream into a strangled croak, "Magnus!"

The windsinger lay motionless for a moment, and Rkard worried that the stone had killed him. Then Magnus raised his head and, with a great deal of effort, pushed himself into a sitting position. The arm that had been hit by the boulder hung limply at his side, and he hardly seemed conscious of the giant's heavy footsteps behind him.

"Get up, Magnus," Rkard whispered. He knew Magnus could sometimes hear messages carried on the wind. Since a gentle breeze was blowing down the butte, the boy hoped his words would reach the windsinger's funny-looking ears. "The giant's coming."

Magnus continued to sit motionless, and the titan stopped behind him. Rkard touched his fingers to the crimson sun on his forehead and felt a warm, tingly sensation running through his arm. Most people assumed the red disk to be a tattoo, but it was actually the sunmark, a birthmark that served as his mystical connection to the sun during times of darkness.

The windsinger suddenly pricked up his big ears and glanced toward the butte. He shook his head and rolled over onto his hands and knees. Rkard breathed a sigh of relief, thankful the windsinger had spared him the necessity of deciding whether or not to cast his spell. After Jo'orsh and Sa'ram had appeared to him, his father had told him that he must never risk his life, not even if it meant saving the entire militia—or his own parents. His father had said more than a few lives depended on his destiny, and that if he got himself killed, everyone on Athas would die with him.

Rkard didn't like what his father had said. And he thought his mother probably didn't either, though she

had not told him as much. After that nasty head—
Wyan—had arrived with the Asticles signet, and everyone had decided that it was time to kill the Dragon, she
had told him to think about his decisions very carefully.
She had said he should never do anything dangerous
unless he had a good chance of succeeding, and even
then he had to think of a way to escape first.

In the valley below, the giant kicked his foot into
Magnus's ribs. The windsinger arced out over the valley, crashing into a jumble of sharp stones thirty paces
away. The impact would have killed a human, and probably even a mul, but not Magnus. He just rolled across
the rocky ground and tried to pick himself up again.

This time, he did not succeed.

The giant grabbed a pointed stone as large as a kank.
Rkard could not decide what to do. Neither of his parents would want him to cast his spell now. The worst
thing he could do to the titan was blind him for a few
moments, and then the brute would probably come to
hunt him and Sadira down. But the thought of standing
by while the giant smashed Magnus gave the boy a sick
feeling in his stomach.

The titan stepped toward Magnus.

Rkard slipped behind his boulder and looked down
at Sadira. The sorceress lay motionless on the ground,
her amber hair glowing softly in the moonlight and her
almond-shaped eyes closed tight. Her chest heaved as
though she were sobbing, and the way her fingers flut-
tered reminded the boy of how they moved when she
cast a spell.

Rkard kneeled at her side and shook her shoulder.
"The giant's going to kill Magnus," he said. "Wake up!"

The sorceress's chest continued to heave, and she
showed no sign of stirring.

"What should I do?" he asked.

Sadira's head rolled to one side, but she did not
answer.

"Okay, I'll decide myself," the boy answered. "What would Rikus do?"

Rkard knew instantly that his hero would not stand by while a giant killed a friend. Rikus would do whatever he could, even if it meant he might die himself. That was why everybody liked him so much.

The young mul stepped past Sadira and clambered to the top of the boulder. The giant was standing over Magnus, just raising the stone to slay the unconscious windsinger.

"Hey, ugly!" he yelled.

The breeze carried Rkard's voice across the valley as though the boy were a giant himself, bouncing it off the rocky scarps on the other side. The titan pulled the heavy stone back to his chest and looked toward the echo first.

"Who's that?" he called, searching the barren slopes at the base of the Ringing Mountains.

"Over here on the butte, you dumb hairy giant!" Rkard yelled.

As he spoke, the young mul pressed his fingers to his sun-mark. Again, he felt a warm tingle descending through his arm. Had it been daylight, he would have pointed his hand toward the crimson sun instead of touching it to his forehead. The feeling in his arm would have been excruciatingly hot rather than merely warm, but he was far from glad to avoid that pain. His spell would have been much stronger during the day, perhaps strong enough to do more than merely distract the giant.

After searching the slope of the butte for a few moments, the giant's dark eyes finally settled on Rkard's small form. "I'm not as dumb as you," he said, squinting at the boy. "I know better than to make fun of—"

Rkard pointed his hand at the giant's face and spoke a mystic syllable.

A crimson ball formed around the giant's head. The

titan screamed and dropped his stone, almost crushing his own foot. He raised his hands to his face and began stumbling about, screeching as though his flesh were melting.

Rkard knew that the giant's reaction was more fear than pain. While the crimson sphere might look fiery, and even feel hot for a brief moment, it was far from a searing ball of flame. The spell consisted entirely of red light, shaped into a bright orb with flickering tails that looked like fire. His father had taught it to him so he could honor the sun on days when blowing sand obscured the real thing, and because it served as a good distress signal.

Anticipating the giant's reaction when he realized the true nature of the spell, Rkard jumped off his boulder and threw Sadira's limp body over his shoulders. Though the sorceress was much larger than he was, he had no trouble carrying her up the steep slope. As a young mul, he was already as strong as most humans. Besides, she did not weigh much more than the huge water pails his mother made him fetch from the village well every day.

By the time the young mul was halfway up the butte, the giant's screams had ceased. Rkard paused to look back and saw his spell rising over the valley, casting an eerie orange glow onto the rocky ground. Once it was high enough, the sphere would stop and hang motionless in the sky, just like a miniature sun.

Now that his head was no longer engulfed in the bright light, the giant had begun to stumble toward the butte. He was rubbing his eyes with one hand and holding the other out before him. The titan had left Magnus where he had fallen, motionless but out of danger for now.

"Papa's going to be angry when he sees this," Rkard said, continuing his climb.

The boy did not even consider trying to deceive his

father, for he had grown up with the certain knowledge that the sun would always bring the truth to light.

As Rkard reached the summit of the bluff, he heard stones clattering below as the giant clambered up the base. The young mul slipped behind the crest of the butte and onto a narrow ledge that overlooked the road to Tyr's iron mine.

"Come back, you little varl!" thundered the giant. "Don't hide—it'll only make me madder!"

Rkard pushed Sadira into the deep crevice that he had selected earlier as a good hiding place, then quickly stacked boulders over the entrance to conceal it. By the time he finished, the giant was so close that his heavy steps were shaking rocks off the ridge overhead. Knowing that the angry titan could easily tear the top of the butte apart, the boy decided to lure his pursuer away from Sadira. He rushed along the ledge until it ended, then scrambled up a rift and onto the top of the butte.

Rkard found himself standing at the giant's feet. Wishing that he were strong enough to cast more than one spell a day, he swallowed and drew his weapon. The glow of his sun-spell sent glimmers of red light twinkling along the edge of his sword's obsidian blade.

"What are you going to do with that thorn?" demanded the giant. "Stick me in the toe when I step on you?"

Rkard stepped forward, raising his weapon. He focused all his attention on keeping his blade from shaking and craned his neck upward to meet the giant's gaze. His mother had always told him that a show of confidence would do more than ten blows to defeat a powerful enemy, and if ever there had been a time he hoped she was right, it was now.

"Leave me alone—and Magnus, too," Rkard said, imagining that it was Rikus and not himself speaking. Without taking his eyes off the giant, he pointed his sword toward the edge of the cliff. "Go away, or I'll cut off your foot and push you over the cliff."

The giant's big belly shook with laughter—until he looked toward the edge of the cliff, where Rkard was pointing. Then the titan's huge mouth fell open and his eyes widened in surprise.

"You?" the brute gasped.

"Yes, me," Rkard replied. He stepped forward and poked the giant's yellow-nailed toe with his sword.

"Now, listen," the boy ordered. "What you want isn't in Tyr—and even if it was, you couldn't have it." Rkard pointed his sword down the hill, then added, "Now go home and tell all the other giants what I said."

The giant looked toward the cliff edge again, then licked his lips as if uncertain of what to do. "I can't go back without the Oracle," he said, his tone more pleading than insistent. "We need its magic to make us smart again! Patch is the smartest one of us left, and he's getting dumber all the time!"

Rkard considered this. Even at his young age, he understood that without a smart leader, any community would collapse into disorder. "Maybe you can have the Dark Lens back after we're through with it," the boy suggested.

Some of the tension drained from the giant's huge face, and he looked directly at Rkard again. "How long will you keep our Oracle?"

The boy paused before answering. In his short life, the only journey he had ever made was from Kled to Tyr, and he could not imagine how much farther away the village of Samarah must be. "We'll be gone a long time—a hundred years," he answered. Having lived all his life among dwarves, who commonly lived three times that long, the guess did not seem unreasonable to the young mul. "Maybe even longer."

The giant shook his head stubbornly. "No! We'll be dumber than kanks by then!"

Rkard raised his sword, expecting the brute to stomp

him, and tried to look confident. The attack never came. Instead, a deep voice behind him said, "Then you will learn to live like kanks!"

Rkard spun around and found two giant-sized heads peering over the top of the cliff—though it may have been an exaggeration to call them heads. One had a hideous, misshapen skull with a sloped brow and gnarled cheekbones, while the other one's neck ended in a knobby stump just above the shoulders. Regardless of whether they had skulls or not, pairs of orange embers burned where their eyes should have been, and coarse masses of tangled beard dangled from where their chins had once hung.

Though Rkard could not see the bodies hidden beneath the cliff edge, he knew they were little more than huge skeletal lumps, warped into shapes scarcely recognizable as manlike. The legs were gnarled masses with knotted balls for feet, and the thighs, knees, and calves were all curled together.

"Jo'orsh! Sa'ram!" Rkard gasped. They were the last dwarven knights, who had become banshees after they disavowed their life focus and died without killing Borys. The young mul had not seen the pair since they had returned his namesake's belt and crown to him, then told him that he would slay the Dragon. "You've come back!"

"We never left," said the one with the lumpy skull, Jo'orsh.

The other banshee focused his floating eyes on the giant. *We have let you giants use the Dark Lens for too long.* Rkard heard the words inside his head, as if a mindbender were speaking them. *You have all grown weak and foolish. It is time you learned to live without it.*

The giant gasped, and a rancid-smelling wind washed over Rkard. "We can't!" the brute cried.

"You can and you must," retorted Jo'orsh.

Do as the boy commanded, added Sa'ram. *Return to*

*Mytilene and tell the others to think of the Dark Lens no
more. We have taken it back, and you must learn to live without it—or perish.*

Rkard looked back up at the giant. The brute had a
stunned and dismal expression on his face, as if he had
just been cast out of his home village.

"And know for every giant your tribe sends to seek
the lens, it shall suffer a century of barbarism," said
Jo'orsh. "Now go!"

The banshee's voice broke over the giant like a thunderclap, sending him stumbling down the hill backward. He took five huge steps before he turned around
and scurried into the valley, giving Magnus a wide
berth.

Once the giant was gone, Rkard's arms and legs
started to tremble. He tried to sheathe his sword, discovered he couldn't hold it steady enough, and gave up.

"Thanks for saving me." He could not bring himself to
face the banshees again, not when he felt so frightened
and foolish. "Are you as angry as my father will be?"

Why should we be angry—or your father, for that matter?
Sa'ram asked.

"Because I disobeyed him." Rkard kept his eyes fixed
on the ground. "I nearly got killed."

"You saved a friend," countered Jo'orsh. "That was
very brave, and your father won't punish you for it."

Rkard shook his head. "I took a foolish chance," he
said. "And when I did that, I risked all of Athas."

Before you can save Athas, you will have to risk it, said
Sa'ram. *You mustn't be afraid to do that—just as you weren't
afraid to endanger yourself to save your friend.*

Rkard frowned. "But I didn't save Magnus." He
looked up at the banshees. "You did."

Jo'orsh shook his head. "All we did was stand behind
you."

Yes, added Sa'ram. *Just as your friends and your parents
will stand behind you when you attack Borys.*

EIGHT

Crimson Dawn

Neeva stood on the ledge between her husband and son, the cold wind raising goose bumps over their naked bodies. They were gazing across the dry lake bed, where the first sliver of morning sun had just appeared over the craggy shoulder of a distant mountain.

"We hail the return of the crimson sun," said Caelum.

The trio raised their arms over their heads. They turned their palms toward the rising sun, except that Caelum held the hand with the strange mouth tightly closed. Although both her husband and son stared straight into its glowing crescent, Neeva fixed her own gaze on the scarlet rays creeping across the salt-crusted lake bed. Unlike the two sun-clerics, she did not have fire-eyes. Had she dared to stare directly into the glorious radiance, she would have been blinded.

"We welcome the beacon that lights the world, the mighty fire that burns away the cold night, the punishing orb that drives the savage beasts into hiding," Rkard said.

"This dawn, we have a special request," Neeva added.

"We ask that you shine brightly and do not let the dust haze obscure your light, so that we may see clearly and choose well from the difficult paths before us today."

Rkard looked up at her. "What paths, mother?" he asked. "Jo'orsh and Sa'ram have said what I will do."

"Not now, Rkard," Caelum said, his voice gentle. "Attend to your devotions."

The young mul remembered himself and returned his gaze to the eastern horizon. Together, the trio stood in silence, the sun's rays spreading a heartening warmth over their skin, fortifying their spirits for the difficult day ahead. The sun-marks on the brows of Caelum and Rkard grew ardent red, gleaming with a deep scarlet luster as they absorbed the sun's radiance. Neeva found herself squeezing her son's hand so tightly that her fingers ached, as afraid of what the future held for him as she was relieved that he had survived last night's battle with the giants.

At last, the bottom edge of the crimson sun rose completely above the shoulder of the mountain. Shimmering red flames briefly flickered from the sun-marks on the foreheads of Rkard and Caelum, then the flares died away. The disks returned to their normal red hues.

"We live by the power of the crimson sun," Caelum intoned.

"The hottest of fires, the brightest of lights, the mightiest of the four elements," Rkard finished.

As the trio retrieved their clothes, Neeva's son asked, "What paths must we choose today, Mother?"

"That remains to be seen," Neeva answered, tying her breechcloth. "The Scourge has been broken, and Sadira has yet to awaken. Perhaps this is not the time to fulfill your destiny."

"But we must!" Rkard insisted. "Sa'ram and Jo'orsh have said—"

"You've told me what they said!" Neeva snapped. "I don't need to hear it again."

The boy flinched, startled by his mother's sharp tone. He bit his lip and rubbed the back of his wrist beneath his eye, then turned to tie his breechcloth in silence.

Caelum raised his brow. "Rkard didn't cause our troubles," he said, laying a hand on their son's shoulder. "In fact, I'd say he did well. It's not every six-year-old that can chase off a giant."

"Of course not," Neeva answered. She dropped to her knees and gathered the boy into her arms. "I know better than anyone how special he is. That's why I won't risk his life if our attack has no chance to succeed. We need both the Scourge and Sadira."

"Jo'orsh and Sa'ram will protect me," Rkard answered, returning her embrace. "Just like they did from the giant."

"I wish I could hear that from them," Neeva replied.

"Why?" her son asked. "Don't you believe me?"

"Of course I believe you," Neeva answered. She glanced up at Caelum, then looked in her son's red eyes. "But once we attack, we'll have to keep fighting. We won't be able to stop and try again later."

"I know," answered Rkard. "The Dragon will try to kill me, just like I'm going to try to kill him. So?"

Neeva smiled at her son's bravery. "So we can't make a mistake and assault too early. If we don't have everything we need, he'll succeed, and you won't," she said. "Let's check on our friends, and hope the sun favors us all today."

She tied her halter around her chest, then led the way over the butte's crest and started down the shadowy hillside. In the valley below, the surviving companies of the Kledan militia were ready to march, while the Tyrian legion, which had arrived late last night, was just beginning to stir.

Neeva went to a small encampment at the bottom of the butte. Early morning shadows still cloaked the site, but the sun's rays were slowly creeping across the valley floor. Soon the camp would be bright with the orb's radiance.

Sadira lay next to a small fire of acrid-smelling cat-claw boughs, still unconscious and as pale as moonlight. Magnus sat next to her, singing a soft song of healing. The windsinger appeared only slightly more healthy than the sorceress, for his knobby hide was crusted with dried blood and marred by large black bruises.

Rikus stood between two boulders at the edge of camp. He held Wyan in the one hand and his sword in the other. The blade was still broken, ending in a jagged stub about two feet from the hilt. But the gray stain had faded from its silvery steel, which now gleamed as brightly as it had before the wraith tried to animate it.

"You're just in time." The mul motioned for Neeva and her family to join him. "I was about to try the Scourge. Wyan says it may not be ruined after all."

"That would be welcome news," Neeva said.

"What I said was that by healing the blade, Caelum *may* have saved it," the head corrected, slowly twisting around to face Neeva. "I didn't tell the oaf to bang it on a rock."

"I don't see what we have to lose," Rikus said. He placed Wyan on top of a boulder. "It doesn't boost my hearing anymore, so the magic's probably gone. But there's only one way to be sure: see if it still has the magic to cut rock."

"Are you sure that's wise?" asked Caelum. "As I recall, it was a boulder that snapped the sword in the first place."

"Only because the wraith had tainted it," Rikus replied. "Before that, I used it to cut things harder than stone."

Neeva motioned for Rikus to perform his test. "Go ahead."

The mul faced the second boulder. The sun's light had just touched the rock, casting a rosy glow over its brown surface. He swung, and his shortened sword struck with a dissonant chime that made Magnus miss two notes in his song. Fearing the weapon would snap, Neeva started to pull her son away, then the blade sank though the stone, trailing wisps of black shadow. The sword did not stop cutting until it had cleaved through half the thickness of the boulder.

Rikus scowled. "It doesn't cut like it used to," he said, bracing a foot against the stone as he pulled the sword out of it. "But it'll do."

The mul returned the weapon to his scabbard, where the tip of the blade was still stored.

"Good," said Rkard. He turned to his mother and asked, "So now we're going to Samarah, right?"

"We'll see." Neeva glanced toward Sadira. The rays of crimson sun were creeping up the sorceress's legs, returning her flesh to the ebon hue it customarily assumed in daylight. "First we must see if Sadira awakens."

"But we've got to go!" objected Rkard. "If we don't, I'll turn into a banshee, just like Jo'orsh and Sa'ram."

Neeva frowned. "What makes you think that?" she asked, squatting down so she could look her son in the eyes. "Muls aren't like dwarves. They don't have to choose a life purpose."

"But your son is no ordinary mul," interrupted Wyan. The head fixed his sallow eyes on the boy's face. "Rkard has a destiny, and who can tell what will become of him if he doesn't fulfill it now?"

Caelum plucked the head up by his topknot. "Don't say such things to my son!" he yelled. "You know nothing of his destiny!"

"I knew the Scourge still had its magic," Wyan countered. "Perhaps I know other things as well."

"Then tell us," Neeva commanded, drawing a dagger.

Wyan's cracked lips twisted into a sneer. "You know the answer," he said. "That's why you're so afraid."

Rkard slipped forward and stood eye-to-eye with the

head. "Nothing scares my mother!"

"You're wrong, brat!" snarled the head. "Your mother's paralyzed with fear. If she lets you attack Borys, you'll be killed. But if she doesn't let you fight, you'll turn into a banshee, more hideous than Sa'ram or Jo'orsh." Wyan showed his gray teeth in a cruel mockery of a smile. "What's a mother to do?"

Rkard took Neeva's hand. "I'm not afraid of the Dragon," he said. "I'll kill him."

"Of course you will—but not until the time's right." Neeva turned him away from Wyan. "Let's check on Sadira and see if the sun's awakened her. We could use some good tidings."

They found the sorceress cradled in Magnus's arms. She was now completely bathed in sunlight, and her skin was as black as ever. The sores and bruises that had marked her body the previous evening were gone, and there were no other signs of injuries from her battle with the wraiths. Still, her emberlike eyes did not burn with their usual intensity, and she lay slumped in a limp heap, rubbing the Asticles signet between her thumb and forefinger.

Motioning for Rkard to wait with his father, Neeva went to the sorceress's side. "Are you well?"

Sadira's eyes flared back to life. She slipped Agis's ring back onto her finger, then reached up and grasped Neeva's hand.

"I'm fine," she said, pulling herself to her feet. "I wish I could say the same for Agis—and for the rest of Tyr."

"What do you mean?"

Sadira took a deep breath, then said, "Agis is dead."

"It can't be!" Neeva gasped. "How could you know?"

"I know," Sadira replied. "I had to fight my way out of the Gray, and the wraiths tried to make me stay by using his spirit as a hostage." Tiny streamers of black shadow began to rise from the corners of the sorceress's eyes. "I destroyed them."

"You can't be sure you were in the Gray," said Caelum, coming to Neeva's side. "It could have been a delusion—"

"Sadira was in the Gray, or it wouldn't have taken me so long to call her back." Magnus pushed his hulking mass to its feet. "And the wraiths are gone, or they would still be attacking us. The only way she could have destroyed them was by fighting them in the Gray."

"Agis is dead," Sadira said. This time, she could not keep from crying as she spoke.

"I'm afraid so," Magnus agreed. "That's the only explanation for seeing him there."

Sadira began to sob, black shadow rising from between her blue lips in puffing billows.

Neeva wiped her own cheek, surprised to find tears running down it. During her days in the arena, she had seen many friends die—some at her own hands, when the game promoters felt particularly cruel—and she had thought all her tears were gone. The warrior was glad to discover that some remained for Agis, the only noble she had ever called friend. She touched her hand to her heart in the gladiator's traditional sign of farewell, then raised it toward the east, where he had died.

When Neeva looked toward Rikus, she found the mul staring at the ground with glassy eyes. His lips were quivering, and he was shaking his head as if he did not believe what Sadira had said.

"Rikus," Neeva said softly.

The mul looked up. "I thought Agis was too smart to die," he said. "I didn't believe what Patch said."

"Neither did I," Neeva said. "But we didn't have much chance to think about it."

"Agis held everything together—the council, the relief farms, our house." The mul stepped past her, reaching for Sadira. "What are we going to do now?"

The sorceress pushed him away. "How do I know?" she yelled. "With Agis dead, what does it matter?"

Caelum quickly slipped in between Sadira and Rikus. "Agis was a friend to us all, and we'll miss him," he said. "But he wouldn't want us to give up. We must consider what to do next."

Sadira shook her head angrily. "Haven't you been listening?" she demanded. "Agis is dead. The only thing that will happen next is Tyr's destruction."

"You may be overreacting, Sadira," said Magnus. "I don't see how one man's death will bring about the downfall of a city that's stood for a thousand years."

"Don't you understand?" the sorceress asked. "The Dragon knows we're coming. That's why he sent the wraiths to kill me."

"And if Borys killed Agis, then you fear he's also stolen the Dark Lens," Caelum concluded.

Neeva's stomach began to churn with a sick, hollow feeling. She could not quite believe that Agis was dead, or that they had lost the Dark Lens before they had even seen it, and something in the back of her mind told her it was not true. Then she remembered what Patch had said: Agis died in the Bay of Woe—whatever that was— and Tithian stole the Dark Lens.

"I don't think Borys killed Agis," Neeva said. She stepped over to Wyan and snatched the head off the boulder. "Where did Agis die? What happened to the Dark Lens?"

"Agis fell in the giant islands," the head answered, smirking cruelly at Sadira. "He and Tithian stole the lens together, but only the king escaped alive. He's the one who sent me."

"Where'd you get Agis's ring?" Sadira demanded. She snatched Wyan from Neeva's hand and held the Asticles signet in front of his nose.

"Tithian gave it to me," Wyan said. "He didn't think you would answer a summons from him, so he wanted you to think Agis had sent me. He's waiting for you in Samarah—with the Dark Lens."

Sadira's blue eyes flared and she stared at the head without speaking. Finally, she asked, "How did Agis die?"

Wyan's long tongue licked his cracked lips. "The giants were warring over the lens," he said. "Agis fell in the final battle."

"With Tithian's dagger in his back, no doubt!" Sadira hissed.

The sorceress pulled the Scourge from Rikus's scabbard and, in one swift motion, cleaved Wyan in two. The head clattered to the stony ground, putrid brown slime seeping from the two halves of the skull.

Rikus stomped on the yellowed bones, grinding them into powder. "He should never have used Agis's ring to trick us," the mul growled. "And when we catch Tithian, we'll do the same to him as he did to Agis."

Sadira did not answer, for she was staring at the Scourge's jagged blade with a slack jaw. For a moment, Neeva did not understand the sorceress's surprise, then she recalled that her friend had still been unconscious when the mul tested its magic earlier.

Finally, Sadira gave Rikus an accusatory glance. "It's broken!" she snapped. "What did you do?"

"It's my fault," Neeva said. "When the wraiths attacked you, I tried to use it against them and tainted its magic. The blade snapped later, when Rikus had to deflect a boulder."

"But there's still plenty of magic in it," Rikus added quickly. "Caelum healed the blade before all the black slime oozed out."

"Black slime?" Sadira asked.

"Yes, it poured from the broken blade," Caelum said, holding his hand out to the sorceress. "This is what happened when I touched the stuff. We were hoping you'd know something about it."

The dwarf opened his fingers so that she could see the strange scales around the edge of his hand, and the fanged maw in the center of his palm. The red lips began to work immediately, twisting themselves into various shapes as the forked tongue wagged in the thing's ebony throat.

"Release me," the mouth hissed, wisps of black shadow slipping from between its white teeth. "Come and free me."

Still holding Rikus's broken sword, the sorceress leaned over and inspected the scales around the edge of Caelum's hand. "This reminds me of what happens when someone suffers a wound near the Pristine Tower."

"Which means?" Neeva was growing more nervous about the fate of her husband's hand.

The sorceress fixed her emberlike eyes on the warrior. "That the magic is Rajaat's."

With a sinking feeling, Neeva asked, "So you can't heal his hand?"

"It's not really a matter of healing," Sadira said. "But it will be simple enough to return the hand to normal."

Neeva breathed a sigh of relief, though her husband seemed interested in things other than getting rid of the mouth. "Why does it keep asking us to free it?" Caelum asked.

"If I'd been trapped inside a sword blade for a thousand years, I'd want out," Rikus said.

Sadira shook her head. "The magic is not a spirit," she said. "It is not intelligent."

"Then who keeps asking us to release him?" asked Magnus.

"I don't know," Sadira replied. "It might be Rajaat."

Neeva felt a knot of fear form in her stomach. "But his champions killed him a thousand years ago!"

The sorceress shrugged. "We don't know that," she said. "The *Book of the Kemalok Kings* says they rebelled. We assumed he was destroyed because the champions survived to become sorcerer-kings. We could easily be mistaken."

"Then it's too bad you destroyed Wyan," said Caelum. "I suspect he would have known Rajaat's fate."

"All you would've heard from him are lies and half-truths," said Neeva.

"Besides, I don't see how Rajaat's fate matters to us. If he's still alive, the sorcerer-kings have him locked away someplace," said Rikus. As he spoke, the mul kneeled down and used a handful of dirt to scrub away the brown gore that had been Wyan's brain. "Our worry now is Borys. It's clear enough from the wraith attack that he knows we're coming for him."

"And our destination," Sadira said. "The wraiths knew enough about our plans to say that they had summoned his spirit from Samarah. I'm afraid Borys may already have killed Tithian and recovered the Dark Lens."

"The Dragon may know where we're going, but he doesn't have the Dark Lens," said Rikus. "If he did, he wouldn't bother sending assassins after us. He'd just attack us himself and get it over with."

"But if he knows our destination, how could he not have the lens?" asked Caelum.

"Our message said to meet in Samarah, but it didn't say that the lens was there now," said Neeva. "Maybe Tithian is waiting someplace else."

"He's certainly cunning enough," said Rikus. "We don't have any choice except to go and see. If we wait here, the Dragon will only try to stop us again."

Neeva nodded. "The battle has started. If we're to win, we need the Dark Lens—even if Tithian is the one who sent for us." The warrior faced her militia and pointed toward the razed farm behind Rasda's Wall. "Go fill your waterskins," she ordered. "We've a long march to Samarah."

NINE

Abalach-Re

The cargo kank scratched at the white-crusted ground with all six claws, protesting Sadira's command to halt. She did not begrudge the beast its impatience. The poor creature had not had water in more than five days, since the legion had started across the glaring salt flats of the Ivory Plain. Now, with the pollen of blade blossom, yellow fan, and other oasis flowers loading its bristly antennae, the insect could probably taste the water it had been denied for so long. The sorceress counted herself lucky that it obeyed at all.

Sadira had stopped two hundred paces from a ring-shaped knoll covered with slender saedra trees. The long-needled conifers grew with upraised boughs that resembled the arms of a sun-worshiping dwarf. Purple-flowered vines with long yellow thorns grew twined around the boles, and beards of moss dangled from the branches.

On the hilltop ahead, two ranks of enemy warriors had formed a battle line among the trees. Most wore green tabards over yellow hemp kilts. In their hands they held square wooden shields and long throwing spears. Obsidian-spiked flails hung at their belts. Unarmed officers wearing light blue turbans stood along the line, interspersed at regular intervals.

"There must be two thousand of them," Rikus observed, coming up behind her. Like Sadira, he led a cargo kank, and he carried young Rkard on his shoulders. "This worries me."

Sadira nodded, and the mul walked to within two paces of her before stopping. This was as close as they had come during the last ten days, for the sorceress could not quite bring herself to forgive Rikus. When she had told him about Agis's death, the mul's first response had not been sorrow or even sympathy. He had wanted to know how they would manage without the noble. Sadira could not even bring herself to imagine life without Agis, and she had let her husband die without the thing he most desired, an heir to carry on the Asticles name. How could Rikus expect her to think about their future at a time like that?

Caelum stepped forward, placing himself between Rikus and Sadira. "That's no raiding tribe," the dwarf said. He reached up and took his son off Rikus's shoulders. "It looks more like a legion."

"That's exactly what it is," said Magnus. "A Raamin legion. When I was with the Sun Runners, we had to flee the city's soldiers many times."

"But we're a good fifteen-day march south of Raam, with Gulg and Nibenay in between," protested Sult Ltak. After the fight against the giants, Neeva had distributed the survivors of the Granite Company among the rest of Kled's militia and asked Sult to stay near her for special assignments. "What are Raamins doing here?"

"Borys sent them," Rikus concluded. "I'll bet he's made the sorcerer-kings spread their armies all over the desert looking for us."

"Whoever sent them, they're between us and water," said Neeva, also joining the group. "We'll have to hope our warriors are strong enough to drive them out."

Sadira looked back to inspect the legion. The three Kledan companies led the column, standing five abreast in thirty disciplined rows. The dwarves had removed their heavy armor and strapped it across their backs to keep from being baked alive in the midday sun. Even this concession to the scorching heat had not saved them entirely, for they had flushed faces and glazed eyes.

The Tyrian humans looked even worse. They stood in a double column behind the dwarves, breathing in short, rapid gasps and leaning on each other for support. Those who owned armor had tied it into bundles and dragged it along behind them, while many others tried to shade themselves from the sun by stretching scraps of cloth over their heads. A few warriors were shifting from one leg to the other in a futile attempt to keep the hot ground from scorching their feet through the thin leather of their sandals. Most seemed too lethargic for such efforts, simply bracing themselves on their weapons and clenching their teeth against the pain of standing in one place.

Sadira saw a small group of stragglers coming up behind the legion, but beyond them nothing rose above the surface of the salt flat: not a boulder, not a single barren stem of spikebrush, not even the whirling wisps of a wind spout. The plain stretched clear to the horizon, glaring white, utterly level. As the legion had crossed that blistering, blinding expanse, the scouts had not found a single trace of animal dung, had not seen so much as a beetle scuttling across the sparkling ground, had not heard the call of even one gluttonous kes'trekel waiting for them to die. There had been nothing, no sign of any other living creature.

Sadira faced Rikus and Neeva. "Should we fight now, or rest for a while?"

The sorceress did not worry that their foes would attack first. No commander would leave a defensive position on a hillside to advance across the open salt flat, especially when he had water and the enemy did not. If they wished, Sadira knew, they could even make camp in the full confidence that the Raamins would wait for them to make the initial assault.

After considering the sorceress's question, Neeva said, "Resting won't do us any good. The more time we spend in the sun, the thirstier our warriors will be when the fight starts."

Rikus nodded his agreement, then turned to face the legion. Before he could say anything, Rkard grabbed his hand. "Rikus, the Scourge!"

The boy pointed at Rikus's scabbard, a cylinder of bleached bone intricately carved with the mul's life story. Tyr's freedmen had presented it to him in gratitude for throwing the first spear against Kalak.

The mul frowned. "What of it?"

Rkard lifted the scabbard. The tip of the cylinder had cracked open, and a short length of the Scourge's broken point was protruding through the hole.

"That's strange." Rikus took the scabbard. "But thanks for noticing, Rkard. Broken or not, I'd hate to lose the tip of my sword."

The mul pulled his sword out of the scabbard, then gasped in astonishment. The broken blade no longer ended in a jagged barb. Instead, it curved to a sharp point at about two-thirds its original length.

"What's happened?" Rikus gasped.

"It's growing back!" Rkard concluded.

Rikus shook his head. "Steel doesn't grow."

"Enchanted steel might," said Sadira. She pointed at the old tip, still protruding from the scabbard. "And that would explain why the broken piece is being pushed out of the scabbard."

The mul rubbed his cheek and studied his revitalized

blade. Finally, he shrugged. "What do I know?" he asked. "I'm just glad to have it returning to normal."

"As are we all," said Caelum.

Rikus tipped his scabbard down and let the broken end of the Scourge's blade slide out. "Since you kept me from losing this, why don't you take it?" he asked Rkard. "Maybe we can make it into a dagger for you."

The boy accepted the gift with a gaping mouth. Even if the blade had not been part of the Scourge, it was steel—and in the metal-poor world of Athas, that fact alone made it a weapon of considerable value.

"Rkard, have you forgotten what to say when someone gives you a gift?" asked Neeva.

The boy blushed. "I'll cherish it as I cherish your friendship," he said, bowing to Rikus.

To Sadira's surprise, Rikus remembered the proper response. "Let it be a symbol of our trust."

Rikus bowed to Rkard, then faced the legion. "Tyrians, flank the dwarves, forming a two rank line!" he yelled. "We must fight before we drink!"

The warriors quickly spread out to both sides of the dwarves. Most of those who had been dragging armor left it lying on the salty ground. In the scorching heat of the Ivory Plain, few humans were strong enough to carry the extra weight into battle without collapsing from heat exhaustion.

As the Tyrians scurried into position, Neeva turned to her warriors. "Form assault wedges!" she called. "I'll lead the Iron Company. *Yalmus* Ltak will take the Boulder Company. Caelum, hold the Bronze Company in reserve."

Unlike the Tyrians, the hardy dwarves did not abandon their armor. Each warrior helped the dwarf to his front unfasten the equipment and put it on. Within a few seconds, the three companies were fully armored in helmets and breastplates. The gleaming steel reflected the sunlight so brightly that Sadira could hardly bear to look at the Kledans.

"That glare will trouble the Raamins." Sadira used her dark hand to shield her eyes.

"Not as much as our axes," promised Sult, cinching down his breastplate.

The Iron and Boulder Companies arranged themselves into wedge-shaped formations, with the points aimed at the center of the Raamin lines. The Bronze Company moved twenty paces back and formed a compact square, each man standing straight and motionless in the blistering heat. Sadira was tempted to suggest they use their broad-bladed axes to shade each other, but thought better of it when she remembered that all Kledans venerated the sun.

"What shall I do?" asked Magnus. "I can't kill all their templars, but I should be able to take out a few."

"You stay here, with Caelum and Sadira," said Rikus.

"But all those Raamins wearing turbans are templars," Magnus objected.

"I know," Rikus replied. "That's why I want you and Sadira to stay back. You'll have a better view and can help where you're needed most." The mul looked to Sadira, an unspoken question in his eyes.

"I understand what you want," Sadira replied. She knew he was hoping she would say something kind or encouraging, but she could not bring herself to do it. The anger inside was too powerful, perhaps because it was something she did not quite understand. When the mul did not turn away, she said, "Shouldn't you be going?"

Rikus spun on his heel and started toward the oasis. Without saying a word, he lifted the Scourge and waved the legion after him.

Neeva eyed the sorceress for a moment. "Don't you think you're being a little hard on him?" she asked. "Rikus isn't the one who killed Agis."

"No, but he's still glad to have my other husband

gone," Sadira said. "He's only upset now because I miss Agis more than he thought I would."

Neeva closed her eyes and slowly shook her head. "Is that what you think?"

"You can't tell me I'm wrong," Sadira countered.

"I shouldn't have to."

Neeva looked away and waved the Iron and Boulder Companies forward. Before leaving, she looked back to Rkard. "Stay with the Bronze Company—and no heroics this time."

The boy frowned, but nodded. "Yes, mother."

Neeva smiled, then stepped into her place at the back corner of the Iron Company.

With Caelum and Rkard, Sadira watched the warriors of Tyr and Kled advance. Seen from the rear, the joint legion reminded Sadira of an ungainly bird. The gleaming triangles of the dwarves represented the body, feathered with silvery breastplates of steel. The human flanks were its wings, ragged, gangly, and barren of plumage. It was a strange creature, born equally of desperation and hope. The sorceress hoped it would prove both savage enough and smart enough to slay its prey.

The formation had traveled about a quarter of the distance to the oasis when a mad cackle rang out from the center of the knoll's summit. Though the voice was female, it sounded more like the bloodthirsty call of a wyvern.

"Who was that?" asked Sadira.

Magnus shrugged. "Even the Sun Runners have not run afoul of every official in Raam," he said. "It could be a high templar—or even the sorcerer-queen herself."

Caelum pushed his son toward the Bronze Company. "Take the kanks and hide yourself behind the formation," he ordered. "And remember what your mother said about heroics."

Rkard took Sadira's switch and tapped the antennae of the two cargo kanks. They clacked their mandibles in frustration, but slowly turned to follow the boy toward the Bronze Company.

"Hiding won't save you, child." The words rolled across the salt flat as clear and distinct as the lyrics to one of Magnus's ballads, though the voice was aloof and cold in a way that the windsinger's could never be.

Rkard started to turn around, but Caelum yelled, "Don't listen to her, Son. Go on!"

As the young mul slipped behind the ranks of the Bronze Company, Sadira searched the oasis hill for the speaker. At the same time, she raised her hand to her mouth and caught a wisp of her shadowy breath, then faced the *yalmus* of the Bronze Company.

"I know you and your warriors prefer sunlight," she called. "But stay beneath this shield. It'll protect you from Raamin magic."

With that, she uttered her incantation and blew the black shadow toward the reserves. The wisp floated over to the Bronze Company, stretching into a long, dark cord as it moved. It dropped to the ground in front of the *yalmus* and snaked its way around the formation. When it had formed a complete square enclosing Rkard and the dwarves, a gray pall crept over the entire company.

The dwarven warriors cast nervous glances into the white sky, muttering and fidgeting. Several even stepped out of line—until their *yalmus* chased them back into place with a sharp command.

Again, a cruel laugh rolled across the salt flat. A chorus of Raamin voices cried out in fear, then a small section of the enemy line grasped their chests and dropped to the ground. Sadira studied the slope behind the fallen warriors carefully, looking for the cause of the men's sudden death. She found only half a dozen saedra trees and several clumps of silverfan. There was not even a blue-turbaned templar standing in the vicinity.

"Did you kill those Raamins?" Magnus asked.

Sadira shook her head.

"Then what—"

Before Caelum could ask his question, a seething orb of white radiance shot out from the gap in the Raamin lines. It skimmed over the legion's flank, vaporizing four Tyrian warriors as it passed. Sadira and Magnus barely managed to duck before it blazed over their own heads, a stench like burning tar riding its wake. The ball crashed into the front rank of the Bronze Company and exploded in a blinding flash. The dwarves shouted in anger and alarm, but no one cried out in pain.

The *yalmus* ordered his warriors to form their ranks. As the spots cleared from her vision, Sadira saw that her gray pall remained intact and had protected the dwarven ranks from injury. Still, the Bronze Company had fallen into disarray. Most of the dwarves had dropped their axes and were blindly trying to find their weapons again, while many others were simply rubbing their eyes and shaking their heads. Rkard stood in the center of the jumble, his eyes pinched shut and his hands clutching the sword shard Rikus had given him.

"By the wind!" Magnus gasped. "That leaves no doubt that Abalach-Re is with them."

"She is," Sadira said. "Only a sorcerer-king—or queen, in this case—could and would call upon the life-force of her own soldiers to cast a spell."

The sorceress turned around to study the area near the collapsed Raamins. She saw no one standing nearby. The sorcerer-queen was using magic to hide herself.

Sadira reached into her pocket and withdrew a bead of amber, crushing the golden gem between her ebony fingers. She tossed the powder toward the oasis and uttered her incantation. A huge billow of flaxen mist formed above the gap Abalach had created in her own lines. A thunderclap crashed over the hillside and the cloud split, unleashing a deluge of yellow beads as large as melons.

As each globe landed, it exploded in a golden spray that coated anything it contacted. The Raamins cursed and yelled, trying to scrape the sticky syrup from their bodies. The stuff hardened almost immediately. Soon hundreds of saffron pillars covered the hillside, each encasing the astonished form of a suffocating warrior. None of the dark shapes trapped inside the diaphanous columns appeared to be a sorcerer-queen.

A great cheer rose from the Tyrian warriors, for Sadira's spell had done more than a little to offset the advantage of the Raamins' defensive position.

"Double-time advance!" called Neeva.

The dwarves broke into a steady run, their formations as tight as ever. The Tyrians began to trot, though their ranks loosened as they picked up speed.

Near the top of the oasis, a huge circle of saedras turned brown and dropped their needles. Before the needles hit the ground, the red bark darkened to black and the barren boughs began to droop. The roots released their hold on the hillside. Tree after tree crashed to the ground, smashing Raamin warriors and raising a large cloud of dust.

The sorceress did not see anyone nearby who could have caused the destruction, though she knew it had to be the result of a defiler drawing the energy for a spell. Since she could not see any other sorcerer in the vicinity, Sadira thought it was most likely Abalach-Re herself who had destroyed the trees. Sorcerer-queens could summon spell energy from plants, as well as men and animals.

Sadira reached into her robe, whispering, "Whoever you are, this will be the last time you defile an oasis."

Abalach surprised the sorceress by answering. "I spoiled a thousand oases before you were ever born, girl." Her voice was a mere whisper in Sadira's ears. "And I'll spoil another thousand after you die."

At the top of the hill, a pair of blue streaks flared

under the dirt. They shot down the slope, glimmers of azure light flashing up every time they passed beneath a stone. Like a pair of sapphire arrows, the bolts sped out beneath the salt flat, each racing straight toward one of the dwarven companies. When they reached the warriors leading the two wedges, a tremendous crackle echoed over the plain. The dwarves went rigid. Their helmets and breastplates erupted into showers of sparks. Dancing cords of energy leaped from their torsos to the men behind them. These warriors also stiffened, and their armor exploded into blue embers. In an instant, the crackling waves of energy fanned out over both companies of dwarves.

At the back of the Iron Company, Neeva screeched and flung the steel battle-axe from her hands. The rest of the Kledans, trapped inside their metal breastplates, were not so lucky. They remained completely rigid and motionless, blue energy cords dancing over their armor and weapons. Soon, their flesh blackened and began to smoke. One after the other, the dwarves burst into flame and disintegrated into piles of ash. An instant later, all that remained of the Kledan companies were two piles of soot-stained armor and Neeva, standing alone and dazed on the salt flat.

Caelum started to call the Bronze Company forward, but Sadira stopped him. "Leave the reserves here, or Abalach will use the same spell against them," she said. "You and Magnus reinforce the Tyrian flanks with your magic. I'll fight from here—and guard Rkard."

The dwarf nodded, then he and the windsinger rushed forward. Sadira considered casting a spell to protect the Tyrian troops from Abalach, but quickly decided against it. If she spent her energies shielding while the sorcerer-queen attacked, Rikus's assault would stall against the superior force waiting on the hill. To win the battle now, she had to reduce the number of Raamins facing her husband, while also putting Abalach on the defensive—

or killing her outright.

Sadira pulled a lump of sulfur and a pinch of bat guano from her pocket. She rolled the two components together into a viscid mass and held it in the palm of her hand. When she spoke her incantation, the wad slowly expanded, emitting a stream of gray, foul-smelling smoke.

As the gummy ball enlarged, the defiled area of the knoll surged upward, forming a huge dome that continued to swell. When the hillside looked ready to explode, Sadira whispered a mystic syllable. The viscid mass she was holding vanished in a billow of smoke.

On the hillside, the swollen dome abruptly collapsed in on itself. The slope trembled, and a murmur of concern rustled through the Raamin ranks. The boughs of the saedra trees began to quiver. From deep inside the knoll sounded an angry rumble, and tongues of flame shot from beneath the defiled ground. Then a mighty explosion shook the entire oasis, hurling a huge section of the knoll into the sky.

A cloud of ash and dust spread over the salt flat, casting a gray pall over the white plain. Splintered trees and Raamin bodies rained down with sharp cracks and soft thumps, most landing within twenty or thirty paces of the hill. Rikus waved his sword, and, with a great cheer, his warriors broke into a full sprint. The cry even seemed to rouse Neeva from her shock, for she picked up her battle-axe and rushed to join the charge.

Rikus and his followers began to leap the bodies and saedra trees littering the approach to the hill. Crackling thunderbolts and sputtering fireballs rained down from slope above. Tyrian warriors fell all along the line. The black streamers of smoke that rose from their bodies were a grisly contrast to the white salt upon which they lay.

Catching up to Rikus's charge, Caelum and Magnus answered the Raamins with their own spells. The dwarf sprayed the slope with a crimson beam that set fire to anything it touched. The windsinger summoned a ferocious southern gale. The squall scoured the hillside with an airborne wall of salt, shredding clothing and flesh alike.

A strand of sparkling green fiber appeared on the ground between Rikus's charging legion and the base of the hill. The right flank reached the green strand first. As the warriors leaped across the line, a loud crack reverberated beneath their feet. The filament became a gaping chasm with a bright emerald glow shining up from its depths. The Tyrians screamed, and a lime-colored tongue of vapor shot up to engulf each one of them. The entire flank simply dissolved, their bodies eaten away even before they fell out of sight.

Magnus stopped at the edge and tried to peer down into the fissure. A green tendril shot up and lapped at his thick hide. He stumbled away, clutching at his throat and coughing.

At the other end of the Tyrian line, where the hill curved away slightly, the warriors had not been so close to the chasm when it opened. Most had managed to stop at the brink and were dragging themselves away on their hands and knees, coughing and choking while tendrils of green vapor lapped at their feet.

From her vantage point across the salt flat, Sadira did not see Rikus among the survivors. She ran her gaze over the tide of crawling refugees and located Neeva and Caelum, but there was no sign of the mul. The sorceress felt a cold lump form in her stomach. Rikus had been leading the charge at his end of the line. Had he fallen into the chasm?

Determined to prevent Raam's sorcerer-queen from casting any more such spells, Sadira pulled a pinch of powdered glass from her pocket. After a moment of searching, she spotted another circle of Raamin bodies near the summit of the hill. It was directly above the chasm's right end, and Sadira felt certain that it marked the place Abalach had been standing when she drew the energy for her last spell.

Sadira tossed the powdered glass into the air and spoke her incantation. As it dropped to the ground, the silvery dust scintillated in the light of the crimson sun. On the hillside, sparkles of red light flashed over the withered saedras. The glimmers quickly coalesced near the heart of the despoiled ground, outlining the distant shape of a mature woman dressed in flowing robes.

The figure turned toward Sadira. "You've found what you're looking for," said Abalach's voice. "What do you think you'll do with me?"

Sadira reached for a spell ingredient.

Abalach barked a sharp command in the language of her city. The Raamin warriors rushed down the slope, their spears ready to throw across the chasm at the retreating Tyrians. For a moment, the sorcerer-queen watched her army charge.

Then, as Sadira pulled a small glass rod from her pocket, Abalach tossed something into the air. A cloud of red smoke billowed into existence and swallowed her figure.

Recognizing the basic nature of the spell, Sadira realized instantly that her foe was using magic to change positions. Still holding the glass rod, she ran her eyes over the knoll, searching for Abalach's new location.

Sadira saw that the Raamins had reached the bottom of the hill. As she watched, they ran up to the edge of the chasm and hurled their spears across the green abyss. Most of the shafts clattered harmlessly to the ground, but enough found their marks to fill the plain with death cries.

A similar squall of screams erupted from the enemy ranks. Green tongues of vapor began to rise from the chasm again, this time licking at Raamin warriors as a whirl of flashing blades and kicking feet knocked them into the abyss.

With a start, Sadira realized that the attacker was Rikus. The mul had landed on the other side of the gap.

Given the width of the chasm, the sorceress could not imagine he had been able to leap across. It seemed more likely that in his typical brash fashion, Rikus had been charging too far ahead of the legion and gotten separated when Abalach's spell created the abyss. For now, that was proving a misfortune for the Raamins, but Sadira did not know how long her husband could continue to fight so savagely.

Already, it seemed to the sorceress that he was tiring. He had stopped advancing and now allowed the Raamins to come to him. Sadira could see at least twenty of them moving toward her husband, whirling spiked flails above their heads. The sorceress pointed the glass rod in their direction and spoke the words to her spell. A bolt of energy arced over the chasm and came down in the center of the advancing Raamins. There was a tremendous bang, and bodies flew in all directions. To Sadira's amazement, Rikus rushed his shocked enemies, sending them to their deaths twice as fast as before.

"Don't be crazy, Rikus!" Sadira cried, knowing even the champion gladiator could not survive such odds. "Wait for help!"

"There won't be any, stupid girl." The voice belonged to Abalach, and this time it came from behind Sadira.

The sorceress felt a strange tingle deep within her belly. The entire Bronze Company gave a deep groan and dropped to the ground in a tremendous clanging of armor. The sensation in her stomach grew more severe, as if a cold hand had reached deep inside her to squeeze her entrails. She did not panic, for she had felt such pain before and knew what it meant: the life-force was being drawn from her body.

Abalach had probably been waiting the entire battle for this moment. With all eyes turned toward the trouble at the front lines, it was the perfect opportunity for the sorcerer-queen to surprise the reserves with an attack from the rear.

Sadira spun around. She found a tangled mass of dwarves clutching at their stomachs as their life-forces were pulled from them. Some had managed to remain on their feet, though they had to brace themselves on their axes and seemed in imminent danger of falling. Others had fallen unconscious and already appeared close to death, with gray faces and sunken eyes. Most simply writhed on the ground, their panicked voices cursing the magic that would rob them of the chance to die with their steel buried in their enemies. Sadira saw no sign of the magical pall she had cast over the dwarves earlier, and she realized that Abalach-Re had been near the company long enough to dispel the magical shield.

In the middle of the confusion stood Rkard, gaping at the dying company with wide, frightened eyes and showing no sign of physical distress. In his hands he clutched the sword tip that Rikus had given him earlier—which Sadira assumed to be the source of his good fortune. Apparently, the shard afforded him the same protection that the Scourge bestowed on Rikus. As long as he held the enchanted steel, the sorcerer-queen could not harm the young mul with any sort of attack, whether physical, mental, or magical.

Thirty paces beyond the boy stood Abalach-Re. The Raamin queen was an ivory-skinned beauty, with peaked eyebrows and huge, round eyes as baleful as they were dark. Her narrow nose ended in a sharp point. She had full lips as red as rubies, a slender chin, and a neck so long and thin it was almost serpentine. The queen's only weapon was a small scepter, which had an eerie green light glimmering deep within its obsidian pommel.

Abalach raised a slender finger and beckoned to Rkard. The claw at the end of the digit was as long as a dagger. "Come here, child," she said, a forked tongue flicking over her red lips. "I only want the banshees. I won't hurt you."

Rkard shifted his grip on the broken blade. "Liar."

Abalach's eyes flared, and she stepped toward the boy. "Then I'll come to you," the queen said. "The banshees will arrive soon enough—when I start breaking your little bones."

Sadira could not tell whether the threat was a bluff or if Abalach did not realize the nature of the shard in Rkard's hands, but the sorceress did not want to put the matter to a test. She directed her palm at the pommel of the queen's scepter, which she knew served as a sort of mystic lens. Through it, Abalach could pull the life-force from men and animals, using it to power her mightiest spells.

Sadira forced a stream of the sun's energy from her hand. The beam was almost invisible as it left her palm, a pink ripple in the hot desert air. With her attention fixed on Rkard, Abalach-Re did not notice the faint shimmer as she drew it, along with the life energy she was taking from Sadira, into her scepter's pommel.

The beam sank into the obsidian ball with a loud hiss. A crimson light flared in the heart of the dark orb, and Sadira felt the outflow of her life-force cease. The pommel burst into shards with a brilliant flash of scarlet, spraying jagged pieces of obsidian in all directions. A ball of scintillating lights hovered briefly at the end of the scepter, then sank into the salt-crusted soil like water.

Abalach-Re threw her useless scepter aside. She scowled at Sadira, then said, "That will not save the child—or you!"

The *yalmus* of the Bronze Company and two dozen warriors, all that remained conscious, pushed themselves to their feet. Looking pale and nauseated, they stepped forward and attacked. Their steel axes bounced off Abalach's ivory flesh without opening a single gash.

The queen began to slap them aside, her claws ripping through their breastplates as though they were flesh. The *yalmus* landed at Rkard's feet, his armor torn open to reveal a gory mess beneath. The young mul backed away, his eyes wide with horror as he watched Abalach savaging the rest of the company. Sadira started forward to protect him.

As soon as Rkard stepped away from the Bronze Company, two lumps of gnarled bone appeared at the boy's sides. They did not arrive so much as wink into existence, emerging from empty air in the flicker of an eye. The figures were as large as giants, and so twisted they could not even be called skeletons. One even lacked a head, though both had long gray beards dangling from where their chins should have been.

Abalach broke the last dwarf's neck, then smirked up at the two apparitions. "Jo'orsh, Sa'ram!" she said. "Come."

Sadira stepped between the banshees and the Raamin queen. "What do you want with them?"

It was one of the banshees who answered. "The lens. Our magic hides it from the Dragon and his minions."

"Only until Borys's spirit lords finish with you," said Abalach. The queen cast a spiteful glare at Sadira, then lashed out, her daggerlike claws arcing at the sorceress's throat.

Sadira twisted away and ducked. The talons raked across her shoulder, tearing away wisps of black shadow. The sorceress struck back, her hands cupped together and glowing scarlet with the power of the sun. The fists caught Abalach square in the jaw. The queen's head snapped back, and her feet came off the ground. She landed half a dozen paces away, among the dwarves she had killed earlier, and immediately started to rise.

Realizing there was no time to cast a spell, Sadira moved to attack again. Abalach locked gazes with her, and the image of a lirr appeared in the queen's dark eyes. It resembled a large lizard with tough, diamond-shaped scales and a tail covered with thorny spines. Sadira realized instantly that the thing was a mental construct, that Abalach was attacking with the Way.

The lirr flared its magnificent neck fan and opened its pink gullet, then flashed across the space separating the two women. It tore into Sadira's mind with such force that the sorceress cried out in pain and actually tumbled over backward, slamming the back of her skull into the salt plain.

The saurian appeared on the shadowy plain of Sadira's intellect, then began to rip great gobs of spongy black matter from the ground. The sorceress's head exploded into pain, and she could hardly believe that it was only her thoughts that the beast was gulping down. She had never felt a mental attack this powerful.

Nevertheless, remembering what her husband Agis had taught her, Sadira focused her thoughts on fighting the terrible beast. She opened a pathway to her spiritual nexus, imagining a dark cord running down to deep within her abdomen. She concentrated on the black matter of her mind, and visualized it hardening into granite. A seering wave of energy rose from deep within her body. The shadowy material hardened into rock, catching the creature in the process of ripping away another large hunk of ground and encasing its claws in solid stone.

A mad cackle erupted from the beast's throat. "How many wenches like you have I killed?" it chortled, speaking in Abalach's voice. "A thousand years of battle, and you dare to think you can stop me!"

With that, the lirr rose to its hind legs, its trapped claws ripping away two great chunks of Sadira's mind. White flashes of pain erupted all through the sorceress's head. The beast dropped back down, smashing the rock encasing its talons, and began to tear away great chunks of black stone. Sadira heard someone screaming and realized it was her. She summoned more spiritual energy, hoping to counterattack, but the only thing that rose in response was a wave of bile.

The sorceress continued to fight, trying to create a wyvern or a baazrag to counter Abalach's construct. She simply did not have the power. The lirr continued to rip through her mind, until at last rays of white radiance began to flood her head, and she knew she would fall unconscious.

Then, from somewhere, she heard Rkard yell in anger as he attacked Abalach. The lirr screeched, then went limp and faded away as rapidly as it had come. Sadira found herself alone inside her wounded mind, lost in a white fog of pain.

"Help!" the young mul called.

Though she did not remember closing them, Sadira opened her eyes. She found Abalach-Re five paces away, thrashing wildly and trying to shake young Rkard from her back. Sa'ram stood at her side. With the rigid shards of bone that served him as arms, the banshee was ineffectually trying to pluck the young mul off the Raamin queen.

Sadira pulled a tiny bead of silver from her pocket and yelled, "Rkard, let go!"

At the sound of her voice, Abalach spun around. Rkard opened his hand and sailed away, crashing down on an unconscious dwarf. He left the Scourge's broken tip planted in the queen's back.

Sadira spoke her incantation and flicked the silver bead at the shard, hoping to drive it through Abalach's heart. The pellet streaked straight to its target, striking the jagged blade at a shallow angle. There was no blast of magical power, as the sorceress had expected. Instead, a pearly aura spread over the steel and it began to hum with a high-pitched chime.

Abalach's eyes went wide. She twisted a hand around behind herself, trying to reach the blade. Sa'ram stepped

closer, lowering his skeletal arm to attack the queen's
back. Before the banshee could touch her, the Scourge
stopped chiming. A huge geyser of black fluid shot from
the shard's jagged end and splattered Sa'ram's gnarled
form.

The inky liquid spread quickly, coating the banshee
beneath a thick layer of ebony slime. Wherever the fluid
stained Sa'ram's twisted bones, they untwined and
rearranged themselves into a less contorted skeleton.
The back grew round and hunched, while the arms
became long gangling things that ended in barbed
talons. The banshee's gray beard disappeared, then a
skull of sable bone rose from the shoulders in its place.
The head seemed remotely human, with a drooping
chin, a small jawbone, and a pair of rather flat cheekbones. Blue sparks replaced the banshee's orange eyes,
while a crown of yellow lightning crackled around his
skull.

"Rajaat!" Abalach gasped, facing the apparition.

"Uyness of Waverly, Orc Plague!" The skeleton stared
down at the queen, billows of black fume shooting from
its nostrils. "I have come for you, traitor!"

Abalach stumbled away. "No! You can't be free!"

Sadira sprang at the queen's back. Slipping one arm
around Abalach's throat, she used her other hand—and
all her supernatural strength—to drive the Scourge's tip
deeper into the queen's body. She felt the steel grate
against a bone, then pass into a lump of softer tissue.

Abalach howled in pain, but abruptly fell silent when
Sadira twisted the blade. A convulsion ran through the
queen's entire frame, and she fell limp. Brown smoke
began to pour from her nostrils and mouth. Her limbs
went stiff, and the muscles of her stomach started to
quiver. A terrible heat poured off her body, and her
clothes began to smoke.

Sadira turned and hurled Abalach away, not bothering to extract the Scourge's tip. The queen spun through

the air with her arms and legs splayed stiffly at her sides. She dropped to the ground a dozen paces away, landing with a hollow thud. For a moment, the body just lay there, staring blankly into the sky while brown fumes rose from its nose and mouth. Finally, the corpse folded in on itself, then burst into a column of bronze flame. The explosion left nothing behind except a salt crater stained brown with soot.

When Sadira looked back toward the black skeleton, she found it melting into a pool of bubbling sludge. The only recognizable feature was the head, and even it was quickly dissolving. The sorceress saw no sign that the ebony mass would reassemble itself into anything resembling Sa'ram. She silently spoke a few words of gratitude for the banshee's efforts to protect Rkard.

A moment later, Rkard took her hand and tugged at her arm. "Come on," he said. "Jo'orsh says that stuff's dangerous."

The sorceress opened her eyes and allowed the boy to lead her to Jo'orsh's massive figure. "I'm sorry about your friend," she said, craning her neck to look into the banshee's orange eyes.

"There is no need for sorrow," said Jo'orsh. "A banshee can hope for nothing except to find rest, and now Sa'ram has."

"And what of that?" Sadira asked, gesturing toward the black pool. "Was that really Rajaat?"

"Yes," the banshee replied. "Your spell allowed his essence to escape the Scourge's shard."

The sorceress swallowed and stared at the bubbling fluid. "How do we put it back?"

"You cannot," Jo'orsh replied. "But there is no need for worry. Like Rajaat himself, it is locked inside the Black. It can harm only those foolish enough to touch it of their own wills."

A shiver of terror ran down the sorceress's spine. "Then the sorcerer-kings didn't kill Rajaat?" she asked, turning back to the banshee.

Jo'orsh did not answer, for he had vanished as quickly as he had arrived.

"What happened to your friend?" Sadira asked, taking Rkard's hand.

"He's still here—like always," the boy said. He scowled thoughtfully, then looked up Sadira. "It's okay that I helped you, isn't it?"

Sadira furrowed her brow and pretended to consider his question seriously. "I don't know. Didn't your mother tell you no heroics?"

"She did," the young mul grumped. "But I don't see why. Rikus gets to be brave."

He pointed toward the oasis. When Sadira turned around, she saw her husband charging up the hill on the heels of the Raamin army, waving his sword and cursing his enemies for cowards. The sorceress could not help laughing. The mul did not seem to realize that Caelum had bridged Abalach's chasm with an arc of flickering flame, or that Neeva was leading four hundred warriors—all that remained of the Tyrian legion— across the trestle to help him.

Sadira started toward the chasm. "Come on," she said. "We'd better let Rikus know the battle's over."

The Forsaken Village

The two inixes stood in the center of the dusty plaza, their saddles empty and their reins hanging loose. Having battered down the bone railing that enclosed the village well, the great lizards had stuck their horny beaks into the dark hole as far as their stocky necks allowed. Apparently, they could not reach the water, for they were bellowing angrily and snapping their serpentine tails from side to side. The beasts' riders, four Tyrian scouts, were nowhere in sight.

Magnus stood at the edge of the plaza, his dark eyes searching for some sign of the missing riders. He counted fifty-two stone huts ringing the plaza, each shaped like a beehive and covered with a scaly roof of gorak hide. He did not see any villagers peering out of the doorways, nor any of their herd-lizards roaming the dirt alleyways between the shacks. The place looked deserted. Even the scouts seemed to have disappeared without leaving any footprints by which to track them.

The unnatural quiet disturbed Magnus even more than the lack of visible activity. As his big ears swiveled around the plaza, he heard nothing—not a child whimpering, not a gorak scratching at a stone wall, not a stifling wind hissing through the streets. The place was as noiseless as death.

"Do you think this is Samarah?" asked Rikus. The mul whispered his question, apparently reluctant to disturb the eerie tranquility of the place.

The windsinger shrugged. "It's in the right place," he replied, starting toward the well. "But the inhabitants seem to have abandoned it."

"Or been driven away," said Sadira. Her voice was loud and sharp as she stepped from a narrow path between two huts.

"What do you mean?" asked Neeva. She was clutching her battle-axe in both hands, as if she expected to be attacked at any moment. Caelum and Rkard were not with her. When the scouts had not returned, she had sent them with what remained of the Bronze Company to examine the village's southern perimeter. The Tyrian legion was circling around in the opposite direction, inspecting the north side. "Did you find something?"

The sorceress shook her head. "No, but I'm worried about what happened to Sa'ram."

"Then tell us why," Rikus demanded. "This is no time to make us guess."

Sadira scowled at the mul, but Magnus interposed himself between the two spouses before she could retort. "Perhaps we should have something to drink first," he said. "Thirst is making all our tempers short."

The windsinger was not being very honest, and they all knew it. After the battle against the Raamins, the coolness that had come between Sadira and Rikus had warmed slightly for about a day. Then something had gone wrong, and now they could hardly speak without quarreling. From what the windsinger had gathered, Rikus had tried to make love to Sadira, and that had angered the sorceress, who was still mourning her other husband's death.

As they moved across the square, Rikus peered around the windsinger. "I'm sorry, Sadira. That was uncalled for," he said. "What were you going to say?"

Without acknowledging the apology, Sadira explained, "Jo'orsh said that Borys wanted him and Sa'ram because their magic was still hiding the Dark Lens," she said. "But that was before Sa'ram was destroyed."

The company neared the well, causing the inixes to look up and hiss. Magnus ignored their threats and began to examine the tackle on their backs, at the same time keeping his enormous ears turned toward the sorceress.

"So you're worried that by destroying Sa'ram, you ruined the enchantment that had kept the lens hidden all this time?" the windsinger asked. He pulled a heavy waterskin off an inix harness.

"That's what I'm afraid of," Sadira said. "It's been ten days since the battle with Abalach. If the Dragon suddenly found himself able to locate the lens, that would be more than enough time for him to come here and take it—along with the villagers, Tithian, and anyone else who happened to be here."

"That's true," Magnus said, opening the waterskin in his hands. The liquid inside smelled too much of leather and lime to have come from the well. "But that doesn't explain the absence of our scouts. Wherever they went, they didn't take their waterskins. In fact, they didn't even change water."

Sadira and the others scowled. Anyone who traveled the Athasian desert knew to keep a waterskin handy, and it was a rare man who did not fill that sack with the freshest water available. That the scouts had not done this suggested they had not lingered at the well for long.

"There's only one way to find out what's going on here," said Sadira. "We'll have to search the village."

"Right, but first things first," said Rikus. He pushed

an inix aside, then retrieved a rope and bucket tied to the toppled rail. "I'm thirsty."

The mul tossed the bucket into the pit. After falling for a moment, it struck the bottom of the well with a muffled sound somewhere between a splash and a thud. Rikus allowed the weighted pail a moment to sink, then pulled it up. He stepped away from the inixes and tipped his head back, closing his eyes in anticipation of a cool drink.

The water that flowed from the bucket was cloudy and pink. Rikus gulped down a mouthful, then made a sour face and threw the bucket across the plaza. "It tastes like blood!"

"That's what it looked like—"

Hundreds of frightened voices cried out from the north side of the village. The screams lasted for only an instant, then faded away in a single, strangled croak. By the time Magnus and his companions spun around to look toward the disturbance, Samarah had fallen silent again. They saw nothing but a hillside of orange stones rising above the scaly roofs of the empty village.

"We'd better see what happened," said Sadira, leading the way across the plaza.

Magnus followed the others. They crossed the plaza in silence, the thick dust cushioning their footsteps, and entered a crooked lane running northward through a small borough of huts. Here, they had to plow through waist-high silt drifts, filling the alley with gray clouds of dust. Neeva and Rikus began to choke and cough, but Magnus simply closed his mouth and breathed only through his huge nostrils. Deep within his nose, several membranes kept his airway clear by filtering out fine particles of dust.

The group emerged beside a small pasture that lay between the huts and the village wall. A blanket of undisturbed silt covered the ground, the jagged shapes of upturned stones visible beneath the gray shroud.

"We should be able to see the legion by now," Magnus said. He pointed across the pasture.

The village wall rose only chin high. If the Tyrian warriors had been standing on the other side, it would have been an easy matter to spot their heads protruding above the crest. Magnus saw nothing but a slope of rock and dust.

"Four hundred warriors don't just vanish," Rikus said.

"The scouts did," Magnus reminded him.

The mul grunted an acknowledgment, then said, "Let's go and have a look." He drew the Scourge, which had grown back to its original length.

Magnus pulled the mace from his belt, and the small company started across the field. The stones beneath the dust were loose and often shifted as soon as any weight was put on them. The companions had to move slowly, picking their way carefully to avoid turning an ankle.

Sadira reached the wall first. She peered over the top and cried out in alarm. The sorceress gave the barrier a hard shove and stones flew in all directions. She slipped through the resulting gap and stared at the ground with a horrified expression on her face.

Magnus and the others followed her through the breach. Along the base of the wall lay the Tyrian legion, still in column formation. Most warriors had fallen with their heads uphill. All were curled into the fetal position and clutched at their stomachs in agony. Their faces were twisted masks of anguish, except that their gaping mouths seemed more astonished than pained and their vacant eyes uniformly stared at the same spot on the slope above. Although none of the bodies were moving, they looked more paralyzed than dead.

Magnus kneeled beside a red-haired woman whose hand still gripped her half-drawn sword. He leaned over her head, cocking one of his ears to cover her mouth and nose.

"Well?" Rikus demanded.

"Her lips no longer sing the song of being," the wind-singer said. He placed a hand on her torso. The flesh remained soft and warm, though it was as still as stone. "Nor does her heart carry the beat of life."

"There are no wounds," Neeva said, rolling over a black-haired man. "What happened?"

"Their life-force was drawn from their bodies," said Sadira. She climbed up the hillside to where the warriors' dead eyes were fixed. "And this is where Borys was standing when he did it."

Magnus and the others joined the sorceress. She stood beside a pair of three-toed footprints such as a bird might make—save that these were a full two paces across. The windsinger had no doubts about who had made the tracks, for he had seen the Dragon attack Kled and recognized the prints from there.

"You were right, Sadira," Magnus observed. "Borys has beaten us to the Dark Lens."

"So let's take it back," said Rikus. He studied the ground, looking for an indication of where the Dragon had gone. There were no other tracks, only the ones Sadira had discovered. "If we can find Borys."

"I have a feeling he'll find us," said Magnus.

"Or my son!" gasped Neeva. She pointed across the village. A short distance beyond the south wall, the sun's rays glinted off the bobbing figures of armored dwarves. "If he knows of the banshees' prophecy, he'll try to kill Rkard."

The warrior had hardly spoken before a gaunt figure as tall as a giant appeared behind the Bronze Company, emerging from thin air as though stepping from behind an unseen curtain. He was the color of iron, with a chitinous hide equal parts flesh and shell. His head sat atop a serpentine neck and resembled that of a sharp-beaked bird, with a spiked crest of leathery skin. He had long, double-kneed legs, and his gaunt arms ended in knobby fingers with sword-length claws. The beast crept up behind the dwarves so silently that they seemed unaware that it was following them.

"Caelum! Behind you!" Neeva yelled. She started down the hill at a sprint.

Rikus followed instantly. Magnus was only a step behind when he felt Sadira's fingers digging into his shoulder. "You go to the well."

"But you'll need help—"

"Do it, Magnus!" The sorceress looked across the village. Outside the wall, the Dragon had almost reached the rear ranks of the Bronze Company. The dwarves, who were too far away to have heard Neeva yell, seemed as oblivious as ever to his presence. "I'm not going to leave Rkard in danger!"

Sadira gave Magnus a gentle shove, and he found himself running down the slope. The windsinger glanced back and saw the sorceress looking toward the Bronze Company, one hand searching her cloak pocket for spell components. He faced forward again and rushed through the gap in the village wall.

Magnus crossed the rocky pasture at a full sprint, stones clattering and slipping beneath his pounding steps. He almost fell as he entered the narrow lane between the stone huts, knocking several holes in the walls as he bounced from one side to the other.

At last he emerged in the square. He saw Borys's gaunt form looming above the huts on the south side of the village. The Dragon was hardly moving at all, simply staring down at the ground. Magnus feared the beast had already destroyed the Bronze Company, for he did not hear so much as a shield clanging outside the wall.

The windsinger rushed across the plaza, his huge feet crashing down on the dusty stones. The inixes looked up and hissed, then slowly backed away from the well to reveal Caelum and Rkard. The two Kledans sat on the ground, looking dazed and frightened.

"Don't worry. Sadira used a spell to move you," Magnus called, still fifty paces from the pair. "The Dragon destroyed the Tyrian legion, and now he's after the Bronze Company."

Rkard was on his feet instantly. "Then why'd she move us?" he demanded. "I can't kill Borys from here!"

Outside the village wall, Neeva's distant voice called, "Bronze Company, halt! Face to the rear!"

Billows of orange smoke poured from the Dragon's nostrils, streaming out of sight as they passed behind the huts on Samarah's south side. Dozens of warriors cried out in anger and fear. They began to cough and choke, but the windsinger did not hear the clang of any armored bodies falling to the ground. Neeva shouted a harsh command, ordering the dwarves to attack.

Rkard drew his sword and started toward the battle, but Caelum grabbed the youth's shoulder to hold him back.

From outside the village came the clatter of dwarven axes striking stony flesh. Borys roared in anger and raised a clawed foot so high into the air that Magnus saw it above the roofs of the huts. The Dragon slammed his heel down. The windsinger heard death screams and crumpling metal.

Rikus screamed in anger, then Sadira's voice rang out with the mystic syllables of a spell. A low growl rumbled through the ground, ending with a tremendous bang. The Dragon stumbled back. The dwarves gave a mighty cheer, and Magnus heard them tramping forward. Sadira called out another incantation, and a black bolt of magic energy blasted a hunk of scaly flesh off the beast's shoulder. Borys sprayed glowing sand toward the village wall and retreated.

Neeva yelled the order to charge, and the clamor of running feet filled Magnus's ears. The windsinger could also hear Rikus disparaging Borys's courage in a futile attempt to lure him back to the fight. At the same time, Sadira was shouting for the company to spread out so that the Dragon could not use a spell to make an easy counterattack.

As Magnus joined Caelum and Rkard at the well, the boy looked up at him. "What are they doing?" Although the Dragon's towering form had already retreated so far that it was no longer visible behind Samarah's huts, the young mul's eyes were still turned southward. "Jo'orsh and Sa'ram said I'm the one who's going to kill the Dragon."

"Perhaps, but we should not complain if your mother and her friends succeed now," said the windsinger.

"Besides, I doubt that this battle will be our last one with Borys," said Caelum. "He is a powerful enemy and will not be slain so easily."

A hut at the plaza's edge suddenly collapsed, spraying stones halfway across the square. Magnus looked toward the sound and scowled. "What caused that?"

"Whatever it was, I don't like it." Caelum raised his palm toward the sun.

"I'll go take a look," Magnus offered.

The windsinger gripped his mace more tightly and started toward the ruined building. He moved across the square cautiously, his dark eyes searching the narrow alleys for some man or creature that could have destroyed the hut. A cloud of silt hung in the air around the fallen shack, but it was thin enough that Magnus could see that there was no one lurking inside it.

Finally, when he had crossed about three-quarters of the plaza, he heard something clatter across a cobblestone ahead. Less than three paces away, a swirl of silt rose off the ground with no apparent cause. Normally, he would have attributed the disturbance to the wind. But the day was a still one. There was not even a faint breeze, and he knew that no air current had caused the sound or the puff of dust.

Something hard and knobby struck Magnus in the
chest. Though the jolt lacked the sharp impact of an
attack, its force was powerful and unyielding. The
windsinger's feet left the ground, then he crashed down
on his back a short distance away. The air over his face
stirred faintly as something unseen passed over him.
The ground trembled slightly as something heavy settled down just a short distance from his head. Then
everything was once again still and quiet.

Magnus regained his feet and rushed toward the well.
"Something's coming, Caelum!"

The windsinger's warning was hardly necessary.
Caelum's palm was already glowing brilliant crimson.
The dwarf pushed his son behind him, then pointed his
hand at the ground and traced a circle around himself
and Rkard. A scarlet glow washed over the cobblestones, sending waves of heat pouring into the sky.

Magnus was twenty paces away, and Caelum's spell
scorched his tough hide even from that distance. Tongues
of orange flame began to lace the shimmering wall,
though the dwarf and his son showed no sign of dis-
comfort inside their protective fire circle. The windsinger's mace burst into flame. He barely managed to
toss it aside before it burned his hand. At the well, the
bone rails surrounding the pit turned black and began
to smoke, then abruptly vanished in a fiery flash.

Unable to endure the terrible heat of the sun-cleric's
spell, Magnus stopped. The fiery curtain around Caelum
and Rkard waved as though something were passing
through it. Even before the windsinger saw the flames
outline the shape of a gaunt figure, he knew the awful
truth. The Dragon had created a double of himself to
lure Rikus and Sadira away.

Magnus burst into song, summoning a hot gale that
swept across the plaza and fanned Caelum's spell. The
flames flared white. Glowing cobblestones shot from the
ground like lightning bolts, trailing blue fire and filling

the air with ear-piercing whistles. The rocks rattled off the Dragon's legs and bounced away with no effect.

Borys passed inside the circle. The only effect the flames had on him was to coat his body in soot, rendering him more or less visible. Caelum raised a glowing hand and sprayed the blackened Dragon with crimson fire. The flames bounced off the beast's chest and curled back.

Magnus rushed forward, ignoring the searing pain that washed over him with each stride. As he ran, he sent a wind-whisper to Sadira. "Borys has tricked us! Come to the well at once!"

Even as he committed the words to the wind, the windsinger worried about all the things that could keep the message from reaching the sorceress. If Borys's magic had caused today's eerie stillness, Magnus's breath would be muffled long before it left the village. Or, if the battle had drifted too far east or west, the wind-whisper would bypass her. And if the words did reach the sorceress, it would take a little while for her to disengage from the fight with the fraudulent dragon and return to the well. By then, Rkard might well be dead.

Inside the fire circle, a loud thud sounded as Borys kicked Caelum in the chest. The dwarf shot into the air, his limp hand still trailing flame. He crashed down on the far side of the well and did not move.

Magnus reached the circle of fire and tried to hurl himself through. He slammed into the flames as though smashing into a stone wall, then his leading flank erupted into blistering pain. The smell of scorched hide filled his nostrils. The windsinger fell away, bellowing in agony and madly slapping at the embers flaring to life on his thighs. He slammed to the ground and rolled. Once he managed to get control of himself, he returned to his knees, already singing a lyric that would ease his pain.

Magnus looked up in time to see Rkard diving forward. The boy's sword flashed, hit the Dragon's scorched leg, and snapped. The young mul cried out in disbelief, then rolled through the fire wall and came up facing Borys. He stood about a quarter of the way around the circle from Magnus, less than a dozen paces away.

The Dragon stepped into the fire curtain and stooped down to pick up Rkard.

Magnus pushed himself to his feet and stumbled forward, his legs protesting each step with fiery pain. "Rkard, over here!" he yelled.

The young mul looked toward the windsinger. When Borys's hand flicked down to cut him off, the boy dodged away and began to run, fleeing toward a hut on the opposite side of the plaza.

The Dragon turned to chase the boy.

Suddenly, on the other side of the fire circle from Magnus, a gnarled mass of bone stood between Borys and the boy. The lump was almost as tall as the Dragon himself, with glowing orange eyes, a long gray beard, and stiff branches of bone protruding from its shoulders. Magnus shook his head, unable to understand where the banshee had come from. The thing had appeared in a flash, standing where there had been only empty air an instant before.

"I won't let you slay our king again," said Jo'orsh.

"I have no intention of killing him," Borys replied. "I'm taking him to Ur Draxa, where I'll return him to you—in return for the Dark Lens. Now, stand aside."

With his arm of stiff bone, Jo'orsh slashed at the Dragon, opening a long gash in Borys's snout. Boiling yellow blood spilled from the wound, hissing and popping as it splashed off the cobblestones.

Magnus circled around Caelum's fire curtain, ducking his face behind his shoulder to shield it from the blazing heat.

Borys tried to sidestep his foe, and Jo'orsh moved to

block his path. The Dragon struck, driving a fist through the banshee's gnarled ribs. A deafening crack reverberated across the square, and the banshee burst apart. Shards of white bone rained down on the plaza from one end to the other.

As soon as they hit the ground, the fragments astonished Magnus by slowly tumbling back toward the place Jo'orsh had been standing.

Swallowing his shock, Magnus lowered his shoulder and charged. Though he was not foolish enough to believe he could injure Borys, he hoped to slow the beast down long enough for Rkard to escape.

Borys stepped away, forcing the windsinger to change courses and rush after him. In two paces, the Dragon crossed to the hut where Rkard had gone. He ripped the hide roof away and tossed it across the square. Apparently, the young mul had left through a back window, for the Beast did not reach down to pluck him out of the building.

"Where are you, little boy?" The Dragon slapped the hut in frustration.

The building exploded into flying stones. Less than a dozen paces away, Magnus had to stop running and duck away to shield his head. When the windsinger looked up again, the beast was tearing the roof off the next building. Again, the Dragon smashed the shack, then he ripped the hide off a third shack.

This time, a red flare shot up from inside and engulfed Borys's slender head inside a glowing likeness of the sun. Unconcerned, the Dragon reached into the hut. When he pulled his hand out, it was curled into a tight fist, with Rkard's head showing out the top.

"No!" Magnus roared.

The windsinger sprinted the last few steps to the plaza edge. He threw himself at the Dragon's bony shin and wrapped his massive arms around it. Borys started toward the tiny silt harbor east of the village, smashing his foot through the nearest hut.

The windsinger grimaced from the impact, but held on easily. His thick hide was as tough as a lirr's, and it shielded him from all but the most serious of blows. He began to sing in his loudest voice, calling up a gale from the Sea of Silt. Borys dragged him through another hut, then another and another. Magnus continued to sing, and soon the sky above was filled with gray clouds of dust. Yellow bolts of lightning crackled out of the gathering storm, each striking the Dragon's head. The windsinger was not foolish enough to think his windstorm could harm the beast, but he hoped it would draw his friends' attention to Rkard's danger.

Borys chuckled, then slammed his foot through the village wall and stepped into the harbor. Magnus sank beneath the silt. He closed his eyes and mouth, trying to breathe through his nose. The membranes protecting his nasal passages were clogged by dust, but at least the filters kept him from swallowing the powdery loess and choking. He would not suffocate for a few more moments.

Holding his breath, Magnus pulled himself up Borys's knee. The storm would continue for a few moments without his ballad, but if he wanted to keep it going, he would soon have to raise his voice again. The windsinger reached up, searching for a handhold on the Dragon's thigh.

Magnus felt a hand slip around his torso. The claw pulled him free and lifted him out of the silt. The windsinger saw that the Dragon had already carried him and Rkard out of the harbor. They were heading toward the heart of the Sea of Silt.

Above Magnus, Rkard had managed to work an arm free of the Dragon's grip and was trying to bend a clawed finger back to free himself. The windsinger knew he would not succeed. Even a mul child could not be that strong.

Magnus snorted, clearing his nostrils, and raised his

voice in song. A peal of thunder cracked over the Dragon, and a dozen forks of sizzling energy stabbed at his head. Borys's eyes flashed even brighter than the lightning.

"Your noise makes my head throb," the Dragon hissed.

Three sharp claws pierced the windsinger's hide, cracking his massive ribs like a storm snapping faro branches. His ballad changed to a howl. He felt the Dragon's arm whip outward, then Magnus found himself soaring over the pearly sea. His black eyes clouded over and he began to arc downward, the wind singing in his ears.

* * * * *

Neeva found her unconscious husband next to the well, one armed draped over the side. The flesh had been scraped off one side of his skull, and a dark streak on the cobblestones marked where he had been dragged across the plaza to the pit. Strangely enough, the wound itself looked clean, as though someone had taken the trouble to bathe it before abandoning him.

"Caelum! Wake up!" She kneeled at his side and shook his shoulder. When his eyes failed to open, she slapped his cheek—not lightly. "Tell me what happened to Rkard!"

The dwarf's eyes did not even flutter.

Behind her, Jo'orsh's bones continued to clatter as they tumbled toward each other. Neeva looked toward the noise and shuddered. The banshee had reconstructed only about half of his gnarled body, most of the torso and one leg, and somehow he looked even more hideous than before.

Rikus and Sadira appeared at the edge of the plaza, leading the five haggard survivors from the Bronze Company toward the well. The rest of the command, nearly thirty warriors, had perished in the battle with the counterfeit Borys. At the time, with its claws ripping through steel breastplates and its heels smashing thick dwarven skulls, the beast had seemed real enough. It was not until the fight had ended and the Dragon had shrunk into a frightened, battered gorak that they had discovered the creature's true nature.

It was then that they had noticed the dust storm drifting out to sea. For a moment, it had seemed to Neeva that she saw a red light in the heart of the tempest, but the others had not been able to find it when she tried to point it out to them. Finally, even she could not see the glow, and the squall had moved out of sight. They had rushed back to the village, finding it as quiet as when they had first arrived.

"How is he?" called Sadira.

Neeva shook her head. "Alive, but that's about all," she reported. "Any sign of Magnus or Rkard?"

The sorceress shook her head. "I'm sorry."

Neeva cursed. "I want to know where my son is," she said. "Why doesn't Magnus send a wind-whisper to tell us where they are?"

"He may have," Sadira replied. "But if he did it after the battle began to drift eastward, we wouldn't have been there to hear it."

"Or maybe he didn't have time," Rikus suggested. "If it came down to a choice of protecting Rkard or warning us, I've no doubts that he'd defend the boy."

"As long as he was able—which may not have been that long," Neeva said. She picked her husband up and carried him a safe distance away from the well. "But what happened isn't as important as how we're going to find my son again."

"Maybe Jo'orsh will be able to tell us something," Sadira suggested. She glanced toward the banshee, who had reassembled his complete torso, both legs, and an arm. "He must have seen what happened."

Rikus nodded. "Until then, maybe this can tell us

something." The mul kneeled at the side of the well. He pointed at the dark streak marking the path along which Caelum had been pulled. "Could Rkard have been the one who dragged his father over here?"

Neeva shook her head. "He'd just carry Caelum," she said. "You know how strong he is."

"Unless he was hurt, and looking for a place to hide," Rikus said. He grabbed the well rope and handed the end to Neeva. "I'll go see."

Neeva barely had time to loop the line around her back and sit before the mul stepped into the dark pit. The rope bit into her waist, and she waited in tense silence while the mul descended. The warrior did not know what she wanted him to find. If Rkard had been injured and dropped into the well, he might well have drowned. On the other hand, she could not bear the alternative—that Borys had taken him and disappeared. She found herself placing all her hope in Magnus, praying that the windsinger had taken her son and hidden where neither Sadira or the Dragon could find them.

The rope slackened as Rikus took his weight off it. The mul groaned in disgust, then cried, "You!"

A muffled thump echoed up from the well, then a bloated head came flying out of the pit. He had coarse hair pulled into a tight topknot, with puffy cheeks, eyes swollen to narrow dark slits, and a mouthful of broken teeth. His leathery lips were caked with fresh blood—no doubt licked from Caelum's head wound.

"Sacha!" Sadira cried.

The head regained his equilibrium and hovered in the air, regarding them with a malevolent sneer. "It's high time you arrived," he said. "Your king has nearly starved to death!"

Neeva ignored the head and leaned over the pit. "What'd you find down there, Rikus?"

"Our scouts—dead," came the reply. Neeva heard the mul grunt, then there were several splashes as he pushed their bodies aside. "And Tithian—at least I think it's him—with something that could be the Dark Lens."

Although this news should have delighted her, Neeva could not rejoice yet. "Anyone else?"

"Rkard's not down here," answered the mul.

"Of course not," Sacha sneered, drifting over in front of Neeva. "If you want to see Rkard again, you'd better hurry and get Tithian out of that hole."

Neeva lashed out, catching the head by his topknot. "Why?"

The head slowly spun around, facing the Sea of Silt. "Because the Dragon is taking him to Ur Draxa, and I don't think Jo'orsh is going to wait very long for you to follow."

Neeva followed his gaze. Having returned his gnarled head to his lumpy shoulders, Jo'orsh was moving toward Samarah's harbor in long, silent strides.

ELEVEN

The Dhow

As the dhow left Samarah's harbor, a gust of wind skipped across the swells ahead. Silvery columns of dust swirled skyward, forming a chain of featherlike silhouettes against the yellow horizon. For a moment, they hung like clouds above the pearly sea, then the bluster died. The plumes slowly melted back toward the surface, forming a low-hanging dust curtain that shrouded Jo'orsh's distant figure in a mantle of gray.

Tithian braced his arm on the tiller and pulled himself upright, sitting squarely on the floater's dome. He peered out toward the open sea and cursed his lack of a king's eye. With Jo'orsh wading through chest-deep silt, it had been difficult enough to see him before the gust came up. Now, keeping the banshee's lumpy head in sight would be impossible.

The effort of sitting upright was almost too much for the king. His time in the well had reduced him to something of a skeleton. The pallid skin dangled from his sticklike arms in loose folds, and each time he exhaled, his breath filled the air with the stench of starvation. He

181

had little desire for solid food, and the few morsels his former slaves had forced him to eat sat in his distended stomach like rocks. The king thought that Sacha's approach to helping him recover, trickling warm blood down his throat, had been much more sensible.

After a few moments of peering into the dust haze, the king let his elbow slip over the tiller and slumped back down. He was careful to keep his bare foot pressed against the Dark Lens, which lay in the open bilge in front of him. He was drawing the lens's energy through his body, using it to feed the dome and keep the ship afloat.

Tithian looked toward the top of the mast, where Sacha had positioned himself to serve as a lookout. "I've lost sight of the banshee," he called. "Can you see him?"

"Through this haze?" the head scoffed.

As Sacha replied, Neeva ducked under the low-hanging boom of the lateen sail and stepped back toward him. Since her days in the gladiator pits, her skin had grown darker and less sensitive to the sun, as demonstrated by the fact that she wore nothing but a leather breechcloth and halter to protect her from its blistering rays. To Tithian's eye, she also seemed more beautiful. Motherhood had given her a fuller figure, while her muscles were more sinuous and less manlike. Her emerald eyes, however, remained as fiery and angry as they had been when the king owned her—especially when they were looking at him.

Tithian met her glare. "What are you staring at?"

Without answering, Neeva picked her way toward the stern. It was not an easy task. They had just entered the open sea, and the dhow was pitching badly as it rode across the dust swells. To complicate matters, the small boat was crowded to overflowing. In the open bilge lay Caelum, crammed in next to a dozen kegs filled with chadnuts and water. His head had been bandaged, but he had not yet regained consciousness. To

Tithian's way of thinking, he was just taking up limited cargo space. Sadira stood along the port side, braced between a barrel and the gunnel, holding the line that controlled the set of the sail. On the opposite side of the boat sat Rikus, his bald head and pointed ears barely visible over the cask tops.

As Neeva came abreast of the mast, she stopped to grab her battle-axe from between two water barrels.

Tithian raised a brow. "I'd advise you to remember that without me, this boat will sink," the king said. "And with it, all hope of rescuing your child."

"I don't care if we sink," countered Neeva. "We've hardly left the harbor and already we've lost sight of Jo'orsh. We'll never catch up to him—or my son."

"The dhow is a sensitive craft," Tithian replied. "We'd be traveling faster if Sadira had left Caelum in Samarah with the other dwarves—as I suggested."

"I doubt Caelum's weight is slowing us down that much." Neeva raised her axe. "Besides, it doesn't matter. We may have lost Rkard, but I want you to die before he does."

"Don't be foolish, Neeva." Sadira laid a restraining hand on the warrior's arm.

The action caused a subtle shift in the sail's trim and the dhow slowed. The sorceress let a little line slip through her ebony fingers, returning the boom to its original position.

Once the dhow had returned to speed, Sadira looked back to Neeva. "Jo'orsh is showing himself because he wants to help us track Rkard," she said. "When he sees us falling behind, he'll wait."

"And let Borys escape with my son!" Neeva spat back.

"That won't happen," Tithian said. "Borys wants the banshee to follow. That's why he took the boy."

"Explain yourself," Rikus ordered. He rose and peered at the king over a water barrel. "If you had something to do with the Dragon seizing him—"

"I wasn't even conscious," Tithian spat. "But I do know Borys wants the banshees alive. In Ur Draxa—his home—he has a way to make them dispel the magic that hides the Dark Lens from him and the sorcerer-kings. The Dragon needs Rkard alive because Jo'orsh was sent to protect the boy."

Neeva frowned. "Sent?" she asked. "By whom?"

Tithian swallowed hard and found himself gripping the tiller so hard his gnarled joints turned white. Nevertheless, the blunder did not cause the king to panic. He simply looked Neeva in the eye and lied: "Agis sent them."

"You don't expect us to believe that!" Sadira snapped.

"Not really, but it's the truth," Tithian said, silently cursing the sorceress. Did she have some way to tell that he was lying? "Jo'orsh and Sa'ram were guarding the Dark Lens when we found it. They were going to kill both of us, until Agis told them about Kemalok being uncovered. Then they left, saying something about the return of the king."

"How'd they come by the Belt of Rank and Rkard's crown?" demanded Neeva.

"Why don't you tell me?" Tithian returned, dodging the question.

This was the moment the king had been dreading since Rikus pulled him from the well. In the hurry to pack the dhow and start after Jo'orsh, there had not been time for his temporary allies to interrogate him. But now, he sensed the questions would begin. As weak as he was, Tithian feared it would be difficult to keep himself free of his own tangle of lies.

Neeva picked up her axe again. "Your raiders stole those treasures from Kemalok." She stopped a pace in front of him, holding her weapon level with his neck. "I know that much, and it's enough to warrant your death."

Tithian did not flinch. "Do you really expect to frighten

me? I know you won't strike—not while you need me to rescue your son."

Neeva's gaze burned with a profound hatred such as the king had never seen before, and he had seen many, many kinds of hate. The warrior's arms began to tremble and tears of frustration welled in her eyes. For a moment, the king feared she would actually lose control of herself and strike. Then she gave a tremendous scream and spun away. Sighing in relief, Tithian committed her expression to memory as a reminder of what would happen if he allowed her to live a moment too long.

As Neeva returned to the front of the dhow, the king noticed Sadira staring at him. Instead of blue-glowing embers, her eyes now resembled a pair of sapphire-colored suns, each blazing with a radiance that nearly blinded him. The sorceress did not move or speak, but merely continued to watch him. In that moment, Tithian understood why she had not asked about Agis: she knew that her husband had been murdered by him.

"You won't kill me, either," Tithian said, not as sure of his words as he would have liked. "We want the same thing."

"No. I want to kill the Dragon. You want to free a monster." As Sadira spoke, a cloud of black fumes shot from her mouth and coated Tithian's body, bringing with it a fearsome cold that chilled his bones to the marrow. "Tell me what you'll gain by helping Rajaat escape," she ordered.

"Wh-what makes you think I want to?" Tithian gasped, his teeth clenched. The contrast between the Dark Lens's heat and Sadira's cold made his bones feel as if they were melting. He expected to burst into flame, or shatter like a block of ice, at any moment. "I thought the champions killed Rajaat."

"Don't lie to me!" Sadira hissed.

Again, the black fumes. "Stop it, wench!" Tithian's

teeth chattered so badly he could hardly force the words
from his mouth. He wanted to use the lens and counterattack, but to use the Way now, he would have to let the
dhow sink. He could not allow that. The king needed
both Sadira and Rikus alive, at least until Borys no
longer stood between him and freeing Rajaat. "I c-c-
command it!"

"You don't have to answer," the sorceress said. "I'm
enjoying this."

"I'm too exhausted," Tithian warned, fighting back
the waves of darkness descending over him. "The dhow
will sink."

"I don't think so," said Sadira.

Tithian heard the sorceress whisper an incantation.
The dhow suddenly rose out of the dust, lifting its
weight off the king's spirit. The boat's speed increased
by half, and it began to slice through the air as smoothly
as an arrow.

"You still need me!" Tithian said. Hoping to use the
Way to defend himself, he tried to lock gazes with
Sadira—but could not bear to look into the blazing blue
suns of her eyes. "What will you do if we don't catch
Rkard before dark?"

"I won't kill you yet," the sorceress replied. "You
haven't suffered enough."

An inky cloud boiled from between Sadira's blue lips,
engulfing the king in cold vapor. He opened his mouth
to scream, but his frozen voice did not rise to acknowl-
edge the pain. He felt his feet slip from the Dark Lens,
then sank into a bitter slumber more icy and black than
his own heart.

Later, after what seemed an eternity of bone-deep
aching, Tithian returned to awareness, not so much
waking as crawling from beneath a terrible, crushing
blackness. His body hurt worse than it had before, as if
that were possible, and he wondered—not idly—if
Neeva had beaten him while he slept. Slowly, the king

came to realize that he was lying on the floor of the dhow, stuffed between the side and the water casks. He heard voices, and the speakers did not seem to realize he had returned to consciousness. Always one to spy, Tithian kept his eyes closed and listened.

"I'm not saying we should let the Dragon keep Rkard," said Sadira. "But I'm not so sure we should kill him. I'm certain that Tithian's helping us destroy Borys only because it'll make it easier to free Rajaat—and we know how much worse than Borys he would be."

"So we should let the Dragon keep collecting his levies?" Rikus asked. "Never!"

"Rikus, that's not what I said—and you know it," Sadira shot back.

The voices of both Sadira and Rikus seemed more harsh than necessary, leading Tithian to suspect they were angry with each other—and wondering if he could use that fact to his own advantage.

"We have the Dark Lens now," Sadira continued. "Borys knows better than anyone how powerful it is. We can force him to return Rkard and forsake his levies."

"But what about the prophecy?" Neeva demanded. "The banshees said Rkard would *slay* the Dragon. We can't just ignore them."

"Why not?" Sadira challenged. "They also said he'd do it at the head of an army of dwarves and humans. Where is that army now? It took Borys and his sorcerer-kings about as much effort to destroy all our warriors as it takes a mekillot to smash a jackal."

"We must have misunderstood what they said about the army," said Neeva. "If Jo'orsh and Sa'ram said that Rkard will slay the Dragon, I have faith he will."

Tithian had to bite his cheek to keep from laughing. The so-called prophecy was nothing more than an elaborate ruse he had invented. Faced with the difficult task of overcoming Jo'orsh and Sa'ram before he could steal the Dark Lens, the king had instead lured the banshees away from their duties by convincing them their thousand-year-old ruler had been reincarnated as a mul child.

It had never occurred to Tithian that his deception would dupe anyone other than the two spirits, but it appeared his former slaves were bigger fools than he imagined. He could hardly wait to see what happened when a six-year-old boy tried to kill the Dragon. The entertainment might even be enough to repay him for the indignities he was suffering at the hands of the child's mother and her friends.

After a moment's silence, Sadira continued the debate. "Neeva, did it ever occur to you that the prophecy might be a warning? That it might be something we *don't* want to come true?" she asked. "Perhaps the fate of our two armies is a portent of what'll happen if we go through with this plan."

"What the prophecy says doesn't matter," declared Rikus. "We've got to kill the Dragon, even if it frees Rajaat."

"Think of what you're saying!" Sadira objected. "As powerful as the sorcerer-kings are, it took all of them together to imprison Rajaat—and he could be even more powerful now."

"I don't care," said the mul, stubborn as ever.

"Borys and the sorcerer-kings are greedy and power-hungry, but their evil is nothing compared to that of Rajaat," Sadira pressed. "At least they won't wipe out every Athasian race except the humans—and wouldn't have the power to succeed if they tried."

"True," agreed the mul. "And I'm as worried as you. But we've got to kill the Dragon. We'd be fools to think we can control him forever. So, if we free Rajaat, we'll just have to destroy him, too. We can't trade one evil for another."

There was a short silence, then Sadira asked, "Neeva, what do you think? It's your son we must risk if we decide to kill the Dragon."

"And it's my son who'll have to live—or die—with the scruples of our choice," she said. "Given that, there's only one thing to do. Rkard must kill the Dragon."

Tithian heard Sadira suck in a deep breath. "Victory or death, then," she said. The declaration was one that Tyrian gladiators had once recited before entering the arena.

"No, just victory," said Rikus. "Death means that we have lost, and we can't allow that—not when we are risking so much."

Tithian heard the soft slap of three hands coming together, then Rikus said, "That leaves us only one problem: Tithian."

"As much as I'd like to kill him, we can't," said Sadira. "He's the only mindbender among us, and we know from the battles we've already fought that we can't get along without one. Abalach used the Way in the Ivory Plain and nearly defeated me, and I suspect that Borys will prove even more powerful.

"We can't trust Tithian," objected Rikus.

"Of course not," replied Sadira. "But we can keep him under control until we've killed Borys."

"And after that?" asked Neeva.

"As soon as the Dragon falls, he'll try to kill us," said Rikus, lowering his voice to a whisper. "If we want to survive, we'll have to kill him first."

Tithian smiled to himself. They could try to murder him, but snow would blanket the Athasian deserts before they outperformed him at his own art.

In his stomach, the king felt the dhow descending. "It's almost dark," said Sadira. "We'd better rouse His Majesty."

A small foot smashed into Tithian's ribs, forcing him to groan in pain.

"Time to go to work," Sadira said. With one hand, she grasped his hair and pulled him off the bilge floor. She sat him on the floater's dome. "I trust you slept well."

Tithian opened his eyes, feigning grogginess. The Dark Lens had been moved to the bow of the craft, and the king could see little more than its red-tinged base showing beneath the boom of the lateen sail. Neeva and Rikus stood directly in front him, their weapons in their hands and glaring at him with open hostility. Caelum still lay in the bilge, his bandage crusted with dried blood.

The king reached up and pulled his coarse hair from Sadira's grip. "You shouldn't separate me from the Dark Lens," he said. "Borys has been looking for me, hoping to find the lens nearby."

"Then I hope he finds you," said Sadira. "It would save us a journey."

"How far have we gone?" Tithian asked, looking around. He saw nothing but dust swells, swaddled in the purple shadows of dusk, with no sign of land in any direction. "Where's Jo'orsh?"

Sadira pointed to a spot off the port bow. "Every now and then we see a furrow of dust over there," she said. "Sometimes he sticks his head up to be sure we're still following."

"That won't do me much good." The king laid his hand on the tiller. "I'll never see him in the dark."

"Don't worry," said Rikus. The mul sat on the starboard gunnel and laid his sword across his knees. "I'll be sitting up to help you look."

"So will I," added Neeva. She took a similar position on the port side. "And if one of us even thinks you're using the Way against the other, or hears anything that sounds remotely like a mystic word, we'll assume the worst."

"That means we'll cut you up into little pieces." Rikus reached out with the tip of his sword and cut the strap of Tithian's shoulder satchel. The bag slipped off the king's shoulder and fell out of the dhow. "Just in case you didn't understand."

Tithian lunged for the sack, trying to grab it before it sank into the Sea of Silt. He instantly felt Sadira's fingers digging into his shoulder, jerking him away.

"You fools!" The king hissed, watching the satchel sink beneath the dust. "That was magic!"

"Which is why I thought it best to be rid of the thing," said Sadira. "Who knows what surprises you had stored in there for us?"

"Now that we've made our point," said Rikus, "is there anything else we should know about—so we don't accidentally throw it overboard?"

The king shook his head. "You've no need to fear me, or anything I have left." He grasped the tiller. "If we're going to kill Borys, we have to work together. I understand that—probably better than you."

"Good," said Sadira. She moved toward the bow. "Then you take over until dawn."

Tithian opened himself to the floater's dome, allowing his life energy to flow into it. Icy tendrils of pain began to spread up through his hips and into his abdomen. He closed his eyes and visualized the ship's hull in his mind, then pictured the gray dust swells changing to blue waves of salt water—the Sea of Silt as it was, long before the sorcerer-kings ruled Athas. The dhow's weight settled on his spirit, filling him with a terrible ache, and again the craft began to pitch as it rode across the endless swells of dust.

That was how it went, day after day. From dawn to dusk, Sadira's magic carried the dhow above the gray waves. Then, as dark fell, Rikus roused the king to float the craft over the silt. The mul and Neeva spent the night sitting to either side of Tithian, watching his every move. At least once a night, one of them smashed him with a fist, just to make certain that he knew they would kill him at the slightest provocation. The king accepted his persecution with a grace that Rikus found vaguely unsettling, never complaining or begging forbearance. Tithian did not even try to win them over with cajolery or false promises, perhaps because he knew such efforts would only bring more abuse.

On the afternoon of the third day, Caelum finally woke. With a great deal of care, more from Sadira than Neeva, the dwarf soon felt well enough to call on the sun. After that, the women left him to his own resources and he quickly grew better, using his healing powers to mend his terrible wound. Other than the dwarf's recovery, the routine never changed. Jo'orsh's head periodically rose out of the dust, his glowing orange eyes serving as beacons in the darkness of the night. Sacha stayed atop the mast day and night, never leaving his post—which was probably wise, since neither Rikus nor any of the others had quite forgiven him for pulling the scouts into the well to feed Tithian.

Deep into their fifth night, with a steady wind blowing from the west and a dust curtain clinging to the sea, Sacha suddenly drifted down from the mast. "Lights," he reported. The head's voice was so hoarse that Rikus could barely understand him. "Behind us."

The mul glanced over the stern and saw nothing but the impenetrable blackness of the dust curtain. "I don't see anything."

"You weren't sitting on top of the mast," Sacha countered. "There were a dozen clusters of them, spread out across the horizon. It's a fleet coming up behind us."

Tithian cursed.

"What do you know about this?" Rikus touched the tip of his sword to the king's throat. "If you've betrayed us—"

Tithian slapped the blade away. "This is no trick," he sneered. "It's the fleet of the sorcerer-kings."

Rikus moved his sword back toward the king and said nothing.

"What do I have to gain by lying?" growled Tithian.

"When the sorcerer-kings came to meet Borys in Samarah, they arrived on a fleet of Balican schooners. It appears they've been summoned to Ur Draxa."

"Why?" asked Neeva.

"To find us, I suspect," said the king. "From my experience, Balican fleets sail in tight formations. If they've spread out, they must be searching for us."

Neeva went forward to wake Caelum and Sadira.

"Bring me the Dark Lens," said Tithian.

Rikus shook his head. "I don't think so."

"You stupid mul!" hissed Sacha. "It's our only chance."

"Our only chance to get killed," Rikus countered. "Even with the Dark Lens, we can't sink a fleet of ships carrying all the sorcerer-kings of Athas—at least not at night, when Sadira's powers are so limited."

"We can't outrun them, if that's what you're thinking," said Tithian. "They have too much sail."

"Then we'll do the next best thing—we'll hide," said Rikus. "The dust-curtain will conceal us."

"It won't," said Tithian. "They have magic cones of glass—king's eyes—that they use to see through the silt haze."

"And what do they use to see through the dark?" asked the mul. When the king did not have an answer, Rikus smiled. "I thought so. The next time we top a dust swell, swing us around so we're sitting across the slope, near the bottom of the wave."

The mul sheathed his sword and went forward to the mast. He waited until Tithian started to bring the dhow around, then lowered the sail, furled it to the boom, and undid the lashings holding the whole assembly to the mast. By the time he pulled the rigging free and laid the boom and sail aside, Neeva had awakened Caelum and Sadira. The dwarf helped Rikus unstep the mast, fold the long yardarm down, and lay the whole thing in the bilge.

"Cover the boat with silt," suggested Tithian.

Rikus frowned. "Won't that sink us?"

The king shook his head. "Why should it? I'm holding us aloft," he said. "We won't be able to move very fast, but with our mast down, we're not going any place anyway."

Rikus nodded, then he and the others began pulling dust from the upslope into the dhow. Soon only their bodies and the tops of the gunnels—made of weathered bone almost as gray as the silt—showed above the sea. The mul instructed the others to lie down, then began covering them with powdery loess, leaving only their faces exposed so they could see and breathe.

"This should hide us from the fleet," said Neeva. "But what about Jo'orsh? We could lose him."

"Perhaps, but he hasn't changed directions in days," said Sadira. "And if the sorcerer-kings are behind us, I suspect we're still traveling toward the Dragon's home."

"Right," agreed Rikus. "But I am worried that the banshee will stick his head up at the wrong moment. His glowing eyes would be hard to miss on a night like this."

"You needn't worry about Jo'orsh," said Tithian. He pushed a liver-spotted hand under the dust to maintain contact with the floater's dome. "He can take care of himself."

With that, the king slid down into the bilge, accompanied by Sacha, who had carefully remained out of everyone's reach during the preparations. Rikus covered the pair with dust, then took a moment to inspect the dhow. When he was satisfied that everything was covered as well as it could be, he drew his sword and lay down, taking care to position himself between the king and the Dark Lens.

They waited in the silt-heavy gloom for what seemed an eternity, listening to their own heartbeats and the wind hissing across the silt. The hollow that they had carved from the dust swell slowly filled in, and loess gathered around Rikus's nose and mouth. At first, he tried to keep a clear air passage by blowing the stuff away, but this did not work and he eventually had to move his hand up to fan the stuff away. He began to doubt that Sacha had really seen any lights, and occupied his time by trying to think of possible reasons for the disembodied head to lie. Aside from Sacha's malevolence, he could not see what the head might gain by making the dhow sit motionless in the dark.

Rikus was just about to rise when he heard the distant creak of straining masts. The others heard it, too, for the dhow fell even more silent, as if everyone had drawn a deep breath and held it. The sound grew louder and steadier, until at last the mul recognized in it the rhythmic cadence of a ship sliding over dust swells.

Far to the dhow's stern, the flickering beams of huge oil lamps began to dance across the silt. The rays roved back and forth in great arcs, creating long columns of bright, windborne silt that pierced the darkness like spears. Even with the lights, the dust was so thick that Rikus doubted the Balican searchers could see more than a few yards beyond their gunnels—at least they couldn't have, if not for the magical king's eyes Tithian had mentioned.

The lights danced ahead to the next swell, then the schooner itself slipped into the trough. If not for muffled voices of its crew and the halos of its deck lamps hovering far above the dust, Rikus would hardly have known it was there. It took many moments for the ship to pass. From the lights shining on the various decks and portholes, the mul formed a fair picture of its size and shape. The thing was huge, at least three times the size of the mighty war wagons Hamanu had sent to attack Tyr during the war with Urik. It seemed entirely possible that the whole village of Samarah could have fit on one of its decks. By the time the schooner's stern lights faded into the dusty night, Rikus felt more certain than ever that he had made the right decision in electing to hide. Fighting the schooner would have been like battling an entire legion.

The ship had hardly passed when the glow of another schooner's lantern stabbed through the darkness overhead. Rikus heard his companions gasp, then the light illuminated a small circle on the crest of the next dust swell. The yellow disk began to sweep slowly down the slope, coming in their direction.

Rikus gripped the Scourge more tightly, preparing to leap up and fight. As his companions tensed to do the same, he heard dust rustling all around him. "Stay still," he whispered. "Don't move unless I say to."

The light continued to come toward them. Rikus guessed the beam would sweep across the ship just about where he lay.

A loud hiss sounded from just in front of their dhow. An instant later, a huge bowsprit drifted over the crest of the dust swell in which they had buried themselves. The spar was as long as a tree, and it gleamed with the reflected rays of an oil lamp. It was passing so close that Rikus could have jumped off their little craft's bow and caught hold of it.

The schooner's lantern beam approached to arm's length of the dhow. At the same time, the prow of the Balican schooner burst through the dust swell, spraying a thick plume of silt high into the air. Rikus closed his eyes and ducked down beneath the dhow's gunnel, pulling himself toward the bottom of the bilge.

The mul felt the bow rise as the schooner's wake pushed their little craft aside. The dhow spun toward the bottom of the swell and began to slip down the slope. It moved easily, for it was still being levitated by Tithian. Fighting the urge to sit up, Rikus opened his eyes to the burning silt. He saw yellow light illuminating the silt over his head. He could do nothing except remind himself that this was the reason they had camouflaged their boat, and to hope that his companions also remembered that.

An instant later, the amber glow vanished. The mul pushed himself up. He thrust his head out of the dust, gasping for breath and expecting to hear an alarm cry rising from the schooner.

Through a thick cloud of dust, Rikus saw the dark wall of an immense hull looming high above them. The mul looked toward the schooner's bow and saw the beam of the lantern sweeping away from their dhow. From his angle below the gunnel, he could not see the lookouts. Nevertheless, he did not think they had seen the dhow. There was no sign that anyone was attempting to shine a light in their direction, nor did he hear anyone shouting an alarm. It seemed that their camouflage had kept the dhow concealed, at least for the brief instant that the lantern had flashed over it.

Rikus saw the heads and shoulders of his companions showing above the dust around him. Neeva was biting her finger to keep from coughing. Sadira and Caelum were both prepared to cast spells, the sorceress holding the dark lump of a spell component in her hand, and the dwarf touching his fingers to the sun-mark on his forehead. Only Tithian seemed calm, leaning against the floater's dome and smirking at them with an air of condescension.

It took only a moment longer for the schooner's stern to hiss past and disappear behind the next dust swell, leaving the dhow alone in the vast, inky darkness of the Sea of Silt. They all breathed a sigh of relief and began to scoop the silt out of the bilge.

TWELVE

The Shoals

The chain of shoals stretched across the entire horizon. In the dusk light, they appeared to be true islands, covered with tangles of water-loving ferns and vine-draped trees. From every copse trilled the warbles of strange birds, underscored at regular intervals by the chilling roar of some colossal reptile. Most of the flats even had a beach of sorts: a broad expanse of crusty, sun-baked mud that ringed the fertile groves in the center.

In the past two weeks, however, the dhow had passed enough shoals for Neeva to know the truth. The inviting isles ahead were little more than a chain of muddy swales, created by water seeping up from springs buried deep beneath the dust. The ground beneath the trees was a thin, sticky sludge only slightly less treacherous than the powdery loess filling the Sea of Silt.

"There's no way the Balicans took their schooners through that," growled Neeva. She leaned over the gunnel and peered into the shadowy labyrinth of channels between the shoals. "We've lost their course."

"We haven't," Caelum called back. The dwarf kneeled in the bow, his eye fixed on an arrow of crimson flame gliding through the silt just ahead of the prow. "Our sun guide still points straight ahead. Judging by how brightly it glows, I'd even say we're catching up to the fleet."

The dwarf cast the spell several times a day, alternately using it to track the Balicans and Rkard. So far, the arrow always pointed in the same direction, though it always glowed much more brightly when Caelum directed it at the fleet.

Neeva looked across the boat to Rikus. "What do you think? Could the Balican schooners squeeze through those channels?"

The mul shrugged. "There's enough space between the trees," he said. "But the shipfloaters would have to lift their hulls high enough to clear the mud crusts at the shoal edges. It wouldn't be easy."

"Or the sorcerer-kings might know of a hidden passage," said Sadira. The sorceress sat in the stern, using her magic to fly the dhow. "If not, their magic is certainly powerful enough to see them through."

When Neeva did not respond, Sadira added, "We'll catch up to Borys and your son."

"How?" Neeva snapped. "We don't know the way through there. It could take days to find a passage."

"We don't have to go through the shoals," suggested Rikus. "We could fly over them."

"No!" Caelum objected. "The Balican fleet is too near. Their lookouts might see us."

Sadira glanced over her shoulder at the setting sun. "Besides, it'll be dark soon," she said. "My powers will fade before we travel far."

Neeva cursed. "We've got to do something," she said. "The last time Caelum's sun guide pointed at Rkard, it was so faint we could hardly see it."

Rikus stepped over Tithian, who was sleeping in the bilge, and took Neeva by the shoulders. "You're right,

Neeva," the mul said. "We don't know how far away the Dragon and your son are, but we're doing everything we can to catch them."

"What if that's not enough, Rikus?" she demanded. "We've already seen that the Dragon's magic is just as powerful as Sadira's. And if he knows we have the Dark Lens, he's probably trying to hide Rkard from us."

"Maybe," the mul allowed, his black eyes holding hers steady. "But you know we won't stop searching."

"Like Borys hasn't stopped searching for the Dark Lens?" she asked. "My son won't live a thousand years. He might even be dead now."

"Yes, he could be dead," Rikus allowed. "But should we do anything different because of it?"

Neeva shook her head, folding herself into the mul's arms. "Damn you," she whispered. "You always were too honest with me."

She had only been there an instant when she felt her husband's hands prying her away. "Are you cruel, or just stupid, Rikus?" the dwarf demanded, interposing himself between her and the mul. "The last thing she needs to hear right now is that Rkard might be dead."

Rikus scowled, more confused than angry. "How do you know he's not?"

"That's not the point," Caelum fumed.

"Then what is?" demanded Neeva. "Do you think I'm stupid enough to believe anything else?"

"Of course not," the dwarf said. "But don't you see what he's doing?"

"What?" demanded Neeva.

"Now that Sadira's spurned him, he wants you back," said Caelum, his red eyes burning with anger. "And he's preying on your emotions."

"I was only trying to calm her down!" Rikus shook his head in disbelief.

Caelum stepped toward him. "I know what you were doing!" The dwarf turned his palm toward the sun.

"And if you try it again—"

Neeva slapped her husband's arm down. "That blow to your head must have shaken your brains loose." She jerked him away from the mul. "Apologize to Rikus."

"He's the one who should apologize," Caelum said. "He's already come between us, whether you admit it or not. You think I haven't noticed how distant you've been?"

Neeva released her husband's arm. "This has nothing to do with Rikus, except that I keep thinking Rkard should have been with him instead of you," she said. Her throat suddenly felt as dry as silt. "I can't help blaming you for what's happened to our son. It's unfair, but I just can't get over the fact that Borys took Rkard from you. I'm sorry."

Caelum's face paled from bronze to ivory. Even his eyes seemed to fade from red to pink. "Don't apologize. I feel the same way," he said. "I've gone over the fight a hundred times, and I still don't know how I could have stopped Borys. I just wish he had finished the job and killed me."

"The fault is more mine than yours," said Sadira. "When I used my magic to move you and Rkard to the well, I played right into Borys's plans."

The dwarf shook his head. "You moved both of us so I'd be there to protect him if anything went wrong," Caelum replied. "But I couldn't. What good is a man who can't defend his own son?"

Neeva felt sorry for her husband, but could not bring herself to offer him consolation. The simple fact was that she could not answer his question. What good was a man who couldn't protect his own son?

Caelum turned toward the bow, then paused and faced Rikus. "Please accept my apologies, my friend," he said. "What I said to you was terrible."

The color rose to the mul's cheeks. "Think nothing of it." He tried to shrug in a good-natured manner, but succeeded only in looking uncomfortable. "We've all been touchy for the past few days. Tithian must be using some mind trick to make us argue."

As if he really believed what he suggested, the mul planted a sharp kick in the sleeping king's ribs.

* * * * *

Rkard woke, gagging on the rotten stench of sulfur fumes and faintly aware that the Dragon still held him. They had stopped flying. Borys stood on a broken hillock of basalt overlooking a vast valley of dust and fire. Before them lay a plain of loose cinders and black stone, laced with yellow channels of molten rock. Scattered geysers spewed ash and viscous fire high into the sky, while cascades of lava poured from the steaming fissures of distant cliffs. A cloud of red ash boiled overhead, and the air tasted as hot as fire.

"Where are we?" Rkard croaked. "Inside the sun?"

"No, Rkard," answered a familiar voice. "Borys has carried you into the heart of the Sea of Silt—his personal lands."

Jo'orsh appeared at the Dragon's side. As always, the banshee arrived instantaneously, as if he had emerged from the vacant air itself.

"Jo'orsh!" Rkard cried. He twisted around to face his friend, fighting against the Dragon's incredibly tight grip. "You found me!"

"I never lost you," replied the banshee. "Why haven't you killed the Dragon yet?"

Feeling guilty that he had not, Rkard tried to pull his arms free. He was too weak. The Dragon had not allowed him any water in almost a whole day, and it had been three times that long since the boy had eaten. Still, the young mul did not think his thirst or hunger made much difference. Borys's grip was as powerful as that of a giant.

Rkard lowered his gaze. "Borys is too strong," he admitted. "I don't know how to kill him."

"That is for you to decide," said Jo'orsh. "After all, it is *your* destiny."

"His destiny?" scoffed Borys. He snorted in amusement, shooting wisps of red-glowing sand from his nostrils. "There is no such thing as destiny—except what a being chooses for himself."

"And Rkard has chosen to slay you," said Jo'orsh.

Rkard frowned. As he remembered it, he had been given no choice in the matter. The banshees had *told* him that he would kill the Dragon.

"Then perhaps I should kill the child now," hissed the Dragon. "Before he makes good on his threat."

Borys's grip tightened, and Rkard heard a crack deep inside himself. A sharp pain shot through his flank, then he could not breathe.

Jo'orsh's orange eyes grew cool and narrow. "Release the boy!"

"Give me the Dark Lens," came the reply.

"If you wish," replied the banshee.

Borys's grip relaxed, and Rkard could breathe again. The effort filled his lungs with fire, confirming that his captor had broken a rib. Taking advantage of the Dragon's preoccupation with the banshee, the young mul pulled his hand free and raised it toward the boiling sky. As he summoned the energy to heal himself, a spout of glowing red ash shot down to lick at his palm. The Dragon paid no more attention to the whirling jet than when Rkard had assailed him earlier with kicks and bites.

Borys kept his beady eyes fixed on Jo'orsh's gnarled form. "After a thousand years, you're going to give me the Dark Lens?"

"Let me have the boy," Jo'orsh answered.

Borys held Rkard out.

Jo'orsh advanced to within a few paces of the Dragon.

He glanced down at a patch of broken basalt in front of him, then stopped. From between the cracked stones shone the orange glow of a submerged lava channel, dappled here and there with flecks of green fire.

"Don't come any closer, Jo'orsh," Rkard said. He was almost ready to cast his healing spell, for his hand now glowed fiery red and smoked from the fingertips. "If you let Borys have the Dark Lens, what happens to me doesn't matter."

"Silence, child!" ordered Borys. His grip tightened around Rkard's injured ribs.

The burning embers beneath Jo'orsh's brow flared yellow, shooting a pair of fiery bolts straight into Borys's beady eyes. In the same instant, he leaped the submerged lava channel and landed face-to-face with Rkard's captor. The banshee drove the jagged nub of his bony arm into the Dragon's wrist.

The claw opened and Rkard fell free.

The young mul bounced off Borys's leathery knee and tumbled to the ground. As his mother had taught him, Rkard tucked his chin against his chest and stretched out to his full length. He landed on his uninjured side, slapping his forearm against the rough basalt to help absorb the impact.

The maneuver did him little good. From his feet to his shoulders, Rkard's body exploded into a stinging ache. He heard himself scream. The sound was choked off as pain filled his chest and the air rushed from his lungs. He could not rise, could not even shift his hand—still glowing red with the sun's healing magic—down to his broken rib.

Far above, Borys jerked his wrist off Jo'orsh's jagged stump, spraying an arc of hot yellow blood over the ground. Though the Dragon's snout and face were scorched, his dark eyes showed no hint of injury—only anger.

"Perhaps I can't destroy you, but there are those who

can," Borys hissed. He stood so close to Jo'orsh that the yellow fumes of his breath swirled over the banshee as he spoke. "The lens."

"Destroy me or not," said Jo'orsh. "The Dark Lens will remain hidden."

"Not from my lords!" Borys's hands shot up and pushed the banshee back toward the submerged lava channel. "Take him, my kaisharga!"

The basalt burst into shards around Jo'orsh's feet. Six gaunt, withered corpses rose from the lava channel, runnels of molten rock pouring off their blackened hides. A little larger than humans, they had emaciated builds and white-hot talons instead of fingers. Their shriveled faces all looked alike, with gaping dark holes where their noses should have been and eyes of green fire. In spite of their other similarities, each had one feature that set him or her apart: lacy wings of fire, smoking horns, fingernails as long and sharp as needles, huge pulsing eyes, chitinous scales of armor. One even had a mouth shaped like a trumpet.

"Jo'orsh, go away!" Rkard yelled.

"Stay!" commanded Borys, his tiny eyes fixed on the banshee. "If you leave, my servants shall have the child in your place."

Jo'orsh made no move to flee, and the dead lords began to close in around him.

"He'll kill me anyway!" Rkard cried. He forgot about his own pain and struggled to his feet. "Disappear!"

Jo'orsh shook his gnarled head. "For better or worse, my long battle is at an end," he said, keeping his orange eyes fixed on his foes. "I knew that when I freed you."

All six of the dead lords leapt at the banshee's gnarled shins and began climbing. The banshee swung his twisted arms at his attackers, knocking the armored ghoul away before they reached his knees. The remaining corpses tore at his legs, ripping away so much bone that the limbs buckled and pitched Jo'orsh backward into a sputtering stream of molten rock.

White flames began to dance over the banshee's twisted bones. He flailed at his attackers, splashing great arcs of fiery rock into the air.

The corpse Jo'orsh had knocked away earlier dived into the fiery river, then all six of the dead lords began tearing his gnarled ribs away. The banshee's eyes grew dimmer, and he sighed, expelling a cloud of golden mist.

Rkard's hand still glowed with the energy he had summoned earlier. The boy stepped toward the fiery stream, intending to cast his sun-spell. He hoped that it would distract the lords long enough for Jo'orsh to escape.

"Rkard, no!" the banshee yelled. "The time has come for you to kill the Dragon—before his minions dispel my magic and learn where the lens is."

Rkard stopped. "How?" The heat of the liquid rock was so terrible that he had to shield his face behind his arm. "Tell me what to do."

Borys stepped forward to straddle the young mul. "Yes," said the Dragon. His wounded wrist dripped beads of fiery blood all around Rkard. "We're *both* very curious."

Jo'orsh's orange eyes remained fixed on Rkard. "I can't tell you how to do it," he said. "If you can't find the answer within yourself, then Athas is lost."

The dead lords pulled away a last rib. Liquid stone poured into the banshee's chest, and the corpse with the huge pulsing eyes rode the viscous stream inside. Jo'orsh's orange eyes began to dim.

The Dragon reached down to pick Rkard up, spattering the boy with droplets of fiery yellow blood. The young mul hardly noticed, for he was concentrating too hard on what Jo'orsh had said to him. If he could find the key to slaying Borys within himself, then it seemed most likely that the banshee meant it was a matter of knowledge.

Rkard's thoughts automatically turned to the greatest source of dwarven knowledge, the *Book of the Kemalok Kings*. His favorite stories described the adventures of King Thurin, who always defeated his enemies by curing the grievous afflictions that had turned them into monsters in the first place. Afterward, the beasts always became either his devoted friends and servants, or they died peacefully, thanking him for releasing them from their eternal agony.

It struck Rkard that as a sun-cleric, his healing abilities were not so different from the way King Thurin had overcome his enemies. He wondered if that was what the banshee had been hinting at. Certainly, as one of Kemalok's ancient knights, Jo'orsh knew the stories of King Thurin as well as the young mul did.

Borys's claws closed around Rkard's body. "So how will you destroy me, child?"

Rkard laid his hand on the seething puncture in Borys's wrist. There was a brief flash as the red glow drained from the boy's hand and into Borys's scaly hide. The wound sizzled and smoked, then the drizzle of yellow fire slowly came to a stop. The hole's jagged edges stretched toward each other and met, leaving a black, smoking scar where the injury had been.

A knot of anticipation formed in Rkard's chest. His magic had sealed the wound—but had it healed the Dragon?

Borys lifted the young mul high off the ground and held him in front of a single black eye. "You are considerate, child," he chuckled. "To show my gratitude, I shall let you live to see your parents—as I kill them."

A sick, hollow feeling formed in Rkard's stomach. The boy could not imagine how he was supposed to kill the Dragon. Back in Samarah, he had used the only other spell he knew when had cast his sun beacon at Borys's head. That had worked no better than healing the beast. And during the long trip to this place, he had tried punching, gouging, biting, kicking, and every other kind of physical assault he knew. Borys had not even flinched. If there was some way for a boy his age to kill the beast, the young mul could not think of it.

Far below, Rkard saw Jo'orsh lying in the fiery stream. The last glimmer of light faded from his orange eyes. His gnarled bones began to smoke. Finally, his skeleton disintegrated in a white flash, leaving nothing behind except a few crusts of black cinder. Within moments, the slow, swirling currents of boiling rock devoured even that trace of the banshee.

The dead lords waded to shore and stepped onto the black basalt at Borys's feet. Orange beads of molten stone dripped from their bodies like sweat.

"The usurper Tithian has the Dark Lens and has joined your enemies," reported the corpse with the pulsing eyes. He was the one who had slipped inside Jo'orsh. "They want the child returned alive, but they are also determined to kill you."

The Dragon nodded. "Good. If we present them with a choice between the two, they may hesitate at a critical moment," he said. "Where will we find them?"

"Jo'orsh left them a day ago, so we cannot be certain," the lord replied. "But the banshee thought that they would be entering the Baxal Shoals by now."

"Less than a day from my valley," hissed the Dragon. His grip tightened around Rkard's chest, sending sharp pangs of agony through the boy's lungs. "It is a dangerous thing to attack them so close to Ur Draxa. If they slip away and enter the city with the lens . . ." Borys let the sentence trail off, shaking his head.

"Then what?" pressed Rkard.

"You cannot imagine, child," the Dragon said. "Even your nightmares are not that terrible."

"The Lord Mariner is lying off the shoals with his fleet," said the corpse with the smoking horns. "With good fortune, he might intercept them—"

"You would like that, wouldn't you, Lord Guardian?" spat the lord covered by chitinous armor. "After the Lord Mariner is destroyed, all his warriors—"

"The Lord Guardian is right. The Usurper and his companions must be intercepted," said Borys. "But the Baxal Shoals are a vast labyrinth. Therefore, all my lords will join in the search. The Lord Mariner will divide you among his ships as he sees fit, covering as many channels as possible." The Dragon looked at the fire-winged corpse. "You will inform the others, Lord Harbinger."

"As you wish," replied the lord, stretching his fiery wings.

"I have not dismissed you!" Borys snapped.

The Lord Harbinger froze in place. Even the flames on his wings did not waver.

"It will be difficult for you to reach the Baxal Shoals tonight," said the Dragon. "If you fail, those who find my enemies must attack during the day."

The dead lords cast uneasy glances at each other, then the Lord Guardian asked, "What of Sadira's sun-magic?"

"She'll destroy you," Borys answered calmly. "But you have only one chance to attack. If you wait for night, or pause to regroup, my enemies will escape and reach the valley in full force."

"If we are likely to lose, why have us attack, Great One?" asked the lord with the chitinous armor.

"Your success will not be measured by victory, Lord Warrior," the Dragon replied. "One of you must steal the mul's sword. The blade was forged by Rajaat, so I cannot attack whoever bears it—but you can. If you can do this one thing, I will destroy my enemies."

"In that case, perhaps we should also take King Hamanu," suggested the Lord Harbinger. "His help—"

"Will be required at the Gate of Doom—along with that of the other sorcerer-kings," interrupted Borys. "I must be ready in case you fail."

Rkard frowned, curious as to what the Lord Harbinger thought Hamanu could accomplish in the battle. From what the boy understood, sorcerer-kings could not hit someone bearing the Scourge any more than could the Dragon.

"Remember that I created you for just such a time as this," Borys said, glaring at his lords. "To survive without the sword is not to survive all."

THIRTEEN

The Spirit Lords

From his post atop the mast, Sacha cried, "Five ships!"

Though Caelum heard the warning, he kept his eyes focused straight ahead and did not rise from his knees. The sun's crimson rays were filtering through the tangled boughs rising from the shoal ahead, and the dwarf could see by the flat bottom of the orb that the red sphere would not rise completely for many more moments. He would not allow the appearance of a few ships to disturb his devotions—especially not when he had such need for the sun's favor.

"Great Beacon, shine upon my enemy, so that his weakness will glare with a scarlet radiance that even my unseeing eyes will find," intoned the dwarf.

Rikus stepped into the bow next to Caelum. "What do you make of those boats, cleric?"

Though he did not respond, Caelum saw the boats. Five of them lay dead ahead, sitting broadside in a single line. The vessels were all cutters. Their single masts billowed with gossamer sails, shaped like bat wings and not supported by any sort of yardarm. The decks bristled with catapults manned by half-decomposed corpses. The hulls were made of burnished basalt and looked far too broad to have navigated down the narrow channels that came together to form the bay.

Caelum returned his attention to the rising sun. "Kindle in me the fires of your vengeance, Mighty Punisher," he said. "Let the flames of your fury pour from my raging heart and char my enemy's flesh, melt his eyeballs, scorch his bones until they crack. I beseech you, let the inferno of my anger sear his body until it is a black and smoking cinder."

"Caelum, get up!" Rikus demanded.

Neeva came to the mul's side. "It's no use, Rikus," she said, pulling him away. "Until the sun has completely risen, my husband's devotion is to it, not us. His own child could be standing on those ships, and still he would not stand."

Caelum resisted the urge to refute his wife. Even if he had not been in the middle of his devotions, there would have been no point to it. She had not greeted the sun since Rkard's abduction, and that fact alone proved that she lacked the faith to understand the depth of the sun communion.

The dwarf continued his intonation, "Wonderful Fire of Life, watch over my absent son and do not let the flame of his spirit darken. Warm his heart, so he will know his father remembers him and searches for him with a fidelity as fervid as your light."

Rikus and Neeva left the bow, each slipping around a different side of the Dark Lens.

At the same time, Tithian called, "Pull in the boom!" The king still sat in the stern of the dhow, for he and Sadira had not yet changed places for the day. "They can't follow us down there!"

Tithian gave the tiller a shove. The dhow tilted to starboard as it changed directions, then abruptly slowed and returned to an even keel as the sail went slack.

Ahead lay a dust channel so narrow that the trees flanking it actually touched fronds over the passage. As Sadira pulled the boom in and caught the wind, the dhow tipped to starboard and started forward again. Caelum dutifully returned his gaze to the sun, scrambling around so that he could watch it over the starboard side of their little craft.

The dwarf tried to still his thoughts, to empty his mind so that it would be refilled with the dawn's radiance. In spite of his efforts, he noticed the cutters' gossamer sails twisting on their masts. He tried to forget them and focus on the sun's crimson rays. If he allowed the impending battle to impinge on his meditations, he would absorb fewer spells than normal, and they would be less powerful.

The dhow's hull began to scrape along the mud crusts ringing the shoals, adding to the difficulty of the dwarf's meditations. He began to hum a single note, as he had taught Rkard to do when the boy was learning to meditate.

At the same time, the ghostly fleet began to move forward. Caelum found himself puzzling over its path. The cutters were trying to cut them off—but their course would take the ships straight through the middle of a shoal.

As the dhow moved deeper into the channel, the fleet's gossamer sails disappeared behind the dense foliage to the dhow's starboard. Sighing in relief, Caelum concentrated on his devotions. This thicket seemed heavier than that rising from the last shoal, so the dwarf had trouble seeing the sun itself. Nevertheless, by the halo of red-tinged leaves in the center of the copse, he knew where to look. He opened himself to the orb and breathed in slow, steady whispers.

This time, the dwarf's meditations were more successful. He barely heard the shrill whistles and eerie cackles erupting from the shoals as the dhow sliced

through the narrow channel between them. Soon, he felt
the sun-mark on his forehead burning hot and red, then
the halo shining through the forest became round and
whole. A crimson flame flared over his brow, and he
knew the sun had risen.

Caelum stood and turned toward his wife. "It seems I
had time to finish my devotions, after all," he said. "For
which we'll *all* be glad when those cutters return."

"Let's hope so," she retorted.

Neeva stood with Rikus, both of them holding their
weapons in their hands and looking past him down the
channel. Behind them, Sadira fished through her robe
pocket with one ebony hand and effortlessly held the
boom line with the other. Tithian sat upon the floater's
dome, his beady eyes darting back and forth between
the shore and the Dark Lens.

The shoal suddenly fell silent. Nothing happened for
a moment, then a cloud of birds erupted from the tangled thicket. Their beating wings filled the air with a
tremendous throbbing as they passed overhead.

Caelum saw a cluster of gossamer sails approaching
through the boughs over the shoal. The diaphanous
sheets passed through the tangled fronds as though
immaterial, not disturbing so much as a leaf. In contrast
to the sails, the cutter's black prows drove through the
muddy shoal like a farmer's plow, cutting great harrows
and uprooting every plant they passed. The majestic
trees fell away almost silently, their heavy boles becom-
ing snarled in a nest of vines and boughs long before
they could crash to the ground.

Neeva and Rikus came forward. His wife hefted her
battle-axe and asked, "Well, husband, can you sink
those ships?"

Caelum raised a hand toward the sun. He waited
until his flesh glowed with a brilliant crimson light, then
pointed back at the dhow's mast. He cast his spell. A
globe of scarlet light formed around the base of the pole

and slowly rose upward. When the shining ball reached the top, Sacha shrieked, shooting off his perch as though someone had kicked him. The head fell, trailing wisps of red smoke, and struck the shoal's sun-baked beach with a hollow thump. The red sphere took his place on top of the mast and shone down on the dhow with a warm, rosy light.

"Stupid dwarf!" cursed Sacha, wobbling into the air. "You could have warned me!"

"What'd you do?" asked Rikus.

"Protected the ship from undead," Caelum replied. "Now the animated corpses on the cutters can't board us."

The dwarf had barely finished his sentence before the clack-clack of firing catapults sounded from ahead. He spun around to see a barrage of small boulders arcing toward them. Rikus and Neeva ducked. When Caelum did not instantly do the same, his wife kicked his feet from beneath him. The dwarf dropped unceremoniously into the bilge.

Most of the volley went wide. The stones crashed through the sun-crusted beaches to either side of the channel, shooting plumes of mud high into the air. Unfortunately, a number of rocks did find their target. Two boulders glanced off the Dark Lens and bounced over the gunnel. Though the impact caused no apparent damage to the lens, it drew an alarmed squeal from Tithian. Three more stones landed amidst the cargo casks, spraying chadnuts and precious water in all directions. One rock even struck Sadira in the chest. The impact drove her down on her seat, but seemed to cause her no harm. She pitched the stone over the side, then stood up again.

Caelum stuck his head up and looked over the gunnel. Two cutters had sailed into the shoal off the port bow and were turning to approach the dhow on a parallel route. The third ship was positioning itself broadside across the channel. The last two vessels remained in the starboard shoal, and were turning their bows toward the dhow. On all five cutters, the ungainly corpses were slowly cranking the catapult spoons back into firing position.

"They're trying to catch us in a crossfire," growled Rikus.

"They won't have a chance," said Sadira. "By the time they're ready to fire again, their missiles won't be able to reach us."

With that, the sorceress took Tithian's place at the tiller and cast her flying spell. The dhow rose out of the channel at such a steep angle that Caelum had to grab the gunnel to keep from sliding. The Dark Lens slipped back against the water casks, pushing them toward the stern. Sadira braced her feet against the last two barrels and held the entire load in place.

"Now, this is magic!" exclaimed Neeva.

"Magic that will betray us to the sorcerer-kings, if they're still near," Tithian complained.

"If they're that close, the battle would alert them anyway," said Rikus, peering over the gunnel. "I doubt we could sink five ships without creating a lot of smoke and thunder."

Caelum also looked over the side, feeling a little foolish for bragging about how his magic would prevent the corpses from boarding the dhow. The little craft was already as high as the treetops and rising. Far below and ahead, the corpses were still loading boulders into their catapult spoons, but the dwarf did not think the stones would come high enough to strike their craft.

As they came nearer to the cutters, Caelum noticed that not all of the corpses on the decks were decomposing. On each ship, one looked strangely preserved, with leathery skin and an emaciated body. The shriveled faces of these figures looked remarkably similar, with gaping cavities for noses and eyes of green fire. But each also had a distinctive feature setting him or her apart from the others: a pair of smoking horns, fingernails as long and sharp as needles, chitinous scales of armor, lacy wings of fire, a sharp beak instead of a mouth.

"What are those things?" Neeva asked. She pointed first at the corpse with the smoking horns, then at the one with the chitinous armor.

"They're the ship commanders—some sort of spirit lords," offered Sadira. "And I doubt they happened on us by chance. Borys probably sent them."

The one with fiery wings leaped off his ship's deck and shot up to intercept the dhow.

"There's no need to worry," Caelum said. He glanced up at the red sphere still shining down from the top of the mast, hoping his spell would prove useful after all. "He can't come into the light."

"Who's worried?" Rikus asked. "But we can't let him follow us, either. Better to kill—er, destroy—him now."

The mul gripped his sword with both hands and stepped into the bow. It was the only place on the dhow where the protective light of Caelum's spell did not extend beyond the gunnels, and so it was the only place the corpse could attack the craft itself.

The spirit lord seemed to sense this, for he streaked straight to Rikus. The mul swung. The corpse fanned his fiery wings and stopped instantly, allowing the Scourge's blade to flash harmlessly past his face.

"Stupid mul!" the spirit lord hissed. "Come with me!"

The corpse slipped to the side of the blade and clamped both hands over the mul's wrists. The lord's wings flapped furiously, trying to back away and pull Rikus from the dhow. Each time they beat forward, long tongues of flame curled off their lacy edges to lick at the mul's face and arms.

Screaming in pain, Rikus dropped down to shield himself behind the bone prow. He braced his feet against the gunnel and pulled, trying to draw his attacker into the glowing circle cast by Caelum's spell. The two foes seemed evenly matched. The mul's wrists remained poised at the perimeter of the rosy light, trembling with strain and agony. The corpse's wings beat madly, filling the air in front of the dhow with yellow whorls of flame.

Neeva ducked under the sail and stepped forward, chopping at the spirit with her axe. The steel did not bite into his flesh, but she caught the crook of the blade behind the corpse's neck. She added her strength to Rikus's and pulled, dragging their enemy across the gunnel into the rosy light of Caelum's spell.

The spirit lord howled in pain. Black tendrils of smoke spewed from his body, and his flesh fell away in flakes of black ash. Caelum could hardly believe what he was seeing. The spell was having an effect, but hardly what he had expected. The corpse had to be as powerful as a banshee. Otherwise, he would have been consumed by crimson flame as soon as he was pulled into the circle.

Caelum turned a hand toward the sun, calling for the magic to incinerate the spirit. A red glow crept over his hand, and he pointed his finger at the corpse.

Before the dwarf could cast his spell, Sadira uttered an incantation from the back of the boat. A bolt of black energy streaked past Caelum's head, striking the spirit in the center of the chest. A tremendous bang shook the dhow, nearly knocking the cleric from his feet and blasting the corpse out of the bow. A ball of ebony fire swallowed the lord, and he plunged toward the shoals below. By the time he reached the ground, all that remained of him was a cloud of ash.

Caelum sighed, feeling more useless than ever. He went to the mul's side and said, "Let me see those burns, Rikus."

The mul shook his head and started to rise. "Later," he said. "They're not serious."

Caelum laid his palm on the mul's blistered arms. "I'll

tend them now," he insisted. "If all I'm good for is healing other people's wounds, at least let me do it well."

With that, the dwarf released his healing energy. The mul hissed as the magic poured into his body. The blisters quickly subsided, leaving only a red tint to show where the mul's skin had been burned.

"Thanks," Rikus said. "That does feel better."

The clatter of catapults sounded from below. Caelum looked over the gunnel in time to see a volley of gray boulders crossing paths beneath the hull. The four ships that had fired the stones were almost directly below the dhow, one pair to each side of the silt passage. The fifth cutter lay a short distance ahead, still blocking the narrow channel between the shoals.

In spite of the catapults' obvious inability to hit the dhow, the mindless crewmen cranked the spoons down to reload. "Go ahead, try again!" Rikus yelled.

As they passed over the last cutter, a loud sizzle sounded from the ship's deck. A brilliant flash of blue streaked from its stern. There was a deafening boom, and the whole dhow bucked. The hull erupted into a spray of gray splinters. Caelum grabbed the gunnel to keep from flying out and felt his feet dangling free. Realizing the dhow had no bottom, he looked down. The cargo casks, the floater's dome, Neeva's axe, the Dark Lens, even the boat's sail and mast were arcing toward the shoals far below. Only the people remained, clinging to the gunnels for their lives.

Caelum watched the dhow's cargo fall. With the sail still attached, the mast was caught by the wind and lost its forward momentum the fastest. It landed about a hundred paces from the cutters, plunging through a shoal's mud crust and standing upright. The water casks and Neeva's axe were strewn over the crusty banks a little distance beyond, while the Dark Lens continued the farthest before plunging into the silt channel.

"No!" Tithian screamed. "The lens!"

The king released his grip and dropped away, raising a plume of dust as he followed the lens into the dust passage.

"What now?" cried Neeva.

"Turn around," answered Caelum.

The dwarf looked back toward the cutters. Already, the spirit lords were leaping off their ships. "I don't care about Tithian, but we can't lose the lens."

"Swing in low near the sail, Sadira," Rikus ordered. The mul pointed at the dhow's mast, which still had the rosy orb of the dwarf's protection spell glowing from the top. "Caelum and I'll drop off to hold them back. Then you take Neeva back to find the lens."

Sadira brought the dhow around. She swooped in so low that Caelum could have counted the cracks in the beach below. The dwarf waited until they passed into the rosy glow of his protection spell, then let go of the gunnel.

Almost before he felt himself falling, Caelum slammed into the crusty mud and felt it crack beneath the impact. He allowed his momentum to carry him forward and tumbled head over heels across the hot ground. He came to a rest on his back, staring straight up the mast at the red sphere of his spell. The mast was wobbling slightly, as if it might fall at any moment, and it was tilting toward the silt channel at a slight angle.

Caelum noticed that he felt nothing from the waist down, and feared the fall had broken something in his back. He tried to kick his legs—and nearly choked on the resulting cloud of dust.

Realizing that he had nearly rolled into the dust channel, Caelum pushed himself back. He stood, already raising a hand toward the sun, and spun around to face the spirit lords.

To his surprise, he did not see any coming after him. The only undead he saw were the decomposing corpses back at the cutters. They stood beside their catapults, staring into the air with vacant expressions and blank eyes. Caelum suspected that their spirits were magically bound to the ships, otherwise they would have been climbing over the gunnels to attack by now.

From across the narrow silt channel, Rikus yelled, "Of all the rotten luck!"

Caelum looked over and saw the mul—at least, he saw the upper half of the mul. Rikus had plunged through the sun-baked crust and was stuck up to his breast in the soft mud beneath. To make matters worse, all four of the spirit lords were rushing toward him. Already the one with the smoking horns was diving at Rikus.

Caelum pointed at the spirit and spoke a mystic command word. A brilliant ray of crimson shot from his finger, bursting into a dazzling spray of light right before the thing's eyes.

The corpse roared in anger, and beams of golden energy shot from his smoking horns. The spirit lord landed at the mul's side, shaking his head in a mad effort to clear the spots from his eyes. The rays from his horns washed over Rikus. The mul screamed in pain and brought the Scourge down across the spirit's neck, sending his ugly head skittering across the sun-baked ground.

Rikus looked back to the other three spirit lords, who were only a dozen steps away. "I can't get out of this mess." The mul drew his arm back to throw the Scourge. "Take this."

"No! Keep it!" Caelum yelled.

Not giving Rikus a chance to argue, the dwarf stepped over to the mast and tried to shove it toward the mul. The shaft was lodged more securely than it appeared and would not tip easily. Caelum continued to push. The pole slipped a little, but did not fall.

Across the channel, the three remaining spirit lords had reached the mul. They spread out around him. The

one with the chitinous armor positioned himself directly
in front of Rikus, while the corpse with the beak approached from the side on which the mul was holding
the Scourge. The last lord, a female with fingernails as
long as needles, circled around behind Rikus.

Caelum continued to push against the mast, for he
could feel it slowly tipping. At the same time, he glanced
up the silt channel to see if he could summon help.
Sadira and Neeva were several hundred paces away, flying low over the silt passage, their backs to him and
Rikus. From what the dwarf could see of their heads,
their gazes were fixed on the channel below, searching
for some sign of the Dark Lens.

Caelum started to call out, but from across the passage one of the spirit lords said, "Now, Lord Warrior!"

The dwarf looked back to see the corpse with the
chitinous armor, apparently the Lord Warrior, dart in
and level a vicious kick at Rikus's head. There was a
loud crack as the mul deflected the assault with his free
arm, then he swung the Scourge at the spirit's legs.

The Lord Warrior jumped the slash. He landed on one
foot, kicking Rikus's sword arm away with the other.
"Now you, Lord Vizier!"

The other male spirit leaped forward, clamping his
beak-shaped mouth around Rikus's wrist. With one
hand, the Lord Vizier grabbed the fist holding the
Scourge and slammed the palm of the other into the
mul's elbow. Rikus screamed but did not release his
weapon, so the corpse tried to force it free by wrenching
the mul's arm.

Caelum heard the mud crust crackle and felt the mast
tip. Growling with determination, he slammed his
shoulder into the pole and pumped his legs madly. It
tilted farther, leaning across the channel. The glowing
sphere on top cast rosy light over Rikus and the area
around him.

The Lord Warrior shrieked and retreated, as did the

female corpse. The Lord Vizier tried one last time to wrench the Scourge free. It proved a terrible mistake, for Rikus reached over and grabbed him by the back of the neck, then held him in place. The spirit lord opened his beak and screeched in pain. Wisps of black, foul-smelling smoke rose from his body. The corpse flailed his arms about wildly in a mad effort to escape.

Rikus pulled his sword across the corpse's stomach. The Lord Vizier gave a harrowing wail and clawed madly at the dry mud in an effort to drag himself away. The mul struck again, and the spirit went limp. The body smoldered for a moment, then a wave of shimmering flames reduced it to ashes.

The last two spirit lords, standing on opposite sides of Rikus, looked toward Caelum. "Can you take care of him, Lady Bliss?" asked the Lord Warrior.

"Gladly," answered the female spirit, spreading her needlelike fingers and stepping away from Rikus.

Caelum circled around to the other side of the mast, as if trying to hide. He could hear the mud crust crackling beneath its weight and knew it would fall at any moment.

Lady Bliss circled the area lit by Caelum's spell, then stopped at the edge of the silt channel. She used one finger to motion for him to come closer, and the dwarf could see droplets of murky yellow fluid dripping from the claw.

"There's nothing to fear, little man," she said, gathering herself up to jump the channel. "This won't hurt."

"This will!" Caelum countered.

Using all his dwarven strength, Caelum shoved the mast. The mud crust gave way with a sharp crack, and the top of the pole swung around. The shaft dropped straight toward Lady Bliss, catching her as she tried to leap into the air. The red globe crashed down on her shoulder. The spirit lord did not even have time to scream before her body erupted into a pillar of crimson flame.

Caelum heard the Lord Warrior curse, then say, "The sword! Give it to me!"

The dwarf did not even take the time to look across the channel. His end of the mast had sunk into the dust, but other end still lay propped on top of the opposite shoal's mud crust. He took a running start and jumped, spreading his arms wide.

Caelum dropped about halfway across. He hit the dust face first, sinking only a short distance before his chest touched the solid shaft of the mast. The dwarf closed his arms around it and pulled himself up, coughing and choking as he came out of the silt. Not even waiting until he could breathe clearly again, he crawled up onto the opposite shoal and turned toward Rikus.

Caelum found himself behind both his friend and the Lord Warrior. Having landed a glancing kick on the back of the mul's skull, the corpse was just leaping away as Rikus tried to twist around and slash at him with the Scourge.

The Lord Warrior slipped a step to the side, positioning himself for his next attack. The dwarf charged, timing his assault to arrive as the corpse stepped forward again. The spirit lord stopped directly behind Rikus. The Lord Warrior raised his leg, preparing to level a vicious thrust-kick at the base of Rikus's skull.

Certain that the blow would be fatal if it landed, Caelum yelled a warning. At the same time, he hurled himself at the Lord Warrior, taking the corpse high in the shoulder blades. The dwarf hit with a bone-jarring impact, his face pressing into the cold, hard scales that covered the corpse's back.

The Lord Warrior cried out in surprise, and the momentum of Caelum's charge carried them both over the top of Rikus's head. The corpse crashed down right in front of the mul, then the dwarf rolled away.

Rikus brought the Scourge down half a dozen times before the Lord Warrior had a chance to react. By the time Caelum returned to his feet, all that remained of the spirit were slabs of putrid flesh.

"Many thanks," Rikus said. "You just saved my life—four times over."

The mul had suffered more during his struggle against the spirit lords than Caelum had realized. His body was covered with lumps, huge purple bruises, and a dozen gashes that were starting to soften the mud around him with blood.

"I haven't saved your life yet," Caelum said. He raised a hand toward the sun and walked over to the mul's side. "The Lord Warrior's beating could take you yet."

Rikus's eyes widened. He stared up at the dwarf's glowing hand with a pained expression. "I'm too sore for that," he growled. "You don't have to heal me right now."

"Of course he does," snarled Tithian's voice.

Caelum looked over and saw the king—or rather, a creature with the king's head—crawling out of the silt channel. Tithian's body no longer looked even remotely human. It was shaped like that of a lizard, with a knobby green hide and squat, powerful legs so broad they looked more like paddles. As the strange beast emerged the rest of the way onto the shoal, the dwarf saw that it had wrapped its long tail around the considerable bulk of the Dark Lens.

The creature crawled over to them and deposited the lens at Rikus's side.

"Now be quiet and let Caelum save your miserable hide—again," Tithian said, looking toward the cutters. "I'll go make arrangements for us to continue. Perhaps we can finish our journey in a style more befitting my station."

FOURTEEN

The Gate of Doom

The ravine was a scar upon the blackened face of the plain, an ugly slash choked with jagged boulders and thick with brown vapor. Its sheer walls were capped with long mounds of loose stone, as if some immense plow had scratched a furrow from a field of solid basalt. The floor was littered with pulsing heaps of yellow stones, while tiny fissures in the cliff faces spat beads of steaming white sludge across the canyon. There was not a plant, living or dead, in the whole valley.

The ravine spilled into a vast, fiery abyss filled with molten rock. At this brink loomed a massive arch of black granite, engraved with squirming yellow runes and twice as tall as the cliffs flanking it. In the shadows beneath the arch stood the Dragon, eclipsed by the edifice and silhouetted against the orange glow rising from the chasm at his back. The claws of one hand were closed around a small, limp figure.

Though Sadira could not see it clearly from this distance, she assumed the figure to be Rkard. The sorceress had been watching for quite some time and still had not seen the boy move.

Sadira felt a hand grasp her shoulder. "It's time," Neeva whispered. "Caelum just received Tithian's thought-message. They're in position."

Sadira looked at the ravine's south wall. The cliff was only about half the height of the great arch itself, but easily tall enough so that Rikus and Tithian would be able to attack the Dragon from above. She saw no sign of the mul or the king, of course, for they would not show themselves until the battle began. Until then, they would remain hidden behind the mound of loose stones that capped the wall.

According to the plan, Neeva and Caelum would make the first move. Protected by Sadira's magic, they would go straight down the ravine. They would try to hold the Dragon's attention on themselves, so that the sorceress would have a better chance of using her powers to sneak up on him.

Sadira's task was to deprive the Dragon of his most dangerous magic. Like the sorcerer-kings, Borys could draw the life-force from men and animals. Also like the sorcerer-kings, he required the aid of obsidian globes to convert it into magical energy. But the Dragon's mighty spells required more of the dark orbs than his hands could hold, so he swallowed his globes and carried them inside his body. If Sadira could get close enough, she could shatter the obsidian in Borys's stomach, thus robbing him of his mightiest weapon.

The loss of the globes would probably also stun Borys, so Sadira would move quickly to rescue Rkard. Then, if necessary, she would return and lure the Dragon from beneath his arch by taunting him, pretending to suffer an injury, or—as a last resort—leaving herself vulnerable to a physical attack. When Borys stepped out of his cover, Rikus and Tithian would attack from above. Hopefully, the ambush would prove fatal. If it did not, the assault would lapse into an unpredictable melee, and their strategy would become, of necessity, a simple one: attack as fast and as hard as possible.

"Sadira?" asked Neeva. "Is something wrong?"

The sorceress shook her head, then followed her friend back behind the ridge they were using as a hiding place. She was sad to see that Neeva did not go to Caelum's side. Sadira had hoped that her friend would make amends with her husband before the fighting started.

The sorceress went to Neeva's side and took the warrior's axe. "Don't you think it's time to forgive your husband?" she whispered. "This will be a hard-fought battle."

"I didn't see you kiss Rikus before sending *him* off," countered the warrior, also whispering.

"That's different. Caelum did all he could to protect your son," Sadira said. "Rikus was glad to see Agis gone."

"That's not true," Neeva replied.

"He thought he'd have me to himself. I saw it in his eyes," Sadira insisted. "He's always been jealous of Agis."

"Rikus?" Neeva scoffed, shaking her head. She lowered her voice even further. "Neither of you are ones to be jealous. That's why you have him and I don't."

"As I recall, you ended that romance—for Caelum." Sadira glanced over her friend's shoulder at the dwarf. He was deep in concentration, one hand pressed to his sun-mark. "And I think you'll find you still love him, if you ask yourself how *you* would have stopped Borys."

Neeva bit her lip and looked away. "Maybe, after this is over," she said. "But all I can think of now is getting Rkard back. Fix my axe so we can get on with it."

Sadira sighed. She rubbed her ebony fingers over the weapon's steel head, speaking several incantations in a row. A dark stain spread outward from beneath her fingertips, coating the double-edged weapon with an ebony sheen as smooth and lustrous as a mirror. Tiny whirlpools of dusky light poured into one blade, while sable starbursts sparkled from the other. Even the handle turned as black as pitch.

"Remember, use the flat of the blade to deflect anything flying at you." Sadira handed the weapon back to Neeva. "When Borys tries to use his magic, point the handle at him. And above all, if you get close enough to hit him, leave the blade buried in his flesh as long as possible—"

"Unless you've changed any of the enchantments, there's no need to go over it again," interrupted Neeva. She cast a nervous glance skyward. "Night could come at any moment."

Sadira looked up and nodded. Although it had been less than three days since they had entered the valley, they had learned to be wary of their sense of time. The boiling ash storm overhead cast the same red pall over this strange land all day long, rendering it impossible to judge the hour by looking at the sky. They could not even create a sundial. The thick clouds hid the sun and prevented even a faint shadow from showing on the ground.

To make matters worse, when night fell, it would do so with no period of twilight or hint of dusk. The sky would simply change from a bright crimson to a dim scarlet, and Sadira's skin would fade from ebony to its normal hue of ivory. And, as Neeva had pointed out, that could happen soon. Morning, such as it was, had arrived much earlier that day, long before Caelum's tracking spell had led them to the Dragon.

Unfortunately, holding their assault until morning was out of the question, for Borys knew their strengths and limitations too well. If they let night fall, he would certainly attack them.

Sadira stepped aside, letting Neeva and Caelum pass. "I'm fairly certain that arch is a mystic gate, though I've no idea where it leads," she said. "So keep a watchful eye. If Borys activates it, our best chance of following him—and Rkard—will be to duplicate what he does exactly."

"What should we watch for?" Neeva asked.

Sadira shook her head. "I wish I knew. A command, or touching a hidden panel, perhaps even something as simple as stepping out the other end," she said. "I doubt that he'll try to use it until he's injured. But just in case, I'll try for your son as quickly as I can."

"Let us hope that Rkard still lives," said Caelum. "And that the hour is not too close to dark."

The dwarf led his wife into the ravine.

As the pair disappeared, Sadira slipped a nugget of dried nyssa resin into her mouth and chewed. She plucked a lash from her eyelid and, when the gum had grown soft, wrapped it inside. Pinching the resulting wad between her fingers, she whispered an incantation. Her body slowly faded from black to gray, then grew translucent and finally became completely invisible.

The clatter of shifting stones echoed up from the gorge, and Sadira knew Neeva and Caelum had begun their descent. She reached into her pocket to prepare her next spell.

*   *   *   *   *

"Did you hear that?" Rikus whispered. "It sounded like clattering stones."

The mul lay facedown on the brink of a small cliff. To one side, the precipice dropped about thirty feet to a plain of broken basalt. To the other side, a mound of loose stones rose fifty paces to a rounded crest that over-looked the Dragon's waiting place. Above the summit of the ridge, Rikus could see the top of the arch, with its snaking yellow runes, silhouetted against the crimson sky. Of course, he could not see over the hill to tell what was happening in the ravine.

"I assume Neeva and Caelum are descending," said Sacha. He was floating beyond the cliff edge, well out of the mul's reach. "Be ready."

"I am," Rikus growled. He drew his sword and peered over the cliff edge at Tithian.

Having transformed himself into something resembling a giant scorpion, the king was using the claws of his six legs to climb the cliff. The Dark Lens was pressed against his back, held securely in place by his curled tail. In place of the arachnid's claws, he had created a pair of arms as long and powerful as those of a half-giant. Only the head remained Tithian's, looking at once demented and pitiful, with his brown eyes glaring from deeply sunken sockets, his hawkish nose slimmed down to a crooked rib of cartilage, and wild shocks of gray hair sticking out at all angles.

"Remember, I'll be watching you," Rikus warned.

The king smirked up at the mul. "We're on the same side in this fight," he said. "It's time you accepted that."

Rikus looked back up the hill. "I've been stung by one scorpion already," he said. "It won't happen again."

* * * * *

Neeva sprang from one teetering boulder to another, her eyes watering and her throat burning from the caustic fumes of the ravine. Most of the brown vapors in the immediate area were swirling around her axe's head, sinking into the enchanted blade and disappearing from sight. The few wisps that escaped were enough to make her glad for Sadira's protection.

They had already traveled most of the way down the gorge. The great arch stood less than fifty paces away, at least five times as tall as a giant. A Balican schooner could have sailed through the gap between its pillars. Even the yellow runes on its face, now writhing madly, were the size of faro trees.

The Dragon continued to stand in the shadows beneath the arch, his head cocked as he watched them approach. The closer they came, the harder it became to see him clearly. The glow rising from the abyss at his back grew brighter with each step, until the glare blurred the edges of his scaly body.

Neeva had expected Borys to attack by now, but it did not disturb her that he had not. The closer he let them approach, the longer Sadira would have to position herself.

The warrior glanced at her axe head. They were all keenly aware that the Dragon ahead could be a double, like the one they had faced in Samarah. One of the enchantments Sadira had cast on the weapon was to make the blade reveal the true appearance of anything reflected in its dark sheen. The image Neeva saw was that of Borys.

"Watch yourself!" Caelum cried. "He may be attacking!"

The dwarf pointed at the top of the great arch. One of the sigils was glowing white and whirling madly. An instant later, it vanished in a bright flash.

Neeva pressed herself close to her husband's side, holding the axe between them and the arch. Before she could ask what he expected to occur, a sheet of steaming white sludge sizzled from a long fissure in the canyon wall. She thought they would be swamped, but the sheet split apart as it neared them. A huge glob struck Neeva's axe and swirled into the blade in a great whirlpool. The rest of the muck fell around them, blanketing the rocks on the ground. A harsh hissing and popping sounded from beneath the white shroud, then it quickly dissolved into brown vapor and rose up around them in a caustic cloud.

Neeva swung her axe through the choking vapors, clearing them away with a single pass of the blade. Both she and Caelum looked back to the arch immediately. To their relief, no more of the runes disappeared.

They advanced farther down the gorge, until they were close enough to see that the yellow runes in the arch's face consisted of flowing ribbons of molten stone. The bright glow behind the Dragon sent blazing daggers of pain shooting through Neeva's eyes, and blasts of fiery wind gusted up from the depths of the abyss to sear her flesh. Determined not to show her weakness, Neeva continued to advance without shielding her eyes or looking away.

A loud, spiteful voice came from beneath the arch. "Stop there, and we will speak."

The warrior and her husband obeyed, keeping a watchful eye on the yellow runes above. "What do we have to talk about?" Neeva asked.

Borys stepped to the front edge of the arch, his body now blocking most of the glare. He lowered his serpentine neck and fixed his scorching gaze on the two intruders. The spiked crest on his head stood completely upright, the barbed tips of its spines gleaming with orange light. A scorching light shone in his beady eyes, and wisps of yellow smoke fumed from his dark nostrils. The Dragon's beaklike mouth gaped open. Neeva brought her axe around, fearing he intended to spray them with his fiery breath.

Borys did not attack. "If you give me Tithian and the lens, I'll return your child and let you live," he offered. "I'll even leave Tyr alone."

Neeva looked up at his hand, far above. She could see Rkard's feet and hands protruding from between the Dragon's claws, but nothing else.

"How do I know my son's still alive?" Neeva asked.

The warrior found herself croaking the words. She did not know whether the dryness in her throat was due to her fear or the parching wind blowing in her face.

Borys poised a claw over the center of his palm,

approximately where Rkard's chest would be. "Would you like to hear him scream?"

"That won't be necessary."

Neeva glared up at the Dragon for a moment, then faced her husband as if to speak with him. As badly as she wanted to agree to the terms, she did not trust Borys any more than she would have trusted Tithian. She had no intention of revealing the lens's location, but was simply trying to buy Sadira a little more time to maneuver into position.

Caelum turned a palm upward, calling upon the sun for his spell. To Neeva's horror, a spout of glowing red ash shot down from the sky to lick at her husband's hand. The dwarf's eyes went wide, and a sound like roaring wind howled from inside the arch.

Neeva spun around, holding the flat of her blade before her. Borys had drawn himself up to full height, his bony chest puffed out with air. His snout gaped so far open that she could see a yellow glow rising from deep in his gullet.

At least we're holding his attention, Neeva thought.

The beast dropped his head and spewed a cone of white-hot sand at the warrior and her husband.

* * * * *

Rikus saw a strange spout of crimson ash whirl down from the sky, descending into the gorge just a short distance from the great arch. Then came a roaring sizzle he recognized from previous battles against the Dragon: the blast of scorching breath. Clouds of blazing hot sand billowed up around the ash. The spout quickly dissolved, drifting away in a fog of gray flakes. Borys's breath continued to roar.

Rikus looked down at the king, who was less that ten feet away, hanging from the cliff face by all six claws. "The fight's started!" the mul yelled. "Hurry up!"

Rikus jumped to his feet and started up the rugged slope. He had taken only three steps when a long chain of yellow runes squirmed off the great arch and streaked down to the mound's crest. They struck with boom after thunderous boom, and the entire summit seemed to explode into shards of basalt and plumes of acrid smoke. The mul covered his head and waited for the eruption to pass. When the choking haze thinned, he saw thirteen obsidian statues standing on top of the ridge. They had round, featureless heads with no faces, and their arms ended in fan-shaped blades.

The statues came lumbering down the slope with plunging, stiff-legged strides that sent loose rocks skittering down the hill before them. As the golems came nearer, Rikus saw a single yellow flame twinkling in the dark breast of each one.

"What's that racket?" called Tithian. He was still hanging on the cliff and could not look over the top to see the approaching golems.

"Nothing I can't handle," Rikus answered. "But watch your head. There might be some falling rocks."

Rikus drew the Scourge and waited, deciding that he could use the cliff to good advantage against the clumsy statues. The four golems in the center reached him first, slashing at his neck. The mul ducked and counterattacked, bringing his blade through the breasts of all four attackers. The enchanted steel cut through the obsidian like flesh. As the sword sliced through the yellow flame inside each golem's breast, the statues burst into shards, opening more than a dozen deep slashes along the mul's side.

Rikus hardly noticed the cuts, except as a warning to be more careful about how he destroyed the other statues. He had not suffered any crippling wounds when these golems exploded, but he might not be so lucky next time.

The mul turned and charged one flank of the golems'

line. He ducked the flailing arms of the first statue, then counterattacked with a series of vicious slashes that took the legs off both it and the next one in line. The third golem stooped over to slash at Rikus's legs, anticipating that he would duck again. The mul leaped over its head and sent it tumbling over the cliff with a stomp-kick to the back. He found himself descending straight into the thrashing blades of the fourth golem.

Rikus flipped his blade around and drove it straight down to the thing's yellow heart. It exploded as the others had, but the shards sprayed out horizontally, and the mul suffered no cuts as he came down before the last statue. This one split its attacks, one arm slicing low and the other high. Rikus leaped back and waited for the appendages to cross, then darted forward and sliced them both off at the elbows. The thing threw itself at him. Rikus grabbed a stump and sidestepped, bracing a foot against its ankle. When he pivoted, the golem's own momentum carried it over the cliff.

As it shattered on the stones below, Rikus faced the last four golems and found them forming a semicircle above him. The mul backed to the edge of the cliff and braced himself. The dark statues closed ranks and rushed, their hands slashing high, low, and through all points in between. Rikus parried for a moment, lopping off a couple of obsidian hands, then stepped back and dropped off the precipice.

As he fell, Rikus drove the tip of the Scourge down into the cliff at a steep angle, catching himself just a yard below the top. Only two golems followed him over the edge, unable to stop their advances in time to keep from falling. Still attacking as they plummeted past, one managed to open a deep gash next to the mul's spine. Then they both shattered against the rocks below.

The last two golems kneeled at the cliff's brink.

The mul thrust his free hand into a crevice and knotted his fist, twisting against the stone to jam it in place.

As the two statues above began to slash at him, he pulled the Scourge free and severed one golem's head. The thing hardly seemed to notice, thrashing at the arm Rikus had thrust into the crevice. When it could not reach, it dropped to its belly. The other golem, now excluded from the combat, returned to its feet and stepped away, where the mul could not see it.

Rikus waited until his attacker's arms spread wide, then pulled himself close and thrust the Scourge up through the brink of the cliff. The blade passed through the basalt easily, driving deep into the golem's chest. The statue exploded, though the cliff edge sheltered the mul from suffering more cuts.

When the last golem did not take this one's place, Rikus began to pull himself up. A pair of heavy steps sounded atop the precipice. A boulder slowly appeared over the brink, held between the statue's glassy arms. Cursing, the mul stretched across the cliff face and drove the Scourge deep into a knob of rock. He pulled his other hand from the crevice and swung away just as the huge rock plunged past.

The golem peered over the cliff and cocked its head at Rikus, then turned away. The mul pushed himself up and grabbed the statue's ankle. As the thing stepped away, it dragged him back onto the cliff top. Leaving the Scourge planted in the precipice, Rikus rolled into the back of the golem's legs. The thing tumbled over his body, landing flat on its back. The mul did not even stand, but simply whipped himself around and pushed it over the edge with his feet.

"Most impressive, Rikus," called Tithian. The king was just crawling onto the top of the cliff. "Aren't you glad now for all that time you trained in my gladiator pits?"

The mul clenched his teeth and reached down to pull the Scourge free. "Stop talking and start climbing," he growled. "The fight's started, and we're late."

* * * * *

Gliding silently and invisibly along the gorge wall, Sadira watched Borys's scouring breath bubble around Neeva and Caelum. He had been spewing sand at them for nearly a minute now, with no sign that he would stop soon. Thanks to the enchantment she had placed on the blade, the scalding wind caused her friends no harm. Nevertheless, the attack did keep the pair pinned close together, and the sorceress suspected that was why the Dragon continued to assault them with it.

The sorceress dove toward the battle, coming down the face of the arch, her hand vibrating with a soft hum. She knew the noise would alert the Dragon to her presence, but she did not care. By the time he cast a spell to undo the magic that made her invisible, her attack would be made. The sorceress descended past several yellow runes and slipped beneath the arch's vault. She saw her target below and dropped.

Borys continued to spew sand at Neeva and Caelum, his arrow-shaped head pushed forward and his beady eyes flashing with rancor. The sharp spines of his crest glistened under Sadira like so many spears. He was stooped slightly forward, presenting his scaly shoulders to the sorceress.

Caelum cast a spell from outside the arch, and a layer of flame appeared beneath Sadira. She lost sight of the Dragon and had to slow her dive. Then she saw a clawed hand pluck the fire from the air like a silk cloth. Borys hurled the spell back at the dwarf. Neeva caught the blazing sheet on the heft of her axe, then whipped it away. The flames blanketed the canyon wall and continued to burn.

Resuming her dive, Sadira looked into the palm in which the Dragon held Rkard. Her stomach twisted into knots, and a cold hand clutched at her heart. The young mul was still not moving, and he looked almost starved.

She could see every rib on his torso, and his stomach was distended with hunger. His skin was flushed and scaly from lack of water, and his limbs were as thin as sticks. Still, the sorceress had to bite her cheek to keep from calling out to Neeva. The boy's eyes were open, and he was touching one hand to the sun-mark on his forehead. He had survived!

As Sadira slipped past the Dragon's bony shoulder, the beast abruptly closed his mouth. He cocked his ear toward her and a knowing gleam flashed in his eyes. The first syllables of an incantation began to slip from his leathery lips.

The sorceress reached Borys's midsection and slapped her hand against his belly. She spoke the command word of her spell. She immediately turned visible, for she did not possess the psionic talents to keep herself hidden after making an attack. A deep hum throbbed through Borys's abdomen, then the tintinnabulation of shattering glass erupted from inside his stomach.

The Dragon roared in pain. He struggled to finish the incantation he had begun a moment earlier, but only managed to belch forth a cloud of black dust—all that remained of the obsidian globes that had been stored in his stomach.

Sadira swung up toward the hand holding Rkard. Far below, Neeva and Caelum charged the arch, yelling and screaming madly. The sorceress streaked past Borys's wrist and swept low over his palm. She reached down and snagged Rkard, gathering him up into her arms—and felt four sharp claws close around her body.

"Caught you, stupid woman," the Dragon chortled. He jerked her out of the air and closed his fist, bearing down with indescribable force. "I knew you'd come for the child."

Sadira wrapped herself around Rkard, protecting the boy from the awful pressure. At the same time, she kicked at the Dragon's gnarled fingers, trying to break one or force them open. It was no use. The sorceress might have been imbued with the power of the sun, but the Dragon was infused with a magical force just as strong.

Borys met the charge of Rkard's parents at the front of the arch. He casually kicked Neeva aside, sending her tumbling across the broken ground, then stomped at Caelum with his other foot. The dwarf saved himself by diving away.

Sadira tried to look toward the top of the cliffs, wondering if Rikus and Tithian could see what was happening. The effort was futile. She could peer between Borys's scaly fingers and see most of what was happening on the ground, but it was impossible to twist around to look up.

"Sadira! You shouldn't have come for me," said Rkard. He was so hoarse that the sorceress could barely understand him.

"Of course I should have," the sorceress replied, her voice strained. It was all she could do to keep her arms extended and her body curled over Rkard so the Dragon's fist would not crush the boy. "You're going to kill Borys."

"I don't think so," Rkard said. "Jo'orsh said something that—"

The Dragon bore down harder.

"Not now, Rkard," Sadira groaned. She tensed every muscle in her body, struggling to keep herself and the boy from being crushed.

Borys stepped from beneath the arch and peered down at Caelum, who was struggling to return to his feet. Sadira took a deep breath, expecting Rikus's war cry to ring off the gorge walls as he and Tithian leapt down from above.

The only thing she heard was Borys chuckling. The Dragon fixed one beady eye on Caelum. From the intensity of his gaze, she guessed that he was about to use the

Way against the dwarf.

"No!" The sorceress started to reach for a spell component, but had to stop when she nearly collapsed on top of Rkard.

To Sadira's surprise, the rugged image of a human man suddenly flashed into the shadowy corridors of her mind. He had blocky features, with a shaven head, round ears, and a long beard with no mustache. His eyes were beady and full of hatred, much as the Dragon's, and he was dressed in a full suit of gleaming plate armor.

At first, Sadira was perplexed about what she was seeing. Then she realized that Borys was attacking with the Way.

The knight pulled a sword and walked until he reached a door of polished ebony, which he kicked open. The doorway opened into a gloomy room with a high, vaulted ceiling. The walls were lined by benches and draped with richly colored tapestries depicting the bearded dwarves of old. In the center of the chamber, a ball of crimson fire hovered over a circle of white marble.

Sadira was confused. She had no memories of such a room. It almost seemed as though she were looking into Caelum's mind.

The warrior crossed to the circle and paused before the blazing globe. "I should have finished my job and cleansed the world of every filthy dwarf when I had the chance."

A few tendrils of flame lashed out and washed over the knight's armor. He simply laughed and raised his sword, then began to chop away great pieces of the burning sphere.

In the ravine, Caelum began to scream, leaving no doubt in Sadira's mind about what she was seeing. The Dragon's mental attack was so powerful that it had penetrated her thoughts, carrying a part of her consciousness into the victim's mind.

"What's happening?" Rkard demanded.

Sadira covered the boy's eyes. "Don't look."

Caelum fell silent, then his body erupted into a spray of blood and flesh. It collapsed to the ground in a dozen neatly sliced pieces. Borys snickered, then turned around and stepped back toward the arch.

Sadira heard Neeva yell. The sorceress shifted her gaze between another pair of fingers and saw Rkard's mother burying the sparkling edge of her axe into Borys's leathery calf. The blade bit deep, and the Dragon's leg began to jerk with rhythmic convulsions.

The spasms brought a feeling of satisfaction and hope to Sadira. She knew that with each contraction, the enchantment she had placed on Neeva's axe was pumping another bolt of mystic energy into Borys's leg. The resulting explosions were not powerful enough to kill the Dragon, but they would certainly serve to slow him down for Rikus and Tithian.

Apparently Borys had no interest in waiting for the pair to arrive. Growling in pain, he limped back beneath his arch without taking the time to remove either the axe or Neeva from his leg. As the Dragon passed between the pillars, he uttered a long series of words in a language Sadira didn't understand.

A loud crackle echoed off the walls of the arch, then a brilliant flash of orange light forced Sadira to close her eyes. She felt Borys step forward, then the mordant stench of boiling rock burned her nose and throat. Her stomach grew queasy, and she suddenly felt as light as a cloud.

"Rikus!" she yelled. "Where are you?"

FIFTEEN

The Broken Plain

Tithian scurried up the slope with just the proper amount of urgency, joining Rikus on the hill's crest. From this high vantage, the king could see that the abyss beyond the arch was filled with a sea of lava. In some places, it bubbled and shot viscous geysers high into the air, and in others torpid whirlpools slowly sank into unseen sinkholes. Scattered spires of scorched stone rose out of the molten expanse, while the black ribbon of a cliff barely showed on the far side of the vast pool.

The king saw no sign of Ur Draxa, the secret city-prison wherein Rajaat was confined. Still, he felt certain that they were not far away from it, for the great arch and its yellow runes had been created to protect something—and the king did not think it was a sea of molten stone. Soon, he would free the ancient master of sorcery and receive his reward: the powers of an immortal sorcerer-king.

But first, Tithian had the Dragon—and a few former slaves—to kill. The king peered over the cliff and discovered that the ravine below was empty. The blood was still draining from the assorted pieces of what the king assumed had once been Caelum.

In a concerned voice, Tithian asked, "Where is everyone?"

As he spoke, the king searched the broken floor of the valley for some sign of Neeva's body. He saw nothing but a few pulsing heaps of stone and the arch, its face still covered with writhing yellow runes.

"They're gone!" Rikus pointed the tip of his sword at the arch. "The Dragon stepped through there with Sadira just as I reached the top of the hill."

"And Neeva?" the king asked.

"Clinging to Borys's leg," the mul reported. "Her axe was buried nice and deep."

Tithian cursed silently. It would have been better if both Caelum and his wife were already dead. Now, Neeva would be one more person trying to kill him after Borys died. Still, the king was not overly concerned. In the weeks since he had stolen the Dark Lens, he had noticed that the higher the sun was in the sky, the more searing the surface of the lens. Judging by the orb's relatively bearable temperature at the moment, the king knew the sun was about to set—taking with it Sadira's powers. If he could time things so that they finished the Dragon just after nightfall, the sorceress would not be a challenge. That would leave only Rikus and his sword to worry about.

Rikus's hand flashed out, grabbing Tithian's long hair. "Bring them back," he ordered.

"I can't do that—"

"Then I have no reason to keep you alive." The mul pressed the Scourge's tip to the chitinous collar connecting the king's head and his scorpion's body.

"Let me finish," Tithian hissed. He was very careful to keep his tail motionless. "Perhaps we can still save them."

"How?" the mul demanded.

"We can follow," Tithian replied, gesturing toward the arch. "And we can do it quickly, if you'll let me fly us down to the arch."

Rikus released Tithian's hair. "We've got little enough to lose," he said. "Do it."

* * * * *

The Dragon's foot returned to the ground, and Neeva felt the chasm's incredible heat at her back. Still clinging to the axe handle, she blinked several times. A wasteland of black scoria sloped gently away before her. It was laced with jagged fissures and twisted ribs of rock, and it appeared more windswept and bleak than any terrain she had ever seen. The plain ended in the far-off distance, where a sheer cliff rose straight into the boiling red clouds of the sky.

In a step, Borys had crossed the sea of molten rock.

The Dragon limped from beneath an arch identical to the one they had departed a moment earlier, then growled in pain. Knowing what would come next, Neeva braced her feet and pulled her axe free. She dropped to the ground just as Borys's claw slapped the place where she had been hanging.

The warrior swung her axe. The sparkling edge bit deep, then began pumping bolts of mystic energy into Borys's wrist. The Dragon's hand swelled to twice its normal size and blew apart, pelting Neeva with beads of fiery yellow blood and bits of bone.

Borys's howl shook the ground.

Neeva dove away. She rolled across her shoulders and came up facing the Dragon's flank, her axe still in her hands. Ignoring the agony of her many burns, the warrior charged, aiming her blade at the leg she had mangled before.

Borys pivoted away. Neeva found herself crossing the open plain without protection. The Dragon fixed an eye on her, and white blazing pain filled her head.

"No!" She used her last act of free will to hurl the axe at him.

Borys's eye widened, and he shifted his gaze to the weapon. The axe tumbled through the air end over end, flying straight toward his abdomen. He brought his good hand—the hand holding her son and Sadira—down to block. The blade sliced across his forearm and bounced toward the arch, drawing a whirling spout of yellow blood after it.

The Dragon's claw sprang open, allowing Sadira's legs to dangle free. Before the sorceress could fall out, Borys flipped his hand palm-up. Neeva saw her son peering out from beneath Sadira's sheltering form.

Borys's fingers twitched but did not close. He glanced down at them, curling the lip of his long snout into a snarl. His claws trembled some more, and Neeva knew her blade had severed a tendon.

"Sadira, get Rkard out of there!" the warrior yelled. When she saw that the sorceress was already reaching for a pocket, Neeva sprinted toward her axe.

Borys cut her off with a single step. "I promised your cur of a child that he would see you die."

The Dragon fixed his eye on Neeva. Again, a terrible pain filled her head as he forced his way into her mind. She continued to run—then a crimson glow lit the field. It was bright enough to cast shadows on the ground, and she knew that Rkard had cast his sun-spell. The agony in her head vanished. She looked up to see Borys's head swaddled in a globe of red light.

Sadira pointed up at the Dragon's face. A bolt of blue energy crackled from her finger, blasting away a large chunk of hide. Then the sorceress gathered Rkard up and leaped into the air. Borys recovered quickly, lashing out at the flying escapees with both maimed hands.

Taking advantage of the distraction, Neeva darted between the Dragon's legs. He lifted his injured leg to stomp her. She dove for her axe, and saw the shadow of a huge foot falling around her. Her face and chest scraped across the rough stone, then the warrior's hands closed around the handle of her weapon. Borys's heavy heel settled across her back. A sickening crack sounded down near her waist, sending a searing wave of agony through her hips.

Neeva screamed and tried to pull herself from beneath the beast's foot, but her legs would not come free. Her toes went cold, then an icy tide of numbness rose through her feet, up past her knees, and spread into her hips. To the warrior, it felt as if her legs had vanished. Her own flesh and bone seemed as remote as the stone upon which she lay.

Growling in anger, Neeva used one hand to swing her axe over her back. She managed only to strain her shoulder and strike a weak, glancing blow. The weapon slipped from her grip and fell to the ground beside her.

Borys stepped away without reacting.

Neeva rolled herself over and tried to sit up. The muscles of her legs and hips would not help her do even that much. She picked up her axe and braced the handle against the ground. As the warrior pushed herself up, the ebony stain suddenly drained from the weapon's blade. The bone hilt faded from black to its natural ivory color, and the light falling over the plain dimmed from angry crimson to murky scarlet.

Neeva heard her son cry out in surprise, then Sadira cursed in anger. The warrior looked across the plain and saw the pair crashing to the ground from a low height. Their limp forms went tumbling across the broken plain. His head still encased in the fiery globe of Rkard's sun-spell, the Dragon turned toward them and watched as the pair came to a stop.

"Get up!" Neeva yelled.

Rkard jumped to his feet and rushed to the sorceress's side. He started to pull her up, but Sadira stood and pushed him behind her. When she turned to face the Dragon, Neeva saw that the sorceress's skin was as white as alabaster.

* * * * *

Rikus and Tithian stepped between the pillars of the great arch, Sacha floating a few steps behind. The edifice looked as though it had been shaped from a single block of stone, for if there were any seams in the construction, they were not visible in the polished face of the black granite. They walked farther down the passage. Rikus counted thirteen empty alcoves lining the interior walls, the same number as the golems he had destroyed. They reached the back of the arch and peered into the fiery sea.

"When did Borys vanish?" Tithian asked. "As he passed beneath the front of the arch, or as he stepped out the back?"

"On the front side," Rikus replied. "A sheet of orange fire covered the opening, and he stepped through it."

Tithian cursed. "He must have touched something, or spoken a word."

"He growled for a second or two," Rikus replied. "That's all."

"That's it!" the king said, growing excited. "The arch must be controlled by a command word. Repeat it exactly."

"If I could sing like a lirr," the mul replied, growing annoyed with the king. "My throat's not built for sounds like that."

"You must—or your friends are doomed," Tithian said. He motioned across the molten sea, then raised the leathery wings he had grown to lower them from the top of the hill. "It'll take hours—maybe days—to fly across that."

"Use the Way to transport us." Rikus raised the

Scourge menacingly.

Tithian shook his head. "I'd have to know what our destination looks like," he said. "We don't even know for sure that we want to emerge directly opposite this point."

"Are you blind?" sneered Sacha. "That must be some kind of signal over there."

Rikus peered closer and saw a crimson dot shining on the edge of the cliff. It was so tiny and faint that he could hardly separate it from the orange glow rising from the molten rock in the abyss, and for a moment he feared he was imagining it. Then he noticed that despite the speck's tendency to shift positions in the rippling heat waves of the lava sea, its brightness remained markedly steadily.

"I see it." Rikus pointed the Scourge at the dot. "That's Rkard's sun-spell."

Tithian shook his head. "It doesn't matter if I know where they are," he said. "Unless I can visualize the place itself, I can't take us there."

"You incompetent!" snarled Sacha. "Must I do everything myself?"

"You couldn't teleport us across a door threshold, much less that." The king gestured at the boiling sea with one of his half-giant's arms.

Sacha ignored him, drifting around in front of Rikus. "I assume the boy's spell is bright enough to cast a shadow?" When the mul nodded, the head swiveled around to look at Tithian. "If you can do as well as a six-year-old mul, then I can get us to the other side."

Raising his brow, Tithian closed his eyes to concentrate—then a tremendous blast sent him skidding toward the brink of the precipice. He scratched at the ground with all six claws, barely saving himself from sailing into the sea of molten rock.

The king managed to back two steps away from the edge, then a shaft of golden light flashed behind him.

His tail and wings disintegrated into a hundred tiny bits. The Dark Lens rolled off his back and dropped to the ground. As soon as he lost contact with the lens, Tithian howled in pain and began the change back to human form. His carapace shrank into a pair of shoulder blades, while the stump of his bleeding tail retracted to become a tailbone and his shredded wings folded down to form the flanks of his torso.

Rikus grabbed Tithian and hurled him toward the lens. Paying little attention to where the king landed, he whirled around to face the front of the arch. At the entrance stood two figures: a silky-haired woman with dark skin and a fang-filled mouth, and an imposing, androgynous figure that resembled a miniature version of the Dragon. Both of their gazes were fixed on Tithian, and it seemed likely to the mul that they were responsible for the spells that had nearly destroyed the king.

Rikus assumed the woman to be Lalali-Puy, the Oba of Gulg, since Sadira had killed the only other sorcerer-queen on Athas. He did not know the identity of the dragonlike figure.

The mul started forward to meet them. Three yellow runes streaked down from the face of the arch and exploded on the ground, spraying rock and dust high into the air. When the haze cleared, three more figures stood outside the edifice: a remotely avian man with a scaly, beak-shaped muzzle and recessed earslits; another man with a muscle-knotted body and a fringe of chalky hair; and a tall figure with the slit pupils, heavy nose, and thick mane of a lion.

Recognizing this last figure from the war with Urik, Rikus gasped, "Hamanu!"

The sorcerer-kings ignored the mul, but the bird-featured man at Hamanu's side said, "Perhaps I should not have doubted this plan of Borys's. It seems to be working well enough."

"Divide and conquer," responded the chalky-haired

sorcerer-king. "When will you learn, Tec?"

"Andropinis, you will address me by my full name," Tec hissed. "I am King Tectuk—"

"Your name is too long," Hamanu interrupted. "We have more important things to do."

With that, Hamanu walked beneath the arch.

Tithian shoved Rikus forward to meet him. "Go on," the king said. "With the Scourge, they can't touch you."

Though Sadira had told him the same thing before, Rikus frowned as he advanced. "Something's wrong with that theory," he said. "I fought Hamanu in the war with Urik. He struck me then—in fact he almost killed me."

Hamanu chuckled. "This time, I won't fail."

The sorcerer-king leaped at the mul. Knowing better than to meet the charge head-on, Rikus threw himself to the ground and rolled. He passed beneath his foe and slashed up at the belly. A blue aura flashed around Hamanu's body as the Scourge sliced through the magic defense, but that was as far as it sank. As it had nearly a decade ago in Urik, the blade simply stopped cutting when it hit the sorcerer-king's flesh.

Rikus rolled once more, then brought his legs around beneath him. As he returned to his feet, he slashed at the sorcerer-king's waist. Again, Hamanu's aura flashed, and the blade clanged off his flesh without biting. The mul did not even see his foe's counterstrike. He merely felt the sorcerer-king's heel smash into his chest, then found himself sailing toward the front of the arch.

Rikus landed on his back, gasping for breath. Throwing his legs over his head, he rolled on his shoulder and glimpsed the other four sorcerers close by. He sprang to his feet and spun, slashing at the androgynous figure that resembled the Dragon.

A golden aura flared around the sorcerer-king's body, and green sparks sputtered high into the air. The Scourge bit deep into the figure's withered shoulder.

The gaunt arm dropped to the ground, sickly brown blood spewing from the wound.

The figure howled in pain and lashed out at Rikus. The mul experienced an instant of blackness, then found himself standing back at Tithian's side. The king had assumed the form of a human-headed viper, with his giant tail wrapped around the Dark Lens. Along his spine were several nasty burns, where he had used the lens's heat to cauterize the wounds he had suffered from the first attack. Tithian and Hamanu had locked gazes, and appeared to be engaged in a battle of the Way.

Rikus felt more relieved than disoriented by his sudden change of location. This was not the first time the blade had moved him. Once before, when he had helped Sadira chase the Dragon away from the village of Kled, it had simply transported him out of harm's way whenever Borys struck.

"Hamanu!" screamed the wounded sorcerer-king, raising the stump of his arm. "This is your fault!"

The distraction did not seem to affect the battle between Hamanu and Tithian. Both men remained motionless, staring into each other's eyes.

Sacha appeared at Rikus's side, gripping Tithian's slender dagger between his teeth. The head dropped the weapon into Rikus's hand.

"Hamanu wasn't one of the original champions," Sacha whispered. "Rajaat created him to kill the idiot Troll Scorcher, Myron of Yoram, so the Scourge's magic works backward against him. The blade won't injure him, and while you're holding it you can't defend yourself against his blows. Use plain steel against him."

Rikus glanced back at Hamanu. The sorcerer-king remained locked in mental combat with Tithian. His contorted face showed the strain of the long battle, with flaring nostrils and beads of cloudy red sweat pouring off his leonine brow.

The mul slipped the dagger into his belt and started

forward. As he advanced, he kept a careful watch on his enemies and held his sword directly in front of him.

The injured sorcerer-king moved back. Rikus guessed that he was Nibenay, since that was the only sorcerer-king's name the mul had not yet connected to a face.

The other three sorcerers hissed spell incantations. Rikus cringed, uncertain as to whether the sword would protect him from their magic. A black shield appeared on Andropinis's arm, while a cylinder of golden light rose up around the Oba of Gulg. King Tec's flesh turned to bronze.

"What's wrong with you?" Sacha screeched, catching up with the mul. "Attack Hamanu."

"No. It makes more sense for me to attack the others," the mul said. "They can't injure me, and Tithian has Hamanu under control."

"Idiot! That's what they want!" Sacha hovered close to Rikus's head and hissed the words into his ear. "Why do you think they're waiting instead of helping Hamanu? They're trying to waste your time while Borys deals with Sadira. Then, after you're tired from fighting the sorcerer-kings, the Dragon will come back and finish what they started."

Rikus stopped and turned sideways, so he could see both into the ravine and back toward the chasm. He was near the front of the arch, less than a dozen paces from the sorcerer-kings.

"This isn't working," growled the Oba. "We'll have to kill the Usurper!"

She locked her eyes on Tithian, as did King Tec and Nibenay. Andropinis stepped to the front of the arch, positioning his black shield between Rikus and his fellow sorcerer-kings.

Tithian groaned, then his tail slackened and began to come untwined from around the Dark Lens. Blood trickled from his nostrils and ears, and his eyes bulged from their sockets. His jaw began to quiver, and Rikus knew that even with the Dark Lens, the king of Tyr was no match for the sorcerer-kings.

Shifting the Scourge away from his throwing hand, Rikus drew the dagger Sacha had given him and hurled it at Hamanu. The blade sailed straight for the sorcerer-king's back, and it looked like it would be a clean kill. Behind the mul, Andropinis spoke the syllable of a mystic incantation.

Rikus spun and leaped, slashing his sword at the sorcerer-king's rising hand. Reacting impossibly fast, Andropinis brought his shield up to intercept the blow. The Scourge hit without so much as a thud and stopped cold.

Andropinis's spell misfired, and a silent burst of silver light flashed between the sorcerer-king and Rikus. The mul felt a tremendous force pushing on his chest, not so much an impact as overwhelming pressure, and his feet left the ground. He sailed a dozen paces through the air before he crashed down, rolling head over heels and coming to a rest at Hamanu's side.

To Rikus's amazement, the sorcerer-king still stood, even with the dagger planted deep in his back. His teeth were clenched in pain, and sweat soaked his entire body, but the injury had not forced him to break off the combat with the Tyrian king. In contrast, Tithian looked ready to collapse, with tears of blood running from his bulging eyes and his serpentine tail barely contacting with the Dark Lens.

Rikus glanced toward the front of the arch and saw that Andropinis's misfired spell had hurled him into the Oba. They were both picking themselves off the ground. The other two sorcerer-kings were still helping Hamanu, their gazes locked on Tithian's face.

Leaving the Scourge on the ground, Rikus leaped up and reached for the dagger in Hamanu's back. Without looking away from Tithian, the sorcerer-king lashed out. The attack was as fast as a viper strike, but at least this time Rikus saw it coming. He twisted sideways, trying to slip past the blow, and felt a hard fist skip along his jaw. Normally, the mul would hardly have noticed a glancing blow, but Hamanu's strike snapped his head around.

Rikus spun with the impact, turning around in a complete circle. He stopped directly behind his foe and grabbed the dagger, pushing it in to the hilt. When the sorcerer-king still did not fall, he twisted the blade and forced it upwards, driving toward the heart. Hamanu screamed and stumbled back, as if Tithian were driving him away.

A kes'trekel came streaking out of the Dark Lens, its curled talons and hooked beak poised to strike. The giant raptor seemed as real as any Rikus had ever seen—which surprised him. The mul was not a complete stranger to the Way, and he knew that battles between mindbenders were fought inside their minds.

When the bird hit, any doubts about its reality vanished. The kes'trekel's talons sank deep into Hamanu's shoulders, bowling him over. The mul released his hold on the dagger, then watched the great bird carry the sorcerer-king's screaming form toward the front of the arch.

As he realized what he was seeing, Rikus did not know whether to rejoice or be sick. With the Dark Lens, Tithian could create physical versions of his mental constructs. While that ability was proving useful now, the mul knew that when the time came to kill the king, it would be every bit as dangerous to him and his friends as it was to the sorcerer-kings.

Rikus rolled across the ground and grabbed the Scourge, then returned to his feet in time to see the kes'trekel hurl itself into the midst of the sorcerer-kings. The mul started forward, knowing he did not have long to attack before his enemies recovered.

"No, Rikus, wait!" Sacha ordered. Then, to Tithian,

the head said, "Give me a light!"

As the king uttered an incantation, Rikus watched the sorcerer-kings counterattack the kes'trekel. They made short work of the raptor, reducing it to a cloud of feathers in an instant.

A bright white light flared behind the mul, causing him to cast a dark shadow. A pair of burning blue eyes and a gashlike mouth appeared in the silhouette's head. The limbs began to thicken, and the figure peeled itself off the ground.

Sacha had summoned a shadow giant.

At the other end of the arch, Andropinis cursed. He and the other sorcerer-kings started forward, yelling incantations and gesturing madly. The shadow giant turned and spewed a black mist in their direction. The passage filled with a thick, impenetrable fog. The vapor quickly rolled back to engulf the mul and his companions in its bone-chilling murk.

"How am I supposed to f-fight in this?" Rikus demanded. His teeth were already chattering, and his flesh was growing numb from the cold.

"You won't have to," Sacha answered. "The sorcerer-kings know better than to enter the Black."

Rikus saw a pair of blue eyes drifting toward him, then he felt an icy hand close over his wrist.

* * * * *

The Dragon turned his remaining hand toward the ground. Sadira saw the telltale shimmer of magic rising into the palm. With both hands injured, she could not imagine he intended to cast a spell, any more than she could imagine where the energy was coming from. The obsidian globes in his stomach were shattered, so the sorceress knew he could not be drawing the power from any animals that might be lurking in this wasteland. That meant Borys was drawing the energy from foliage.

Sadira did not see so much as a blade of grass anywhere on the desolate plain, but she knew there had to
be plants somewhere. She turned her own palm toward
the ground and began to draw. Even when the sun was
down she was a powerful sorceress and could rely on
the normal energy sources to cast her spells.

It took a moment, then she felt the familiar tingle of
magic rising through her arm. The energy seemed to be
coming from the cliffs at the edge of the plain. She
would have to be careful not to draw too much power
too rapidly, for fear of robbing all the life-force from the
unseen plants and destroying them.

Before the sorceress's eyes, the gash on Borys's forearm slowly began to seal itself.

"We'll never kill Borys if he can heal himself!" Rkard
exclaimed. The boy stood at her side, staring in horror at
the Dragon's closing wounds.

"We'll find a way," Sadira replied, infusing her voice
with more confidence than she felt.

The sorceress closed her hand to the flow of energy
and pulled a small piece of brown tuber from her
pocket. Keeping one eye on the Dragon, the sorceress
uttered an incantation over the root, then held it out to
Rkard.

"Eat this. It'll make you so fast Borys won't catch
you." As Sadira spoke, she saw the fingers on Borys's
useless hand begin to wiggle.

The boy refused to take the root. "You should eat it,"
he said. "I tried to tell you before—I'm not supposed to
kill the Dragon."

Sadira frowned. "What are you saying? Of course you
are."

Rkard shook his head. "Jo'orsh told Borys that *I*
decided to kill the Dragon," the boy explained. "But
that's wrong. When he and Sa'ram came to Agis's
house, I asked them why they were giving me the Belt of
Rank and King Rkard's crown. They said it was because

I was going to kill the Dragon—so I thought—"

"They were telling you it's your destiny," Sadira interrupted.

Rkard did not answer right away, and the sorceress watched the fingers of Borys's hand close into a fist. She thought he might come after them then, but the Dragon summoned more energy and did not move. Apparently, he intended to leave them no weaknesses to exploit when he attacked.

After a moment, Rkard said quietly, "Borys told Jo'orsh there's no such thing as destiny. I didn't believe him at first, but then Jo'orsh said people choose their destinies." He paused, then added, "Only, I never chose mine."

"Then how come he and Sa'ram gave you the belt and crown?"

Rkard shook his head. "I don't know," the boy replied. "And I'm not sure how they got them in the first place. The belt and the crown were stolen from our treasuries when the slavers raided Kled."

"Tithian!" the sorceress hissed. For some reason, the king had made up the whole story about Rkard being destined to kill the Dragon—and used the belt and crown to convince the banshees that it was true. "I'll kill him!"

"Only if you kill Borys first," Rkard answered. "So eat the root yourself."

"No, I want you safe."

"You can't make me safe," answered the boy. "Besides, Borys isn't as worried about me. He'll come after you first."

The Dragon was still drawing energy from the ground. The wound on his leg had already healed, and the nub of a hand had appeared on the stump of his severed wrist.

"Go see what you can do for your mother," Sadira said.

The sorceress put the root in her mouth and fixed her eye on the crimson globe encasing Borys's head. Given that Rkard's spell had prevented the Dragon from using the Way, she suspected that he would dispel it when he recovered the full use of his hands. Sadira turned her palm toward the ground, wondering if the beast would find it any easier to use his mental powers from inside a sphere of darkness.

*   *   *   *   *

It seemed to Rikus they had been floating in the Black forever, the shadow giant's icy fingers entwined around their wrists and icy strands of gossamer filament brushing across their faces. The mul ached to the bones with cold, and only the vibrations of his constant shivering kept the ice crystals from completely encasing his body. Save for the red shimmer of the Dark Lens, glimmering a short distance to his side, Rikus could see nothing.

"It's t-taking t-too long," Rikus said, hardly able to speak because his teeth were chattering so badly.

"In the Black, time has little meaning," the shadow giant replied. Earlier, he had introduced himself as Khidar. "But I will deliver you to the other side in a matter of instants in your time—provided Sacha was not mistaken about the light. Normally, we cannot approach Ur Draxa because there are no shadows in this land."

"A few instants is still too long," the mul worried. "If the sorcerer-kings know the arch's password—"

"That knowledge will do them no good," replied Khidar. "My people will keep the arch filled with the Black until you have killed Borys. If the sorcerer-kings step into it, they will never leave."

Rikus still wasn't convinced. "They have powerful magic," he said.

"Which they will eventually use to dispel the fog in the arch's passage," Khidar replied. "But even for them, the shadow people are not easy to battle, and they were not prepared to meet us. You may believe me when I say that by the time they follow, your battle with the Dragon will be won—or lost."

A crimson globe appeared in the darkness ahead, partially obscured by a thick wisp of blackness that reminded Rikus of a sand streamer blowing across the face of a moon.

"Now you must be quiet," Khidar urged. "That's our destination."

As they drifted closer, the wisp of blackness grew thicker and more substantial, until it resembled a pair of gnarled tree boles rising up to meet high above ground. Only after studying the image for another moment did Rikus identify the dark band as a pair of huge legs. Khidar was bringing them up directly beneath Borys.

In the next instant, Rikus emerged from the Dragon's shadow and found his head protruding above a vast plain of broken scoria. As his eyes adjusted to the red light of Rkard's sun-spell, he reached up with sword in hand and braced his arms on the ground. He started to pull himself up, leading the way out of the Black.

The mul made it as far as his waist before Borys's voice cried an incantation. The red light of Rkard's sun-spell abruptly vanished, and a terrible, crushing agony gripped Rikus's hips as he found himself clamped in solid stone.

Biting back the urge to scream, Rikus looked around and saw no shadows anywhere. Below the ground, he could feel Tithian tugging at his cold-numbed legs.

The mul raised his sword and stretched toward Borys's foot, but held his blow when he heard Sadira's voice behind him. Rikus looked over his shoulder. He saw a black sphere leave her hand and shoot up toward Borys's head.

The mul cursed silently, then stretched out to slash at the back of the Dragon's ankle. The blade struck with a mighty clang, spraying blue sparks in all directions, then red smoke and yellow blood poured from the wound.

Borys howled and stumbled away, his head engulfed in a sphere of darkness. He turned a palm downward, then Rikus felt an eerie tingle as magical energy sizzled through the ground around him.

Sadira made her second attack, firing a storm of flaming blue ice at the Dragon. The pellets scoured long, smoking scars into his thick hide, but did not penetrate. Borys growled in frustration and dodged, apparently expecting another attack and fearing that it would have more effect.

"Over here, Sadira!" Rikus called, waving his sword in the air.

"Rikus!"

The sorceress rushed toward him. She moved with incredible swiftness and was at his side in an instant, reaching into her robe for a spell component.

"Where have you been?" The words came so fast Rikus could hardly understand her.

"That's not as important as where I am now—trapped halfway in the Black!" the mul growled. "We need a light."

Fifty paces away, Borys uttered an incantation and touched his hand to his head. The sphere of darkness evaporated instantly.

"Light, Sadira!" Rikus urged. "Now!"

Sadira spoke a mystic syllable and touched the Scourge. A brilliant glow flared on the blade, casting a long shadow behind Rikus. He felt his waist come free. Before the mul could pull himself out of the ground, a pair of arms shot out of the Black and grabbed the rocky plain. Rikus felt Tithian's shoulders pushing him up from beneath, then the mul was free of the cold murk.

Rikus stood and held his sword steady. Tithian's head and torso emerged from the mul's shadow. Sacha came with him, cleaving to a mouthful of long gray hair. The king stopped climbing when he noticed Sadira staring at him with a murderous light in her eyes.

"What's wrong with you?" he demanded.

"Ask later," Rikus said. "We're in enough trouble—"

Sadira's head snapped toward the Dragon. She launched herself forward, giving Rikus a hard shove.

Rikus heard the sizzle of a magic bolt crackle from Borys's direction, then everything went dark. An instant later, the mul found himself standing near the brink of the abyss, staring back toward the center of the plain. Where he had been standing a moment earlier, there was now a smoking crater the size of the Golden Palace. Rikus could not see how deep the hole was, for it was surrounded by a rim of broken stone as high as Tyr's city wall.

"By Ral!" The mul was so shocked he could do little but gape at the immense hole. "Sadira!"

"What are you doing, giving up?" asked a familiar voice.

For the first time, the mul realized that he was standing near an arch similar to the one on the other side of the lava sea. Lying near its base, her head cradled in Rkard's lap, was Neeva. Though Rikus could not see any injuries, her motionless legs revealed all he needed to know.

"Neeva!" he gasped.

"Go." She pointed toward the crater. Borys was already limping down into it. "I'll be fine with Rkard looking after me. See what happened."

The mul started forward, then heard a strange voice at his feet. "St . . . ning . . . oaf!"

Noticing that he only heard the voice when his feet touched the ground, Rikus halted and looked down. Out of the shadow cast by his sword came Tithian, followed immediately by Sadira's pale form.

"How did you—"

"It was the only place to go," Sadira replied, cutting him off before he finished the question. "Where's the Dragon?"

Rikus pointed toward the crater.

"We'd better hurry," Tithian said. Still in serpent form, the king started to slither toward the crater.

"Wait," Sadira said. "I've got an idea."

"It'd better be a good one," Tithian said. "We don't have long before Borys realizes we're not in that crater."

The sorceress took the Scourge, then touched the blade to the Dark Lens. A flash of crimson light flared from beneath the enchanted steel. The sword began to glow red, and Sadira gasped in pain.

"What are you doing?" Rikus asked, horrified at the thought of what the heat might do to the temper of his blade.

"Remember what happened the first time you broke the Scourge?" she asked. "And how terrified Abalach-Re was in the Ivory Plain?"

The mul smiled, then looked to Tithian. "Weaken the blade," he ordered.

"Are you mad?" the king gasped.

"If you want to kill Borys, do it!" Rikus ordered.

Tithian frowned but directed his gaze at the weapon. His brow furrowed in concentration. Where the Scourge's blade touched the lens, a white flame danced over the steel. Sadira cried out and dropped the sword.

Rikus tore a strip off the hem of the sorceress's robe, then wrapped it around the Scourge's hilt and picked the sword up. About midway down the blade, a black scorch mark stained the steel.

"That'll do fine," the mul declared.

Rikus led the way back to the hole, Sadira sprinting at his side. Tithian crawled behind them, holding the Dark Lens in his tail. When they reached the crater, Rikus signaled the others to hide, then climbed to the top and peered down on Borys. The Dragon was on all fours,

still digging through the rubble at the bottom of the pit.
The mul picked up a rock, intending to let it drop on
Borys to get his attention.

There was no need. The Dragon drew himself up to
his full height, and Rikus found himself standing eye-to-
eye with the beast.

"Where's my lens?" Borys demanded.

The Dragon raised his hands, but resisted the temptation to strike, obviously aware that Rikus would vanish
if he did.

Allowing some of his very real fear of the beast to
show through, Rikus replied, "I d-don't have it."

Rikus raised the Scourge as if to strike, then pretended to slip on the treacherous ground. He flailed his
arms wildly, flinging the Scourge down the slope below.
The instant the sword left the mul's hand, Borys's
mouth gaped open, and his head darted forward. Rikus
hurled himself down the hill backward, watching the
Dragon's snapping jaws snake after him.

Tithian struck first, slipping from behind a boulder to
make contact with one of Borys's beady eyes. Rikus saw
the psionic image of a winged serpent striking from the
Dark Lens toward their foe. The Dragon swiveled his
huge head around. The glowing figure of a lava golem
shot from the beast's eyes and intercepted the viper. The
snake bit into the burning giant, then erupted into
flames.

The serpent continued its attack, coiling its body
around the figure and constricting. The two constructs
began to wrestle, shifting forms into birds, lirrs, lions,
and a dozen other ferocious creatures. The battle raged
with such fervor that tongues of real flame came flying
off the two images, scorching stones and searing Rikus's
flesh.

Leaving his construct to carry on the battle against
Tithian by itself, Borys looked back to Rikus. The mul
was still sliding down the hill, grasping madly at the

Scourge. Wisps of smoke began to ooze from the Dragon's nostrils, and his mouth opened to exhale.

Sadira leaped from her hiding place. She lunged at the beast's eye with a dagger of hissing blue smoke. Borys closed his mouth and looked away. The sorceress's blade missed its intended target, but still slashed down across the Dragon's snout. The attack drew only a trickle of blood, but it bought Rikus enough time to find the Scourge and spring to his feet.

Borys's hand flashed from behind the crater rim and closed around Sadira. Now that she was no longer protected by the power of the sun, his claws sank deep into her abdomen. She screamed in pain. Blood began to seep from between the beast's fingers.

Still holding the sorceress, Borys swung his head back toward Rikus. The mul charged up the hill and drove his sword down through the Dragon's snout.

The blade sank through both jaws, drawing a spray of boiling yellow blood. Borys threw Sadira down and snapped his head high into the sky, trying to flip Rikus off. The mul hung on tightly, locking his legs around the Dragon's snout and desperately trying to snap the blade.

He heard Sadira yell from on the crater rim, "Keep fighting, damn you!"

Rikus looked down and saw that Tithian had ceased his mental attack. Instead of combating Borys with the Way, the king was slithering away with the Dark Lens in his tail.

One of the Dragon's gnarled claws rose into sight, blocking the mul's view of the scene below. Rikus cursed, knowing that if he allowed his enemy to strike at him, he would find himself standing near the arch—and away from the combat. Gripping the Scourge's hilt with both hands, he flung himself away from the claw and braced his feet against the other side of the snout. He pulled with all his might. The blade flexed with a resilient chime, but did not break.

Far below, Sadira called Tithian's name. Rikus looked down and saw the sorceress throw something. The king ducked behind the Dark Lens, then a web of sticky white filaments formed in the air above him and began settling over his head.

Tithian laughed.

Borys whipped his head around in an angry attempt to shake Rikus loose. The Scourge snapped with a sour twang, and the mul fell away. As he dropped, he saw a fountain of black syrup spraying from the blade still half-buried in the Dragon's snout.

Rikus slammed into the crater rim. His body exploded into pain, and the Scourge's hilt slipped from his grasp. He tumbled down the slope, the Dragon's roars filling his ears. Soon, he managed to bring himself to a stop. Everything hurt so badly that he could not tell whether he had broken all his bones or none of them.

The mul rolled over and, grasping a boulder, pulled himself to his feet. To Rikus's relief, attacking him was sure to be the last thing on Borys's mind. A huge fountain of black fluid was shooting from the Scourge's broken blade and had already coated the Dragon's head beneath a thick layer of ebony slime. With angry red plumes of smoke pouring from his nostrils, the beast was madly scratching at the steel shard lodged in his snout. He accomplished little, save to coat his claws with the same dark sludge that covered his face.

The Dragon bellowed in horrid pain. He sprayed a fiery red cloud high into the sky, and his hands dropped limply to his sides, his beady eyes glazing over in agony. A series of convulsions ran through his slender face. With each spasm the snout grew shorter and thicker, until the thing looked more like a nose and drooping chin than a beast's muzzle. The spiked crest on top of his head broadened into a sloping forehead. Borys gave one last roar, then fell silent and dropped behind the ridge.

Feeling fairly confident that the Dragon would not return to attack him, Rikus looked across the slope. He found the king bound tightly to the Dark Lens by a sturdy mesh of silver filaments. As the mul watched, a huge red spider emerged from the depths of the lens. The creature lowered its head to the web and drew the glistening strands into its mouth. Once Tithian was free, the creature sprang at Sadira. It sailed across the intervening distance in a flash, then landed square on the sorceress's face and began savaging her with its maw.

Rikus started forward to help her. As he stumbled across the slope, he watched helplessly as four lacy wings sprouted from Tithian's back. Still holding the Dark Lens in his tail, the king rose into the air and flew toward the cliff on the far side of the plain. His size dwindled rapidly, and the mul knew that he would quickly pass out of sight.

Tithian flew away, and Sadira rolled down the slope and pinned the spider beneath her. She pulled her head away from its maw. Her face was covered with red welts that looked like burn marks, but there were no punctures to suggest that the thing had been injecting poison into her body. The sorceress grasped her attacker in both hands and picked it up high over her head. She brought it down on a sharp rock. The thing vanished in a fiery flash.

Sadira screamed in shock and covered her face.

Rikus reached her side. "Let me see," he said.

"I'm not seriously hurt—which is more than Tithian will be able to say when I catch up to him," Sadira said. She lowered her arms, revealing a face with singed eyelashes and reddened skin. Rikus was relieved to see that there were no critical burns.

"What about the Dragon?" Sadira asked.

The mul pointed toward the top of the rim. "I snapped the sword," he said. "What's left of Borys fell inside."

"We'd better have a look," Sadira said.

They climbed the slope and peered cautiously over the top. In the bottom of the crater, a huge skeleton of black-stained bones lay curled into a fetal ball. Its shoulder blades were fused into a single large hump, and its gangling arms were wrapped around its knees. The thing's face was the remotely human visage that Rikus had seen replace Borys's, with the Scourge's shard still lodged in the nose and spewing dark slime into the air.

As they watched, sparks of blue energy began to dance in its empty eye sockets. From its fleshless mouth came a sibilant voice.

"Borys of Ebe, Butcher of Dwarves, Leader of the Revolt," the voice hissed. "Your master has claimed his punishment."

Inky fluid began to bubble up between the skeleton's teeth. The ribs broke open and began to gush ebony syrup from the jagged ends. The arms and legs separated at the joints, then the pelvis split down the center, and finally the spine collapsed into a line of disconnected vertebrae. With each separation, more dark slime poured into the basin, until the skeleton itself disappeared beneath a pool of bubbling, frothing black sludge.

SIXTEEN

The Blue Age

A stone shifted beneath Rikus's foot and went tumbling down to the boiling black pond below. The mul's legs went out from beneath him, and he dropped to his seat, landing hard on the crest of the crater's rim. He managed to keep Neeva cradled tight against his chest, but she groaned anyway.

Rkard was at their side in an instant. "Careful!" The boy scowled at Rikus. "We're not even supposed to move her."

"I'm sorry. We have no choice," said Rikus.

Sadira came over the rim and joined them. "The sorcerer-kings might come through the arch at any moment," she said, bracing herself on Neeva's axe to rest. Rkard had sealed the punctures in her stomach and dressed the burns she had suffered when Tithian used the lens against her, but the sorceress still looked pained and fatigued. "You don't want our enemies to find her, do you?"

"I want you to kill the sorcerer-kings," said the boy.

Neeva took her son's arm. "Haven't we talked about this?"

"But they killed Borys," the boy retorted.

"And maybe they'll kill the sorcerer-kings later," Neeva said. She winced with pain, then added, "But they can't do it now, not with the Scourge broken and Sadira's powers gone until morning."

"This is dangerous, Mother," Rkard protested. "I'm supposed to heal you at least one more time before moving you. Otherwise, you might not walk again."

"If the sorcerer-kings find me, I won't live long enough to walk," Neeva said, her voice growing stern. She looked up at Rikus. "Take me down."

"Don't drop her this time," Rkard ordered. He went down the slope first, kicking loose stones out of the mul's path.

"He doesn't mean to hurt your feelings, Rikus," Neeva said. "After what happened to Caelum, he's scared to death that he'll lose me too."

"I won't let that happen," the mul said.

"Sshhh." Neeva touched her fingers to his lips. "During the war with Urik, I thought you learned not to make promises you can't keep."

The mul shrugged. "Some things never change, I guess."

Rikus shifted his gaze down the hill. A dozen paces below, the black sludge from his sword had filled the bottom of the crater. Dark wisps of shadow rose from its surface, while yellow eyes blinked in the center of slow-spinning eddies. In places, warped spouts of slime oozed up to form disfigured silhouettes of four-footed birds, two-headed men, and mekillots with long writhing tails at both ends. Sometimes, the weird beasts even seemed to take on lives of their own, making their way to the shore and crawling a short distance up the slope before they dissolved into sticky messes and drained into the ground.

Rikus thought it a mark of his company's desperation that they had picked this place to hide Neeva, but he had been unable to think of another plan to protect the injured warrior from the sorcerer-kings. As Neeva had told her son, with the Scourge gone, he and Sadira would not be killing any more sorcerer-kings—at least not until the sorceress's powers returned in the morning.

Rikus followed Rkard to a jagged tumble of boulders that offered shelter both from searching eyes and splashing ooze. He kneeled down and deposited Neeva in the center of the cluster, bracing her back against a large stone. She glanced through a gap toward the black pond, just a few steps below.

"This should do," she said, nodding. "The sorcerer-kings won't be anxious to come down here. You two go on."

Rkard's eyes widened. "Go? Where?"

"Now that your mother's safe, we must find Tithian," Sadira said.

"No!" The boy grabbed Rikus's arm. "The Dragon's dead. You have to stay here."

Rikus's heart grew as heavy as stone. "There's nothing I'd like more," he said. "But I can't. If we let Tithian go, he'll release an evil even more powerful than the Dragon."

"I know—Rajaat," the boy answered. "But without the Dragon to keep him locked away, isn't Rajaat going to escape sooner or later anyway?"

"Not if we capture the Dark Lens," Sadira explained. "When I touched Rikus's sword to it, I felt magic as powerful as the sun's. I think we can use the lens to keep Rajaat imprisoned."

"And that means you have to leave my mother in danger?" Rkard asked.

"I'm afraid so," Rikus answered.

The boy turned away. "My father wouldn't leave her."

"Rkard, don't . . ."

Neeva let her command trail off and raised her hands to wipe away the tears suddenly brimming in her eyes.

"Look at this," she said, staring at her wet fingers in amazement. "I haven't cried since I was a child, when Tithian bought me for his gladiator pits."

"Water for Caelum," Sadira said. "Don't hold it back."

"I couldn't if I tried." Neeva watched her tears tumble to the ground, shaking her head with unspoken regrets.

Sadira laid a hand on the warrior's arm, but seemed unable to find the words to comfort her friend. Rikus realized that the sorceress knew the same thing he did: it was too late to apologize now. The spirits of the dead did not hear the voices of their loved ones, or even remember their names.

Sadira touched Rikus's arm. "We'd better go."

The mul pulled his dagger and held it out toward Rkard's back. "I don't know if this blade will do you any good, but it might."

When the boy did not turn around, Neeva said, "Rikus is leaving now, Rkard. Do you want this to be the way he remembers you?"

"No," the boy said. He turned around and, without meeting Rikus's glance, accepted the dagger. "Good luck."

The mul patted the boy's shoulder. "Take care of your mother," he said. "And if we're not back by the time she's walking, leave without us."

Rkard looked up, his eyes wide with fear. "You've got to come back! If you don't . . ." He paused, collecting his composure, then said, "I don't even know the way."

"If we must, we can find it together." Neeva took her son's hand and pulled him to her side, then fixed her green eyes on Sadira. "Don't make the mistake I did. Say everything."

The sorceress gazed at Rkard and did not answer for several moments, then finally said, "I will."

Sadira handed the axe to Rikus, and together they climbed the hill. As they started over the top, the mul paused and ran his eyes over the crest of the rim. "I dropped the top part of the Scourge up here some-where," he said. "When the sorcerer-kings come, it might be useful to have the hilt in my scabbard. Maybe we can bluff them into leaving us alone."

"It can't hurt to try," Sadira said. She pointed to a location several dozen paces away, near the top of the small hill. A small circle of ground was covered with an ugly black stain. "Look over there."

The mul walked to the area. He found the Scourge behind a boulder, with the hilt lying uphill above what was left of the blade. Black slime continued to ooze from the jagged break, creating a bubbling pool of sludge tipped at the angle of the slope. As with the larger pond inside the crater, wisps of shadow rose from its surface, and yellow eyes peered out from the center of slowly swirling eddies.

Rikus considered the amount of sludge still oozing from the blade, then decided it might be better to leave the shard alone. He started to return to Sadira.

The mul stopped a step later, when he glimpsed an orange light flash beneath the great arch. When the glow faded, the four sorcerer-kings and the remaining sorcerer-queen stood between the pillars of the great edifice, their eyes roving over the broken plain. The distance from the crater to the arch was just small enough for the mul to see his enemies clearly. The runt of a limb had sprouted from the stump of Nibenay's severed arm, and Hamanu showed no sign of discom-fort from the dagger that had been plunged into his back.

Rikus dropped behind a boulder and signaled for Sadira to come over. She slipped behind the crest of the crater rim, trying to stay out of sight as she ran over to join the mul. Her precautions were of little use. The sorcerer-kings stepped from beneath the arch and walked across the plain toward the crater.

By the time Sadira reached Rikus's side behind the

boulder, the sorcerer-kings stood at the rim's base, directly in front of the pair's hiding place. The five figures were less than twenty paces away, and perhaps half that distance lower.

Hamanu stepped forward and looked up the slope. "You fools," he growled, angrily shaking his mane. "What you have unleashed may destroy us all."

"In your case, the loss will be a welcome one," called Sadira. She rose to peer over the boulder.

Rikus joined her. If the sorcerer-kings attacked, a few feet of stone was not going to save them.

"Give us the Dark Lens, and your deaths will be mercifully quick," said the Oba.

"I'm in no hurry to die." The mul looked at Sadira. "How about you?"

"I'll take my time," the sorceress replied. She glanced down at their enemies, then said, "If you want the lens, you'll have to find it and take it."

Hamanu started forward, but the Oba caught him by the shoulder. "Wait. They're too anxious."

"They're blustering," the sorcerer-king snarled.

"Perhaps, but they did kill Borys," she countered. The Oba pointed at the dark stain on the slope below the mul. "Do you really want to take the chance that they haven't set a trap?"

Hamanu's huge nostrils flared, but he stepped back. "You have something else in mind?"

The Oba nodded, then called up the slope, "How much do you know of Rajaat?"

"Enough to know that you betrayed him, which, at the moment, makes him our friend," Rikus replied.

The Oba chuckled, though she sounded more nervous than amused. "Rajaat would slay you two as soon as he finished with us."

"His shadow people have proven helpful so far," Sadira replied.

"Of course. They wanted you to kill Borys," said

Andropinis, shaking his fringe of white hair. "But if you knew the truth about Rajaat, you would know better than to rely on his gratitude."

"Why don't you enlighten us?" requested Sadira.

Andropinis glanced at his fellows.

"Go ahead," suggested the Oba. "After hearing the truth, they'll yield the Dark Lens without a fight."

Andropinis turned his palm toward the ground.

"No magic!" Rikus yelled.

The sorcerer-king fixed an icy glare on the mul and drew the energy for his spell. "Watch and learn," he said, waving his hand across the sky.

An image of the Ringing Mountains appeared above the horizon, but they were not the barren crags Rikus knew from his life in Tyr. A howling wind tore great plumes of snow off the highest peaks, while large sheets of ice ran off their lofty shoulders. Lower down, the slopes resembled the wild forests of the halflings, with thick, verdant timberlands clinging to the steep slopes. Pearly clouds of mist hung low over valleys filled with gurgling streams and thundering rivers.

As majestic as the mountains were, they interested Rikus little compared to what he saw at their base. Between two ranges of foothills lay a hollow about the size and shape of the Tyr Valley. There the semblance ended. Instead of the barren waste of rocks and thorns the mul knew, the vale was filled with a vast swamp of vine-draped trees and floating islands of moss.

At the edge of the valley a strange, beautiful city of graceful sweeps and brilliant colors rose directly out of the swamp. The buildings seemed not so much constructed as grown, for they were marked by an architecture of gentle curves and elegant spires, with no straight edges, sharp points, or abrupt corners. The material was a uniformly porous stone that radiated blazing crimson, emerald green, royal blue, deep purple, or any of a dozen other hues. Where there should have been streets were canals, filled with long slender boats guided by child-sized figures with adult faces. If not for their elegant tabards, their short-cropped hair, and their handsome features, the mul would have sworn they were halflings.

At the city's edge, the swamp gave way to the sparkling waves of an immense blue sea. It appeared to stretch clear to the horizon and beyond, covering ground that Rikus knew to be nothing but sandy wastes and rocky barrens.

"Tyr, during the Blue Age," said Andropinis.

"Blue Age?" Sadira was studying the scene intently.

"Before your time or ours, when only halflings lived on Athas," explained the Oba. Making no effort to conceal her admiration for the halflings, she continued, "They were the masters of the world, growing homes from a rocklike plant that lived beneath the waves, harvesting the sea for everything they needed to maintain a vast splendorous society, able to create anything they needed by manipulating the principles of nature itself."

As the sorcerer-queen spoke, a fetid brown tide spread over the blue sea. It crept into the swamp surrounding Tyr, causing the floating moss islands to shrivel and sink. The vines went next, withering into the brown sludge like the sloughed skin of a serpent. The trees themselves died last, dropping their leaves and losing their bark. Before long, the grove stood naked in the swamp, an army of gray boles mired in a valley of putrid slime.

"Despite their vast knowledge, or perhaps because of it, one day the halflings made a terrible mistake that destroyed the life-giving sea," the Oba continued.

"A good story, but don't assume I believe it just because Andropinis spreads it across the sky," Rikus said.

"Believe it," said Sadira. "On my way to the Pristine

Tower, I saw halflings and stone just like that. So far, they're telling the truth."

"We've no reason to lie," snapped Andropinis. "We care nothing for your opinion."

The sorcerer-king waved his hand. The Ringing Mountains receded into the distance, until they looked like no more than blue clouds hanging low on the horizon. In their place stretched a vast, featureless plain of mud, brown as dung and as thick as clay. In the center of the flat rose a single spire of porous white stone, capped by a beautiful citadel with alabaster walls and a keep of white onyx.

"The Pristine Tower!" Sadira gasped.

A long file of halflings left the citadel, descending the narrow staircase that spiraled down the outside of the spire. Their tabards hung off their bodies in dingy strips, while their hair cascaded over their shoulders in tangled snarls. Their features had grown haggard and wild, and they gestured with the quick, darting movements typical of the feral race Rikus had known during his own time.

The halflings started across the brown plain toward the Ringing Mountains. The mud cleaved to their feet like torch pitch, and soon they could not take a step without also raising a huge clump of brown earth. In their wake sprouted tall grasses, leafy bushes, and magnificent trees that loomed above the tableland like towers. Soon, the plain became a verdant paradise, teeming with foliage of every sort.

Creatures began to appear in this forest: horn-covered lizards, bright-feathered birds, and graceful herd-beasts such as Rikus had never seen, with racks of white horns and long thin limbs. Some of the animals perished almost immediately, falling prey to the great hunting cats that prowled the newborn wilderness, while others lived long enough to create others of their kind.

The flowering of this new paradise did not come

without pain. As the halflings traveled across plain, the weak collapsed and were abandoned where they lay. Their bodies began to transform into strange shapes. One grew stocky and hair-covered, while another tripled his height without gaining much bulk. Still others became both thicker of limb and taller, and some developed scales, sprouted feathers, or even grew carapaces. By the time the surviving halflings reached the distant mountains, they had left more races behind than Rikus could count. He recognized many of them, such as the dwarves, elves, and humans. Others, he had never seen, or only knew about from legends. There were frail, winged characters even smaller than halflings, and ugly swine-faced beings that could scarcely be called people. Like the animals, many of these individuals perished quickly, while others went on to populate the world with whole races of their own kind.

"Realizing their own vanity had destroyed their civilization, the halflings seeded Athas with the beginning of a new world," said the Oba. "This is the Green Age, the age before magic, when the Way dominated the world."

As she spoke, villages and castles sprang up in the forest, rapidly growing into walled towns and cities connected by an intricate series of cobblestone roads. Powerful mindbenders wandered the wooded lanes on floating ivory platforms, traveling from their majestic towers to the sylvan citadels of the elves and the gloomy cities of the dwarves.

Andropinis gestured, and the scene shifted to an isolated turret in one of the smaller villages, where a single figure sat by a glass window poring over a stack of books. There was no way to describe the man's appearance except as hideous, for he had a huge head with a flat, grossly elongated face. His eyes were half-covered by flaps of skin, while his long nose, lacking a bridge, ended in three flaring nostrils. He had a small, slitlike mouth with tiny teeth and a drooping chin. His body was contorted and weak, with humped shoulders and gangling arms.

The figure looked up from his book and held his palm over a potted lily growing in the windowsill. The plant quickly withered and died. He tossed a pinch of dust into the air, and a gray fog filled the room.

"Rajaat came to us early in the Green Age, one of the many hideous accidents spawned from the Rebirth," said the Oba. "His only blessing was a supreme intellect, which he used to become the first sorcerer. He spent centuries trying to reconcile his brutal appearance with his human spirit. In the end, even his powerful mind could find no answer. He came to revile himself as nothing but a deformed accident.

"Soon, Rajaat turned his hate outward. He declared the Rebirth a mistake, and proclaimed all the races it had spawned to be monsters. He dedicated himself to wiping the blight of their existence from the world, so that he might return Athas to the harmony and glory of the Blue Age."

The gray haze faded. Rajaat stood atop the Pristine Tower, looking out through a crystal cupola. He seemed immeasurably older, with long shocks of gray hair, a wrinkled face, and white, burning eyes. A company of armored figures marched out of the base of the keep. They descended the tower's spiraling staircase and went into the wilderness. Soon, great patches of forest began to wither and die as they waged a terrible war.

"He created us—his champions—to lead the armies of the Cleansing Wars," said the Oba. "Rajaat told us to destroy all the new races, or they would spawn monsters like him and overrun the world."

The forests steadily vanished, leaving most of Athas the barren and lifeless place that Rikus knew so well. Then, abruptly, the destruction ceased, and the champions returned to the Pristine Tower.

"We had almost won," said Andropinis. "Then we realized Rajaat was mad." He sounded regretful, perhaps even angry, that they had not finished the war. "We stopped fighting."

"You didn't stop because Rajaat was mad. That had to be clear all along," Sadira said. "You stopped because you learned the truth about who would survive when he returned the world to the Blue Age."

"That's right," admitted the Oba. "All during the Cleansing Wars, Rajaat told us that humans would be the only race left when we finished. We didn't learn that he was lying until it was almost too late."

"And then you rebelled, imprisoning Rajaat," finished Sadira.

Andropinis allowed his spell to fade. "I see you know the rest of the story."

"Not all of it," said Sadira. "How did Borys lose the Dark Lens? I'd think he would be more careful with something so valuable."

"The transformation into a Dragon is a difficult one," answered the Oba. "Shortly after we changed him, Borys lost his mental balance and went on a rampage. No one realized the lens had been stolen until he recovered—a century later."

"I don't believe this tale of yours," Rikus said. "If Rajaat was trying to give the world back to the halflings, why did he make his champions humans? Why didn't he use halflings?"

"He couldn't make them sorcerers," answered the Oba. "Because their race harkens back to the Blue Age, before the art of sorcery existed, they cannot become sorcerers."

"You're lying," Rikus said. "I've seen halflings use magic."

"Elemental magic, yes—like Caelum's sun magic or Magnus's windsinging," said Sadira. "They draw their powers directly from the inanimate forces of the world:

wind, heat, water, and rock. But normal sorcery draws its power from the life-force of plants and animals."

Rikus started to object that Sadira drew her power from the sun, then thought better of it. Her sorcery could no longer be considered normal.

"I think the sorcerer-kings have told us the truth," Sadira said.

"Then give us the lens," said Hamanu, moving forward. "It's the only way we can keep Rajaat imprisoned."

"The Dark Lens isn't here," replied Sadira. "Tithian took it."

"Sacha and Wyan told Tithian that Rajaat would make him a sorcerer-king," the mul added. "We think he's on his way to free Rajaat."

"How unfortunate for you," sneered Nibenay. The sorcerer-king stepped toward the slope, emboldened now that he was sure they did not have the Dark Lens. "Then there's nothing to stop me from repaying the mul for my injury."

The Oba grabbed him by the stub that had sprouted from his severed arm. "Leave them for later," she ordered, looking toward the cliff rising above the edge of the plain. "If the Usurper frees Rajaat, we'll need your help. It would be a shame if we didn't have it because they were lucky enough to kill you."

Nibenay jerked away, leaving his freshly grown stub in the Oba's hand. "It wasn't your arm he cut off!"

"Then attack if you wish, but you'll do it alone." The sorcerer-queen pointed at the distant cliff, where a dark spout of energy was rising into the sky. It had punched a hole in the stormy red clouds of the ash storm. Through this breach poured the golden light of the Athasian moons, casting eerie shadows over the edge of the plains. "The rest of us have other concerns."

Andropinis cursed. "The fool Usurper has taken the lens into the city."

Andropinis started toward the city at a run, simultaneously preparing to cast a spell. The other sorcerer-kings turned and followed. Only Nibenay lingered behind, his palm turned toward the ground.

"This won't take a moment," he hissed.

Rikus grabbed the Scourge's hilt and hurled the broken sword at the sorcerer-king. The weapon tumbled end-over-end, beads of black resin flying off the blade and creating a line of dark spatters down the slope. Nibenay lunged away, rolling over his shoulder across the coarse scoria. The shard clanged to the ground two paces behind him.

The sorcerer-king jumped to his feet and looked toward Rikus. He started to speak an incantation, but suddenly stopped and stared at the hillside in horror. The black bubbles from the Scourge had connected with each other and stretched into a long thin line. The two sides pulled apart like lips, revealing a mouthful of huge fangs.

"Soon, Gallard," the mouth said. It was using the name by which Nibenay had gone when he was a champion. "Very soon."

A long green tongue shot from the dark fissure, lashing out for the sorcerer-king. Nibenay cried out in alarm and pointed his finger at the thing, screaming his incantation. A red bolt streaked from his finger, blasting the appendage into a hundred pieces. The mouth laughed, and another tongue snaked out from between its lips.

Nibenay backed away, then turned and ran after the other sorcerer-kings.

SEVENTEEN

Ur Draxa

His serpent's body coiled tightly about the Dark Lens, Tithian lay beneath a looming wall of granite, just outside the tunnel he had bored through an enormous foundation block. Before him stood a silent thicket of trees, with supple trunks that quietly swayed in the moonlit night, like slave dancers welcoming him to the city. Each had only a single blue leaf, as large as a sail and stretched tight over a dome-shaped network of branches. Neatly groomed paths curved through the shadows beneath their boughs, suggesting he had entered in some sort of park.

Tithian hardly noticed the beauty of the place; his attention remained fixed entirely on the Dark Lens. When he had emerged from his tunnel, a surge of energy had risen from the ground, through him, and into the lens. Dozens of smoky tendrils had begun to dance over the top of the orb. They had twined themselves together in a crackling spout of force and risen into the sky, parting the red storm raging overhead.

"Get moving," said Sacha, floating through the

tunnel. As the head's words carried into the thicket ahead, they faded without an echo. "The sorcerer-kings are flying across the plain."

Tithian gestured at the black spout. "Something's wrong," he said. "I didn't do this."

Sacha rolled his sunken eyes. "Try not to be such a cretin," he said. "Rajaat's watching."

Tithian began to uncoil himself, keeping the lens gripped in his tail. "What's happening?"

"The lens is overloaded, so its discharging its excess energy."

"Overloaded?"

"You're near Rajaat's prison. The lens is drawing energy from the spell that keeps it intact," Sacha explained, his tone deliberately patronizing. "Did you think the lens took its power from the sun alone?"

As a matter of fact, that was exactly what Tithian had thought, but he did not give Sacha the pleasure of hearing him confess his mistake.

"Which way now?" he asked, looking deeper into the silent park.

"How would I know?" demanded Sacha. "How many times do you think I've been to Ur Draxa?"

A man slipped from behind one of the trees ahead. He wore a peculiar suit of armor fashioned from brightly painted human ribs, with a massive helmet carved from the squarish skull of some fanged race of half-man. The stranger carried a steel halberd with an ornately shaped blade that looked more suitable for displaying on a palace wall than fighting. Though the man moved with no particular care, his footsteps fell as softly as those of an elven hunter—leading the king to suspect the wood's eerie silence had more to do with magic than tranquility.

The newcomer pointed his weapon at Tithian and motioned for him to lie on the ground. When the king did not obey, the man raised his halberd, and a hundred more warriors stepped from behind the trees. Their leather armor was not so fine as that of their leader, but the spears they carried looked much more practical than the man's halberd.

"We don't have time for this," Sacha snarled. "Kill him."

Deciding to take a lesson from the Dragon, Tithian visualized a great storm of fire erupting from his mouth. An incredible surge of energy gushed from the Dark Lens, blazing through the king's body with such ferocity he feared he would explode. A blinding white cone of flame erupted from his mouth, engulfing the officer and the warriors behind him. Tithian did not even see the thicket burn. The huge leaves and the branches vanished in a flash, then the ground was littered with scorched boles and blackened skulls. Only the edges of the small wood had escaped the instant devastation, and even they were starting to burn.

"Well done," said a voice at Tithian's side.

The king whipped his head around. At first, he did not see the speaker, then he glimpsed a pair of flickering blue eyes. They were looking up at him from the faint shadow his moonlit body cast on the ground. As Tithian watched, the silhouette slowly peeled itself off the dirt and changed into a more manlike form—though it was only about the size and shape of a halfling.

"Who are you?" Tithian watched a nose and a pair of lips form on the thing's face.

"How quickly you forget," the silhouette responded. "I led you through the Black less than an hour ago."

"Khidar?" Tithian gasped. "I thought you were a giant!"

"Of course not, you imbecile," Sacha chided. "The shadow people are descended from the last of Rajaat's halfling servants."

"Shadows play strange tricks with size, do they not?" Khidar added, grinning. He now had a fully featured face, with short-cropped hair, blue eyes, an upturned nose, and bright white teeth. "Your ignorance is understandable. There weren't many of our people. Most halflings of the Green Age wanted nothing to do with the Cleansing Wars."

Tithian ran his eyes over the devastated park, not at all interested in the history of the shadow people. "I don't suppose you can tell me where to find Rajaat."

Khidar pointed a black finger toward the edge of the burning thicket. Although the halfling's head was now completely solid, the rest of his body remained a mere shadow. "Rajaat has told me you must look for him in the heart of Ur Draxa," Khidar said. "When those trees are gone, you'll see a great boulevard running toward the center of the city. My scouts tell me that it ends beneath a great arch embedded in the inner wall."

"What then?" Tithian asked.

"By the time you reach it, we will know for certain whether Rajaat lies beyond," he said. "If so, one of us will take you to the other side."

Tithian shook his head. "If I slither down a major street with the lens in my tail, I'm going to attract a lot of attention."

The king illustrated the problem by sending a series of squirms down his serpentine body.

"So disguise yourself," snapped Sacha.

"As what?" Tithian countered. "Anything large enough to carry the lens will draw attention. I can probably destroy whatever they send at me, but it'll take time we don't have."

"Don't worry about a disguise," said Khidar. "I'll make certain the Draxans are too busy to concern themselves with you. Besides, until you destroy Rajaat's prison completely, my people can emerge from the Black only partially. With us wandering through the city, you'll be only one of many strange things loose in the streets."

The halfling led the way toward the burning trees at the edge of the park.

* * * * *

Crossing the plain took longer than Sadira expected. She and Rikus ran until her breath came in painful gulps, filling her lungs with fire and racking her ribs with agony. They slowed their pace, continuing until fatigue so numbed the sorceress's legs that she could hardly stumble along.

"We'd better walk for a while," she said, breathing hard. "If I turn an ankle, we won't catch Tithian at all."

The mul slowed his pace and came to her side. "I don't suppose you've any magic left?"

Sadira shook her head. "I've already used the enchantments that could help us."

During the day, when she was imbued with the sun's power, Sadira could shape her magic with little more than a thought. But at night, she was like any other sorceress. She could use only spells whose mystic runes she had impressed on her mind through hours of rigorous study. Unfortunately, speaking an enchantment's incantation erased its runes from the mind, so the caster could not use the spell a second time until she studied it again.

"There's no use worrying," said Rikus. "Before he can free Rajaat, Tithian'll have to find him—and with the sorcerer-kings after him, that could take some time."

"Let's hope so."

Sadira glanced at the sky ahead. The black spout still rose from the top of the cliff, and she could see by the lengthening gap in the red clouds that it had begun to move. The sorceress returned her gaze to the ground, picking her way across the jagged stones as quickly as she could.

After a few steps, Sadira said, "There's something I need to say, Rikus."

The mul raised an eyebrow, but kept his attention fixed on the broken ground. "What is it?"

"I owe you an apology," Sadira said. "When I found

out Agis was gone, I felt guilty for letting him die without the heir he wanted. I've been using you as a scapegoat for those feelings, telling myself that the only reason I didn't carry his baby was because it would make you jealous."

Rikus continued forward. "Was that the reason?"

Sadira hesitated before answering. She had made her apology, as she had promised Neeva, and did not know if it was necessary to discuss her feelings any further.

"Then I'm the one who owes you an apology," said Rikus. "If I stopped you from giving Agis something so important—"

"That wasn't why I refused," Sadira interrupted. "I didn't want a baby because I was afraid."

"Afraid?" the mul scoffed. "How can the woman who braved the Pristine Tower, who faced down the Dragon, be frightened of something as common as childbirth?"

"Common or not, childbirth's no little thing," Sadira scolded. "But you're right. The pain isn't what worried me—it was the trust. By having a child, I'd be giving myself to Agis forever, and trusting him to do the same."

"And that would have meant leaving me."

"That's what I told myself," she said. "But the truth is, after Faenaeyon abandoned my mother, I've never really trusted love."

"Agis was no elf. He'd never have left you or his child."

"I'm not saying he would have. He was much too loyal," Sadira said. "But people change, and so do their feelings. The love might have vanished, then we would've been stuck with each other."

"And it might not have. You can't predict what happens in life, but that's no reason to retreat from it." The mul paused for a moment, then came closer and took her arm. "But children aren't a concern for us. Even if you wanted one, I couldn't give you a baby. Let's just go on like before."

Sadira shook her head. "I'm not sure that's a good idea," she said. "For me—or for you."

Rikus frowned. "What do you mean?"

"It wasn't until after Agis died that I realized I needed him."

"And you don't need me?" Rikus asked, looking hurt.

Sadira smiled weakly. "That's not what I mean," she said. "But there's someone else who needs you. And you need them, too."

"If you're talking about Neeva—"

"Not just about Neeva," Sadira said.

"This is useless," Rikus said. He released her arm. "If you think we can decide for Neeva—"

"I'm not deciding for Neeva," Sadira interrupted. "But I know what she—and Rkard—will need."

Rikus looked away, uncomfortable. "What they need is for us to catch Tithian and get back to them," he said, starting to trot. "If you're up to running again, we'd better move on."

Sadira fell in behind the mul. By concentrating on where his feet landed, she found it easier to secure her own footing, and they crossed the plain at a steady pace. As they approached the cliff, it became clear that the precipice was not natural, but a wall constructed of granite blocks as large as houses, with seams so tight a dagger blade could not have slipped between the stones. Crackling forks of lightning shot down from the ash storm overhead to lick at the rampart's loftiest heights, and the summit itself was lost in the boiling red clouds.

"I can't believe Tithian would fly over this wall," Sadira said. "Lens or no lens, if one of those bolts hit him, he'd be scorched to cinders."

"I don't think he went over."

The mul pointed down the way, where the black circle of a tunnel opened into the bottom of the wall. They veered toward the circle. They soon saw that it was perfectly round, with smooth edges and a glasslike finish. It had been driven through the heart of a granite block, and was so long that the light at the other end was only about as large as a thumb. Sadira followed Rikus into the passage.

When they emerged on the other side, the sorceress saw that they had entered the corner of what had once been a forested preserve, though it no longer bore much semblance to a park. A fiery blast had ripped through the area, toppling the trees and leaving them limbless and smoking. Scattered among their blackened boles were hundreds of charred skeletons, along with the cracked obsidian points of incinerated spears.

"Whoever they were, they weren't much of a challenge for Tithian and the lens," Rikus observed.

"It doesn't look like they even slowed him down." Sadira pointed into the distance, where the energy spout from the Dark Lens continued to rip through the storm overhead. The black pillar seemed only slightly less distant than it had when they started across the plain. "We'd better hurry."

They picked their way across the devastated park, emerging on a processional boulevard that ran straight toward the heart of the city. To the sorceress, it appeared incredibly long, passing through an endless series of arches and vaults with no apparent purpose except ostentatious decoration. Hundreds and hundreds of monuments to stern-faced warriors and shrewd-looking bureaucrats lined the great avenue. Given the softness of the light descending from the golden moons, the edifices cast surprisingly harsh shadows across the street. Behind the statues rose the high towers and looming emporiums of a great and ancient city, though its sharp and blocky architecture seemed designed to belittle rather than impress its observers.

The citizens of the city, or at least those Sadira could

see, were rioting. Terrified nobles wearing suits of painted bone armor ran haphazardly through the streets, swinging obsidian swords and axes at mobs of slaves dressed in nothing but hemp breechcloths and carrying pieces of wood for weapons. Here and there, small groups of warriors were trying to mount counterattacks against their rebelling subjects, but the oppressors were too badly outnumbered, and Sadira knew it would only be a matter of time before the slaves put them all to the blade.

Rikus and Sadira started down the bustling avenue, the mul using the shaft of his axe to part the crowd while the sorceress kept her eye on the black energy spout. Although Tithian, and presumably the sorcerer-kings, were too far ahead to see, she did not worry they would be difficult to find. The rift in the clouds was directly over the great boulevard, and it pointed like an arrow straight ahead.

"Something about this doesn't make sense," said Sadira. She was sticking close to the mul's back. "It should take longer than this for the city to come unraveled. How can the slaves already know that the Dragon is dead? And even if they do, how did they overthrow their masters so quickly?"

The mul shrugged. "The sorcerer-kings seemed upset about Tithian bringing the lens into the city. Maybe it has something to do with that," he said. "But who cares, as long as slaves are winning their freedom?"

Sadira shook her head. "The rebellion's just a symptom. If the revolt bothered the sorcerer-kings, there wouldn't be a slave left alive on this avenue."

As the pair advanced down the boulevard, they were occasionally accosted by riot-frenzied slaves or panicked nobles. When they were attacked by slaves, Rikus simply disarmed the aggressors and sent them on their way. When nobles assaulted them, Sadira and the mul did not hesitate to kill, happy to assist in the city's liberation.

Soon, they came upon three strange beings leading a dozen slaves after a portly templar. The creatures resembled the ancient halflings of the Blue Age, save that they were part shadow and part person. The leader had a material head and a shadowy body, while another had solid limbs but nothing else. The third was split down the center, half silhouette and half physical.

When the leader of the half-shadows saw Rikus and Sadira, he called out in the strange language of the city. Though she did not understand the words, the sorceress recognized the voice speaking them.

"Khidar!"

The halfling led his two fellows and the slaves toward her. "You would have been wiser to leave after you killed Borys," he said. "Rajaat is not fond of half-breeds like you and your husband."

The slaves spread out, preparing to come at Rikus and Sadira from all sides. Most were armed with wooden sticks, but three had obsidian axes, and one carried a steel sword.

"Get out of here!" Rikus motioned the slaves back with his axe. "I'd hate to have to hurt you."

The slaves began jabbering at each other, no more capable of understanding the mul than he was of understanding them.

"Call them off, Khidar," Sadira ordered, slipping one hand into her pocket and using the other to summon the energy for a spell. "They'll only get killed."

Khidar hissed something at the slaves in their own language, and they launched themselves forward. Eight went for the mul, while the other four, all armed with sticks, circled around to come at Sadira. The sorceress saw Rikus swing his borrowed axe, smashing the flat of the blade into the swordsman's skull. As the unconscious slave dropped to the ground, the mul continued his swing, severing the heads of two obsidian axes with his steel blade. At the same time, he sent the third axeman tumbling away with a stomp-kick to the chest, then the club wielders were on him.

Having slipped past Rikus, the other four slaves charged Sadira. She pulled a handful of sand from her pocket and flung it in a wide arc before three of them, uttering her incantation. A mesmerizing golden light glimmered over the grains, capturing the gaze of the three men. Their heads slowly tilted forward as they watched the sand drop. When it hit the ground, their eyes closed and they fell on their faces, fast asleep.

Screaming some Draxan curse that Sadira did not understand, the fourth halfling brought his club down in a vicious overhand strike. The sorceress twisted her body to the side and slipped inside the attack, blocking at the wrist, just as Rikus had made her practice a thousand times. She looped her hand over the warrior's arm, guiding the elbow down toward her own knee, which she was bringing up beneath the joint.

The elbow snapped with a sharp crack, and the slave's hand opened. Sadira caught his club as it fell, then drove the point of her elbow into the screaming halfling's throat. He stumbled away, gasping for breath, and the sorceress stepped toward her husband.

Sadira could hardly see Rikus beneath the flailing clubs, yet the mul still seemed intent on defeating his attackers without killing them. Three of the eight lay on the ground, unconscious but showing no sign of an axe wound. She saw one of the warriors double over and stumble away, then the hilt of her husband's axe flashed up beneath his chin, knocking him off his feet. The slave shook his head and started to rise again.

"You don't have to be so careful!" Sadira yelled.

She smashed the butt end of her club into the man's temple. His eyes rolled back in his head, then the sorceress waded into the fray with her husband. Though she did not deliberately try to kill anyone, neither did she take pains to safeguard them. She knocked one slave unconscious by smashing her stick across the back of his head, snapping the club off at the midpoint, then drove the jagged end deep into the small of another man's back. He dropped to his knees instantly, in too much pain to scream.

A wave of bone-numbing cold shot through the sorceress's wrist. She looked down and saw a black shadow creeping up the arm, then heard Khidar's voice.

"I can still take you to the Black," he said. "Come along."

Sadira spun toward the half-shadow and raked her fingers across his eyes. Her nails bit deep and Khidar screamed, but he remained attached to her. The dark stain of his cold touch slipped up over her elbow, and it was no longer possible to tell where his hand ended and her arm began.

The sorceress drew back to strike again and felt another icy hand grip her shoulder. She looked back to see the another halfling, the one who was split down the center, grasping her by the collar. A terrible numbness began to creep through her torso.

"Rikus!" she yelled.

Her husband had problems of his own. Although he had knocked the last two slaves unconscious, the third half-shadow had thrown himself on the mul's back. Rikus was whirling around madly, trying to hurl his attacker off. The halfling's arms and legs were flailing wildly, but he and the mul remained joined at the torso.

Then she remembered Rikus's description of his fight with Umbra. Even with the Scourge, the mul had been unable to defeat the shadow giant until he dropped his torch. The weakness of Khidar's people, she realized, was that without light there could not be shadow.

Sadira turned her palm toward the ground, preparing to cast a darkness spell. She felt the energy flowing up her arm—then the familiar tingle abruptly vanished when it reached the black stain on her shoulder. The half-shadow gripping her by the collar screamed in pain, then suddenly released his grip and fell away. He looked as though a bolt of lightning had blasted away part of his body, with wisps of black smoke streaming off the empty place where there had once been the silhouette of a shoulder.

At first, Sadira did not understand, but then she realized what had happened. Shadow people had no life-forces of their own; they existed only as silhouettes marking the absence of energy—usually in the form of light. So direct contact with a mystic power—one of the most potent forms of energy—annihilated them.

Sadira turned her palm toward the ground again. Already Rikus's entire back had turned black, with the stain rapidly spreading around his ribs and down over his hips.

"Let go, Khidar!" the sorceress hissed, pulling more magical energy into her body.

"Why? So you can save Rikus?" he sneered. "You might escape, but your husband comes with us."

"No!" Sadira threw herself forward.

She thrust her hand into the stain on Rikus's back. The half-shadow did not even scream. His body simply exploded into black vapor, casting his arms and legs, still material, in all directions. The blast hurled Sadira through the air, then she heard a loud crack as the back of her skull slammed into the cobblestone street. Her vision started to dim, and a terrible ringing filled her ears. The sorceress pushed herself upright, fighting back the curtain of oblivion that threatened to descend over her.

"Fine," said Khidar. He reached across Sadira's body and grabbed her free hand. "We'll take you instead of Rikus."

Sadira turned her palm toward the ground. Already her hand was swaddled in shadow up to her wrist. She began to pull, trying to summon more magic. Sadira succeeded in drawing nothing but a bone-numbing chill into her body.

"Don't be afraid," Khidar hissed, his blue eyes locking onto hers. "You'll grow accustomed to the cold."

"Not likely," said Rikus, stepping up behind the halfling.

The mul brought his hands down on either side of Khidar's head, driving his palm-heels into the ears. The halfling's eyes bulged out, then his skull collapsed with a loud crack. The Black ceased to spread from beneath his shadowy hands.

Rikus stepped back, pulling Khidar's head away. The Black came with it, peeling off Sadira's body like wet silk. The mul tossed Khidar's lifeless head aside.

"At least we know we're not too late," Rikus said.

Sadira rubbed the lump that had appeared where the back of her skull had hit the cobblestones. "And why's that?"

"They wouldn't have attacked unless they thought we could stop Tithian," the mul answered. He pulled her to her feet and started down the street. "All we have to do is figure out why they were so worried."

* * * * *

A searing wave of pain hissed through Tithian's serpentine body. He contracted into a tangled knot of coils. His scales rose on end and quivered, bending back against their natural pattern to point toward his head. Fighting to keep his tail wrapped around the Dark Lens, the king clenched his teeth and waited for the spasm to pass.

He was in the Dragon's sanctum, a beautiful grove of a thousand exotic trees. There were tall conifers with red needles as long as daggers, stubby palms, each topped by a spray of barbed fronds, and majestic hardwoods with crowns as white and billowy as clouds. A carpet of blue moss covered the forest floor, decorated at odd intervals by a blossoming bush or a curving hedge of brightly colored leaves. An eerie calm hung over the place, for there was no wind, and the king had not heard the cry of a single bird, insect, or creature of any kind.

"Don't stop now!" Sacha's screech shattered the ghostly silence. "We're almost there."

A short distance ahead, two more paths emerged from the silent forest and joined this one to form a circle of polished jet. In the middle of this plaza, a dull black sphere hovered in the center of a sable-sheened basin. The orb was pulsing madly and spinning in all directions at once. Torrents of dark energy poured from it into the hollow below, then came billowing out to gush toward the Dark Lens in a roiling stream.

"Crawl, worm!" commanded Sacha. "Use the Way."

Tithian closed his eyes and visualized himself uncoiling, slowly stretching forward. He felt no surge of energy from the Dark Lens, but his body slowly stretched out, utilizing the energy already pouring through it. Once he had pushed his head forward, the king allowed his muscles to contract, dragging himself closer to the black sphere.

Progress came slowly, for Tithian had to call upon the Way each time he stretched out. His belly scales would not lie flat, and they began to break off as he dragged himself forward. The pain searing through his body grew steadily worse as he neared Rajaat's prison, and he felt sure he would burst into flame.

When he reached the edge of the plaza, the Dark Lens turned crimson. The black spout stopped rising from its glassy surface. Dark fumes began to swirl off the king's scales, streaming into the pit ahead. The heat of boiling blood filled Tithian's body, and he screamed.

"Crawl," urged Sacha. "The Dark Lens has drawn away the magic of the caging spell. Touch the Black, and Rajaat will be free!"

Tithian pulled himself forward and reached across the pit. He lowered his hand, and his fingers brushed the numbing cold of the Black. A crimson glow flashed from the king's flesh, and his body erupted into fiery pain. His teeth clenched so tightly that several of them cracked, and his muscles clamped down on his bones so hard that he feared they would break.

The black sphere burst open, spraying wisps of cold gloom in every direction. A seething cloud of blue steam boiled up into Tithian's face.

* * * * *

From beneath the protective shadows of an ornamental tunnel vault, Sadira peered over Rikus's shoulder. Fifty yards ahead, a granite wall blocked the way, though it seemed incorrect to say that the boulevard ended there. The cobblestone pavement ran clear to the base of the rampart, passing beneath an imbedded arch as though the street continued on the other side of the wall.

Before the arch stood four of the sorcerer-kings, their gazes fixed on the stone blocks in their path. As Sadira and Rikus watched, Andropinis floated down from the top of the wall. He shook his head and said something they could not hear, though Sadira guessed that he was telling the others they could not fly over the wall. This seemed to anger Hamanu, who cast a ray of golden light against the stones beneath the arch. The beam sprayed back over the monarchs, showering the street with flickering yellow sparks that ate through the cobblestones as though they were cloth.

When Hamanu finally lowered his hand, Sadira saw that the spell had not even scorched the wall.

"Borys sealed it against even them," Sadira whispered. "He must not have trusted his sorcerer-kings entirely."

"Or never thought that they would need to get inside without his help," Rikus suggested.

"Perhaps. But if five sorcerer-kings can't get past the wall, how could Tithian?"

"The same way he and I crossed the lava sea—with Khidar's help," Rikus answered. "Do you think you can get us to the other side?"

"Perhaps, when the sun—"

The crack of a distant explosion interrupted Sadira. It came from somewhere far beyond the arch, and the sorceress could tell from its sharp report that the blast was a powerful one. A patchwork of cracks raced through the granite wall, then the entire rampart blew apart with a deafening boom. The sorcerer-kings vanished beneath a maelstrom of billowing dust and flying boulders.

Sadira grabbed Rikus. Before she could turn to run, a tremendous shock wave slammed them to the ground. The vault blew off its foundations. The walls clattered down at their sides, and the arch crashed onto the street behind them. Sadira covered her head and curled into a tight ball, protecting herself from the dozens of fist-sized stones that rained down on her body. When the bruising shower ended, she found herself choking on a thick cloud of rock dust.

Rikus's strong hand grasped her arm. "Are you hurt?"

"I'm fine," Sadira said, allowing the mul to pull her up.

The sorceress saw that they were surrounded by an arc-shaped pile of debris. They had escaped serious injury only because they had been standing at the front of the arch when the explosion blew it over backward.

At the end of the street, it did not look as though the sorcerer-kings had been so lucky. The wall they had been trying to cross was now a mountain of rubble. Sadira saw no sign that any of their enemies had escaped the devastation.

"By Ral!" Rikus cursed. "What's that?"

The mul pointed over the top of the boulder heap. In the distance beyond, a blue spout of water was rising into view. For a moment, the sparkling pillar held steady, its frothing white cap just visible above the rubble ahead. Then, seeming to gather strength, the shimmering column shot toward the boiling ash storm above. It struck the red clouds with an almighty crash, then swept the billowing ash from the sky on the tide of a cerulean storm.

EIGHTEEN

The Cerulean Storm

Tithian opened his eyes to a turquoise dawn. He blinked several times, trying to clear his vision, but the firmament did not change color. He saw that it was streaked with blazing rays of azure light, while a bank of puffy blue clouds slowly formed overhead.

The king sat up and looked eastward. He did not recognize the luminous sphere he found hanging just above the horizon. The orb resembled a huge sapphire, with shining blue facets and an azure fire burning deep in its heart. It was the sun, but not the sun he knew.

Tithian stared at the blue sphere in amazement, until his eyes began to ache and he realized the glow would blind him if he stared too long. He forced himself to look away and saw that the forest around him had been utterly destroyed. The trees all lay on the ground, their tips pointing away from the grove's center and their boles ripped clean of limbs. In the far distance, there was no sign of the huge wall that had once surrounded the sanctum, or of the great edifices that had stood outside it.

As he surveyed the devastation, the king saw that he still sat in the plaza where he had found Rajaat's prison. The Dark Lens lay on the cracked cobblestones at his feet, murky and cold. Tithian remembered using his serpent's tail to cling to it when the Black exploded, anchoring himself to the ground and calling upon its energy to keep himself from being torn apart by the blast. The effort had finally proven too much for his body, and he had fallen unconscious as the storm began to subside.

On the other side of the Dark Lens lay the marble basin that had held Rajaat's prison. The bowl was now filled with a bubbling, foul-smelling ichor as black as obsidian. In the center, the yellowed bones of a hand protruded above the pool. Its crooked digits looked more like talons than fingers, slightly curled and ending in barbed tips.

"What are you waiting for?" snarled a familiar voice.

Tithian looked over his shoulder and saw Sacha floating toward him. The head was badly battered, with deep lacerations on his scalp, a smashed nose, and yellow bruises covering his face.

"Pull him out!" Sacha demanded.

Tithian lay down at the edge of the basin and stretched an arm across the bubbling soup. He closed his fingers around the hand's naked bones and tried to draw the thing out, but only succeeded in pulling himself toward the ichor. The king opened his grip—then hissed in pain as the hand dug its barbed talons into his palm. It dragged him forward, until his shoulder and head both hung over the dark sludge.

Tithian saved himself by thrusting the fingertips of his free hand into a cracked paving stone. He stopped his slide and slowly drew himself back onto the plaza. Once he had anchored himself securely in place, he began pulling the hand toward him. First the arm, then the shoulder, and finally the head rose from the ichor.

The skeleton had a flat, grossly elongated skull with a sharp ridge crest and a sloped forehead. Beneath its heavy brow, crooked forks of blue light glimmered deep in each eye socket. Wisps of white mist puffed from its nasal cavity. Its jaws were lined with curved yellow needles, while a huge mass of knobby bone formed a long, drooping chin.

"Rajaat?" Tithian gasped.

"Who else?" answered Sacha.

Rajaat sank the talons of his free hand into the stone. He ripped his other claw free and drove it down on the other side of the king, pulling himself to the basin edge. Tithian scrambled back on all fours, barely saving himself from being stepped on as Rajaat pulled himself from the dark pool. The ancient sorcerer's frame was about as tall as an elf and completely skeletal, with hunched shoulders, gangling arms, and ivory-colored thighbones as twisted as they were thick.

The creature's eyes lingered on Tithian's face for an instant, then flickered over the barren trees lying around the plaza's edge, and finally returned to the Dark Lens. Rajaat stared at the black orb for several seconds before finally looking skyward. The fleshless jaws parted in a crude imitation of a smile, then Rajaat opened his mouth wide.

"Free!" he bellowed, his voice rumbling over the sanctum like thunder. Streamers of blue fog gushed from his mouth, condensing into tiny droplets and falling to the ground like rain. "Let the traitors tremble and wail! I have returned, and my retribution shall be bloody and painful!"

As Rajaat spoke, a strange ripple ran through his warped thighs, then through his ribs, arms, and the rest of his bones. Before Tithian's eyes, his yellowed skeleton grew to the size of a half-giant.

The king gathered himself up, then took a deep breath and walked forward. He stopped before Rajaat and bowed. "I am Tithian," he said, not looking up. "I opened your prison."

Rajaat stepped over the king's head without answering. The black ichor trailed after his heels, rising out of the basin and spreading itself over the ground like a shadow. Tithian leaped back, not wanting to have any contact with the foul-smelling stuff, then spun around to request his reward.

"Wait," advised Sacha, staring at Rajaat with an astonished expression.

The ancient sorcerer now stood at least two full heads taller than any half-giant. Although he had only a skeleton for a body, the ichor serving as his shadow had arranged itself into the silhouette of a manlike figure, fully fleshed and with an immensely powerful build.

As Tithian watched, Rajaat raised an arm into the sky as though reaching for something. Far above, a turquoise cloud vanished from sight, then reappeared in his grasp. The ancient sorcerer began to work it with both hands, flattening it out like bread dough, then stretching it into a thin sheet. Once he seemed satisfied with its consistently, he stooped down and pressed it over his foot. The misty fabric stretched over his bones like flesh.

Sacha's jaw fell open. "He's changed." A knowing smile crept across the head's lips, and he said, "This time, he won't fail. Athas shall return to the Blue Age."

Another wave of ripples rolled through Rajaat's yellow bones, and he grew to the height of a ship mast. The ancient sorcerer took a few more steps, positioning himself beneath another cloud, then reached up and plucked it from the sky. He began to work it like the first, fashioning another piece of skin.

Behind Rajaat, the ground became porous and white wherever his shadow passed. A moment later, circles of brilliant color—scarlet, sapphire, saffron, emerald, and a dozen others—burst across the surface, rising from somewhere deep inside the stone. In the center of these vibrant circles sprouted round nubs, like the seedlings of some strange plant.

Rajaat continued to walk around the sanctum, plucking cloud after cloud from the sky and using them to cover his skeleton. Soon, he stood half-again the height of a giant, with no indication that he would quit growing any time soon. Tithian waited until the ancient sorcerer wandered back near him, then moved boldly forward to present himself. He turned a palm toward the ground to prepare a spell that would amplify his voice.

Before the king could begin to draw energy, Rajaat looked down at him and boomed, "No! Not here." The ancient sorcerer waved an enormous hand at the strange rock plants that had sprouted from his shadow. "Never in the Blue Lands."

Tithian closed his hand, satisfied that he had finally won Rajaat's attention. "I am King Tithian of Tyr."

"I know who you are," the ancient sorcerer replied. He looked away from Tithian and plucked another cloud from the sky, then began to work it without paying the king any more attention.

"And do you also know of the promises that were made to me?" Tithian asked in a polite voice.

Rajaat fixed his diamond-shaped eyes on the king and said nothing. Another series of ripples rolled through his body, and he grew even larger.

"Can I expect you to honor those promises?" Tithian called.

"If you wish to serve me, you must learn patience," Rajaat said, stepping away.

"Serve him!" Tithian hissed quietly. He turned to Sacha. "That wasn't part of our bargain."

Rajaat surprised the king by turning around. "You do not wish to serve me?" he asked, a malicious light glimmering in his eyes.

"I wish what I was promised," Tithian said, swallowing nervously. "The powers of an immortal sorcerer-king."

The gleam in Rajaat's eyes grew warmer. "In time," he promised.

The sorcerer held a closed fist far above Tithian's head. The king looked up and saw the hand open high above. A cascade of salty water poured down from the enormous palm, hitting with such force that it swept him off his feet. The deluge did not stop for many moments, until Tithian felt a frothing tide of water rising beneath him.

* * * * *

Sadira peered over the tangle of floating logs, studying the looming figure she took to be Rajaat. He stood twice as tall as any giant, with a crown of lightning crackling around his head. A constant crash of thunder belched forth from his fang-toothed mouth, and whenever he exhaled, billowing blue fog shot from his gaping nostrils and dissolved in a torrent of rain. His entire body was swaddled in roiling clouds the color of turquoise, and great torrents of salty water poured from the claws at the end of his gangling arms. Even his shadow was part of the tempest, causing the water to churn and froth wherever it fell.

"How're we going to kill that?" asked Rikus, crouching at Sadira's side. "He's a walking storm."

The sorceress shook her head. "I don't know, but we'd better think of something fast," she said. "This water isn't getting any shallower."

Using the log tangle as camouflage, Sadira and the mul were wading through a shallow lake that, not long before, had been a vast grove of trees. It was filled with fish and strange, scuttling creatures that vaguely resembled scorpions. The sorceress pushed the heavy load of timber before them instead of Rikus, since her ebony skin and magical powers had returned with the peculiar blue dawn. The mul devoted most of his efforts to his axe, trying to keep it out of the water without letting it show above the logs. Glowing eddies of red and green light swirled over the blade, the result of a magical spell Sadira hoped would prove effective against Rajaat's vapor-covered form.

"There's Tithian," Rikus said.

The mul pointed at a jumble of logs, about fifty yards away and sticking out of the lake at all angles. In the center of the heap sat the king, resting cross-legged atop the Dark Lens. The black orb seemed strangely dark and murky, with only a single flicker of blue light showing deep within it. At Tithian's side hovered Sacha. Both the king and the disembodied head were watching Rajaat, and so far they seemed oblivious to the presence of Sadira and Rikus.

Sadira pushed the log tangle in Tithian's direction, sending a school of fish with squarish heads and writhing tentacles scurrying away. "We'll take the lens first."

"Good thinking. That'll keep Tithian out of the fight," agreed Rikus. "Then what?"

"I'll try fire," Sadira said.

"It makes sense, given what Rajaat's made of," Rikus agreed. "Still, I'm beginning to wish the sorcerer-kings were doing this, instead of us."

"Be careful what you wish for," Sadira said. "A little thing like being trapped under a collapsed wall isn't going to kill the sorcerer-kings."

Rikus frowned. "I suppose that's true," he said. "Maybe we should wait and let them attack first."

"So they can send Rajaat back to his prison and make another Dragon to keep him there?" Sadira scoffed. "I'd rather take our chances attacking him ourselves."

Rikus gave a reluctant nod, and they continued

toward Tithian in silence. As the pair approached, they saw that the logs around the king were covered with a lumpy brown crust of minerals and shells. Sadira cursed silently. They had seen several areas where the tree trunks were covered by similar crusts. Such places were usually surrounded by hedges of submerged rockstem, brightly colored plants that grew in fingerlike formations as hard as rock and as sharp as obsidian.

Sadira heard a muffled clack as one of her logs hit a finger of the rockstem. She and Rikus ducked down, watching through the tangle as Tithian and Sacha spun around. The king and the head peered in their direction for several moments.

Finally, Tithian's voice drifted across the water to Sadira's ears. "It's nothing, just floating logs," the king said, facing Rajaat again.

Sadira motioned for Rikus to ready himself, then pulled a splinter of a log and held it in her open palm. As she whispered her mystic syllables, the sliver floated out of her hand, growing to the size of a war lance. Red smoke poured from all along its shaft, and scarlet sparks shot from its end. The sorceress leveled her finger at the king's head and the spear sizzled away.

The lance had hardly passed out of the log tangle when Rajaat's head snapped around. A blue spark flashed in his eyes as his gaze fell on the sputtering shaft, then he flicked a finger toward it. An enormous bug-eyed fish leaped out the lake and snatched the weapon from midair. The spear exploded in the creature's mouth, blowing its head into a thousand small bits.

"Tithian is my servant," boomed the ancient sorcerer. "Only I may destroy him."

Rajaat stepped toward Sadira and Rikus, crossing two dozen yards of water with a single stride.

"Go, Rikus!" As she spoke, Sadira slipped a hand into the pocket of her wet cloak.

Rikus stepped forward, swinging his axe at the rock-stem. The blade's enchantment sent great geysers of water spiraling into the sky, and the mul smashed a large notch into the top of the hedge.

Tithian leaped off the Dark Lens and disappeared into the tangle of crusted trees.

Sadira pulled a ball of wax and sulfur from her pocket and threw it toward Rajaat, crying out her spell. The yellow ball erupted into a huge sphere of flame. It streaked up to Rajaat's face and engulfed his head—then began to sputter as soon as it contacted the clouds serving as the ancient sorcerer's skin. The fireball died away without raising so much as a puff of steam.

Rajaat reached for Sadira with his claw-fingered hand.

Rikus stepped away from the submerged hedge and swung his axe at the ancient sorcerer's wispy wrist. The steel passed through harmlessly, with no geysers of vapor or swirling fountains of cloud to suggest that Sadira's magic was working. In fact, it came out the other side clean and shiny, the enchantments on its blade dispelled.

Sadira tried to dive away, but Rajaat's fingers closed around her waist before she could submerge herself. The enormous hand felt wet and soft, yet as unyielding as her own dark flesh. The ancient sorcerer lifted her up before his blue eyes and studied her.

From the high vantage point, Sadira could see much of Ur Draxa. It was a huge city of forests and magnificent buildings, with a wide band of destruction encircling the clear waters of Rajaat's spreading lake.

"Stupid half-breed," hissed the ancient sorcerer, pelting her with a gale of cold rain. "Did you really think to use my own magic against me?"

He squeezed, filling Sadira with pain. She pushed against his crushing grip with both arms. It was all she could do to keep her ribs from collapsing. As strong as her sun-enhanced muscles were, Rajaat's were far more powerful.

Sadira looked down and saw Rikus far below, thrashing about madly in the crystalline waters as he vainly chopped at her captor's ankle. It was like trying to cut smoke, save that the blade did not even cause an eddy as it passed through. She tried to yell at him to run, but could not expand her chest far enough to draw air into her lungs.

Rajaat continued to squeeze for several more moments, forks of lightning dancing in his diamond-shaped eyes. Then, as Sadira's muscles began to quiver with fatigue, he relaxed his grip. He looked away from his prisoner and gazed down at the lake below. A school of five huge fish were slipping through the gap Rikus had opened in the rockstem hedge and swimming toward the Dark Lens.

Rajaat smiled and, in a voice so soft Sadira could hardly hear it, whispered, "Finally, the traitors have come!"

The sorceress felt Rajaat's hand tense and realized he was about to throw her. She dug both hands into her captor's vaporish flesh, then the ancient sorcerer hurled her down toward the Dark Lens.

A wisp of turquoise cloud came away in Sadira's hand. As she spoke the single word of her incantation, the vapor spread out beneath her, stopping her fall at the height of Rajaat's waist. The ancient sorcerer took an absentminded swipe at her, sending her cloud drifting away on an invisible tide of air, then fixed his attention on the water at his feet. The crown of lightning around his head began to crackle and dance more madly.

Sadira peered over the edge of her cushion, and saw King Tec rising from beneath the waters with the Dark Lens balanced on his back. He turned toward Rajaat and stared up at the ancient sorcerer, his beak clattering. A short distance away, the water boiled around Nibenay

and Hamanu as they summoned the energy to cast a
spell, leaving a huge expanse of rockstem colorless and
defiled in the process. The Oba and Andropinis stood
nearby, staring intently into the lens as they prepared to
use the Way.

Tithian and Sacha abandoned their hiding places and
started toward the Dark Lens. Rikus, who had continued hacking at Rajaat's ankle until Sadira was freed,
stepped away from the ancient sorcerer and moved to
attack the king.

"Rikus, no!" Sadira reached into her cloak pocket.

From the way Rajaat had reacted when he first saw
the sorcerer-kings, the sorceress suspected he would
attack before "the traitors" could execute their plan. She
did not want Rikus near the Dark Lens when that happened.

The ancient sorcerer's crown of lightning suddenly
fell silent. His gaze went vacant, and a tempest of sapphire hailstones began to build in his diamond-shaped
eyes.

Sadira tossed the tough belly scale of a rock adder
toward her husband, uttering her incantation as it fell. A
shimmering gray shield appeared over the entire area
surrounding him.

Two streams of smoking hailstones hissed down from
Rajaat's eyes. With a deafening roar, the pellets crashed
off the sorceress's shield and bounced away. They
dropped into the lake many yards away, sending steaming plumes of water high into the air.

When the storm subsided, Rajaat's eyes were almost
white with anger. He raised a foot to step toward Sadira,
flashing sheets of lightning crackling off his crown.

Hamanu and Nibenay pointed toward the Dark Lens,
roaring the incantations to cast their spells. Tiny streams
of absolute blackness shot from their fingertips into the
orb. The currents came out on the other side magnified
into great rivers and washed over Rajaat, swallowing

Rikus and Tithian on the way.

The Oba and Andropinis attacked next, facing each other and moving their hands through the empty air. They kept their eyes fixed on the ebony murk that had engulfed Rajaat, and soon the dark mass began to assume the shape of a sphere. When the globe was perfectly round, the two sorcerers moved closer together. The black orb holding Rajaat began to shrink.

Sadira felt far from relieved. The sorcerer-kings' plan had been an efficient one, and her intervention on Rikus's behalf had kept Rajaat's counterattack from interrupting it. Still, the ancient sorcerer had clearly been expecting the sorcerer-kings—even looking forward to their arrival. Given that, it seemed strange that he had relied on only one spell to stop them, and that his last act before being captured had been to come after her.

This battle, the sorceress suspected, was far from over. Nevertheless, she had learned something valuable from it. The Dark Lens was not only a mindbender's tool. The sorcerer-kings had used it to increase the power of their spells a hundredfold. Unfortunately, Sadira had already seen that her own magic had very little effect on Rajaat, and she did not think the lens would change that. But she knew of someone else who might be able to use the orb to good effect.

Sadira took a deep breath, then turned and uttered a soft incantation. When she exhaled, her cloud began to move as though a stiff wind were blowing it across the sky. The sorceress cupped one hand and held it out to her side. Her flying cushion turned toward the Dark Lens. Keeping a watchful eye on the sorcerer-kings, she flew over and slowly circled the area.

Nibenay raised a hand to wave her down. "You've served us well," he said. "You have nothing to fear from us."

Sadira did not fly any lower. Watching both him and

Hamanu even more closely, she asked, "And what of Rikus?"

"In there, with the Usurper and Rajaat," said Hamanu, gesturing at the black sphere. The Oba and Andropinis had already managed to squeeze the globe down so that it was no taller than a small giant.

Sadira tried not to be afraid. She had retrieved people from the Black before, and she saw no reason that she would not be able to do it again.

Her hopes must have shown on her face.

Nibenay said, "Don't think that your powers can call your husband back. He's beneath the Black, not part of it."

"What's the difference?" Sadira asked.

"The Black is shadow. It shows what is by what is missing," explained Hamanu. "But beneath the Black is the Hollow, where nothing is missing because nothing remains—not the future, not the past, not even the Gray. Nothing—simply nothing."

"Now, come down here as I told you to do," Nibenay commanded, his voice growing irritated. "It will be better for you and us if we declare a truce."

Pretending to accept the sorcerer-king's offer, Sadira circled around to have one last look for her husband. She angled her hands so that her cloud descended, swooping low over Rajaat's new prison and the Dark Lens. When she saw nothing but the white, lifeless rock-stem that Nibenay and Hamanu had defiled, the sorceress curved away.

That was when she noticed a black shadow swimming through the water behind Andropinis. Though only about the size of an elf, the silhouette retained Rajaat's basic shape. It was slithering along the bottom of the defiled lake, so that only someone looking down from directly above was likely to see it.

Rajaat had learned a new trick in his prison. While the sorcerer-kings concentrated on capturing his body, he had been lurking in his own shadow all along.

Sadira smiled to herself. Now she knew how to defeat Rajaat. All she had to do was steal the lens and return to the crater with it.

Nibenay turned his palm downward and defiled more rockstem, preparing to cast a spell. The sorceress continued to fly, trying not to watch Rajaat's shadow. The sorcerer-king raised his hand, pointing toward Sadira.

In the same instant, Rajaat's shadow emerged from the water and threw his dripping arms around Andropinis's throat.

"For you, eternal confinement," Rajaat hissed.

Andropinis screamed in alarm as his ancient master's silhouette swallowed him. The sorcerer-king's cry fell silent almost at once, and no sign of him remained.

Nibenay changed his aim from Sadira to Rajaat and fairly screamed his incantation. A net of pulsing white energy shot from his hand. It passed through the ancient sorcerer's shadowy form without effect, but the Oba, who had been standing across from Andropinis when he was seized, had to duck to avoid being hit. Deprived of any chance to cast a spell or use the Way against her former master, she dropped into the water and pushed herself away from him.

Rajaat ignored the sorcerer-queen and stepped toward the Dark Lens, which was still being supported on King Tec's back. Nibenay and Hamanu, standing between the ancient sorcerer and the lens, retreated in opposite directions, one summoning the energy for a spell and the other furrowing his brow as he prepared to use the Way.

Sadira circled around and lined herself up behind Rajaat. She moved toward the back of her cloud so there would be room for the Dark Lens, then angled the nose downward and started to descend.

On the other side of the lens, the Black stopped shrinking. "I need help!" King Tec yelled, still trying to keep the lens focused on the shadowy sphere. "Nibenay, Hamanu—"

Rajaat stepped up behind him, plucking the Dark Lens off his back. "For you, death."

He brought the orb down. Tec's skull split with a tremendous bang, spraying foul-smelling smoke and sizzling drops of fiery red blood in all directions.

Sadira smiled. She was coming up directly behind Rajaat. The sorceress hoped to lift the Dark Lens out of his grasp as her cloud passed through his shadowy body. But if her tactic resulted in a collision instead, she would have a better chance than anyone of recovering the Dark Lens. With her body imbued by the sun's power, the impact would not harm her, and at least she was anticipating it.

Rajaat faced Nibenay, raising the lens in both hands. "For you, a thousand years of torment."

Rajaat stepped toward the sorcerer-king, causing Sadira to pull up the front of her cloud and execute a tight bank. She rose along the side of the ancient sorcerer's shoulder. For an instant, the sorceress feared he would glimpse her in his peripheral vision, then she was staring up at the Dark Lens.

The cloud lifted the heavy orb out of Rajaat's hands—then abruptly dove as the extra weight pushed the nose down. Sadira found herself dropping straight toward the dark sphere in which Rikus and Tithian were imprisoned. Behind her, Rajaat cried out in surprise and sorcerer-kings began shouting orders. The sorceress hardly heard them, for she was too busy trying to pull the Dark Lens toward the rear of the cloud so the nose would rise.

As Sadira approached the Black, a surge of searing energy rushed up from the depths of the Dark Lens. Forks of blue lightning crackled over her body, and she began to suffer muscle spasms. Surprised, she could not prevent her cloud from continuing its dive, and it crashed straight into the murky sphere the sorcerer-kings had created.

Sadira saw a black flash. The explosion that followed was not as large as the one that had destroyed the Dragon's sanctum, for the lens was only partially charged. Still, the sorceress found herself soaring through the air backwards. She splashed into the shallow lake some distance away, with the Dark Lens pressing down on her chest and water filling her lungs.

NINETEEN

Flood Waters

Rikus kicked off the hipbone of a massive skeleton and sailed through the colorless ether. He grabbed Tithian by his long braid of gray hair and used it to pull them together, then slipped an arm around the king's throat and squeezed. The king coughed and rasped for breath, digging his fingers into the mul's arm in a futile attempt to free himself. Rikus only tightened his grip.

The mul, the king, and Sacha were floating inside a black sphere with a huge skeleton Rikus assumed to be Rajaat's. It was impossible to tell the size of their prison. The place seemed entirely filled by the ancient sorcerer's yellowed bones, yet Tithian had tried several times to push off an ankle or hand and float out to the dark walls. He had never seemed able to reach them, and when Rikus caught up with him, they had always seemed to be next to the skeleton.

Rikus glimpsed Sacha floating toward his back from behind a thighbone. The mul gave his torso a sharp twist, but used too much power and spun himself past the disembodied head. More accustomed to maneuvering through the air, Sacha took advantage of the mistake to streak forward. He clamped his teeth around the warrior's ear and began to rip.

Screaming in pain, Rikus shoved Tithian away, and, with a stomp-kick to the back, sent the king tumbling toward the skeleton's skull. The mul reached up, grasping Sacha by the nose with one hand and by the chin with the other. He snapped his attacker's mouth open, drawing a loud crack from the lower jaw, then brought his knee up and smashed Sacha against it. Sacha's eyes went glassy and blank, then brown, foul-smelling ooze began to pour from his nostrils and ears.

Rikus tossed Sacha's crushed skull aside, then turned back toward Tithian. The king was floating near the skeleton's head, his dark eyes locked on the mul. Fearing that the king was preparing to attack with the Way, Rikus ducked under the skeleton's leg.

As Rikus started to pull himself forward, crooked lines of lightning began dancing across the walls of the black sphere. His first thought was that Tithian was responsible. He peered over the skeleton's torso and found the king staring in confusion at the dark shell of their prison.

The lightning cords suddenly connected with each other, forming a crackling net of energy. With a shrill hiss, the black walls dissolved into wisps of shadow. A blinding blue flash filled the sphere, then the mul felt himself being drawn upward.

Rikus tumbled through the air for what seemed a long time, his eyes filled with spots. Finally, he began to arc downward, and, through his erratic vision, he saw turquoise clouds and a blue sun above him. He hit the water so hard that it felt as if he had slammed into a granite plain instead of splashing into a lake. The air rushed from his lungs, and he went under.

Rikus felt himself touch bottom, then pushed off and shot back to the surface of the lake. He came up coughing water and flailing his arms. Somehow, he managed to keep his head above water long enough to see a floating tree trunk, then swam toward it with choppy, uneven strokes.

When he reached his goal, Rikus threw his arms over the log and spent several moments clearing his lungs of water. His flesh stung and his joints ached from the impact of the fall, but he did not feel any serious injuries.

A loud boom echoed across the lake from behind Rikus. Fearing a magical attack from Tithian, the mul twisted around. More than fifty paces away, he saw a black orb streaking into the sky. Sitting on top of it was the figure of an ebony-skinned woman, her long amber hair waving in the wind. Sadira had recovered the Dark Lens.

Rikus started to call out for her to come back, but stopped when he saw the figures of three sorcerer-kings rising from the lake to go after her. He could hear their voices shouting, but was too distant to understand their words. Two of them turned their palms downward, and frothing spouts of water rose toward their hands as they summoned the energy to cast spells.

Rikus cursed his inability to aid Sadira, then watched as the sorcerer-kings closed their hands and pointed toward his wife.

"Sadira, watch yourself!"

As the mul called the words, Rajaat's skeleton rose out of the lake between the sorcerer-kings and Sadira. It was not as large as when Rikus had first seen it, now standing only about as high as a full giant.

"No!" boomed Rajaat's angry voice. "You shall wait here for your punishment."

The skeleton pointed three of its curled talons at the sorcerer-kings. Glittering blue bubbles shot from the digits, and each engulfed one of the figures flying after Sadira. The shimmering balls of water brought their prisoners to a quick halt. They began to drift over the lake in a lazy circle, small bulges appearing in their liquid walls as the occupants tried to free themselves with magic spells, the Way, and physical blows.

After watching them for a moment, Rajaat's skeleton turned around. Sadira had already disappeared with the lens. The ancient sorcerer stared after her for a moment. Finally, he plucked a cloud from the sky and began to flatten it into a sheet of vaporish skin, walking after Sadira as he worked.

Rikus pushed himself to the end of his tree and began to kick his legs, but quickly realized there was no need. A brisk tide was flowing after Rajaat, carrying the mul and an ever-growing jumble of logs along with it. Rikus tried to raise himself above the debris, searching for a glimpse of what he hoped would be Tithian's dead body.

Rikus saw no sign of the king, and soon he could not afford to look. The current was beginning to froth and bang logs against each other. It took all of his mulish strength just to keep his head above water and not lose his grip on his makeshift raft.

* * * * *

As the current carried Tithian out of the shadows, a sharp crack sounded from the roof of the arch. The king ducked under the frothing waters, narrowly escaping before a shower of splinters erupted from his log. The river throbbed with the pulse of the blast, battering his ears with terrible pangs of agony.

Staying submerged, the king swung under his log and came up on the other side, looking toward the top of the arch. He saw the small figure of a halfling male. The man was peering into the tangle of logs, no doubt searching for Tithian's body, and at the same time slipping a cone-shaped pellet into the groove of a tiny crossbow.

Tithian ducked back under the water, knowing from experience how deadly the little crossbows could be. During his short float trip down what had once been Ur Draxa's processional avenue, he had seen dozens of halflings using the weapons, indiscriminately killing the former residents of the city. They seemed entirely determined to murder every non-halfling in sight.

Once the king judged the floodwaters had carried him safely out of range, he pulled himself onto his log and gasped for breath. Although he was using the Way to augment his strength, the effort of clinging to the tree in roiling floodwaters was wearing on his old man's body. If this chase did not end soon, he feared he would be in no condition to steal the lens back from Sadira.

Tithian propped himself up on his log and looked ahead. All he could see in front of him was a bizarre, watery city that had once been Ur Draxa. The stern architecture had been replaced by flowing bends and gentle curves, with not a sharp corner in sight. The granite arches and marble buildings were now made of colorful rockstem, while the monuments lining the avenue depicted mild-mannered halflings. Instead of axes and swords, these small heroes held writing quills and vials of peculiar shapes, their placid expressions and serene smiles strangely at odds with the murderous behavior of the bloodthirsty warriors now roaming the canals.

Finally, Tithian spotted Rajaat's looming form at the end of the avenue, a walking storm of cerulean clouds. Once again, a crown of lightning crackled around his head and gales of rain poured from his hands. As Tithian watched, the ancient sorcerer lifted a foot and kicked open the enormous gates. Rajaat ducked beneath the keystone and vanished from the king's sight. The floodwaters rushed after him, pouring onto the plain beyond.

* * * * *

Sadira descended toward the crater and saw that the lake of bubbling black goo had evaporated from the basin, leaving the interior as smooth as a glass bowl. In places, the sheen rose almost as high as the rim, reflecting the rays of the blue sun back into the center of the valley. There, the azure beams gathered in an ethereal ball that the sorceress found as discomfiting as the new color of the heavens. As beautiful as they were, blue skies and blue suns had no place above the deserts of Athas. They harkened back to a gentler age, an age that could only be restored by killing most of what now lived on the dusty planet. As much as Sadira longed for a better world, she would not pay the price that Rajaat demanded. She had to stop him.

As the sorceress circled the basin, cold fingers of apprehension spread through her chest, for she saw no sign of Neeva's hiding place. The rocks where Rikus had concealed the warrior were gone, fused into the lustrous veneer of the caldron. Sadira tried to stay calm by reminding herself of Rkard's strength. The boy was more than strong enough to carry his mother to safety— assuming that whatever had scoured the crater clean had allowed him the chance.

With an increasingly heavy heart, Sadira crossed to the outside slope of the rim and continued her search. She did not call out. A gentle breeze was blowing toward the city, and it would not do to have it carry her voice across the plain. She could already see that Rajaat's towering form had left Ur Draxa and was coming toward her, and the last thing she wanted was for him to hear her calling for Rkard and Neeva.

Sadira landed on the north side of the crater, where a high section in the opposite rim would shelter her from Rajaat's view. She climbed up to a notch in the crest and deposited the Dark Lens in the nook. She filled the gaps around the orb with dirt and rocks, her magic-enhanced strength making quick work of the task. The sorceress was not trying to hide the lens so much as prop it up and camouflage it well enough to keep it from being seen at first glance.

After pausing to look around the area one last time, Sadira climbed up to the rim's crest. She slowly circled back toward Ur Draxa, scanning the exterior slope of the crater and forcing herself to resist the temptation to call the young mul's name.

The sorceress did not know what she would do if the boy had left or died. She was counting on his spell to do what she could not: exterminate Rajaat. Sadira's powers, based as they were on the ancient sorcerer's own magic, would be of little use in the coming battle. But Rkard's powers were the opposite of Rajaat's. They were based in the element of fire, while the ancient sorcerer was closely allied with the element of water. If anything could destroy Rajaat, it would be Rkard's magic.

The sorceress stepped around a jagged crag and the ramparts of Ur Draxa came into sight, glowing scarlet and emerald with the brilliant hues of living rockstem. Rajaat had already crossed most of the plain. As he came forward, forks of lightning shot down from his crown to strike at the ground, and torrents of rain poured from his hands. Thunder rumbled from his mouth, and dark, seething plumes of vapor shot from his nostrils. On his heels came a frothing wall of water, rolling across the broken ground and rapidly flooding the whole plain.

Sadira ducked back behind the crag to prepare for the coming battle.

"Where's Rikus?" whispered a familiar voice.

Sadira bit her tongue to keep from yelling and spun around. Rkard stood a few steps away, crouching behind a small boulder. The sorceress went to his side.

"I was afraid—I thought you had left," she whispered, hugging him tight. "Is your mother safe?"

The boy nodded. "The black stuff started to boil, and

we had to move. She sent me up to get you," he said. "Where's Rikus?"

"We'll look for him later," Sadira said, standing. "Right now, I need your help."

Tears welled in Rkard's eyes. "Rikus isn't coming back, is he?" he asked. "He's dead, just like my father!"

Sadira kneeled in front of the boy. "We don't know that, Rkard!" she snapped, grasping his shoulders tightly. "But we have to worry about ourselves and your mother now. Rajaat's coming, and I need your help to stop him."

Rkard looked away and bit his lip, gathering himself together. "What do you want me to do?"

"Nothing you haven't done many times before."

Sadira guided him toward the Dark Lens, explaining her plan as they walked. When she finished, she made the young mul repeat it twice. The sorceress did not think Rkard would have trouble understanding what she required, for the task was simple and he was a smart boy. She just wanted to make sure he knew that the plan would work even if she were killed.

After helping Rkard find a good hiding place, Sadira climbed a quarter of the way around the crater. When she came to a place where the outside slope fell away in a sheer drop, she stopped. This would be a good place to wait. She could jump behind the crater rim to shelter herself from Rajaat's magic, while her ebon-skinned body would not be harmed by the plunge to the sharp rocks below.

Rajaat's flashing crown appeared above the opposite rim, filling the caldron with echoes of crackling lightning. The entire basin shook with the power of his thunderous bellows. The ancient sorcerer started to climb, and frothing floodwaters began to whirl around the base of the crater.

Sadira turned a palm toward the ground, summoning the power to cast a normal spell. As the energy flowed into her body, she pulled a stick of incense from her pocket and watched Rajaat's head appear above the far crest. His vaporish skin hung from his face in billowing folds, with dark creases that gave him a fierce and sinister appearance. From the size of his eyes and the diameter of his crown, she guessed the ancient sorcerer was about the size of a giant.

Sadira waited until Rajaat had stepped onto the crest of the ridge, then pointed the incense at him and uttered her incantation. The end of the stick flared and started to burn. As the smoke rose into the air, plumes of steam began to trail off the ancient sorcerer's misty flesh. Long gashes and round holes quickly opened, exposing the yellowed bones beneath.

Rajaat waved a wispy claw over his body and muttered a counterspell. The incense in Sadira's hand went out, and the steam stopped rising from the wounds on his body. The ancient sorcerer stepped into the crater. When his feet slipped on the slick sides, he spread his arms and floated down the steep slope like fog. He never took his eyes off Sadira.

"I created sorcery," Rajaat hissed, stepping across the basin. "How can you think your pitiful skills a match for mine?"

Rajaat pointed a curved talon at her head. Sadira spun away, confident her plan would work as she intended. Another step forward would bring her foe into perfect position for Rkard's spell.

A string of mystic syllables rumbled from Rajaat's mouth. The throbbing roar of a mighty whirlwind howled over the basin, and a spout of dark clouds shot from the ancient sorcerer's finger. It streaked toward Sadira, hurling lightning and pounding columns of water at her side of the crater.

The sorceress jumped off the cliff. The spinning winds hit behind her, ripping the rim into an explosion of broken rock. The storm caught Sadira before she hit the ground and lifted her into a swirling tempest of boulders and water. Lightning bolts stabbed at her from every direction. When they struck, they did not die away, but crackled over her body in an endless loop. She was quickly enclosed in a sizzling cage of energy, which flashed twice around the whirlwind and disappeared into the dark clouds. The cyclone sped out across the flooded plain.

A quarter of the way around the crater, Rkard peered over the Dark Lens and watched the storm disappear. His breath came in gasps, and his heart was pounding so hard his chest hurt, but he forced himself to stay calm and concentrate on what he had to do.

Rkard turned his gaze into the crater, where Rajaat's cloud-wrapped figure stood in the middle of the basin. The ancient sorcerer's shadow lay against the western rim, looking distinctly insignificant. Resisting the temptation to attack—and not at all certain he was doing the right thing—the young mul waited. He did not take his eyes off his target for even an instant, and hardly dared to blink.

Sadira had said that Rajaat would chase her, and that Rkard should not cast his spell until the ancient sorcerer's silhouette fell across the bottom of the crater. It was the shadow they wanted to destroy, not the cloud body.

Rajaat did not go after Sadira. Instead, he remained in the crater, pulling blue clouds out of the sky and using them to patch his wounds. Rkard watched with an open mouth, more in wonder than fear.

The ancient sorcerer continued to heal himself for several moments, stopping only when he had covered all the holes on his body. Rkard braced himself for the attack, ready to call on the sun's power as soon as his foe moved to follow Sadira. Rajaat did not cooperate. Not even glancing toward the distant cyclone, the sorcerer ran his gaze over the interior of the crater, searching for the Dark Lens.

Rkard touched his hand to the sun-mark on his fore-head, not trusting the strange blue orb in the sky to sup-ply the magic he needed. He considered casting his spell at that moment, before his enemy's glowing eyes could fall on the lens. Then he remembered what Sadira had told him about how the sorcerer-kings had imprisoned the cloud, only to be attacked by the shadow a few moments later.

"Rajaat isn't like us. He doesn't give form to his shadow," she had said. "It shapes him."

Rkard studied his foe's shadow more carefully. From the other side of the Dark Lens, he could angle his spell to strike the silhouette where it lay now. Hoping this small change wouldn't ruin Sadira's plan, but seeing no other way to do as she had instructed, he crawled across the hot surface of the lens to the other side. He would have gone around the bottom of the orb, but it was so big that he would not have been able to see Rajaat—and no matter what happened, he was determined not to take his eyes off his prey.

Rajaat locked his eyes onto Rkard's face and stepped toward him. Although the boy could still see most of Rajaat's shadow, one flank and part of a leg were hidden behind the sorcerer's body.

"Give me my lens, filthy child," Rajaat growled. He gestured at the Dark Lens with a clawed finger.

The young mul pressed his palm to the warm obsid-ian and cast his sun-spell. Rajaat's eyes flared white, though the boy could not say whether it was with alarm or anger, then a ruby light flared deep inside the orb.

Rkard did not expect what happened next. The lens flashed scarlet, then searing red flames spread over the surface. The boy cried out in alarm and backed away as the Dark Lens erupted into a miniature version of the crimson sun.

* * * * *

Neeva heard a booming voice from inside the crater.
"I created sorcery," it said. "How can you think your
pitiful skills a match for mine?"

The warrior looked up. From her hiding place on the
uphill side of a boulder, she could see both Sadira and
her son. The sorceress stood on top of a small cliff, about
a quarter of the way around the crater rim from where
Rkard hid with the Dark Lens. Neeva could not see the
speaker, though she felt certain from what she had
heard that it was Rajaat.

A string of mystic syllables rumbled from inside the
crater, then Neeva heard the throbbing roar of a whirlwind. Sadira jumped off the cliff. Her feet had barely left
the rim before a dark cyclone ripped it apart. A ball of
lightning formed around the sorceress as the spinning
winds swallowed her up, then the storm raced away
over the flooded plain.

"No!" Neeva gasped.

The warrior pushed herself up, bracing her back
against the boulder. The effort of standing made her
cold legs ache to the bone, while the small of her back
felt like someone had plunged a burning dagger into it.
Still, Neeva was thankful that she could stand at all.
When her son had cast his healing spell on her at sun-
rise, it had taken a long time for the feeling to return
below her waist, and she had begun to fear that her
injuries were too serious for him to repair.

Leaning against the boulder, Neeva turned to watch
the cyclone, hoping to see what became of Sadira.
Instead, she saw a gaunt and bedraggled figure pulling
himself from the floodwaters. Even from twenty paces
away, she could see that he had a hooked nose and a
long braid of gray hair.

"Tithian!" she hissed.

The king looked up the hill toward Rkard, whose
attention was raptly fixed on the crater basin. Not even
pausing to gather his breath, Tithian rose and started up

the slope on trembling legs.

Neeva grabbed a fist-sized rock and, gritting her teeth against the pain, took her first step across the slippery hillside. Rkard had told her that it was risky for her to walk, but with Tithian on the loose, she knew it was more dangerous not to. The warrior managed half a dozen steps before the king glimpsed her and stopped.

Tithian faced her and sneered, turning his palm toward the ground. "I thought you'd be dead by now."

Neeva braced her feet and threw the rock in her hand, aiming for the throat. Tithian ducked, and the stone struck him in the temple with a sharp crack. The king dropped to the ground. Though it was possible the blow had killed her target outright, the warrior knew better than to count on that. She hobbled over to her prey and found his eyes rolled back in the sockets. She grabbed a large stone and raised it over his head, taking no chances with the treacherous king.

Tithian's hand suddenly shot up, directing a brilliant flash into the warrior's eyes. Neeva's vision instantly went white. She slammed the stone down and heard it clatter harmlessly off the ground. The warrior went into a blind-fighting pattern. She pivoted away from the last place she had seen the king and circled her hands in front of her body, frequently changing directions to prevent her enemy from predicting where the gaps would appear.

A cruel chuckle sounded at Neeva's side. Sweeping her arm around in a circular trapping motion, she stepped toward the sound—then stumbled and nearly fell when her lethargic legs did not respond as she expected. The warrior felt Tithian's hot breath on the back of her neck and realized that he had used a spell to throw his voice.

Expecting to feel the bite of a dagger blade in her kidneys at any moment, the warrior arched her stomach forward and swung her head back. She heard a loud crack as her skull smashed the king's nose, then felt his arm draped across her shoulder. He had been trying to cut her throat. Neeva drove her hand up inside Tithian's arm and forced his wrist away from her neck. She bent forward, pulling him over her back, and heard him land in a heap in front of her.

Neeva tried to raise her foot to stomp the king's head, but succeeded only in sending a fiery pang of agony shooting through her leg. Tithian clattered across the rocky ground, rolling or crawling away, and the warrior lost track of his exact location. Gray spots were beginning to appear in the white glare of her vision, but she still could not see. The king stopped moving and fell silent. Neeva felt sure that he was preparing a spell, but had no idea of how to avoid it.

She heard something rising out of the water, then Rikus's voice shouted, "Dive roll, quarter right!"

The command called for a maneuver they had used during their days in the arena together, and Neeva knew exactly what it meant. She threw herself forward at an angle, crashing into Tithian's soft midsection before she hit the ground. The king cried out in surprise. She heard the hiss of mystic energy discharging into the air, then came down on top of his body.

The air left Tithian's lungs in a sharp grunt, but he did not stop fighting. Neeva felt him pull both arms out from beneath her body. She raised her arm to block the right one, assuming it held the dagger.

"No, left!" Rikus called. By the sound of his voice, he was almost upon them.

Neeva could not switch blocks, so she rolled toward the king's left arm and pinned it beneath her weight. She brought her hand down and found his wrist, then gave it a sharp twist and heard the hollow pop of a bone coming out of its socket. Tithian cried out in pain, then smashed his right hand into his attacker's back and shoved her off.

Neeva heard him scrambling away, then found the dagger on the ground where he had dropped it. Her vision was now growing clear enough that she could make it out as a gray blur lying on the black smudge of the ground.

Tithian began to run up the hill toward Rkard, as Neeva could tell by the sound of the rocks clattering beneath his feet. At the same time, she heard Rikus's heavy steps charging up from her other side. Neeva took the dagger by the blade.

"Knife, Rikus!"

Neeva flipped the dagger into the air, angling her throw so it flew toward Rikus hilt first. An instant later, the weapon came hissing back above her head. Tithian screamed, but she did not hear him fall.

"Damn!" Rikus snapped, stopping at her side.

Neeva felt the mul take her arm and pull her up. Terrible pains shot through her legs as her weight returned to them, but they did not collapse beneath her. She also discovered that she had recovered her vision well enough to see the mul's face. He looked as haggard and weary as had Tithian, with beads of water running off his body and dark circles beneath his eyes.

"I've been trying to catch Tithian since Rajaat flooded Ur Draxa, and now he's disappeared again," Rikus said.

Neeva pointed toward the Dark Lens. "I doubt it," she said. "He was trying for the lens when I attacked him."

The mul's face went white, then he started up the hill at a sprint. Neeva followed more slowly. Each step was a struggle, but she was determined not to wait idly by while Tithian took the lens.

A few steps up the slope, she confirmed her suspicions. A trail of blood led up the toward the Dark Lens. Neeva looked up, preparing to call a warning.

She did not have the chance. Her son had crawled over the lens to the other side and was staring into the basin, his attention consumed by Rajaat. The ancient sorcerer's crown of lightning showed above the top of the lens, but that was all Neeva could see of him.

"Give me my lens, filthy child," growled Rajaat's booming voice.

Rkard pressed his palm to the Dark Lens and cast his sun-spell. A ruby light flared deep inside the orb, and the entire lens flashed scarlet. Neeva caught a glimpse of Tithian's gaunt form pressed against the bottom half of the obsidian globe, his arms spread wide and gripping the lens. The king screamed in agony. Searing red flames burst over the Dark Lens's glassy surface, and the orb erupted into a miniature version of the crimson sun. Tithian's silhouette vanished into the inferno.

* * * * *

Rkard heard Tithian scream and glanced down in time to see the king's silhouette vanish in the inferno. The boy wondered briefly where Tithian had come from, then cowered down behind the crater rim, waiting for Rajaat to cast the spell that would obliterate him and half the hillside.

The ancient sorcerer did not attack. Instead, he reached for the crimson fireball that was the Dark Lens. When his hands came near, the scarlet flames suddenly left the surface of the orb and shot across the basin. As the fire stream passed Rajaat, the flame evaporated half the clouds on his torso, then washed over the far wall with a tremendous roar.

Rajaat's shadow vanished beneath the fire storm. His cloud-covered body stopped moving, and his arms froze in place over the lens. The fire curled back toward the center of the basin and formed a roiling ball of flame a dozen yards behind Rajaat. The fiery ball did not look so different from Rkard's normal sun-spell, except that it was a hundred times as large and a thousand times as bright. Squinting against the brilliant light, the young mul stood to get a better look over the rim.

"What are you doing?" cried a familiar voice. "Get down!"

A pair of powerful arms seized Rkard by the waist and pulled him away from the rim.

"Rikus!" The boy twisted around and threw his arms around the warrior's neck. In the distance beyond, Rkard noticed that the storm that had carried Sadira away was breaking up. "You're alive!"

"Of course I am. Let's make your mother happy and keep you that way, too," Rikus responded. "What's going on here?"

Rikus pointed at Rajaat's hands, which were still hanging motionless over the Dark Lens. The lens itself was no longer burning, but its surface was glowing red. There was no sign of Tithian, save for a puddle of liquid steel that had once been his dagger.

"I'm not sure what happened," Rkard answered. "I cast my spell at Rajaat's shadow, just like Sadira said. But I don't think it worked. He just stopped moving." Rikus frowned. "We'd better have a look."

Together, they crawled to the top of the rim and peered over. Rajaat's cloud-covered body was beginning to boil away in the heat of Rkard's giant sun-spell. The fireball was blazing so brightly that even the young sun-cleric could not look at it for more than a second. Nevertheless, what he saw in that time was more than enough to concern Rkard. A pair of blue diamonds stared out from inside the flaming orb, and they were staring straight at his face.

Rkard ducked behind the rim again, pulling Rikus down beside him. "I think Rajaat's caught inside my sun-spell."

Rikus smiled. "You trapped him?"

"For now," he said. "But what happens when my spell expires?"

"We'll just have to make sure that doesn't happen,"

said Sadira's voice.

Rkard looked back to see the sorceress stepping off a small cloud. She was still dripping wet, but appeared otherwise unaffected by her battle with the cyclone. A few paces below Sadira, the young mul's mother was laboriously climbing up the hill.

Rkard frowned and started to chastise her for walking, but Rikus caught the boy's shoulder. "I wouldn't say anything right now," the warrior advised.

Rkard nodded, then asked, "Are you well, Mother?"

"Just fine, thanks to you," she said.

Rkard smiled, then turned to Sadira. "I don't know how the Dark Lens will affect my spell," he said. "But it usually only lasts for a quarter-hour or so."

"We won't need nearly that long," the sorceress said. She reached into her pocket and fished out a small sliver of diamond. "This should keep your fire burning forever."

Sadira stepped near the Dark Lens and cast her spell. The diamond shard disappeared from between her fingers, and a stream of white light flowed into the obsidian. It emerged on the other side as a silvery river of magic energy, engulfing the fiery orb of Rkard's sunspell. Pearly wisps of flame began to shoot through the fireball, and it burned with a new brilliance.

Rajaat's crown exploded into a furious storm of energy, spreading a sheet of blue lightning across the sky. With a deafening thunderclap, the ancient sorcerer's mouth fell open, spewing a stream of hail out over the flooded plain.

For a moment, Rkard feared that their enemy would free himself, then Rajaat began to dissolve. The skeleton came apart first, slipping from the cloud-body and clattering into the basin in a heap. Next, the arms and legs floated away. The torso flattened out into a platter-shaped wafer, and the shoulders and head slowly melted into it. The ancient sorcerer's crown was the last thing to disappear, forks of blue lightning still dancing in a circle as a turquoise fog spread over the entire basin.

The cloud hovered near the top of the rim for a moment, then suddenly spun up into the heavens and spread over the entire sky. Bolts of lightning crackled down from the dark shroud, while peals of thunder echoed off Ur Draxa's distant walls. A heavy rain began to fall, pounding Rkard like a ruthless enemy, but the boy did not care. A short distance above the eastern horizon, he could see the sun's halo shining through the angry tempest, and it was crimson.

EPILOGUE

Seven figures stood on the hill above the Gate of Doom, all lost in their own thoughts. Neeva and Rkard kneeled at the edge of the cliff, looking down into the valley where Caelum had died, their heads bowed in silent contemplation. Sadira sat a short distance away, near Rikus, save that the Dark Lens rested on the ground between them.

The two sorcerer-kings, Nibenay and Hamanu, and the sorcerer-queen, the Oba of Gulg, waited at the end of the ridge. They were looking across the Ring of Fire, at the massive wall of steam that had arisen when Rajaat's flood finally overspilled the Draxan plain and cascaded into the boiling lava lake below. More than anyone, the rulers seemed to sense that the time had come to rethink old ways, to forget old enmities, to find new approaches to the challenge of life on Athas.

Rikus found himself wondering what this moment looked like to them, through cruel eyes that had already seen a countless chain of passing days. They appeared neither sad nor happy, and the mul wondered if it was even possible for them to have such emotions. Would this day be a turning point in their long lives, or was it simply a time when it had become necessary to form new alliances? He did not know the answer and suspected they did not either. For now, only one thing was important: a truce had been struck, and once the terms were met, there would no longer be a reason to fight—at least not until they had all returned home and recovered enough to think of new reasons.

The Oba turned to Sadira and nodded. The sorceress stood and wrapped her ebony arms around the lens, then picked it up. Rikus did not stand with her, for those were not the terms of the agreement. Sadira had to do this alone, for Nibenay and Hamanu were as weary and mistrustful of the Tyrians as the Tyrians were of them.

As Sadira started forward, a thunderbolt crackled down from the sky and another torrential downpour began. No one paid it much attention, for it was not the first rainstorm that had burst over the valley.

Then a sharp voice boomed. "Stop!"

Rikus leaped up, his empty hands tensed into weapons, and Sadira put the Dark Lens down, already preparing to cast a spell through it. Rkard also stood, raising his hand toward the crimson sun, and even Neeva, wincing with pain, pushed herself to her feet. The Athasian rulers reacted just as quickly, the Oba and Hamanu furrowing their brows as they prepared to use the Way, while Nibenay turned his palm toward the ground.

"You can't do this!" said the voice. Something about it seemed faintly familiar, but there was a strained, sizzling tone that made it difficult for Rikus to place. "Stop. I demand it!"

A sphere of blue mist formed in the rains, hovering in the space between Sadira and the sorcerer-kings. It began to ripple and waver, slowly taking on the ghostly features of an old man's gaunt, sharp-featured face.

"Tithian!" Rikus gasped. "I thought you were dead!"

Another bolt of lightning danced across the sky, and a peal of thunder shook the entire ridge. "Not dead, imprisoned. Before you destroy the lens, free me."

"To do what?" demanded Neeva, limping to Rikus's side. "Become king of Athas?"

"No," the head replied, his face suddenly growing pained and lonely. "Kill me if you wish, but you can't leave me here."

"And what will happen if we do, Usurper?" demanded Nibenay, a crooked smile spreading across his thin snout. "Will you make it rain on us?"

The sorcerer-king lowered his hand and chuckled. Hamanu and the Oba also began to chortle, their faces growing more relaxed and less suspicious.

"If you can strike me down, do it now," said Sadira, staring into Tithian's watery eyes. "That's the only way you'll stop me."

The wind began to howl, and the rain came down harder. More thunder crashed over the ridge, and forks of lightning danced through the sky—all without touching Sadira or anyone else.

"I thought as much," said Sadira, stepping straight through the king's misty face. "Make it storm all you like. Athas needs the rain."

Another crash of thunder rumbled overhead, and more lightning danced through the dark clouds. Rikus chuckled, then tipped his head back and opened his mouth, allowing the cool water to pour into his mouth. So did Rkard, and Neeva as well. Soon, everyone on the ridge was drinking water straight from the sky, making good use of Tithian's bluster.

Tithian finally grew tired of his humiliation. "Without me, you would never have slain the Dragon," he said, letting his image dissolve into mist. "All I ask is that you repay me with a merciful death."

"You killed Borys because you wanted to be immortal—now you are," scoffed the Oba, signaling Sadira to come forward.

The rainstorm died as suddenly as it had arisen, and the sorceress carried the Dark Lens to the edge of the ridge. Without pause, she hurled the obsidian orb into the lava lake. She and the others watched it fall. When it hit, a long, steady rumble rolled up from deep within the Ring of Fire, and the entire hill began to shake. At last, there was a deafening crash, and a plume of black flame shot up from the lake. It rose high into the sky, piercing Tithian's storm clouds like an arrow, and arced toward the sun.

When it finally disappeared, the Oba nodded. "It is done," she said, and began to walk away.

Nibenay cast a cold glance in Rikus's direction, then also started toward home.

Hamanu waited a few moments before following, pausing as he passed the mul's side. "I once told you that there is a difference between daring and insolence," he said. "I trust you will remember that difference in future dealings between Tyr and Urik."

Rikus nodded. "As long as you keep in mind the difference between men and chattel—at least as far as Tyrians are concerned."

"I always do," replied the sorcerer-king. "It is my slaves who forget."

Hamanu left, leaving Rikus and the others alone. They watched the three rulers for a short time, until the trio grew tired of walking and each took flight in a different direction.

Once they were out of sight, Rikus let out a deep sigh of relief. "We made it this far," he said. "We should start for home ourselves."

Neeva's mouth tightened with sadness, and tears began to well in her green eyes. "I guess we'd better." She looked away and wiped her cheeks, then laid her hand on Rkard's shoulder and began to limp down the hill. "Home is a long way off."

Rikus felt Sadira's hand pushing him after the warrior. When the mul looked back, he saw wisps of black shadow rising from the corners of her emberlike eyes.

She smiled with genuine joy. "Go," she whispered.

The mul returned her smile, though with a little more sadness than hers, and kissed her on the cheek. "I love you."

"And I love you," she replied, giving him another gentle push. "But Neeva and Rkard need you."

The mul nodded, then turned and caught up to Neeva and her son. "Have you given much thought to where home will be now?" he asked.

The warrior shrugged. "In Kled, I suppose," she said. "It is Rkard's home."

"Maybe he'd like to live in Tyr," Rikus suggested. "We could take him to Kemalok as often as he likes."

The boy's face lit up. "You mean we could live with you and Sadira?"

The mul frowned, not quite sure how to answer this question.

"No, you'd just live with Rikus, in his townhouse," said Sadira, stepping to Neeva's side. "When I return I'll stay at Agis's estate—but you could come to visit."

Neeva looked from Sadira to Rikus, her brow furrowed and her lips tightly pursed. "You two have this all worked out, don't you?" she asked.

Rikus felt the heat rising to his face. "Yes," he said. "I guess we do."

Neeva shook her head in amazement, then slipped her arm through Rikus's. "Then it seems Rkard and I have no choice in the matter." She grasped Sadira's hand and squeezed it warmly. "We'll go back to Tyr."

"Good," said Sadira. "I'm looking forward to seeing you there."

Neeva frowned. "Seeing us there?" she asked.

Sadira nodded. "I'll be staying here for a few weeks,"

she said. "There are some wards that I must place around Rajaat's new prison. Tithian is not the only mortal on Athas who lusts after immortality, and I intend to be certain that I know if anyone else attempts to achieve it by freeing Rajaat."

Rikus and Neeva glanced at each other. "I guess that means we'll be staying, too," Rikus said. "We can't cross the Sea of Silt without you."

Sadira smiled. "Of course you can."

The sorceress pursed her lips and began to blow. Black shadow billowed from her mouth, and she used her hands to form it into the shape of a boat. Soon, the wispy image of a dhow sat before them, although it had no sail or keel. Sadira tossed a jagged piece of black basalt into the bilge and spoke her incantation. The dhow turned as solid as stone, then rose off the ground and hovered in the air before them.

"Don't try to fly too far in one day. You have to set down on a mudflat or island each day before dark." The sorceress reached over the gunnel and pointed to the rock she had thrown into the bilge. "In the morning, hold the stone up to the sun, and the boat will form again."

Rikus helped Neeva into the boat. As Rkard climbed in beside his mother, the mul faced Sadira. "Hurry back," he said. "We'll miss you until you return."

Sadira took Rikus's arm and guided him toward the boat's tiller. "You have a long journey ahead," she said. "And remember, you need to make landfall before dark."

The mul climbed into the stern. Sadira kissed him on the cheek and gave the dhow a shove. The little craft streaked into the sky, climbing through a thin layer of clouds and into the full fury of the crimson sun.